THE PACK

E.C. SAULNESS

5 PRINCE PUBLISHING
5PRINCEBOOKS.COM

Published by 5 PRINCE PUBLISHING & BOOKS, LLC

PO Box 865, Arvada, CO 80001

www.5PrinceBooks.com

ISBN digital: 978-1-63112-390-0

ISBN print: 978-1-63112-391-7

Cover Credit: Marianne Nowicki

F102024 vII040225

For Sarah, Sam, Audrey, and Michael.
My Pack.

ACKNOWLEDGMENTS

Thank you to everybody who made this possible with their support, inspiration, and feedback.

You don't know who you are, and I'm not about to tell you.

Where would the fun be in that?

Now this is the
Law of the Jungle,
as old and as true
as the sky;

And the Wolf that shall
keep it may prosper,
but the Wolf that
shall break it must die.

As the creeper that
girdles the tree trunk,
the Law runneth
forward and back.

For the strength of the
Pack is the Wolf,
and the strength of the
Wolf is the Pack.

-Rudyard Kipling

THE PACK

PART 1

ABOUT A GIRL

CHAPTER ONE

BELLINGHAM, WASHINGTON,
    MARCH 1995

It was about ten-thirty in the morning, early March. According to the calendar, spring was just around the corner, but the slushy snow lingering along the sides of the road made the calendar look like a damn liar. There hadn't been much snow all winter. *El Niño*, they called it. With the end of the season in sight, people seemed to think that they were going to get off easy. No. Winter hadn't been going easy on us so much as it had been waiting to deliver a sucker punch once our hopes were up and our guard was down.

I parked my old Chevy Blazer between two newer cars in front of the nursing home. It could have been embarrassing to be seen getting out of the battered old SUV between a pair of over-waxed sedans, but luckily I had left my pride in my other jeans, the freshly washed pair without any holes that I hadn't been able to find for a few years now.

Larrabee Assisted Living & Memory Care, the sign at the

entrance proclaimed in print big enough for the geriatric residents to decipher even from a distance. The building was a big two-story number, built ten or fifteen years ago in a tree-filled area just south of town. It was clean, and simple, and completely devoid of any sense of character or history, but hey, the view of the bay was nice.

I sat and admired the view for a moment as I finished my smoke and scratched my dog, Blue, behind the ear, just the way she likes. I try to tell myself that I take the old girl along for her sake, the motherly cattle dog is always at the car door before I get there, but if I'm being honest, I take her for me. Blue rides with me whenever I feel like I might need a soothing influence to keep me from losing my temper. I can't remember the last time I left her at home. Blue keeps me calm. Rubbing my fingers through her fur probably does more for me than it does for her. Not that I'd ever tell her that. She's a good dog, but there's no sense in inflating her ego.

Keeping calm isn't always easy, and I need all the help I can get. My dogs help, the cigarettes too, but that's not enough. A stiff drink, a couple Vicodin, or maybe some good old-fashioned morphine when I can get it, are all good tools, especially together. I don't hesitate to use any or all of them when I need to. I'll use anything but needles, they scare the hell out of me. No doubt that sounds dangerous, and for most people it would be. But I'm not most people; I'm a monster. "Dangerous" is what happens when I can't keep my cool.

Places like nursing homes don't look too kindly on walking in with a lit cigarette, a bottle of Jack, or even a dog as sweet and even tempered as Blue. With that in mind, I tossed back another handful of Vicodin with a swig from my hip flask to top off the three or four I had taken before I'd left my trailer, just to be safe. I rolled another cigarette, lit it, and rolled yet another to tuck away for later. Blue looked up at me from where she lay on the passenger seat, disapproving.

"Don't give me that," I said as I rolled the window down for her and snatched a small paper bag from the floor of the passenger side before getting out of the Chevy to finish my smoke.

The cigarette helped to smother a lot of the smells that hit me once I stepped outside. That muffling quality was a large part of why I smoked so regularly, but cigarettes could never completely suffocate the world of scents that perpetually flooded my senses. This close to the full moon, they were less effective than usual.

Luckily, at that particular moment, it was some of the more pleasant smells that were the strongest. Icy salt mist greeted me from the nearby bay, and the fresh, sticky-sweet smell of the spruce and fir trees surrounding the building beckoned me to come stalk among their fallen needles. The trees themselves were a sort of greyish-mustard color to my colorblind eyes, but they still smelled green.

As I neared the building, the ocean and pine smells gave way to the astringent aromas of disinfectants and medications. They covered the faintly lingering scents of tea and coffee as well as tendrils of steam coming off a bland, tasteless lunch being prepared somewhere in the back of the building. Fumes of processed turkey, mashed potatoes, peas, and an artificially sweet lemon custard that made my stomach recoil still couldn't quite mask the one scent that was inescapable in a place like this. The subtle but unmistakable smell of death.

My unsettled stomach growled in conflicted hunger and disgust. Somewhere in a dark corner of my mind where I tried to keep it sedated and locked away behind bars of opiates and white-knuckle willpower, my inner beast growled its own hunger and unrest in sympathy with my stomach.

No! Get back! Sleep. I'll feed you soon. Go. Sleep.

I pictured myself leaning against a cage door in a vast, dark place, pushing with all my might against the thing behind the bars, all shadow and claw, instinct and rage. There was no reasoning with the beast. It had to be coaxed or forced. Slowly, a welcome numbness suffused my imagined arena, and the beast faded back to sleep as my pharmaceutical reinforcements arrived like a well-timed, warm blanket. Better late than never.

"Sir, there's no smoking here."

A small and matronly woman in a pastel uniform stood surprisingly close to me, a gaudy paper shamrock pinned to the breast of her uniform. I'd been so absorbed in my internal struggles that I hadn't seen, heard, or smelled her approach. I hadn't even realized that my eyes had been closed as I'd stood there fighting the beast in the back of my mind. How long had I been standing in front of the automatic doors? My cigarette had turned half to ash in my hand and the Filipina woman, 'Jeanette' on her nametag, was glaring at me impatiently. No doubt she assumed I was loaded on some drug or another. She wasn't wrong.

"Mister Shepard, you'll have to put out your cigarette."

It puzzled me for a moment that she knew my name, the warm blanket on my mind taking the edge off the clarity of my thoughts. Of course she knew my name, I'd been coming here for years now to visit Maggie. It would be odd if they didn't know me by now, even though they were perpetually strangers to me.

Wordlessly, I acknowledged Jeanette by dropping the cigarette to the slushy pavement and grinding out the butt with the heel of my worn leather work boot.

She huffed at me with evident frustration and judgement that she saw no point in concealing from a bum like me. "It's almost lunch time, sir. If you'd like to see your grandmother before then, you should hurry up."

I didn't say anything. Sometimes it was best to let people keep their assumptions. It was certainly easier than lying, and infinitely simpler than the facts. I nodded a silent thanks to her and shuffled into the plastic-smelling lobby, letting her walk me to the check-in counter where I filled out the necessary fields in the book.

```
Resident:    Magdalena    Adler.    Visitor:    F.
Shepard.
```

I kept my eyes low and my unseasonable sunglasses on as I followed Jeanette to the common room. It wouldn't do to meet some old lady's gaze and have the beast look back unexpectedly at her from behind my grey eyes. Some of the people in here could be blown over by a stiff breeze and seeing something like that might well give them a heart attack. Besides which, the less I saw in a place like this, the better. It wasn't an old building, thankfully, but people came here to die. It was full of ghosts, and they weren't who I had come here to see.

Ghosts aren't so bad, but just like anybody else they can be a pain in the ass if they decide to take notice of you. The thing about looking at somebody, alive or dead, is that they tend to look back at you. If you want to be left alone, it is best to pretend that you *are* alone. People leave you be, that way, whether it is the janitor waxing the floor, or the ghostly old man walking through the door to the staff room hoping to catch a peep show of one of the nurses changing uniforms between shifts. That particular old goat had been haunting this place for two or three years now, lingering far longer already than most specters.

He was none of my business. I took the stairs to the second floor, adding to Jeanette's obvious frustration. I hate elevators, damn cages that only open and close when they damn well feel like it.

Chet Baker played the trumpet on the common room stereo from an old record. The large room smelled of tea, ointment, and traces of sickness and urine. A large mirror covered one wall in what was probably an attempt to make the room seem bigger and better lit than it was. I caught a glimpse of my own reflection and was briefly reminded of why Jeanette had such contempt for me.

My hair was longer than I'd realized, uncombed and hanging to my eyes and over my ears. The mousy-grey color that I saw appeared as a dark red to anybody else. Unruly whiskers covered my face as fully as the smoky sunglasses covered my eyes. It wasn't quite a beard, and it certainly wasn't clean, but it did do something to help conceal the cleft lip which gave me the perpetual semi-snarl I'd had since birth.

The right arm I'd broken as a child was noticeably shorter than my left, to me at least, but the loose sleeves of my rumpled field jacket probably hid that detail from others. My wrinkled and stained jeans and button up work shirt had clearly been slept in more than once. I looked more worn than I'd expected. Tired. If I were a stranger, I'd have guessed my age somewhere in the thirties or forties, and I'd have fallen short of the mark by half a century. I looked like a vagrant, a junky, a complete loser, proving that now and then you actually can judge a book by its cover.

I looked away from the mirror. Not because of my reflection, which was reason enough to look away—believe me— but because of the other things that I see in mirrors. The ghosts that I sometimes glimpse walking among us are much more present in reflections. They are nearly always there in mirrors, especially in a place like this, and I wasn't the only one who saw more clearly by looking through mirrors. They can see me just as easily.

Still, I was ashamed at how disheveled I looked. If there was one person left in the world whose opinion mattered to me, it was Maggie. With that in mind, I combed my shaggy hair with my fingers before vigorously rubbing the film off my teeth with a finger in lieu of a toothbrush.

Nurse Jeanette sighed impatiently and gave me a look that told me I was fighting a pointless battle. Still, I tugged a little at the collar of my field jacket and brushed imagined dirt off my shoulder before clearing my throat and nodding to her that I was ready to go on. She rolled her eyes and led me to my destination.

There were perhaps a half dozen elderly men and women in the common room. Two old men sat in front of a television and talked over it, not caring what was on. The rest sat alone, listening to the music or their own thoughts, perhaps tapping their feet or sipping at plastic cups of tea designed to look like porcelain. A staff member sat in one corner, reading *Maxim Magazine* and humming to himself. He closed the mag and made a show of looking busy once he noticed nurse Jeanette walking in.

Jeanette walked us to the windows overlooking the cloudy bay where a willowy old woman sat in a wheelchair. She had a knit blanket wrapped around her shoulders and a familiar old quilt lay folded on her lap. A pair of thick glasses and a cup of cool chamomile tea sat on a table beside her as she stared vacantly at the clouds.

"Lena," Jeanette said as she reached out and gently touched the old woman on the shoulder, "look who's come to see you."

She turned her head and raised her cloudy eyes to look at me uncertainly. She seemed utterly lost for a moment, unsure of who I was, where she was, or even who she was, but a look of recognition crept slowly over her face after Jeanette helped her put her glasses on.

"There she is," Jeanette said.

A tentative smile dawned on the fragile old face and her lips parted, showing surprisingly perfect dentures.

"Paul?" she whispered the name of her long-dead husband.

"I guess she's having one of her bad days," Jeanette said. "I'm sorry."

Jeanette and the other nurses were used to this. Whenever I came to visit, I'd been 'recognized' as any number of people over the years. Sometimes I was her dead husband Paul. That was hard. Other times she thought I was her dead father whom I strongly resembled. That was harder. Now and then she was absolutely certain that I was her older brother. Those times could be the hardest of all. The truth often is.

"That's alright," I said. "I'd like to sit with her a while anyway."

"Certainly," Jeanette said with a sad smile. "Lunch is in twenty minutes. Of course, you can stay and visit after if you want to..."

"No, I won't be long," I said. Her family would likely be visiting her in the afternoon, and seeing them was the last thing I needed.

Jeanette nodded and gave that same judgmental and disapproving look she'd given me in the parking lot and then went to talk to the worker with the magazine. She left him looking chastised and embarrassed before taking his magazine and going back to her work downstairs.

The disoriented old woman in the wheelchair sat quietly and looked at me with familiar grey eyes, smiling faintly as if it were expected of her. I sat in the chair beside her and didn't say anything until Nurse Jeanette was gone, then I leaned forward and put my hand on hers. Her skin felt like tissue paper.

"Happy birthday, Maggie," I said in her ear as I leaned in to kiss her cheek, using her girlhood nickname.

"Happy birthday," she repeated to me.

"No, it's *your* birthday, Maggie," I squeezed her hand, "not mine."

"My birthday?"

"Yes."

"No," she said in disbelief.

"Cross my heart."

"How old am I?" she asked.

"Today, you're ninety years old," I told her.

She laughed softly, taking what I had told her as the sort of meaningless nonsense I'd have said to make her laugh when she was nine instead of ninety. Her eyes drifted back to the window where the dark grey clouds were moving more quickly, and a large V-shaped flock of white geese flew past.

"I brought you something," I said as I reached into the small paper bag I'd brought with me, pulling out a deep, blue cellophane package and placing it on her lap.

"What's this?"

"Candies. Your favorite flavor."

She furrowed her brow, not recognizing the candy any more than she had recognized me. Her eyes drifted back to the clouds as Chet Baker played *Blue Thoughts* over the speakers. I sat with her for a moment longer before a thought came to me.

"I'll be right back," I said to her, patting her hand.

I walked to the corner of the common room, where Dale, the recently chastised employee, according to his name tag, sat sullenly monitoring the room. A table of coffee, tea, and water sat beside him on one side. To the other side was the record player along with a shelf of old albums beside a collection of books that most of the residents here could never read.

"Can I help you, sir?" he asked as I began to browse the

albums. I ignored him as I searched the titles, lots of mellow stuff from before any of the staff were born. The employees seemed to think that anything recorded before their own births would please the old folks who lived here. Old music for old people. But there's old, and then there's *old*. The songs playing right now were recorded when Maggie and those her age were already middle aged. I needed something with deeper roots.

"Sir?" he asked again as he stood guard over Chet Baker. I'd found what I was looking for. I pulled out the album and handed it to the boy.

"Yeah, play this," I told him, pointing to a track on the record.

He examined the cover, and took his time about it, flexing his imagined authority over his corner of the universe. I turned to face him and peered over the top of my sunglasses, meeting his eyes briefly.

People react in all kinds of ways when they see my eyes. If I'm especially angry, or they are especially skittish, the results can be dramatic. I've seen people faint or piss themselves in extreme situations. One guy even ran into a brick wall in a panic and knocked his lights out. When the beast is rattling its cage in the back of my head, something in the primal part of a person's brain sees a predator when they look into my eyes, something other than human, and it scares the sense out of them.

I wasn't especially angry at that moment, just my usual surly and impatient self who didn't want to waste time playing power games with a kid. Whatever Dale saw in my eyes in that brief glance was enough. He didn't say anything else, merely stopped the record player with shaking hands and took old Chet Baker off before putting on what I'd given him.

I pretended not to notice his trembling hands, figuring that the poor kid should keep some shred of dignity. I filled a fresh tea cup with hot water, picked out a packet of peppermint tea, and let it begin to steep before adding a heavy dose of honey. I gave it a stir until it smelled just right.

"Here, Maggie," I said, carefully offering her the cup.

She looked at me without recognition but raised the cup to her mouth and breathed in the smell of mint and honey. Just then, Dale finished the task I'd given him; an old familiar song started through the speakers above us. One that I knew Maggie had loved when she was a young woman.

She closed her eyes as she took in the scent of the steaming cup, and I noticed a slight movement in her foot as she began to hesitantly sway it to the music.

"I know this song," she said, half questioning.

"You always loved Gershwin," I said.

"*I'm a little lamb who's lost in the wood, I know I could always be good...*" Sinatra crooned a show-tune that had been decades old before he'd recorded it.

Maggie hummed along almost inaudibly as she struggled to recall the next line but couldn't quite come up with the words. She furrowed her brow in frustration.

"Sing it for me?" she asked.

For anybody else, I wouldn't have even considered it, but I'd always been willing to do anything for her. I cleared my throat.

"*Although I may not be the man, some girls think of as handsome, to her heart I'll carry the key,*" I croaked along with Sinatra, for her ears only.

She hummed the next line with more confidence and then opened her eyes, a light coming on in a dark room.

"*...Someone to watch over me,*" she sang in a sweet, brittle voice and met my eyes.

For a moment I didn't hide my eyes from her. For one thing, we don't like to hide things from each other. We never have. But more importantly, I felt that there was nothing there for her to fear. At least at the moment. I'd never hurt her; I was certain of it.

But I'd been sure of that with others, and I'd been wrong. I looked away.

"Francis?" She recognized me, using the name that only she and our mother had ever gotten away with calling me.

"Happy birthday, Maggie," I put my hand on her knee but kept my eyes lowered.

"Is it really...ninety?" she asked.

"You don't look a day over eighty-five," I teased.

"Sweet talker," she swatted my hand.

We sat there together and listened to the song, enjoying each other's company.

"I think Ella Fitzgerald sings it better than this guy," she said.

"Beggars can't be choosers."

"Those colored girls," she said, "they sure can sing, can't they?"

"I don't think they like to be called that anymore, Maggie," I said.

"What's that?"

"Never mind."

We sat in the silence a moment longer, watching the clouds. I unwrapped one of the candies I'd brought for her and offered it.

"Mmm. Blackberry. My favorite," she said, after tasting it.

"Always was."

"How did you know?" she said.

"Maggie, it's me," I took her hand. The lights in her eyes were flickering, growing dim again. I pulled a silver necklace from beneath my shirt, showing her the familiar Saint's medal that I'd worn for most of my life.

"Francis?" she asked.

"Yes, Maggie, it's me," I assured her.

"Oh!" she sat up excitedly. "Did Evelyn come with you?"

That hurt.

"No, honey," I said. "She's not here."

"She was..." Maggie trailed off, confused.

"If you say so," I said, trying not to let her hear the hurt in my voice.

"You two are such a sweet couple," she said. "She seems so angry, though. You should apologize for... for whatever you did."

I had nothing to say. Correcting Maggie could only bring her pain. Reality is overrated.

"She's so pretty," Maggie mused.

"Always was," I agreed.

"What's that?"

"Nothing."

"Well, you be sure and give her my love when you get home."

"I will," I promised.

We held hands. I listened to her smacking her lips as she sucked on the candy, the smell of it mingling pleasantly with the aroma of the peppermint tea. Sinatra was singing *My Way*.

"Do you know my husband?" she asked suddenly.

"Yes."

"He's a good man, my Paul."

"Always was," I agreed.

"What?" she asked, unsure again of who and where we were as Nurse Jeanette appeared in the doorway with other staff members to gather everybody for lunch.

"Nothing," I whispered as I stood and prepared to go. I kissed her on the head. "Happy birthday, baby sister."

"Do I know you?" she smiled up at me.

"Sometimes."

. . .

"Did you have a good visit with your grandmother?" the receptionist asked as I signed out at the front desk.

"Peppermint," I said as I scratched at the paper.

"Beg pardon?"

"She likes peppermint tea, not chamomile," I said.

"Oh, alright," she smiled nervously.

"With honey," I added as I ambled through the automatic doors, not waiting for a response.

I let Blue out of the Blazer so that she could tend to her needs after being cooped up and retrieved the cigarette I had prepared earlier. I lit it with the battered old zippo I keep in my left pocket.

I sucked the smoke down like water from a straw until the fresh tremble in my hands subsided. Maggie had looked... old. Too damn old.

She'd looked older than me since sometime in the Hoover administration, and she'd been able to pass as my grandmother since disco, but it was clear that she was nearing the end of the line. I didn't like thinking about that. Maggie was the only person left who really knew me. Sure, I had a contact or two who had some idea that I was something... else, who knew that I was older and tougher than I looked, but they didn't know it all. Maggie knew me from the beginning. She was family, and she was going to be gone soon.

Hell, who was I kidding? She'd already been gone for a while in a lot of ways. She'd started forgetting things a dozen years ago. Just little things at first, the things you expect when you get on in years. Keys, appointments, the occasional name. But one day, she'd left her house and hadn't come home.

It was warm, an Indian summer, so she hadn't frozen when night fell, but her family was alarmed. I wasn't close with any of them, not anymore, but one of her grandchildren had called me after the police had gotten involved, and they had scoured the neighborhood with no luck. They thought of me as a cousin, as the grandson of Mama Lena's big brother Frank who had died in the war. I was Lena's favorite nephew. Frank Shepard the third or fourth, a distant cousin that they didn't even see at holidays but who kept in touch with the Adler family matriarch.

It had taken me twenty minutes to find her after the criminally quick drive to her North Seattle neighborhood. Not because I knew where she would go, but because her scent is more familiar than any I know. My old-little sister smelled like peppermint and honey, like years of sun speckled on warm skin. She smelled like holding hands on the way to school, like snowball fights, and like the tears she left on my shoulder while our father beat our mom and we held our breath in the closet.

She had walked down an old trail behind an elementary school and sat on a bench near a creek in one of those wooded swaths that Seattle is riddled with. It had gotten dark, and she had forgotten which way she had come. She wandered for a while, ripping her clothes on a patch of devil's club. The pain in her leg had made her cry out, but that just made it easier to find her. I heard her cry from a half mile upstream and was at her side a minute later, cradling her in my arms like I had when she was three years old and I had been nine, when she'd had a nightmare but had already known better than to wake our parents.

Her son had pulled some strings and arranged for her care in an expensive new nursing home in Bellingham, the town where we'd grown up. I think it was the idea of going home that made her agree to finally give up living in her own home. She'd never have agreed if she could see the ghosts of our past the way that I can. A month later, I'd moved back to the area too, to be near her.

She'd been scared. Scared of losing herself more than she was of dying. She didn't want to live like this. Never like this.

"Francis, I don't want to," she'd said and clutched my hand fiercely, "don't let me..."

She couldn't come right out and say it. She couldn't ask me to promise. She was still a good Catholic, like our mama raised us to be. She wouldn't ask me to commit a mortal sin. She never said the words. But we both knew what she wanted.

I'd killed for her before, but we were both young then. Now I was old and tired, even if I didn't show it the way that she did, and she was all I had. I was a coward. Selfish.

But she still had her moments, didn't she? She'd known who I was today, if only briefly. It took the tea, and the music, and the taste of blackberry hard candies, but she had come back. She was still in there. She wasn't gone yet.

CHAPTER TWO

A cold wind off the bay hit me just right under my glasses and made my eyes water.

"Okay girl, time to get to work," I said to Blue as I hurriedly finished relieving myself behind a tree. I had that uncomfortable crawling feeling at the back of my neck that comes sometimes when I'm being watched. Damn pervert ghosts. It served me right for pissing outside an old folks' home.

I kept my eyes down and quickly let Blue into the Chevy, ladies first, and then took my spot in the driver's seat, rolled and lit another smoke, and started the engine.

I drove a couple of miles and then pulled onto the interstate headed south. It took Blue a few minutes to realize we weren't headed straight home, but by the time we were passing the lake she knew. She cocked her head and snuffled at me.

"Don't blame me, this is Mack's idea," I told her.

She looked at me skeptically, cocking a single ear at the mention of Mack's name.

"Won't take long," I promised the dog.

She lay back down with a theatrically long exhale and kept one skeptical eye on me from between her forepaws.

I kept one hand on the wheel and reached with the other, picking up a torn piece of brown grocery bag that I had scribbled my notes on.

Andy Morgan. Edison Court. Bikers. Rita. Yellow Trailer.

More info than that and I wouldn't have been able to fit it on the paper scrap. Mack had wanted to give me more details, he'd been a little pushy about it in fact, but I'm not one for long conversations.

The ringing phone had woken me up the day before, sometime after sunset.

At first, I didn't know what the hell I was hearing. An alarm? A siren? That was the first impression formed in my drowsy mind. I'd fallen more than rolled out of the nook in my trailer where I slept, but I was in a fighting crouch by the time I opened my eyes. The painful ringing in my ears drawing a reflexive growl and an angry snarl.

Tybalt, my furry feline pest control system, who had been sleeping behind my knees, hissed angrily in protest. The phone rang again, and I realized what it was.

"Who is this?" I growled after picking up the receiver.

"Who do you think it is, Sherlock?" the deep and familiar voice on the other end chuckled.

"Mack? How?"

Mack Watson was a private investigator and bail bondsman who ran his own business out of Everett, just outside of Seattle. We'd been partners once, before I'd decided that it would be better for everybody if I just crawled off into my little trailer in the woods. Alone with my dogs where nobody else could get hurt. He'd still show up at my place with a bottle occasionally, and we would talk about old times until it was empty. Now and then I'd help him with a case when he could pique my interest, or if my funds were low enough.

"Now Red," Mack laughed, "I know you're a little slow, but do I really have to explain how a telephone works?"

"What? No," I said, "I just— it was off. The bills. They turned it off..."

"Yeah, and then they turned it back on. They do that when somebody pays the bill."

"But I didn't." I was still getting my bearings and clawing to catch up. My head was killing me.

"I did. How else am I supposed to get a hold of you?" He knew that just showing up at my door unannounced this week was a good way to get mauled, either by Blue and her pack of misfit strays or by myself on the wrong day.

"You had no right," I barked.

"You're welcome," he said.

I took a second, cursing under my breath as I opened a warm can of beer and wet my cracked lips.

"I've got a job for you," Mack said.

"That's not how this works, Mack," I said. "You know better. I call you."

"On the phone you stopped paying for?" he said. "I need your touch on this one."

"I'm busy," I lied.

"No, you ain't."

"It's not a good time," I said honestly. It was Maggie's birthday, as well as the nearly full moon that was already in the cards for the next day.

"I know, it's your time of the month," he laughed at his own old joke.

"It wouldn't be safe," I said.

"It's already not safe. I've got a skip I've got to get in court in two days, and none of my other people are willing to go to this location. But you've got your thing."

My thing, as Mack liked to call it, was exactly the reason I couldn't get mixed up in whatever this was.

I've heard a lot of words in a lot of different languages for what I am, but I don't care for most of them. Vrykolaka, Ulfhednar, Wendigo, Maicoh, Warg, Lycanthrope—none of them exactly rolled off the tongue.

Werwolf was the German word for it, as well as the term most familiar to people who have seen too many movies. I hate that one, and not just because of the tacky and inaccurate Lon Chaney bullshit that it makes people think of.

In France we were called Garou, and I like that as good as any.

Mack knows better than to call me a werewolf, so he just refers to my 'thing' in a way that makes it sound like I'm a capo in some supernatural mafia. He had some idea of what I was and some of what that meant I could do, and here he was trying to use it like it was a qualification on a resume. There's a reason these things are best kept secret.

"I don't care," I said. Two days would be the full moon. I started to hang up the phone, but Mack's tiny voice in my hand convinced me to wait.

"It's a kid!"

Damn him.

"Bikers?" I asked. Mack had known me long enough to know just how to push my buttons. A goddamn kid. *Shit.*

"Yeah," he said. "These hard cases who call themselves Los—"

"Where?" I interrupted.

"A trailer park, near Burlington. Edison Court, it's called," he said. "This kid—"

"Name?" I said.

"Andy," Mack said. "Andy Morgan. But listen Red, this is—"

"Got an address?"

"No," Mack said, "but the tip, some biker's girlfriend named Rita, says the club has the kid stashed in her trailer. Says it's the yellow one. Red, I'd send somebody else, but everybody is scared of these motherfuckers. See, this kid Andy got mixed up with—"

"I'll get him to you tomorrow," I snarled. "Don't call me again!" I slammed the phone back into the cradle, cracking the plastic. I ripped the cord out of the wall for good measure and then scribbled my notes on a piece of the grocery bag that the beer had come in. After that, I finished the beer and then opened a second to wash down a handful of Vicodin before nodding off for another twelve hours or so.

I knew this trailer park, Edison Court. It was out on the tide flats, about a half hour south of Bellingham. Not all that far from where I lived. That area was full of just three types of people: farmers, bikers, and slow-driving tourists who flooded the area every year to stare dumbly at fields of brightly colored tulips – but the 'Tulip Festival' was still a couple months away.

I pulled off the interstate and headed west on the flood plains. On the horizon, seagulls danced around smoke from the distant oil refinery as it rose to join the equally grey clouds. Clouds that threatened to add another dose of slush to the dreary Northwest afternoon.

"Damnit Mack," I cursed to myself, and Blue cocked an eyebrow. There was a reason I tried not to go out this close to a full moon. the thing in the back of my head was already stirring fitfully. It took a lot to keep the beast in check for these few days.

I fished the pill bottle out of my pocket and was disappointed to hear how few pills remained as I shook it. I pocketed the cap and tossed back about half of what was left inside, leaving only three or four more.

I didn't like walking into a situation like this with my senses dulled and my mind foggy, but it was better than walking in howling for blood. With any luck I could get this Andy kid out of there and down to Mack's place without the need to bust any heads. Then I could get home to the dogs and curl up into a Vicodin coma for the next few days until the damn moon had moved on to a calmer phase. All I had to do was keep the beast in his cage and get in and out without any bloodshed.

Deep in my mental cage, however, the mere thought of spilling blood set my other self to growling in groggy anticipation. I wished the damn pills would hurry up and kick in.

CHAPTER THREE

I was hungry and high as I neared Edison Court. The Skagit floodplain out by Edison was a flat open area without many trees, typical for this part of the state. It felt exposed. The bright spot in the clouds where the sun was hiding told me that I had a couple more hours of daylight ahead of me. A leather-clad man on a motorcycle had pulled out ahead of me as I approached, one of the bikers that had Mack's people so nervous, I supposed. The Harley he rode was functional if not pretty. Too much matte black and not enough chrome. The pipes had been cut short to make as much noise as possible, serving no purpose that I could see other than to announce to strangers what an asshole the rider was.

I kept driving past the entrance to the trailer park as the biker pulled out so that he wouldn't see me pulling in. I drove behind him for a short time and got a good look at the patch on his black leather jacket before he opened the throttle and pulled away and out of view. "Los Perdidos," the top rocker proclaimed in yellow and the deep yellow-grey that human eyes would probably see as red, above a picture of a smiling skull with a shushing skeletal finger placed vertically against its bony mouth.

Los Perdidos. The lost ones? The lost boys? I reached through the warm fog of my medicated brain for the translation. One advantage of living a long time is that you have the opportunity to pick up a lot of things, like languages. In my time I've learned about a half dozen languages. I only speak them incomprehensibly, but I can usually understand a fair bit more than people expect.

I pulled off at the next country road and circled back around to the trailer park from the other direction once the rider was long gone.

Edison Court was the kind of place that trailer trash ended up after the unemployment benefits ran out, and where junkies moved once they were tired of even pretending to want to get clean. I fit right in.

Paint peeled from two rows of rusted metal boxes that sat on cluttered little muddy lots, where tufts of untrimmed grass stuck defiantly out of the slush. A twisted metal swing set stood between two of the homes, a neglected plastic tricycle and a few abandoned pieces of children's clothing lay discarded on the frozen mud. It made me angry to think of children being raised in that place, but angry was the last thing that I needed to be if I was going to keep this thing from turning bloody.

I killed the ignition on the Blazer and scratched Blue behind her ear. She raised her head for a moment to see where we were and quickly reached the conclusion that there was nothing much to look at. She licked my fingers twice, curled back up on the passenger seat beside me and half-closed her eyes.

Now what? I didn't have an address, a picture, or even a scent. Just a name to go with a yellow trailer, but there were three goddamn yellow trailers. Hell, to my colorblind eyes almost half of them seemed some shade of yellow. Maybe I should have heard Mack out for a second after all, but I'd just been too damn startled by the phone call, and my hackles had been up. I looked around at a few of the trailers, looking for anything that might give me a place to start. A broken window, covered in plywood, another that had burned out Christmas lights gathering cobwebs. A couple of run-down trucks were the only vehicles in residence, the place looked nearly abandoned.

No motorcycles. That might be a good thing, unless this faceless Andy had ridden away on one. Any kids were still at school, and any resident with an unlikely job was away at it now. It was a good time of day for this sort of thing, less chance of complications.

A figure caught my attention out of the corner of my eye. Looking more closely, I saw that the lone pedestrian was another ghost. This one, an apparition of a middle-aged woman, was walking around and occasionally stopping to put her hands to her mouth as if to amplify her voice as she called out. She appeared to be looking for somebody, a missing dog or child perhaps, that she would never find.

Most specters are like that, endlessly running through the same futile actions. They single-mindedly carry out some compulsion based on the deep-rooted obsessions that consumed their dying thoughts. If they were left alone, they usually wouldn't take notice of anything else. Usually.

People like me, Garou, are an exception. We see the ghosts when others can't, with growing clarity as the moon waxes full, but we are also more noticeable to them in turn. I could feel the hairs on my arms and legs prickle as she stared at me, trying to puzzle out what was different about me. I kept my eyes forward while Blue nuzzled my leg.

After busying myself by rolling and sparking another cigarette, the spectral seeker finally lost interest and continued her search for... whatever.

Ghosts like that aren't uncommon, in my experience. I was

just glad that there weren't more at hand. I had more mundane worries to occupy me.

How the hell was I going to find this kid? I had no idea what I was looking for. As I didn't even have a scent to try and follow, my eyes and nose were of no particular use. That left my ears. I rolled the window half down and closed my eyes, the better to not see any more ghosts for the time being. I listened.

The first things I heard were closest to me, the rise and fall of Blue's breathing on the seat beside me, the grumbling of my own stomach, the clicking of my cooling engine. Nothing helpful there. I tuned those out and concentrated, hearing the distant roar of the ocean in one direction and the steady hum of the interstate highway in the other, miles off. I pulled in, focusing on the couple of hundred feet around me in every direction. In one trailer I heard snoring. In another I heard a young child crying in a way that made it sound like it was beginning to realize there was no point, nobody was listening. How old was this Andy kid supposed to be, anyway? Mack knew better than to expect me to change diapers. Again, I wished I'd taken the time to get more detail before smashing my phone.

I kept listening. I heard a television, people chanting a name again and again, 'Jerry?' Then I heard a phone ring from the trailer with the crying and ignored child and a woman's voice answered it quickly. I could hear her speaking in hushed tones, then a door opening and closing before she continued speaking in a bathroom or closet. I could almost make out what she was saying, almost but not quite. I strained but couldn't bring the words into focus. Everything was too... fuzzy.

Drugging the beast in my head in order to avoid tearing somebody apart was a practical necessity, but the downside was that the more dormant the wolf was within me the less I could draw on the abilities that came with it. Put plainly, I was having trouble performing. It happens.

As I saw it, I had two options. First, the cautious approach. I could take my sweet time out here looking for leads or going door to door until I found something, but that would take time that I wasn't willing to spend. Or second, the expedient choice. I could rattle the cage a little bit and see if I could wake up the wolf just enough to let me get this done and trust that I could keep the lid on things once I had his attention.

Since I didn't want to be out here any longer than I had to and because as far as I knew a pack of bikers could show up at any moment, I chose expediency. I took my impatience and anxiety at the situation, along with a bit of the sadness I'd had thinking about my sister, and tossed in a bit of the reflexive rage I'd felt when I'd been jolted awake by Mack's call the day before. I held on tight to these feelings and fed a trickle, just a few drops really, into that part of my mind where I kept my inner monster.

The results were immediate. A ripple of adrenaline surged through my body, sharpening my senses and clenching my limbs as well as my jaw. With the alertness and tension came a wave of predatory instinct, the urge to find something to stalk, to chase, to rip and tear. I clamped down tight on the emotions I'd been feeding to my wolf, cutting it off. Too much of that and the thing I kept locked down could burst out of the chains and bars that I imagined held it in place. It would take the driver's seat entirely. I'd be the one locked in the back of my mind, barely aware of what I was doing as the wolf ran wild. I'd be stuck there, a prisoner in my own body, until the wolf-spirit that shared it had either exhausted itself or I managed to wrest control. Considering how close I was to a full moon, it could well be a day or two until I managed to regain full dominance.

If I hadn't been drugged to the gills, I wouldn't have tried drawing on the wolf, but then I wouldn't have had such a hard time focusing in the first place. As it was, I nearly lost control, but the warm opium daze that the pills had brought with them helped me lull the beast back to a rest once I had what I needed.

"—that bitch out of my house, now!" hissed a woman's voice.

I could *almost* make out the reply by the male voice on the other end of the phone, but not quite. I could draw on the wolf again, but after how precarious my control had been the first time, there was no way.

"No Rudy, not today," she said, "now. I'm kicking her ass out. I don't give a damn what Lodi says!"

She was silent for a moment as the voice on the phone adopted that tone that some men like to use with upset women, somewhere between placating and patronizing.

"You think I don't know why you keep her here? I know you guys've been passing her around! Well, I ain't gonna babysit your fuck-toy for you anymore. I already told her to pack her bag. I've got a baby to take care of!"

Suddenly she's mother of the year, I thought to myself sarcastically. Was the baby even hers? No way was Andy a small child. Babies don't post bail. I was looking for a teenager. She listened to the phone for a minute before responding in a calmer, conspiratorial tone.

"Yeah?" she said. "How much? Damn. That's a lot of money. Okay, yeah, I won't let her leave. Yeah, probably better I don't know."

She listened again.

"Y'know baby, if I let her shoot up first it would make things a lot easier," she offered.

A pleased male voice on the other end gave approval in words I couldn't quite hear.

"Damn right I'm smart, that's why you love me. Just be careful baby, I don't want you going to prison for this shit."

He responded in sinister whispers.

"Yeah, you do what you gotta do to get patched in. Just make sure nobody finds her. I love you too, baby. See you soon. Hurry."

Did I hear what I thought I'd heard? Were they going to kill some lady? It sure sounded like it. Damn. Not my business. But I couldn't just ignore it either, could I? The decent thing to do would be to tip off the police, let them handle it. After all, I was here for a kid, not to get between a gang of bikers and some floozy. But I'd developed a habit of not talking to the police a long time ago, and habits that old are damn hard to break. I got out of the car.

"Stay," I whispered to Blue. She sat up attentively but didn't move. I continued to listen closely as I made my way to the yellowish trailer with the neglected baby and jealous woman. Who else was in there?

"I'm sorry, Rita, I'm ready to go. Can I just use the phone? I'll get a ride," a new voice said.

Rita? Wasn't that the name of Mack's snitch? I supposed this might be my business after all.

"No, there's been a change of plan," Rita said, "you can stay. Rudy will be back to pick you up in a little while."

"Pick me up? Where am I going?"

"Hey, I'm gonna cook up some of that good shit the guys left. You want some?" Rita asked.

There was a pause before the other voice responded skeptically. "Why are you being so nice to me?"

Clever girl, I thought as I stalked up the stairs of the trailer's flimsy front porch.

"I feel bad for before," Rita said. "I know how it is with these guys sometimes. What happened isn't your fault. I want to make up for what a bitch I was to you before."

I flicked the butt of my cigarette into the nearby bushes and knocked on the door. Quick and hard. The sudden noise startled the two inside, judging by their quick intakes of breath.

"That was quick," Rita said, confused.

"I didn't hear a bike..." smarter than Rita.

"Who's there?" Rita called through the door.

"Mack sent me," I said. What the hell, I may as well try honesty. She was supposed to be working with Mack after all.

"Shit," I heard Rita hiss under her breath, no doubt thinking nobody could hear her. "I don't know what you're talking about. Fuck off!"

So much for the best policy.

"Just open the door," I said, massaging the growing ache from my temple with my left hand. "Please," I added as an afterthought. No point in being rude.

"Andy, get the fuck to the bedroom and hide in the closet," Rita hissed in a voice she mistakenly assumed I wouldn't be able to hear through the door. I heard hesitant footsteps obey her.

Andy? Well shit, what's in a name? It didn't occur to me that Andy could be a girl. Kids these days.

"Hold on," Rita yelled theatrically, "Jesus!"

Rita was tall for a woman. She cracked the door and exposed an angular face with shadowy brown Latin eyes and excessively painted full lips. Her dark hair had honey-colored streaks and was still settling around her shoulders. I guessed that she had just let her hair down moments before answering the door, in preparation to use her most familiar weapon, her looks, against the stranger who had come knocking. A quick, involuntary glance at her impressively exposed bosom and uncomfortably tight jeans left little to my imagination and seemed to support that guess.

Rita did a passably fair job of pretending to be confused by my arrival, looking lost in the woods. She even went so far as to quickly look me up and down and give a coy, flirtatious smile, implying that she liked what she saw. I looked like shit, and she was full of it.

"What do you want?" she asked.

"Mack sent me." I repeated.

"Who?" she said.

I rubbed my temple again and grimaced. Why did people have to make things harder than they had to be?

"Listen, Rita," I said, her brows lifted when I said her name, "cut the crap. I'm taking Andy."

"She's not here," Rita lied.

"Right," I said, "that's somebody else hiding in your bedroom closet."

"I—I don't know what you're talking about," she stammered.

"Have it your way," I said, and shouldered my way through the door.

"Hey!"

I ignored her protests and walked toward the only door in the back of the small trailer. The place smelled like sour garbage, wet diapers, old beer, full ashtrays, and sex. Underneath it all was the faintly sweet-vinegar smell of heroin. I sniffed. Rita hadn't been lying about one thing. It was the good stuff.

Suddenly, she was on my back, screaming and spitting as she hit my head again and again with her small fist. The pain and surprise shot down my spine, and I had to fight to keep the anger from spilling into my wolf. I don't hurt women, as a rule, but the wolf and I differ on these things. I'd promised myself, long ago, that I'd let myself die before killing another woman. That didn't mean that the urge wasn't strong.

I reached behind me and caught her arm, pulling her off and in front of me as she kicked and cursed me. I held her against the flimsy wall by her upper arm, trying not to bruise her. She continued to strike at me with her other arm and she scratched at my face a couple of times and even knocked loose my sunglasses before I caught her other arm in mine and pinned her against the wall.

"Stop!" I snarled as I locked eyes with her.

That was all it took. Having drawn on my wolf recently, I didn't doubt that my eyes had begun to change. They're the first things that do. She saw it, the wolf in my eyes, and she reacted instantly to the dominant predator in front of her. She submitted, completely. Instantly. A Garou's eyes can have a powerful and immediate effect on some people. Fear and panic are most common, but there were other reactions. Rita was one of those unfortunate women who have learned through painful experience to associate fear and submission with intimacy. Her skin flushed, and her scent changed from anger to a disgusting combination of fear and arousal.

It may have been a disgusting combination to the man that I struggled to be, but it was utterly intoxicating to the beast that I wanted to deny. I felt him, my wolf-self, pressing against the bars of his cage, salivating. Hungry.

Yes, the thought bubbled to the forefront of my foggy mind. *Take the bitch. We are dominant. It is right. She knows.*

I found myself staring at her, feeling the urge to pounce on her trembling body and satisfy urges I'd been denying for years. I'll admit that I was tempted. I was no monk. It wouldn't be that bad, would it? She wanted it. I could taste it on the stale air. She was taking short, shallow breaths, her large nipples drawn to sharp points beneath her tight shirt. My hand clenched that shirt.

Yes. Rip. Take!

From some deeply Freudian corner of my psyche came the thought of my mother, of the woman she had been and the things she had endured. I thought then of my father, of the man he had shown me I could have become, but never wanted to. An ancient childhood full of religious sexual repression and Catholic guilt rose to the fore. I looked down at Rita, vulnerable and willing, completely at my mercy, but I saw my wife. I saw Evelyn. A flood of shame came rushing with the thought of my wife's face. I took that shame, that guilt, and poured it into the wolf.

Disgust. Shock. Confusion.

There are feelings that feed the wolf. Hunger. Lust. Pain. Fear. Anger. Most of all anger. These are fuel for a Garou. A little of them can empower us, but too much of them can bring a total loss of control, no matter what the phase of the moon may be. There are other feelings though, feelings that are alien to the wolf. Guilt. Shame. Regret. A wolf doesn't understand these things. *Can't* understand them. I drowned my other self in those feelings now, utterly dousing the burning need that had been spreading and threatening to take over.

I felt the wolf within me back away. He didn't retreat, but he stepped back as if smelling something rotten and allowed me to reassert control for the time being. My senses dulled. Whatever was in my eyes must have dimmed as well, Rita scrambled away from me and crossed her arms in front of herself.

Deciding that it would be best to be done here as soon as possible, I recovered my sunglasses and turned to push open the bedroom door. It was locked, but the wall was flimsy and split when I applied a little force.

The diaper-sex-heroin smells were strongest here, along with a hint of something else, something strange and familiar that I couldn't quite place. A twin bed with dirty sheets sat in a corner. A chewed and soiled crib stood beside it holding an ugly baby, his face swollen and red from crying. He stared at me with snot covering his chin and his saturated diaper hanging nearly to his knees. Rita's eyes stared at me from his unwashed face.

Babies and ghosts have a lot in common. They both want things that I don't have the time or skill to deal with, and I've found they are best handled by pretending that they aren't there. At least in the short term. I opened the closet door.

The girl huddled fearfully in the corner of the closet, partially obscured by a pair of men's boots and a few longer shirts on hangers. She looked to be about fifteen years old. She was a willowy little thing, five-foot-nothing. If pounds were pennies and you guessed her weight at a dollar, I'd expect at least a nickel in change. Fashionable holes in her loosely fitting jeans showed pale bony knees, under an overly large, unbuttoned flannel shirt, she wore a black t-shirt with a wacky white stick figure under the words, "Pearl Jam," whatever the hell that was. Her hair was artificially dark, bobbed short on one side but long and streaked blue on the other. Her face prominently displayed a black eye and split lip. She'd had a rough go of it lately. Her nose dominated her face and seemed a bit out of proportion with her thin lips.

What stood out, even in that moment, were her eyes. Giant, blue, stormy things that glared defiant daggers at me from a bruised face, and they didn't quite match. One eye was deep blue, almost indigo. The other had a patch covering less than half of her iris which was startlingly emerald-green. Especially surprising to me, as I haven't been able to see that shade of green outside of memories and dreams since I'd become Garou. It startled me to see a fleck of this lost color now. So, this was Andy Morgan?

She looked at me and sort of past me with those strange eyes, like she saw something that wasn't there. A look somewhere between puzzlement and recognition came over her, and the smell of fear subsided somewhat. She seemed to have decided that she didn't need to be afraid of the strange man who had just stormed into the place where she was hiding. Maybe she wasn't as smart as I'd given her credit for earlier when I'd been eavesdropping.

The smell of the girl intrigued me, but there was a more powerful scent emanating from the closet which grabbed my attention and held it in a vise. It was obvious that this closet was where they kept the dope that Rita had been talking about. A small black duffel bag, the kind people take to the gym, sat on the top shelf and seemed to be the source of the aroma. Then there was the smell of the girl herself. She had a pleasant underlying smell of lavender and vanilla, but she also reeked of a smoky combination of tobacco and heroin. Under the receding wave of her diminishing fear, I caught another scent. I sniffed once to be sure. No mistake. This girl was pregnant. Also, that familiar smell that I'd barely noticed before was strongest here, coming from the girl herself, though I still couldn't define it. The closest I could come was to say that it smelled green. The smell of leaves and growing things, of buds about to blossom, of the first hint of spring pollen. It was faint, but distracting, an itch in my awareness.

No time to puzzle about strange eyes and mysterious scents, we had to leave while that was still possible.

"Get up," I said.

She obeyed, scrambling to her feet with a mouse-like alacrity.

"Who are you?" she asked, her eyes on my feet.

"The guy who is taking you out of here," I said.

The pregnant teenager half-squeaked and half-screamed as I heard Rita approach from behind me. As the first gunshot went off, Andy dropped to the ground. The kid had good instincts. The shot had missed me and punched a small hole in the thin wall with more of a crack than a bang. I spun around, keeping a tight grip on the leash in my head.

Rita stood there holding a very small target pistol, a .22 I'd say. It was the sort of gun you used if you were desperate, not the sort of thing you used to put down a man. Not if you were smart. But I didn't give Rita credit for being overly bright. In fact, she wasn't even pointing it at me convincingly. I heard Andy scrambling behind me to the cover of the bed and watched Rita's gun follow her. She was trying to kill the girl!

I moved without thinking as Rita pulled the trigger two more times. I'd planned to knock the pistol away, take it from her, maybe put her on her ass again, but the final shot tore into my hip and struck bone as I reached her.

Pain.

I was on her. The wolf was on her. The gun was knocked across the room, forgotten. I had her on the floor, beneath me, my hands around her skull. I was roaring, filling the room with the pain and anger that flooded my senses.

Yes. Yes! Kill!

The pain of the little bullet grinding within me had knocked me from the driver's seat. The wolf was in control now. I could feel her pulse through the palms of my hands, just as I felt the itching in my gums and fingertips as the change threatened to wash over me. Fangs and claws ached to burst free, to tear into her, to taste her. I could push my thumbs through her temples and into her skull. It would be easy. Her fear was primal and absolute, flooding my nose, intoxicating me. I wanted to taste it. To taste the hot blood gush over my mouth as I ate her heart. It would be so good.

Rita's baby wailed, and I was dimly aware of motion across the room. It drew my eye. Andy moved and covered the child with her body, not wanting to let him watch his mother get torn to wet meaty shreds. Andy herself stared directly at me and met my gaze with her blue and emerald eyes. Something in her eyes gave me pause, sent a small shiver through me that had the effect of somebody snapping their fingers beside my ears or dousing me with a small splash of cool water. I saw her worry and fear, not for herself, but for the baby she was shielding.

Children shouldn't have to see something like that. They shouldn't have to carry the memory of their mothers being attacked–being beaten in front of them. I know.

No. I struggled to assert myself against the wolf. *Not a woman. Never. Another. Woman.*

I heard myself laugh, heard the wolf laugh through my mouth, a nasty snarling sound. *Yes,* it thought back to me. *Meat is meat.* My hands tightened on Rita's skull. I could feel more than hear the creaking of her skull as it began to give out under my strength. I could smell everything. Taste everything. The panicked hammering of Rita's heart, the smell of the urine spilling from her as she squirmed uselessly, and the hushing noises that Andy made to the baby as she began, herself, to quietly sob.

No! I'll kill you. I'll kill us both. This time I won't fail. God help me, if I kill another woman, I will end it. I promise you!

The wolf took notice. It could feel my sincerity. My self-loathing. It couldn't understand it, but it knew I meant it. Catholic upbringing be damned, if suicide was the only way not to live as a monster, I'd do it.

The wolf hesitated, and in that moment, I had him. I saw myself with my hands around his bestial throat, wrenching him away from the front of my mind. He snarled and snapped, but I didn't care. Let him tear me to pieces if that was what it took. I wasn't letting go. Andy and Rita only saw me sitting there, hands on Rita's head, not moving. But internally, I was throwing myself against the wolf. I kicked. I clawed. I bit. I fought like a wolf. I felt his grudging respect as I forced him back down into the depths of our mind. He would challenge me again, soon, but for now at least, I had won dominance. I was the alpha of my own mind, for the moment.

I released Rita and sat with my back against the faux-wood wall, pressing my left hand to my hip to staunch the bleeding. Rita rose with a grimace, white marks in the shape of my fingers already darkening on her forehead. She scrambled across the room to her baby. Andy gave him to her without hesitation and Rita held the filthy, squalling boy and sobbed over him in the corner. The wolf watched through my eyes, still salivating with the thought of tearing into her. She was prey to him now.

I forced some slow, deep breaths as I gathered my wits. I waited for the ache in my muscles to subside. The itching in my gums and fingertips lingered, though. Finally, I stood painfully and looked at Rita. She was no threat anymore. She was incoherent. She had given up completely on the thought of killing Andy or keeping her from leaving with me. The man on the phone would be angry, but Rita wasn't thinking that far ahead. She was just glad to be alive. I'd seen it before. I'd felt it before.

"Move," I said to Andy, my voice raw and guttural now with the lingering influence of the wolf. She moved to the door, trembling.

I took a last cleansing breath in the unclean bedroom air, and a thought occurred to me. Walking to the closet, I grabbed the gym bag where I had smelled the dope. For a moment I stood there, holding it, and looked to Rita where she sat on the floor with her child, daring her to object to my taking it.

She didn't.

CHAPTER FOUR

Andy was a smart girl, smart enough to know not to give me any trouble after what she'd just seen. She got into the front seat of my Blazer when I wordlessly directed her to do so. Blue gave a little whimper of submission when she saw me. She could smell the wolf near the surface, and she moved back to let Andy have the front seat. I was in no state to trust the girl enough to let her sit behind me as I drove.

I'd be okay for now; the bullet could wait. My side burned, but the bleeding had already stopped, a benefit of having had the wolf so close to the surface.

I'd almost killed that woman, Rita. It had been so close. Things could so easily have gone the other way. It made me feel sick. I stopped at the driver's side door for a moment and emptied my stomach into the wet snow. The muscle spasms made the pain worse, but I compartmentalized the sensation and kept it away from my other self. I was overcome again by the unnerving sensation of being watched. The wolf had washed away the opiate shield I'd been hiding behind, and I felt exposed. I kept my eyes on the ground. I didn't want to see the specters that I was certain were staring at me.

I got into the Blazer and immediately found my bottle of Vicodin. I emptied it into my mouth and choked them down. Andy looked at me with a queer expression but didn't say anything. I glanced back at her. *Say something, I dare you.* She looked away. Blue came up from the back seat and lay protectively across Andy's lap. She looked up at me and whined softly.

I started the Chevy and we drove out of the trailer park in silence, headed for the interstate. Minutes later, we passed two bikers in Los Perdidos patching headed the other direction. Back to Edison Court. They were in for disappointment. Andy ducked as they passed us. I turned my head as they passed—I don't have a rearview mirror—and saw that one had the full patch and rockers on his back. The other wore a single rocker that only said "Prospect" across his lower back.

"Friends of yours?" I said, finally breaking the silence.

She shrugged.

"Who are they?"

"Just a couple of guys I know," she avoided the question.

"I'm sorry," I said, "I must have accidentally given you the impression that I'm a patient man having a good day."

She took the hint.

"That's Rudy and Lodi. That was Rudy's house. He's Rita's guy."

I nodded. It fit. Rudy had been the guy on the phone.

"They were going to get rid of you," I said.

"I know. I need to find a new place to stay."

"No," I said. "They were going to kill you. Rudy called Rita about it right before I got you. That's why she was trying to make you stay."

She didn't say anything for a moment. I could practically hear the wheels turning in her head. She wanted to know how I had known about the phone call. Had the phone been bugged?

It was a reasonable assumption. Blue must have picked up on the girl's anxiety. She licked at her hand reassuringly. That surprised me. Blue is a sweet dog but doesn't often show that side of herself to strangers. Andy stroked the dog's muzzle gratefully.

"What's her name?" she asked.

"Blue."

"She's sweet," she said.

"Yeah," I grunted.

She found the spot behind Blue's ear, her favorite spot to be scratched, and the dog slapped the seat with her happy tail in appreciation.

"Are you a cop?"

"Do I look like a cop?" I asked.

"No."

We drove in silence a little longer, and I left her to her thoughts. Her smell was distracting me. Lavender, vanilla, and that puzzling, verdant scent that made me think of springtime. It was nice, too nice, and the wolf wasn't entirely settled. I didn't need the distraction.

"Do you know how to roll a cigarette?"

"I know how to roll a joint," she said.

"Same idea." I reached into a pocket and gave her the pouch of tobacco and papers. Her fingers were cold. "Roll me one."

She froze for a moment after our hands touched and looked at me again, like she was seeing something else that she hadn't seen before.

"What?" I asked.

"It's... nothing," she said and turned her attention to the job I'd given her.

She nimbly rolled a cigarette with both hands, nice and tight. Better than I could do it. I took it and lit it, cracking the window a little for her benefit and turning on the heat.

"Can I have one?" she asked.

"Suit yourself," I said, lighting it for her after she finished rolling.

"Thanks," she took a drag and coughed, hard. Most people had a hard time without filters.

"Do you think that's good for the baby?" I asked.

She almost dropped the cigarette along with her jaw.

"W—what?" she stammered.

I didn't answer. She ground out her smoke in the Blazer's unused ash tray.

"What are you?" she asked, wide eyed.

"Just a guy doing a job," I said.

"What job?"

"You've got court. I'm making sure you show up."

Now she smelled afraid. Not of me, but afraid.

"So, you're like, what, a bounty hunter?" she asked.

I shrugged.

I finished my cigarette as we drove south on the interstate. We passed a couple of small towns in silence. Andy settled herself by stroking Blue. The dog twitched her tail contentedly and pretended to sleep.

"So, do you have a name?" Andy asked.

"Yeah."

She rolled her eyes at me.

"Are you going to tell me what it is?"

"No."

She glared at me, unafraid.

"Holy shit, you're bleeding!" I'd stopped bleeding before I'd gotten into the driver's seat, but she noticed the blood on my shirt and pants. Rita's bullet had missed my field jacket, luckily, but the jacket had opened enough now that the wound was just visible to the teenaged girl.

"It's fine," I said.

She stared at me, disbelieving.

"What?" I said.

"Those scratches on your face," she said, pointing at the marks Rita had left when she'd jumped on me, "they were bleeding a few minutes ago. Now they look old, like they happened days ago."

I didn't say anything.

"What *are* you?" she asked again, but she still didn't seem scared of me. Strange girl. I didn't answer.

She looked at me like she was studying me, like she saw something. I wondered what she thought she saw, but I didn't want to talk any more than I had to. She'd already seen too much, and I didn't want to give her anything else to remember about me.

The cigarette was out, and her smell was beginning to distract me.

"Roll me another one, kid," I said.

She stared at me, stubbornly.

"What's your name?" she finally said.

I sighed.

"Frank."

"Oh," she said and turned away.

I could smell the change in her attitude. Something was making her skin crawl. She started to roll another cigarette with her long, nimble fingers.

"What?" I asked her as I lit the cigarette.

She shrugged.

"Spit it out."

"It's just... I really don't like that name," she said, obviously thinking of somebody else.

"Ah," I said. "Me neither."

She smiled.

"What kind of name is Andy?" I asked.

"Cassandra," she said, "it's short for Cassandra."

We drove for about a half-hour after leaving the trailer park. We didn't say much. I pondered who the hell this girl was with her distracting smell and emerald fleck in her eye. Why could I see that? I wanted to look at those eyes again, to savor the color that had been lost to me for so many years, but I knew better than to meet her eyes. With the wolf this close to the surface, it would be an unkind thing to do to her. I pulled off the interstate in the city of Everett, where Mack had his offices.

"Listen," she said, "can you just let me go? You don't have to bring me back."

I shook my head, no.

"Please?" she begged. "I'll do... anything."

She emphasized that last word in a clumsy but well-practiced attempt at seduction. It was clear to me what she meant. The kid had gotten used to trading her body for safety. Judging by the bruises on her face, and the bikers ready to kill her, that hadn't been working out the way she'd hoped.

She was pretty in a rough and tumble sort of way, more fierce than beautiful, but she was just a damn kid. The fact that she thought I might take her up on an offer like that made me angry. The fact that there was a part of me that liked the idea made me even angrier.

She reached her hand out and rested it on my knee, creating a curious and pleasant warmth. I pushed her away, roughly.

"Don't," I growled.

We were getting close to Mack's. She was puzzling me. After everything she'd just seen, she should be scared to death of me. She was scared, but not of me. That wasn't right. I didn't get it.

"Why aren't you scared of me?" I asked her.

She looked at me again with those strange eyes in that way of hers, like she saw something I couldn't. I didn't meet her glance, but I could feel the weight of those eyes on me. Then she smiled. It changed her face, that smile. She was still the same scrawny bruised kid who had seen and done ugly things to get by, but there was a warmth there when she smiled. A fire that crept into her mismatched eyes and made them sparkle.

"Why do you want me to be?" she asked.

The kid had guts. Against my better judgement, I decided that I liked her.

I pulled the car into an alley and parked in front of an old house not far from the train station. A blue neon sign read "Watson Bail Bonds." We were there.

He must have been watching for us, because the side door opened, and the familiar shape of Mack Watson walked down the three steps. Blue recognized him. She sat up and started to whine excitedly, one paw pressing against the window.

I saw Mack suddenly as Andy must see him, struck by how old and fat he'd become. I'd first known him when he'd been young and fit, a negro soldier in a segregated unit who still had both of his hands. The old, bearded man in front of me breathed heavily just from walking down the stairs, his prosthetic left hand tucked into his coat pocket as usual. His bushy white beard and prominent gut suited him well each winter when he dressed up as Santa Claus for the local foster kids. He'd practically been a kid when I met him, not much older than Andy, but now he looked like a grandfather.

"Kid," I said, "Mack is a good guy. You don't have to be scared."

I didn't know what I was doing. I wanted to reassure the girl but didn't know how. I put a hand on her shoulder. She stiffened. I pulled it back. I was bad at this.

"You're clueless," she said as she angrily got out of the car.

"Probably," I agreed under my breath.

"Miss Morgan," Mack's deep voice greeted Andy, "I'm glad you could make it."

She didn't answer, just stared at her feet ashamedly. He stepped forward and got a good look at her bruised face, as good as he could get in the fading daylight.

"Goddamn," he said with disgust. "Let's get you some ice, honey. Marilyn!"

A handsome blonde woman in her fifties came to the door and briefly glared in my direction while I sat in the Blazer and pretended not to see her. We had history. Blue hopped out and nuzzled Andy's hand in farewell. The girl took a knee and let the dog give her a proper kiss goodbye.

"Bye-bye, Blue," she said to the dog.

"Your father is going to be here soon, Andy," Mack said. "Go on inside with Marilyn, and she'll get you something to eat while you wait."

Andy continued to watch her feet as she walked reluctantly inside and didn't object as Marilyn ushered her into the building with a motherly hand on her back. Blue shimmied excitedly to Mack who smiled and gave her his real hand to lick.

"Hey there, girl," Mack said in the voice that grown men reserve only for dogs and small children. "How're you doing, Blue? Still hanging around with this loser?"

Mack thinks he's funny. Always did.

CHAPTER FIVE

"What the hell happened?" Mack said when he saw the blood on my shirt. I was puffing away on one of his customary menthols while Blue did her business in the alley.

"Don't worry," I said. "It's mine."

"Oh, well *that's* a relief," Mack said. He has a long relationship with sarcasm.

"I said don't worry about it."

"Did Andy do that? You didn't do that to her face did you?"

I couldn't muster enough self-righteousness to be offended. Considering how close I'd come to ripping the head off the woman who had actually shot me, I couldn't blame Mack for wondering. But it hit me like a punch in the gut to think that he wondered if I could have done that to a young kid like Andy.

"No."

"I'm sorry, Red," he said. "It's just—I've seen how you can lose it when you get hurt. In the moment, you know."

He wasn't wrong. We stood there for a minute, thinking about memories we both would rather avoid discussing and averting our eyes to give Blue some modicum of dignity while she hunched her back and dropped a steaming load beside somebody's freshly washed Volvo.

"You look like shit," he said, no doubt inspired by Blue.

"Thanks," I said.

"Seriously Frank," he lowered his voice, "I know you're tough. You've got, y'know, your 'thing'. Hell, we've known each other—what now—fifty years?"

"I don't keep track." Fifty years sounded about right. "What's your point?"

"My point? When I met you, you were older than me."

"I still am," I said.

"Right, well, you don't look it. You look younger than my damn son."

"Healthy living," I said, taking a long drag of the borrowed cigarette for emphasis. He didn't laugh.

"My ass," he said. "You look like hell. You've got rings under your eyes. You've lost weight. I swear, you look like you should be singing in one of those grunge bands."

"I don't sing," I lied.

He sighed and dropped the subject. Finally taking the hint.

"So, what happened at the trailer park?"

"They were getting ready to off her," I said.

"No kidding? Damn, she's in deeper than I thought."

"In what?" I asked

"Drugs," he said. "She's been hanging around the wrong people and got picked up on a bust. Her old man talked her into cutting a deal and testifying."

"But she got scared and ran off?"

"Yeah, about a week ago."

"Smart kid," I said.

"What's that supposed to mean?"

"It means she knows better than to turn stoolie on guys like this."

"Guys like who? And Jesus, Red, stoolie? Who talks like that anymore?"

I ignored his jab.

"Some bikers. A newbie named Rudy and some shot caller called Lodi, ring any bells?"

"Yeah," he said. "One of them anyway. Lodi. I've heard that one. Bikers and their dumb nicknames."

"What've you heard?"

"His real name's Vargas, Carl Vargas, out of California. He's connected. I think he's done some time. He has what they call *anger management issues*. He served, too. Lots of these bikers have. I think he was a Marine. Like you."

"Well, this Vargas character was on his way with the new guy to ice her when I got there. I overheard a phone call to your snitch. She had a last-minute change of heart."

I touched my waist where Rita's bullet was making me wish I'd brought more Vicodin. I thought longingly of the bag of heroin I'd lifted, just waiting for me in the back of my Blazer.

"You didn't make a mess, did you?" Mack sounded concerned.

"No," I said, finishing the menthol and holding my hand out for another. "No bodies. It was close, though."

Mack let out a relieved sigh and handed me another smoke. I lit it and then whistled for Blue. She came running.

"I'm sorry about the timing," Mack said, "but you can see why I couldn't send somebody else."

"What about your kid?" I asked. "Isn't your boy still a cop?"

"Owen? Yeah," Mack beamed. "He's a Detective Sergeant now."

"So why not have him pull some strings, raid the place?"

"Wrong county. Those bikers live out in the sticks by your place for a reason. Jurisdiction bullshit. How do you think it would have gone if some country sheriff had come knocking on doors?"

"Yeah," I said. My side hurt. "I guess so."

"Frank," Mack sounded serious, "do you even know what county you were in?"

Mack means well, but he worries about the dope. He always has. He thinks I'm going to hurt myself, and he doesn't understand that my body doesn't work the same as everybody else's. What would kill most people just gives me a pleasant nap.

"How about your girl? She still acing school?" I asked. This wasn't the time to talk about me.

"School? Shit Frank, you don't even know what year this is, do you?"

I took a long drag of the cigarette and tried not to look like I was thinking too hard about that question. Luckily, the tags on Mack's SUV were always current.

"1995," I said casually. The number surprised me, but I wasn't about to let Mack know that he'd been right.

"Yeah. *Ninety-Five.* Marie finished med school in *eighty-four,* and Owen hasn't been in school since he joined the force in *seventy-eight.* Frank, you worry me sometimes."

"Drop it, Mack," I said quietly.

"Alright, Frank, alright," Mack said. "I'm sorry again that I pulled you into this. Thanks for handling it."

"Forget about it," I said. "Just pay up and let me get home."

"Why don't you come in for some coffee?" Mack offered, "Clear your head. Let Marilyn patch you up."

"Just pay me, Mack," I said. "It's getting late."

"Right, okay." Mack sounded disappointed.

Mack turned to his big blue Suburban, a newer model that he kept waxed and sparkling. He pulled out his keys and opened the door, then turned to rummage around in his back seat. He returned, struggling to hold a cardboard box which he attempted to hand to me. I didn't take it.

"What the hell is this?" I looked in the box and saw... groceries? Canned stew, a few pounds of hamburger, and dog food. No beer.

"Consider this a bonus," Mack smiled, breathing heavy.

"A bonus is what you give somebody on top of their payment," I said as Mack walked past me and set the box on the hood of my Chevy.

"After that phone bill I paid for you, you're lucky not to owe *me* any money," he said, frowning.

"I never asked you to—"

"You're welcome," he said.

I was too tired to be angry. Besides, the dogs and I needed the food. But I'd be damned if I was going to thank him. I opened the back seat and slid the box in. Mack raised an eyebrow as he saw the gym bag on the floor behind the driver's seat.

"What's that?" Mack asked.

"Mine."

"Red..."

"The kid's a junkie," I said, dodging the subject.

"What?"

"Andy, she's a dope fiend. I could smell it on her."

"Damn. I thought so, but I was hoping I was wrong."

I don't know why I told him that. I'd like to think it was because I was worried about Andy and her baby and knew that Mack would help her. But honestly, I think it may have just been to shut him up about the bag. I thought about letting him know that she was pregnant too but decided that I'd already spilled enough of her beans. That was her business to handle. She'd tell him if she wanted to.

I wanted to ask about Andy, but Mack probably wouldn't

know anything that would explain the things about her that puzzled me. The emerald in her eye, or the way she smelled like springtime. Besides, the longer I let Mack talk, the more chances he'd have to try and talk me inside for coffee so he could try another damn intervention. I was in no mood.

I opened the door to the front of the Blazer and Blue jumped in to take her customary place riding shotgun. Mack gave her an affectionate rub on the jowls, and she lolled her tongue blissfully before he closed the door. I opened my door and got in.

"Red, I'm worried about you."

"Don't be."

"It don't work that way."

"Too bad."

"Don't be an ass, Frank," he said. "We've got to talk. I'm gonna come up to your dump on Monday to see you. That should give you a couple days to ride out your 'thing'. So, don't bite my head off when I show up."

"Fine," I said, and started the engine.

The western sky was clearing to my left as I drove home, giving me a good view of the last bits of sunset over the water and, further behind, the snow-capped Olympic mountains. To my right, the Cascade foothills were still shrouded in the clouds that had recently given us our late blanket of slush. It looked like it was going to be a clear sky tonight, but it would be a bad evening for stargazers. The moon would be reaching her fullness a little after two in the morning, and her light would be overpowering.

That thought, along with the pain in my hip, made me break out in a cold sweat. I could do a lot to hold back the wolf. I had done a lot in the last few hours. But after everything I'd just gone through, there was no way I'd have what it would take to keep him locked down when the moon crested. The actual moment of the full moon is another matter. People think of a full moon as something that happens over the course of a night, or even a couple nights, and they aren't far wrong. Actually, there is one precise moment, just a heartbeat really, when the moon is *full*. Sometimes it happens at night and sometimes in the middle of the day. Each month is different. This is the climax of the lunar cycle, when she stops growing in the sky and starts waning, and this is the moment when the wolf in me gets his way. No matter what. I make damn sure to be locked up and far away from people when that moment comes.

I spotted Andy's unfinished cigarette in my ashtray and lit it, drawing deep to steady my nerves. The taste of her was still on it where her lips had been. She tasted like maple blossoms. I tried not to think about that. I finished the cigarette as I crossed the Skagit River and rolled down the window to toss it out, but I hesitated and put the cigarette out in the ashtray where Andy had left it, for a change.

I drove past the exit where Andy and I had pulled onto the interstate, too close to home. A couple of miles later I was passing out of the Skagit valley and climbing into the wooded hills where I lived. The slush along the road was more serious up here, almost snow, but not quite. They were building something along the interstate by my exit. A big construction project. Some kind of hotel or casino, I'd heard. That was too close, too. I didn't like it.

It didn't take more than ten or fifteen minutes on the country roads to arrive at the entrance to my place, not that anybody else would think of it as an entrance. I pulled off at a locked gate that seemed to be restricting access to a thin spot between trees and blackberry bushes.

"Stay," I told Blue as I hopped out and fumbled with the combination lock, unwrapped the chain, and swung the rusty gate open with a push. I then climbed back into the Blazer, pulling past the gate, and leaving Blue once more to lock the gate behind us. The entrance to my place was almost completely overgrown with grass, low-hanging tree branches, and blackberry bushes to the point that it was nearly impossible to tell that the place was there at all, and I liked it that way. Sure, I couldn't get in and out of a car to close the gate without getting a few scratches on my hands or leaves in my hair, but I judged that inconvenience a small price to pay for a little extra privacy.

I carefully pulled a particularly thick branch of blackberry thorns from the side of my field jacket before squeezing back into the driver's seat.

I was feeling my years as I pulled forward through the brush. Branches and thorns scraped against my Blazer—a few more scratches would make no difference—and parted to reveal the mossy clearing where I kept the old aluminum travel-trailer. Blue sat up excitedly as the rest of her pack came bounding and barking toward us into my headlights. I put the Chevy in park and opened the passenger door first, allowing Blue to exit and accept the brunt of the welcoming frenzy. Smedley, the only member of the pack who rivalled Beatrice for reliability and character, took the lead. But soon the seven other dogs that made up our pack of strays all joined the fray, and I couldn't help but smile a little despite myself. If a pack of happy dogs making fools of themselves doesn't make you smile, then nothing can.

When I stepped out of the car, all nine dogs ran to surround and welcome me. They knew better than to jump or nip at me as they had with Blue. They recognized the predator in me as the biggest and most dominant member of the pack and were instinctively submissive. Cold noses politely nudged the back of my hands as others snuffled at my pant legs. I rubbed their heads and patted their sides in descending order of their rank in the pack hierarchy.

Even though she had been with me on my outing, I acknowledged Blue first along with Smedley so that the others would know that I recognized the pair as dominant over the rest of them. After that, I rubbed the ears of Patton, the scarred black-and-white pit mix who was a close runner-up for dominance. Then came Winston, a pudgy bulldog who demanded his share of respect in the pack with sheer stubbornness and an absurd sort of dignity. Next in the hierarchy, by virtue of his ridiculous size, was Lenny. The good natured—and slightly stupid—mutt weighed more than I did. He was easily the biggest, the dumbest, and possibly the sweetest member of my little pack. I wasn't sure of his heritage, but his shaggy grey hair and floppy ears made me think there was some wolfhound in his bloodline somewhere along with a generous serving of horse. Next came Fred. The anxious mutt looked part Doberman and part Collie and could never seem to hold still. He was skittish and prone to biting any hand but mine. I suspect he'd been beaten before he joined my little pack. Norma Jean and Nettle, one as elegant as the other was prickly, came next. Last came Oliver, an old, stubby-legged mutt with some obvious beagle ancestry and an obnoxious tendency to beg and whine. He was the oldest, but also the smallest and least dominant of the group.

Reaching back into the Blazer, I pulled out the box of groceries that Mack had pushed on me and placed it on the hood. I held up one palm for the dogs to see and they immediately fell silent, sitting in place. I ripped open a bag of dry kibble and emptied it on the ground beside the Blazer, all the dogs wagged their tails and licked their chops ferociously but knew better than to make a move yet. Oliver let loose a pathetic whine before Patton snarled and snapped at him, shutting him up. I went on to empty a pack of hamburger meat onto the bag's contents, courtesy of Mack's generosity. I took a small pinch of the hamburger and ate it, letting the pack see me do it. The alpha eats first.

I like my meat rare, but not raw. I intended to cook my supper inside.

The metallic and juicy sensations of the cold meat on my tongue had the wolf rumbling in his cage.

Wait. Almost. Soon.

The dogs stayed in place, watching me attentively as I retrieved the gym bag from the back seat, and limped with the box of groceries and my bag of ill-gotten gains toward my trailer.

"Okay."

As soon as I whispered the word that released them to their feast, Blue and Smedley dove into the food and took their pick of the meat and kibble before Patton and the rest of the pack joined in. I set the box on a rusted folding chair beside the door and took off my jacket and sunglasses. No point in making a mess inside.

I peeled off my bloodied shirt and tossed it into the steel drum that I occasionally used for fires and took off my belt before pulling my pants down a couple of inches, examining the hole in my hip where Rita had shot me. It was swollen and crusted over, purple around the edges. This was going to hurt.

Shirtless in the snow, I walked to the nearest tree, a mossy birch, and braced myself against a low hanging branch thicker than my leg. I doubled the leather belt over in my hand and then folded it over again before putting the thumb-thick hide between my teeth.

Alright you son of a bitch, do your thing.

I looked up at the night sky and my eyes found the nearly full moon peeking at me from behind the retreating clouds. I felt the wolf inside me rise up like boiling water against a pot lid, heat filling my limbs and shooting into my fingers and toes. My nails hardened and dug into the tree branch, my teeth sharpened and punctured the belt, and a low, rumbling growl began to grow in my chest and throat.

I felt a burning in my hip and a writhing sensation, like worms crawling through my flesh where the bullet had lodged itself. I looked down and saw the flesh pucker as something moved beneath my skin. Then the bullet, the size of a child's tooth, pushed itself out of the hole and fell to the ground. The wound itself oozed a small rivulet of blood but then sealed itself before my eyes. The injury wasn't gone, but nobody who saw it would believe that it had happened today.

The belt dropped from my mouth and the wolf howled at the waves of pain. I let him have his moment. The dogs grew silent and hid behind or beneath the Blazer, laying low to the ground in submission. They were in no danger if they stayed out of the way. They were our pack.

The pain and anger of the day's events, along with some portion of the residual frustration and pain of my unnaturally long life, found its way to my arms. The tree branch, thicker than my leg, snapped like a twig. The rest came out of my mouth in something like a scream. I heard the biggest dog, Lenny, whimper in fear. They knew better than to run. Pack or not, if they ran, the wolf would have had to give chase.

In the dim corner of my mind, I decided to redirect the wolf by giving him something he wanted. Instead of anger and pain I focused on my hunger, on the burning emptiness in my gut. I felt it more keenly now after healing. My nose twitched and my heightened Garou senses locked on to the rich, coppery scent of the bloody meat sitting in the grocery box. All thoughts of cooking it had fled my mind.

I tore into the packaging with my teeth and scarfed the pound of raw meat. Its weight in my stomach gave me just enough control to open the next package with my hands, but I ate it just as greedily. It was glorious.

After eating, I crouched there in the snow and revelled in the feeling of a full belly and the night air on my bare skin. Soon, my dogs joined me, they licked the beef blood from my hands and face while I nuzzled at them affectionately. Slowly, exhaustion took hold and the wolf gave way again to the man.

I rose from the ground, stiff and cold. I grabbed a handful of wet snow in my hands and rubbed it on my face before walking back to the now broken birch tree. I felt almost like I should apologize to the poor thing. On the ground, I saw the small spatter of blood I'd left before, and I bent to retrieve the ridiculously small piece of metal that had been causing me grief all afternoon.

I didn't risk looking at it again, but I could feel in my bones that the moon hadn't yet crested. There was time yet, and when it came, the wolf wouldn't be satisfied with some broken wood and a couple pounds of hamburger. It was time to get inside.

I unlocked and opened the door to step into the dark trailer. I was quickly joined by Tybalt. I fumbled with my old Coleman lantern and it burst to life with a low hiss, casting deep shadows with its dim light.

I closed the door and dropped the bullet into the mason jar by the stove, adding it to my collection. It was cold in the trailer, maybe colder than it had been outside. I'd run out of propane sometime in February. But at least it was dry and there was no wind.

"Maggie sends her love," I said.

Evelyn sat in her chair, exactly where I knew she would be waiting for me. She didn't say anything. She sat quietly and looked at me with that sweetly sad smile she always had for me. I couldn't look at her.

"She's not doing too well, but she misses you," I said.

Evelyn didn't speak.

I found a half-finished beer that I'd left open who knew how long ago and upended it. It was flat but very cold. I pretended not to notice what was probably a fly.

"I had a hell of a day," I told my wife. "Mack sent me after this kid. She was tough. Reminded me of you. You'd like her."

Evelyn didn't say anything.

I placed the gym bag on the kitchen table and sat down to finally open it.

"Let's see what we have here."

There were pounds of heroin, neatly wrapped and packaged inside. I'd known that the bikers were in the dope selling game, but I had no idea they were in it so deep.

Damn. Pounds of it. If the stuff was any good, and it smelled like it was, I was holding hundreds of thousands of dollars' worth of heroin.

I sat and pondered the contents of the bag for a few long minutes.

"Well, no point just staring at it," I said as I walked past my wife to fetch the pipe from my bed.

Evelyn didn't say anything.

I loaded the pipe well beyond what anybody else could expect to smoke alone and carried it back to my bed. Given the choice, smoking was my preferred road to oblivion, but I'd just eat the stuff if I had to. Whatever it took to get the job done. Well, anything but needles. I'm deathly afraid of needles, I ain't proud of it, but if I'm being honest, nothing triggers my fight or flight instincts like somebody coming at me with a syringe. It is an old terror of mine and one that isn't going anywhere anytime soon.

Sitting down, I found the handcuffs and combination bicycle lock and steel cable that I left attached to the frame. I cuffed my ankle to the trailer and threw the key across the room, out of my reach.

Getting loose was no problem for me, all I had to do was enter the combination to the padlock and I'd be free to walk over and get the key to the cuffs. Easy. Easy for a man, anyway. Not so easy for a wolf. What *would* be easy would be to use that Garou strength to rip the cable from the frame. At least, it would be easy if I weren't so high on heroin that I couldn't open my eyes. The moon would crest, and the wolf would take over, sure. But by then all he'd be taking over would be my limp body and drug-addled dreams.

It was a system that hadn't failed me since I'd started it several years earlier.

From the corner of my eye I could see Evelyn looking at me with disgust and disapproval. I deserved it.

"I'm sorry," I said as I lit the pipe.

Rita really hadn't been lying, the dope was good.

"I'm sorry, Evelyn," I said again as I took another hit.

Evelyn didn't say anything.

Soon I had finished the pipe and I could feel the warm wave of the high washing over me, burying the wolf in the comfortable oblivion. The moon was almost full. My eyes were closed, and I lay curled on my side on my shabby bed. I felt my wife join me, slipping into the bed behind me, pressed against me.

"I'm sorry, Evelyn," I said, the tears starting to come.

The ghost of my long dead wife put her arm over me and held me there as I started to fade.

"I'm sorry I killed you."

Evelyn didn't say anything. She never did.

CHAPTER SIX

"Dreams are the touchstones of our characters." Thoreau said that. If he was right, I hate to think what that says about my character. I'd avoid my dreams if I could. They are sad and pathetic things full of guilty memories. On most nights, the dope does a decent enough job of helping me avoid, or at least blunt, those dreams, but not when the moon is full. On those nights, the wolf is too strong to be kept in without constant, conscious effort, and so when I sleep, I dream wolf dreams.

The wolf isn't one to wallow in self-pity and regret. He doesn't even know what those feelings are. When he does our dreaming, he spits those emotions of mine aside like indigestible tufts of gristle and hair without a second thought. The wolf dreams first of the hunt, always the hunt. The dreams always start the same way, in a forest unlike any that exists today, if it ever existed at all. I think it did exist, somewhere, sometime. Maybe on some other world if not in this one. It has the feel of a memory. The smell of home.

I find myself bathed in cold, green light, between tree trunks bigger than houses. I'm standing on four paws upon a soft bed of pine needles, so thick and soft that my steps don't make a sound.

This is the only green I know anymore, besides the green of memory. This place, this wolf-wood, is painted in colors that don't exist in the living world. The thick branches of prehistorically enormous trees reach into the clouds and leave me with no sense of the position of the sun or stars. The light that streams through is like moonlight, but from all directions, bright enough to create an eternal twilight but too dim to cast shadows. A cool, silvery green. The perfect light for my wolf eyes.

It smells clean, this primeval forest of dew and pine, of sap and soil. A familiar smell. I am the wolf, and I am at peace. A contradiction to my waking life. But only at first. Before long I become aware of a hunger, like antlers piercing my guts, and I know that I must hunt. That I must kill if I'm ever to feel that peace again. The clean smell of the forest is joined by the distant, savory smells of warm, living meat, and I am off. Four legs carry my furry body along in search of my prey like a terrible, swift wind.

What comes next is often different in the specifics, but I always find it, the source of that unbearably sweet smell. Sometimes it's a stag, other times a boar. I've taken down bison and moose and even great beasts that I don't recognize, with strange horns and snouts. Sometimes, it's something like a man.

Tonight, it was Rita, the woman who had shot me.

I see her kneeling by a spring, cupping water to her mouth and looking about herself nervously like the prey she knows herself to be. There is no clothing here in my forest, only flesh and fur. She doesn't see me with her blind doe eyes. I creep on my belly, closer and closer. I can almost taste her. But this is no sport, taking her unawares. I crave the chase. Before I am close enough to pounce, I raise my head and howl a challenge. I dare her to escape. I dare any other beast to come between us. She is mine. She sees me then. Our eyes lock and she knows. She is mine. Fear and arousal flood my nose as her heart beats hard enough to hear. She runs.

Yes.

I am after her. She has no chance. I close quickly, too quickly. I nip at her heel to turn her left and then right. I bite at her naked flank, just hard enough to draw blood. I let her pull away then as I savor the taste of her fear of me, her need for me. It fills my senses. She disappears quickly into the cover of the forest, but I can hear her still, the careless snap of twigs and her panicked, greedy gasping. It is simple to circle around her again and catch her off guard. A cub could do it. I nip at her again and again, turning her, spurring her on, tasting her.

Finally, she stumbles, exhausted. I've prolonged the hunt as long as I can. She backs against a tree and watches me, her breasts heaving, her tears flowing as I approach. There is no hurry now, the outcome is certain. She wants it every bit as much as I do. More. She needs this. It is what she is for. She is prey.

Her screams mingle with my howls and fill the forest. Sex and blood and triumph and satiation fill me, fill her. It is over too soon, always too soon, but as I lay there among her remains, cracking bones and lazily licking at the marrow, I can feel it again. The peace. Contentment.

Yes. This is right. This is what we are. Brother.

Glowing eyes watch me from the boughs, flickering lights of countless colors that dance from branch to branch. They're always there, the wisps, winking in and out. Among the lights I see two that seem to be focused on me. Blue sparks that seem intrigued by the sated wolf as he prepares to sleep. Blue, but not completely. The sapphire on the left is different, a pairing of sapphire and emerald, blue and green.

Andy?

I wake to the smell of Evelyn. Evelyn and my own piss and

vomit. My bed is full of them both. I'm at once disgusted with myself, and I'm sure she is too. She sits in her old chair, looking at me, full of silence and pity. I don't meet her eyes. I never do.

"Leave me alone," I say.

The moon isn't quite gone. I can still feel it pressing on me, stoking the wolf in his cage. It is too soon to be up and about; I can't risk it. I don't want to be conscious. I'm not ready to face myself.

I reach out for the bag of dope and can't quite grab it. I crawl towards it and realize something is wrong. The handcuff is still around my ankle, but the steel cord that anchored me to the trailer is broken.

That's new.

I look around to assure myself that I am indeed in my trailer. I am. The door is slightly ajar, and the night air has left a frost on the inside of my modest home. On my table, on my floor, on the walls, even on my beard. What had happened?

That had been some dream, stronger than most. I'd been shot. I'd been exhausted. No doubt I'd snapped the restraint as I thrashed in my sleep. That had never happened before. It scared me. Badly. My fear threatened to spiral out of control, into a panic that would wake the wolf again. I couldn't allow that.

Forcing deep breaths, I stumbled to the door. I heard Blue whimpering outside the door, but I ignored her. This time, I made certain that the damn door was closed and locked. I was going to have to rely on the drugs to get me through the rest of the weekend. I didn't half mind the thought of getting loaded again. If anything, I was grateful for the excuse.

My numb fingers fumbled with the frosty unwashed pipe, spilling some of the fine powder on the floor as I did. That didn't matter, there was more than enough. I struggled with my lighter to produce a flame, but it was too cold. Damnit.

Evelyn shifted in her seat. I knew that the moon was still full because I could hear the creak of the old wooden chair as she moved. Spirits are strongest during the full moon, more corporeal, better able to influence the world around them. Hell, she might even be stopping the old zippo in my hand from lighting. She'd never done that before, but it was a night for firsts. I wasn't in my right mind.

"Fine," I shouted and threw the lighter across the trailer. There was more than one way to get loaded.

I sat on the floor beside the bag and reached into it with my fingers, producing a sizeable pile of the white powder in my hand. Hundreds of dollars in the palm of my hand. I brought it to my face and snorted deeply. The dry vinegar taste hit me like a truck.

Had I already been on my ass or had it knocked me there? I didn't know. Damn. This was a lot. Too much? A night of firsts indeed. I felt the warm wave crashing down my limbs, engulfing me. A thought occurred to me. Could this kill me? Surely even I had to have a limit. But I knew better. The wolf would never let that happen. Survival was the strongest instinct it had, stronger than the urge to hunt or to mate. Above all, the wolf was a survivor.

Still, I may as well give it the old college try. Mama Shepard didn't raise a quitter. My vision was growing dark. I was sinking into the abyss. Before I completely lost control of my limbs, I brought the handful of dope back to my face and snorted again, doubling down. This time I didn't stop. I fell to my back on the floor and rubbed it into my face, into my nose, into my mouth.

The last thing I saw with my glazing eyes was Evelyn standing over me, looking down at me. She had just the hint of a bitter smile on her familiar mouth.

"Tsk tsk," I hear the reproachful sound as I sink into the floor. Out of the blue, and into the black.

I was gone.

I didn't dream much after that. At least, I don't remember them if I did. I remember flashes. It's a sad cliché that your life flashes before your eyes before you die. That may be true, but I'm no good at dying so I can't be sure. I may have come a little closer than usual that night. Though, brief flashes of my life are all I can remember dreaming. My mother's sad face. My father's fists. Holding a frightened Maggie. The Corps. The trenches and barbed wire of France. The wolves. Evelyn. Most of all Evelyn. Meeting her. Loving her. Killing her. Some life.

When I finally woke up, my mouth was cracked with thirst, and my head was pounding like I'd just fallen to the floor. I lay in a cold puddle of my own piss, and I was fairly sure that somebody had shit in my pants. So much for any thought of salvaging those jeans. At least my stomach had been too empty to add another dose of vomit to my mess.

I glanced around the filthy trailer and saw no sign of Evelyn; her old oak rocker was sitting empty. The worst of the full moon had passed. I crawled to where the handcuff key was sitting on the floor. The cable really had been snapped—I'd hoped I'd dreamt that—and released myself from my disappointing restraints. At least the door was still closed.

Despite my nausea, I was ravenously hungry. My nose was dripping and sweat poured from me, despite the cold. I don't get sick, at least not the way most people do. The wolf was silent in his cage, so I didn't need to get doped up, but I wanted to. Still, Mack would be here in a day or two, depending on what day it was now, and I knew I had to clean up a bit before I could afford to drift off into oblivion again. I took a pinch of the heroin I'd spilled on the floor, just enough to take the edge off the withdrawal and snorted it. My stomach settled and the tremor in my hands eased up a bit as the comforting warmth hit me. I sat for a couple minutes as my head cleared, then I got up and got to business.

I stripped off my pants, tossed them on the pile of filth that I'd been sleeping on and staggered out into the rainy winter daylight, naked and noticeably cold.

CHAPTER SEVEN

"Is that what passes for a pecker where you come from?"

The wolf growled in my skull, and I clenched my fists reflexively, but I kept from jumping out of my skin, the benefits of a waning moon.

"Jesus, Mack," I snapped, squinting and shielding my eyes against the daylight. "How long have you been here?"

Mack Watson leaned against the hood of his old grey Ford Taurus beneath a flimsy prefabricated cover he'd set up a couple of years back for rainy days like this. He kept this car for the occasional surveillance job, and he preferred to take it through the gauntlet of my driveway when he visited rather than risk scratching up his prized Suburban. I regretted giving him the combination to the padlock on the gate, but it was hard to keep such things from the guy who bought it. He had lit a fire in the fire barrel, and it smelled like it had been going long enough to build some coals. He sipped from a can of Coors in his hand and Blue sat dotingly at his feet, keeping the less hospitable members of the pack at a distance where they soaked up what heat they could from the fire. Several empty cans sat at Mack's feet and a cooler rested on the hood beside him. He glanced at his wristwatch.

"Oh, I've been here for about three or four beers now," he grinned and waited for me to marvel at his wit. As usual, I let him wait.

I walked toward the rain barrel where I collected my runoff.

"I thought you knew better than to show up unexpected," I was bothered that I hadn't heard him arrive. His approaching car should have been enough, and my dogs certainly would have alerted me if I hadn't noticed that. But he'd been sitting out here for over an hour, opening and draining cans practically under my nose.

"I told you I was coming up."

"You said Monday," I cupped my hands and slurped greedily at the water.

"It is Monday, Frank."

Rita's dope really was good. I dunked my head into the icy water and splashed some of it onto my body to rinse off the filth while I processed the fact that four nights had passed since I'd seen Mack. My stomach growled in corroboration.

"Damn," Mack shivered, "How can you stand that? Makes me cold just watching you."

"So, don't watch," I said, dunking my head again.

"Have you been sleeping this whole time?"

God, I hope so, I thought to myself.

"Toss me one of those," I held out my hand as Mack passed a silver can. I opened it and drained it without pausing. It was good to have something in my stomach, but it was only a start. I dropped the empty can and extended my hand for another.

"First, maybe you should use that thing or put it away," Mack said with a brief downward glance.

"Alright, alright" I said. I relieved myself against the broken birch and went back into the trailer for a change of clothes.

After wiping myself off with an old towel and throwing on a relatively fresh pair of jeans and a tattered T-shirt, I came back out carrying my boots. My hair and beard, significantly thicker after the full moon, still dripped with water.

"Damn, you look cold," Mack said as he tossed the promised beer.

"I'm not," I said as I opened the can, drinking this one more patiently. Most people don't know what real cold is, especially here in Washington where it seldom snows. Of course, most people didn't have a bloodthirsty wolf spirit sharing their bodies and making them unnaturally resilient. Still, after spending a couple of hard winters barefoot in the Wyoming Bighorns during one of my more reclusive phases in the mid-sixties, I barely noticed what passed for cold anymore here in the northwest.

"Well, I am." Mack said. "Can we go inside? I brought you a tank of propane for the heater if it's still working."

"No," I said. I thought about the piss and puke and shit I'd have to clean up and decided to do Mack a favor. I knew he'd been through the wringer in the war, but some things you can't unsee.

"Well, I ain't staying out here," he said. "Come on, I'll buy you dinner."

Dinner? I glanced at the sky and realized it was late afternoon. Damn.

"Sounds good, let me feed the gang first."

I upended another twenty-pound bag of kibble for the pack and waited for Blue to have her share before putting on my boots and field jacket. Blue looked slightly put out when Mack took her customary place in the passenger seat of my Blazer, but she hopped into the back without much complaint. I don't like to travel without Blue when I can avoid it, she has a way of keeping me level.

"Smells like dog in here," Mack said.

"Can't imagine why."

Blue panted happily over his shoulder and he gave her snout a pat as we pulled through my bramble gauntlet and onto the road. Now that we were in the car together, I noticed that Mack smelled uneasy. He had something on his mind.

"Burgers?" he asked.

"Burgers," I agreed.

I didn't pry, I knew that Mack had come to talk, and he would tell me what was on his mind when he was ready. He made small talk as I took us to Boomer's, an old-style drive-in burger joint in Bellingham that I like. Mack ordered a bacon burger, fries, and a coke. I ordered ten plain burgers and water. Bread and meat, why mess with a good thing? He showed me pictures of his grandkids while we waited for our food. I looked at them politely but didn't really know what to say. There was something on his mind, and I was never good at small talk.

We took our food to a quiet, wooded spot at the nearby lake. I ate two of my burgers on the way and tossed one to a grateful Blue in the back seat. The lake had trails all around it where college kids liked to run or bicycle or take their dogs for walks, and the whole thing was a bit too close to a golf course and the suburbs for my taste. But it was a hell of a lot more comfortable for me than sitting in an enclosed space with a bunch of strangers.

The rain eased up for a while and Blue found a gnarled stick that she managed to bully Mack into throwing for her. It was nice, a couple old friends and a dog having burgers at a lake. I felt almost normal. But it couldn't last.

"So, Red," Mack began nervously, clearing his throat as he searched for words.

Here it comes, I thought to myself. This was the part where he tried to save me. To get me clean, to get me to go to church, to get me to move back into town, to get a life.

"Spit it out, Mack," I said.

"You told me there wasn't any mess—at the trailer park, I mean," he said, "right?"

"That's right," I said. A couple of bruises and some light property damage hardly qualified as a mess by my standards. Well, that and a few hundred thousand dollars in missing heroin. I knew that was going to come back to bite me in the ass. I braced for it.

"Nobody got hurt? You're sure?" he asked.

"That's what I said."

"Okay," he said, "okay, I believe you."

"What is it, Mack? Is the kid okay?"

"Andy? Yeah, she's okay. She's with her dad. She testified. She was scared as hell, but she did good. Real good. Tough kid."

"Then what the hell is it?"

"My informant. She's dead."

"Damn," I said. "Rita? That's a shame. Can't say I'm surprised, though."

"You're not?"

"Well no," I said, "not if her fella found out that she snitched."

Or he found out that his club's dope was missing, I thought to myself.

"Well yes, we already knew that they're not shy about hurting women. We talked about that when she called and told me about Andy. I told her she shouldn't hang around after we got her. But she said that she had that handled."

"Apparently not." I thought about the bruises on Andy's face and the way that Rita had clearly associated force with sex. I found myself wanting to pay a visit to some bikers.

Yes, the wolf liked that idea.

"But that's the thing, Frank," Mack said, "this didn't look like something some angry bikers did. This is something else."

"Oh?" I said. Maybe Los Perdidos were smarter than I gave them credit for. Mack had said that this Lodi guy, Vargas or whatever his real name was, was connected. Maybe he knew how to send a message and cover his tracks.

"It looked like, well, Frank, it looked like some kind of animal got to her. Tore her apart."

"What?"

"The county guys said they'd never seen anything like it. Thought it was a bear attack, or maybe a pack of dogs or some rabid coyotes, or something. But they don't know what we know."

"W—when?" I asked.

"Late Thursday night or early Friday morning," he said, "the night you brought Andy."

"So, you think that I..." I broke into a sweat. I remembered my dream. Rita. The taste of her blood. Her screams. The way she'd felt under me. The way my fangs sank into flesh as I tore into her. It had been so vivid.

"No, Frank," he said, "of course not. I know you. I'm saying that there's someone else out there. Someone like you."

I stared out at the lake, the rain was starting again. Blue knew something was wrong. She sat at my feet and rested her jowls on my knee, whimpering.

"I'm sorry, Frank," Mack went on, "I didn't mean to make it sound like I thought it was you. I know what kind of man you are. I know you'd never do anything like that."

I thought about Evelyn. I remembered the blood on the walls where I'd torn into her. The way she screamed. The way it excited me.

"Frank?"

The dream. The broken cable. The open door.

"Frank?"

"You're wrong," I said.

"What?"

"You're wrong about me, Mack."

"What the hell are you talking about?" he asked.

"I did it," I said under my breath. "I'm a killer. I've done it before."

PART 2

SCHOOL DAYS (WHEN WE WERE A COUPLE OF KIDS)

CHAPTER EIGHT

THE PAST.

I wasn't always a monster. At least, I don't think I was. I can't remember a time, though, when I didn't feel like one. A child believes what their parents tell them, and my parents told me I was a monster, a disappointment, a freak.

I was born in 1899 to a young girl in Montana who had been seduced by a scoundrel. A good Catholic upbringing and a wealthy German father were the main reasons she felt obligated to keep me, but being born deformed didn't help to endear me to my family. My case wasn't bad as far as cleft lips go. I've seen much worse, but I can't remember my mother ever looking at me without a hint of regret. Disgust. The scars on my face were a reminder to her. A punishment for the sin that conceived me. My grandfather, an influential brewer in Butte saw to it that I received what passed for cutting edge medical care at the time. He also saw to it that my father married my mother, whether either of them wanted to or not.

My father, a drunkard and petty criminal of Irish stock, was not the sort of man that Wilhelm Roth imagined for his daughter. But once I was on my way, Grandfather would be damned if his precious Etta would give birth out of wedlock. So, Harriet "Etta" Roth married Frank Shepard in the summer of '99. There may or may not have been shotguns involved. I couldn't say. My mother gave me her red hair, her love of reading, and her religion of perpetual guilt. My father gave me his grey eyes, his quick temper, and his name—Francis Shepard —with all the stains he'd left on it. Both of them blamed the other for my deformity.

I don't remember much about those early years in Montana. I remember my grandfather only as a presence, really. In my mind, he is a silhouette with a deep voice and cartoonish mustache, who smelled of beer and spoke broken English with a heavy accent. I know he kept things in order and kept food on our table when my father would disappear for weeks at a time.

I was too young then to know why my father was gone so often, but knowing him as I do now, I think it likely that he spent more than one of those absences in a jail cell and the rest in a brothel, until poverty forced him home. It wasn't too bad, really. My mother was distant, and my father was absent, but I was warm and fed and tended to with a sort of benevolent neglect.

I was four years old when I remember everything changing. My mother wept, my grandfather thundered, and my father left, again. Mrs. Frank Shepard was expecting again, and grandfather said it was past time that his son-in-law sobered up and began to provide for us himself. My father left to seek his fortune and after a time we didn't hear from him. We didn't mind. I watched my mother's belly growing, nobody explaining to the ugly little boy what it all meant. I think my mother was scared that she was going to have another deformed baby. Another little monster to hide and to remind her of her sins.

Then my sister was born. Magdalena. Magda, as my mother and grandfather liked to call her, was perfect. Everybody loved and doted on her in a way that bewildered me. I didn't know that my mother could smile like that at anything. I wasn't jealous though, after all, it wasn't her fault that they smiled at her and tried not to look at me. I loved her too. More than I'd ever loved anything before. She didn't look away from me when I stood over her crib. No, she squealed and smiled at me and held my finger as she slept. She had my heart, completely.

Then, after almost a year, our father came back.

He had found work out on the coast and had come back to fetch his young family. I can't prove it, but in hindsight I think my grandfather must have promised him a handsome payoff if my father managed to sober up long enough to get a job and a home. I don't know why else he would have come back for us.

We left my grandfather and the rest of my mother's family and travelled by train to the northwesternmost corner of Washington state, where the small towns of Whatcom and Fairhaven had only recently consolidated to form the city of Bellingham. It was there that our disreputable father had found work as a policeman, of all things. That didn't last long.

Things were tolerable early on. Father was rough but not cruel. Mother was distant but hadn't abandoned us. As a five or six-year-old boy, I taught myself to stay out from underfoot to avoid being shoved roughly out of the way. Our father would shout at our mother, and I saw him slap her a few times. Nothing all that unusual for the time, but he ignored Maggie and I if we didn't do anything to irritate him. Mother ignored me in any case.

It was when grandfather died that things took a turn. We'd been in Washington perhaps a year when we received the news. Mother was inconsolable. Nobody would tell me what had happened, only that my grandfather had died. Mother told me to pray, but I didn't know the right words. I knelt by my bedside, closed my eyes and mostly just thought of Grandfather. I don't think I cried. I honestly don't think I really understood what death meant yet. Grandfather was gone? So what? We'd been gone for a long time now.

Mother cried a great deal. She didn't even stop when father slapped her and shouted at her to stop. "Shut up! Do you think you're the first person whose father died?" Slap. Slap. "Stop it!" Slap. She only cried more loudly. That scared me, and it scared little Maggie too. That was when I first learned to take care of my sister, seeing to it that she was fed and clean when Father would disappear again for days at a time and Mother wouldn't leave her bedroom.

Finally, Mother went to the doctor and was given medicine. From that day forward she was never without her medicine. I remember thinking that doctors truly were miracle workers, because she never cried again after that. Not even the night later that year when father lost his job and came home drunk.

I don't know what she said to him that night, but whatever it was, he didn't like it. He beat her bloody while I shushed Maggie under the bed, singing her nonsense songs and trying to drown out the yelling and sickening sounds of meat on meat. I wished that I could have done something. I remember thinking that I was supposed to protect my mother but didn't know what I could do. I was scared, and I was ashamed.

I thought that maybe if I'd had medicine to make me braver then I could have done something. After all, even after he beat her until her eye swelled shut and she couldn't move for weeks without wincing, Mother never cried. She just took her medicine.

Our father had always fancied himself something of a prize fighter. He was often in trouble with the law for getting in some fight or another at the saloons, usually after losing his latest job.

When he lost his job at the cannery, he beat a man to within an inch of his life and was locked up for a time. Mother fed us from our meager garden and her limited skills as a seamstress. When his boss at the lumber mill said something he didn't like, father broke his nose and lost himself another job. The shame of being so frequently arrested by men he'd once worked with ate at him, and he spent what little money he made at the saloons where he got in still more fights.

He didn't have any great talent as a pugilist, despite his opinion of himself, but our father was a mean son of a bitch and was always willing to fight. Between jobs, he made some money in prize fights by the waterfront. Indulging his love of drinking, fighting, and whoring, he all but lived in the saloons and brothels.

Other children wanted nothing to do with the poor Catholic boy with the harelip, so when our father was out of the house, I spent my days in the wooded hills outside of town. The city itself was all mud and wooden buildings, but the forests were wilder then than they are now. I befriended crows and stray dogs that didn't seem to notice the holes in my shoes or the way I lisped when I talked. I never left Maggie alone when Father was home. I was always there to keep her quiet and out from underfoot, but when he was gone, we were all free to do as we liked.

Every good memory I have of my earlier years, that doesn't center on my sister, takes place alone in the woods. I skipped stones, built bridges, caught fish, climbed trees, and generally behaved as a little savage, as my mother liked to say. I remember imagining that the crows would tell me secrets or that little lights in the trees would sometimes dance for me in a rainbow of dazzling colors. My mother told me that I had an overactive imagination. I may not have always been a monster, but I think I've always been something of a misanthrope.

CHAPTER NINE

I was twelve years old when my father broke my arm. Maggie was seven and had made friends with another boy who lived nearby, Paul Adler. Paul and his family were Jewish, a detail that didn't mean much more to me or Maggie other than the fact that some people were Irish while others were Swedes or French. But our father cared a great deal.

When we first met Paul, he stared at my lip like everybody else and asked me what had happened. I made up a lie like I usually did when asked about my deformity.

"A horse kicked me," I told him.

"Oh," he said. And that was all. We weren't friends, I didn't have any of those, but I decided that I liked him. My mother had been very strict with me when I spoke and by the time I was twelve years old I'd almost completely overcome my lisp. Almost, but not quite. Other children still mocked me for it when I spoke, so I rarely did. Paul didn't mention it once.

When Maggie played with Paul and his dog Goliath, an enormous shaggy sheep dog, I went along to keep an eye on Maggie and to play with Goliath. We'd always wanted a dog of our own but were never allowed to have one. Maggie and Paul became good friends. He was a little older than her but a bit younger than me, and when the weather was good the four of us would often spend time together.

Until my father found out.

"No child of mine is going to play with a goddamn Yid!" He was furious.

Mother nodded, Maggie cried, and that was the end of it. At least for a week or two. Maggie and I were playing by the creek when who should come bounding up to us but Goliath, all happiness and friendly wagging tail. Paul was close behind.

"We're not supposed to play with him, Maggie," I reminded her.

"Francis, please?" she said, all pout and sweetness. I'd seen how much she had cried when she was told that she couldn't play with him anymore, and I wasn't about to break her heart again by forcing her to go home.

Later, it was the dog hair that gave us away. Father was drunk and had fresh bruises on his face. He was ignoring us in his usual manner.

"Oh, your dress is filthy," our mother complained, and he took notice.

"What's that?" he said.

"It's nothing, Frank," mother said. But it was too late.

He was angry at first, he was always angry when he took notice of us, but when he realized that the hair on Maggie's blue dress had come from Goliath, he was purple with rage.

He'd never hit Maggie. It never even occurred to me that he would. Mother took the brunt of his anger, and I was accustomed by then to an occasional cuff or whipping, but Maggie was everybody's darling. She was untouchable. So, it shocked us all when he raised his arm and knocked her to the floor with the back of his hand.

"What did I say!" he roared. It wasn't a question.

I don't know if he was done hitting her, or if he might continue by kicking her or shaking her as he did Mother. Perhaps he'd take off his belt and whip her a while to teach her a lesson, the way he did with me. I didn't wait to find out. I saw my sister on the floor, a trickle of blood beginning to flow from the fresh split in her lip, and I acted without thought.

I was on him. I punched at him, clawed, kicked, I may even have bitten at him. I don't know. I only know that I wanted to kill him. That I would kill him.

I didn't have a chance.

He outweighed me by almost a hundred pounds. He yelled in surprise and anger, and then the wind was out of me. His fist was buried in my stomach, and I thought I was dying. Rather than leaving me to my fate on the floor beside my sister, he lifted me to my feet by my right arm, my legs dangling limply.

"You ugly bastard!" he spit the words at me, I could smell the liquor on his breath, "You think you're a big man now, do you?"

He punched me again in the ribs and pain exploded inside me. I still couldn't catch my breath.

"You think you're a man?"

He hit me again. Something cracked. I gurgled.

I saw my mother with her hands to her mouth, staring in horror but not daring to move or to speak. I knew that fear. I saw Maggie, a flash of red hair and blue dress, shaking her head violently in silent denial of what she was seeing. And I saw my father's face, bruised and whiskered, purple with rage, a smile growing.

"Maybe it's time to teach you to be a man, little *Franthith*," he mocked my name, his name, with the lisp I'd worked so long to overcome. "Here's your first lesson."

He grabbed my right arm in both hands now, I was completely limp, and he held me by it. My vision was dimming.

I couldn't see what happened next. I felt a pull, a twist, a bend, and then I heard it more than I felt it. A series of splintering cracks, and I fell to the floor as he released his grip.

My arm bent in a way that it never had before. It was as if I had three elbows. I was confused at first. There was a wailing scream, I think it was Maggie's, but it may have been mine. Then the pain caught up with what I was seeing, and it was more than I could bear. He kicked me in the head and spared me the rest of it, I don't remember what came next.

Several things changed after that day. Both of my parents began to pay attention to me. My mother's attention, as with most things she did, was based on guilt. I think I earned some of her respect that day, if not her love, and she took pity on me. She read to me and gave me some of her medicine. I remember the unique taste of laudanum, but mostly I remember the way it made everything feel tolerable, like it didn't matter. It dulled everything, the pain, the anger, the loneliness.

Maggie looked at me like I was some sort of war hero after that. She sang to me as I healed and brought me dandelions she'd picked while out playing without me. She'd come home with less dog hair on her dress, she was getting clever, but I could still spot it. Mother probably could too, but we didn't say anything. She was still sneaking off to play with Paul, this time alone. Father didn't make anything of it after that. He had a new pastime.

"If you think you're a man then I'm going to treat you like one," he said to me one night. He gave me a bottle and commanded me to drink from it. I'd had wine at communion, but the taste of cheap whiskey was something unexpectedly strong. I knew better than to spit it out, broken bones or not, he would punish me for that. I remember the burning as it went down and settled into an ember in my stomach. I didn't like it. Not yet.

Although it never really healed properly, once my arm healed to my father's satisfaction, he decided that I was to learn to box. His lessons consisted of getting drunk and making me spar with him. He didn't really intend to teach me anything. I was to be his punching bag as he trained for his next bout. I could block or dodge, but God help me if I ran or tried to hit him back. He told me that if I got good enough that he'd take me down and enter me in a fight of my own, but he never bothered to show me how to throw a punch, except by example.

Over the next several years, I learned a lot from my father. How to take a punch. How to take a drink. But mostly I learned how to hate somebody. People don't think that hate is something that needs to be taught, and maybe they're right. But I doubt that I'd have been nearly as good at it without such a good teacher.

CHAPTER TEN

My father never stopped hating Jews. He hated everybody, but at least he stopped being so openly antisemitic after Solomon Adler, Paul's father, hired him to work at the Blue Diamond coal mine. Paul must have begged his father, we all knew it, and if anything, my father hated the Adlers even more for that perceived charity. But he took the job and kept his mouth shut. After all, he was getting older and his best boxing days were behind him.

But mine were just beginning.

After a hard week in the mines, my father would take his ugly son to the prize fights and make his drinking money on side bets. I didn't win. I wasn't supposed to.

"This time, you go down in the fourth round," he said. "Do you hear me? Round four. Say it."

"But I can win," I said, earning myself a hard slap. I could have ducked it, but it would have just made him angrier. Besides, he didn't hit as hard as he thought anymore. The slap was nothing. I stared at him, seventeen years of hate in my eyes.

"Round four, say it!"

"Round four," I said. He pushed me into the ring, and I took my beating.

He made less and less by having me throw the fight, the odds got worse with every loss. I'm sure some of the lowlife idiots who let my father hang around were onto him. If he'd had any faith in me at all he'd have realized it would be better to have me win some.

So, I ducked, I slipped, I parried, and I took enough hits to make it look convincing when I eventually went down, but I made sure to get a few good hits in along the way. I needed them to know—my opponents. I needed them at least to worry that this might be the day that Frank Shepard Jr. finally cut loose and put them down. Even more, I needed to see my father sweat. I needed to glance over to the corner and see him worrying that I might land too many hits. That I might knock some poor kid out before I got to my own appointment with the floor. Most of all I wanted him to worry about what I could do to him; in my head it was always him in the ring with me.

I never saw any of the money. Why should I? In his eyes, I was his property, not his protégé. No different than a dog he'd fight into the grave. He drank it all. It was worth it, though, because it kept his attention on me and away from Maggie and our mother.

Maggie was popular in school. At twelve years old she was a lovely red-headed girl with a disarming smile and infectious laugh, facts that seemed to overcome our poverty and opened the door to friendships with half the school. She was still friendly with Paul Adler, but her popular friends weren't much more accepting of the Jewish kid than they were of the harelip with holes in his clothes.

Paul was one of the only people who talked to me. I suppose that made him my friend, but I'd just as soon have kept to myself. The other students stopped teasing me after I started boxing. I was always coming to school with new bruises and cuts. I was clearly somebody who got in a lot of fights, and as I grew, I was treated with less contempt and more fear. I was almost grateful for my father for giving me a new story to explain my cleft lip–I don't think anybody ever believed that I'd been kicked by a horse. By this time the scar from my cleft lip wasn't as prominent as it had been as a small child. It would always be there, but the small line, and the hint of a snarl, were now just a part of my face instead of its defining feature. It's strange what you can grow into.

I did Maggie a favor in public and kept my distance from her as well. She'd never have asked me to do this, but I knew that I wouldn't be doing her popularity any favors by reminding people that I was her brother. I still watched over her, just from a distance. I watched as the boys started to look at Maggie differently, admiringly, the way a hungry cat admires a bird. More than once I chased older boys away from my twelve-year old sister.

I spent my free time alone in the forest when the weather permitted, and sometimes even when it didn't. I was always borrowing books from the library. I loved Jack London and Rudyard Kipling, but I wasn't picky. I read almost anything I could get my hands on. I was especially fond of dime novels and pulp magazines, especially escapist adventure books like *Argosy* and *Detective Story Magazine,* which I'd read under a tree on some Mondays or even Tuesdays when I'd cut school until the swelling on my face would go down after a weekend fight.

I came honestly by my habit of escaping life in the pages of a book. Our mother spent hours poring over old novels. She loved her Bronte and her Austen, but disapproved of my "common trash" magazines. She threw them away, at least until I learned to hide them better. One of the only other things she seemed to care about was church. "Father Riley says..." was the beginning to half of the things she said to us, and the only times she missed mass were when she couldn't hide a fresh bruise or swollen lip from my father. In addition to prayer and novels, she found her comfort in her 'medicine.'

I didn't have my mother's faith or love for the church. I don't think I ever did. Perhaps there was a time when I was very small that I blindly trusted the adults who told me about the Garden and the Fall and the Flood, and Jesus and the Saints and all of it, but I can't remember ever seeing it as more than just another story that my mother sought comfort from. Maybe it comes from having a father that I hated. I could understand the concept of God as a father to be feared, floods and plagues sounded fatherly to me, but the idea of worshipping the mean son of a bitch for it never made any sense to me. Just give me my beating and be damned, but don't expect me to thank you for it.

Mother and Maggie attended all the services faithfully, but our father had other plans for me. Our weekends were sacrosanct. That was when I played Isaac to his Abraham, when he offered his son as a sacrifice to the gods of liquor and cash. But no angel of the lord ever appeared to save me and have a ram take my place in the ring.

Father had his alcohol and whores, mother had her priests and her medicine, Maggie had her friends and her faith. I had my books and my trees.

As they always do, things changed. War had been raging in Europe, and more and more there was talk of America throwing her hat into the ring. The temperance movement and "those damned Protestants" were pushing for a dry and sober America, and people seemed to like the idea. Washington state was an early adopter of Prohibition, and my father had to turn to illegally bootlegged Canadian whiskey as the saloons were shut down and driven underground. He and a lot of the other miners

spent more and more time with the bootleggers after the Blue
Diamond coal mine played itself out and closed down.

Eventually, I was done with school. I'd have loved nothing
better than to get as far away from my parents as possible, but
there was Maggie to think of. I got a job working at the cannery
and came home each evening smelling bad and feeling worse,
but I kept my mother and sister fed, since our father seemed not
to give a damn anymore.

That spring, President Wilson asked congress for a
declaration of war against Germany, and they gave it to him.
Mother didn't like it; her father had been from Germany and
she spoke enough of the language that Maggie and I both had
picked up a fair amount of it when we were small. Our father
had been a soldier once, before I'd been born, and he talked a lot
about how he'd love to sign up and go over and fight "the Hun".
He talked a lot about how ashamed he was that his son wasn't
eager to go do his part and uphold his good name. I didn't bother
to point out to him that I was now the only one putting food on
the table. It would only have earned me a fresh beating. I was
still too young to be drafted, but in another year that would no
longer be the case. I stayed up at night worrying about what
would happen to my mother and sister if I was conscripted and
sent off to war. I couldn't leave them alone with him.

Jobless, we saw more and more of our father around the
house. He didn't have enough money to spend as much time as
he'd like at the brothels and bars, but he stole a good portion of
what I brought home and used it for just that purpose when he
could. Mother's looks had faded a bit over the years. She'd
always been a beautiful woman, her figure and the same fiery
red hair that she passed on to her children had always turned
heads. Maybe it was the 'medicine', maybe it was the beatings,
maybe it was just the years, but she wasn't beautiful anymore.
She was just tired, sad, and dim. A shadow of who she used to

be. She didn't turn anybody's heads anymore. Not even our father's. He'd been looking elsewhere for years. At whores, at strangers, and finally in 1917 he started to look at Maggie.

I caught him one day, unshaven and smelling of cheap liquor, admiring her through the washroom window. 'Admiring' her in that same way that he'd stare thirstily at a cold beer.

CHAPTER ELEVEN

People think of the past as being black and white, as if nostalgia were painted only in sepia. That's not my experience. I may have stopped seeing the world in full color when I was changed, but before that, when I was only an angry young man, I saw every shade of verdant green and every hue of bloody red. No amount of blood I ever saw matched the angry crimson that filled my world when I saw my father staring at my baby sister, his own daughter, his eyes gleaming with filthy desire. His arm moved in a disgusting rhythm beneath his jacket as he leered at her.

It had been five years since he'd broken my arm, the first and only time I'd ever struck him, but the arm still ached. I hadn't forgotten my lesson. I still dreamed about it, and I'd never raised a hand to him again. I'd taken every beating without fighting back. I'd lost every match he'd forced me into. Every time, I'd gotten back on my feet. I tried to show defiance in my eyes, and I'd come back for more. But I never hit him back. Not until that day.

I'd finished a shift at the cannery. It was summer work, but it was more than my father seemed able to hold down. I reeked of fish oil and the salty smell of salmon, and I'd hurried home precisely because I knew that my father wasn't working, and I didn't like leaving Maggie when he might be coming home. Most of the time he'd occupy himself with some debauchery or other in town and wouldn't return until long after I did, but his money must have run out that day.

I liked to take the alleyways when I walked home, just an old habit that came with preferring my own company. I don't think he knew that about me, or even what time I came home in the evening. If he'd ever cared about me at all beyond the thought of what he could use me for, he'd have known better than to think that there'd be nobody to see him in the back yard that day. Or maybe he really believed that I was a pathetic broken thing and was too drunk to care if I saw him or not. His back was to me when I hopped the fence into our meager yard.

At first, I thought he was taking a piss against the corner of the house. Then I saw through the window the washroom where my sister was taking her bath. I couldn't see her, I could only see her clothes hanging behind the closed door and the traces of steam on the window, and I could hear her singing to herself as she always did in the bath. I saw the reflection of his face then, staring down at her in the tub from behind, smirking and twitching as he worked at himself. Then, in the reflection, he saw me. His grey eyes went wide in shock, but then he recognized who had caught him. He tucked himself away in his britches and spun on me.

"You got some nerve," he said.

Me? I was in the wrong? I stared at him in disbelief. I didn't move.

"Go on," he said. "Git! Before I bust your ugly face."

I didn't move. My knuckles were white with pressure as I clenched my fists and stared at this man who had tormented us for my entire life. I remembered all the times I'd held Maggie under the bed and wished I'd been brave enough or big enough to help our poor mother.

"Boy, you're asking for it!" he said.

Suddenly, he didn't look as big as I'd always thought he was. I realized for the first time that I was looking him in the eye, instead of looking up at him. He pulled his belt out and gripped it in his right hand, the way he always did before he'd whip me with it.

Crack.

He snapped it at me. It struck my upper left arm and slashed down across my chest. I knew it would leave a welt, it might even be bleeding, but I didn't feel it. What I felt were Maggie's eyes on us as she pressed her face against the glass. She must have been startled by the sound of our father's voice and had come to see what was happening. I looked at her face, and I remembered the split he had left in her lip the day he had broken my arm, the day he had hit my sister.

Crack.

The leather slapped against me again, but this time I reached out with my right hand and snatched it, tearing it away from him and throwing it on the uncut grass between us. His eyes widened in outrage, pure shock that I would disobey him, that I would resist him. He swung at me. A right hook as slow and as telegraphed as I'd ever seen. If I'd been in the ring, I'd have thought it was a fake out. Nobody could be so pathetically clumsy. It would be the easiest thing in the world to move out of the way or even to duck it entirely. Had he always been this slow, or was I just faster? It didn't matter. I let him have the hit. I knew he couldn't hurt me anymore.

His fist cracked into my jaw and my head snapped back, the blow ringing in my ears. I think he expected me to drop, or at least to stagger under the force of that blow. I disappointed my father for the last time.

I moved in close and low and lay into him with a pair of punches to the liver. He made a strange sort of choking grunt that sounded almost like, "Oh?" as he staggered back against the house. He started to slide down against the wall to the ground, but I caught him, pressing against his throat with my left forearm as I stared into his face. I'm sure I showed all my teeth in some sort of snarl. I was absolutely feral.

I saw it then, the fear in his eyes. He looked at me and he was scared. I knew it, and it made me feel stronger. The shocking thing was that the fear wasn't something that suddenly appeared in his eyes. It had always been there; I just hadn't seen it for what it was until that moment. He wasn't powerful. He was a weak and cowardly wretch and always had been. That was what made him cruel. He struggled to pry my arm away from his throat with both of his hands. He clawed at me and drew blood from my forearm, but I didn't notice until later.

"You don't touch her!" I screamed in his face as I punched him. His head bounced against the house.

"You don't hurt her!" I swung again.

"You don't look at her!" I hit him again, putting into the punch the full force of the right arm that he had broken years earlier.

"You don't!" Punch.

He gurgled as his head bounced off the house and into the next punch with a series of wet thuds.

"You!" Punch. I was barely aware of the crack in my hand. Something in it had broken as I punched him. I didn't care.

I don't know how long I stood there, beating his head in against the house. I know that by the time my mother was in the yard, shrieking at me, I had stopped forming words with my mouth and was just screaming into what had been my father's face as I hit it again and again with my broken hand.

The past is not black and white to me. That red moment is

seared into my memory and has never faded. The red in our mother's crazed eyes as she yelled at me to stop. The red of my sister's wet hair in the window as she stared at me in silent horror but didn't lift a hand or say a word to object to what she watched me do. Especially the red of blood. Mine and my father's, it was all the same. It covered my broken fist and dropped onto and from the forearm that held him there. It bubbled and covered the pulpy mass of his face where teeth and bone protruded in splinters that had cut into my skin. And it streaked the pale green of our house where the back of his skull had broken and painted the wall as he slid slowly toward the ground.

"'...and children will rise against parents,'" Mother said, "'and have them put to death.'"

She wasn't making much sense. Maggie and I had gotten her to take her 'medicine' to calm her, and now our mother was just sitting there and babbling pieces of sermons. She wouldn't look at me. She kept looking at her rosary, or out the back window, where my father's body lay where I had beaten him to death.

"Sorry," Maggie apologized as she cleaned and bound my hand. I hadn't said anything, but she knew that it hurt. She could always tell.

I didn't speak. Nobody had said anything about what had happened. My mother had just screamed and screamed until Maggie had come out. My little sister had taken the tarp from the shed and draped it over our father's body before taking our mother and I each by a hand and leading us into the house.

I hadn't said anything. I hadn't had to. Nobody had asked me to. Maggie had seen everything, and our mother was incoherent. In that moment Maggie had taken charge with a gentle firmness, and just as I had become aware of the fear that had always been in our father's eyes, I now saw the warm strength that burned in my sister's.

For the first time in my life, with a body in our yard and our mother in hysterics, I wasn't worried about my sister.

"We have to hide it," she finally said, avoiding my eyes.

I thought about it, about enlisting Maggie in some desperate attempt to hide our father's body. I thought of the places in the woods where it wouldn't be found for days. I thought of a cove I knew where the tide might sweep it away, and I thought of my strong and beautiful sister throwing her life away by aiding and abetting a murderer, by concealing a patricide.

"No," I said, "we have to tell the authorities."

"What?" Maggie almost shouted. "That's crazy, they'll lock you up! What would that solve?"

"Therefore, confess your sins to one another and pray that you may be healed," our mother said as she fidgeted with her rosary.

"We tell them the truth," I said, "just not all of it."

"They'll see your hands," she said, "the scratches."

"Not if I'm not here."

"You're going to run away? That's even worse!" Maggie wasn't having it.

"You will be a restless wanderer on the earth." Mother quoted more scripture and we ignored her.

"No," I said. "Not run away. I could...enlist."

She furrowed her brow in confusion for a moment. Maggie didn't like to talk much about the war or politics, and I wasn't sure how much she understood about what was going on in Europe. Apparently, she knew enough not to like the idea.

"No, Francis, no," she was starting to cry. I put my arm around her and held her close.

"I'll probably have to go anyway; I'll be old enough in October..."

"But the war is going to be over by Christmas. Everybody says so," she argued, tears flowing freely now.

"You will hear rumors of war but be not alarmed." Mother rambled on. "Such things must happen..."

"Mother, stop it!" Maggie snapped.

"Magda..." our mother muttered in shock that her daughter would raise her voice to her, but she stopped talking.

"Maggie, look," I said, "it's the best option. I'm going to be conscripted anyway, but this way I go on my own terms. Would you rather I rot in a jail cell while you and mother starve? Or live on the run like Billy the Kid?"

"But what if you're hurt, or..." she couldn't make herself say the other.

"I'd rather take the chance," I said. "This way I can at least send money home. Besides, who knows, I might just make something of myself. I could become... *something*. That's more than could happen if I stayed."

"Francis, I don't like it!" she said. "I don't want you to go."

"Since when has what we wanted ever made a difference?"

"I don't care! We can all go away, together. We can start over somewhere," she pleaded.

"With what money?" I asked. "Maggie, think. You know this is the best choice."

She didn't agree, but she didn't disagree either. Her eyes drifted to my feet and she was my baby sister again, pouting tearfully that she couldn't have her way. I put my arms around her and kissed the top of her head.

"After I'm gone, wait as long as you can," I said, "until tomorrow morning if you can, then go to the police."

"No! I'm not going to turn you in," she argued. "I'll get rid of the body. People will think he ran off."

"No," I told her. "I don't want you getting caught covering

up for me. You'd be a criminal. I won't have you paying for what I did."

"But Francis—"

"Maggie," I interrupted her, "I won't have it. Now promise me you won't hide him."

"Fine," she glared at me. "I promise. I won't move him. But I won't turn you in either!"

"Alright," I said. "Just go to the police and tell them that you found father's body in the backyard. It's the truth. Then they can assume what they like. Lord knows he was mixed up in enough bad business that they won't have any difficulty coming up with ideas."

"But they'll want to know where you are, won't they?"

"Tell them the truth. Tell them that I left to enlist."

"Won't that look strange?" she asked.

"Yes, probably," I agreed, "but I'll be gone."

"I still don't like it," she said.

"I know," I agreed. I held her.

I changed out of my bloody clothes, Maggie promised to burn them, and I had to take a pair of our father's slacks and shoes in order to have anything decent to wear. I didn't like wearing his things, but I didn't like having his name either, and now I supposed he didn't have any need for either of them.

I took his wallet and his silver saint's medal that he'd always worn. I figured that leaving him without a wallet would make it look more likely that he'd been attacked by somebody he owed. There was barely any money in it. The silver medal of Saint Francis I gave to my mother, she had bought it for father back when they had been married. It showed the saint, hand extended to touch the head of a submissive wolf.

Mother rocked silently in her chair and took the medal when I placed it in her palm. I couldn't help but notice how frail and cold her hands were. She looked up at me then, something she'd rarely done in all my life. She looked me in the face. She raised one trembling hand to my lip and traced the line there that she had been so ashamed of, so reluctant to even look at.

"'Then the Lord put a mark on Cain so that no one who found him would kill him...'" she whispered the words and reached out to place the medallion around my neck.

My eyes started to sting and water as she squeezed my shoulder. She'd never shown me any motherly affection. That small touch was the only time I can remember that she expressed anything like care for me, anything like love. I didn't know how much I'd needed it, and it hurt now that I glimpsed it.

It didn't last. She put her head down and resumed her rocking, muttering to herself. Something about sin and fathers and sons. It didn't matter. I stood up and turned away.

Maggie wanted to walk with me to the train station in Fairhaven, but it was going to be dark soon, and it wasn't a short walk. I wouldn't hear of her walking home alone at night.

She kissed me goodbye at the front door, her arms around my neck, unwilling to let go. It reminded me of all the times she'd held on to me like that as I'd carried her when we were younger. Now she didn't even have to stand on tip-toes to kiss my cheek. I felt her tears against my cheek as I squeezed her one last time.

We didn't say anything else; we didn't need to. What was there to say? That I loved her? That I'd be worried sick about her every day? Should I have told her that I'd come back as soon as I could? That she was my whole world, the only person who meant a damn to me? That without her, I'd have never made it this far? If she didn't know all that by then, no words could have done the job. She knew. We both did.

"You're a good man, Francis."

It was sweet of her to say. She must have known how badly I needed to believe it, even if we both knew it wasn't true. I'd just killed my father, and now I was abandoning my family. My father had known all along what I was. I was no good.

I wiped her tears from her red cheeks with my good hand and forced a smile for her. She returned it. That's the way I think of her, even today. As a red-faced young girl with fire in her hair and tears on her cheeks, a stubborn smile matching the spirit in her watering eyes.

I walked down the street and looked back once as I rounded the corner, to make sure she wasn't following me. She stood by the front door, watching me go, the light from the sunset competing with the color of her hair. The sunset didn't even come close.

I hadn't told Maggie, but I had one last piece of business to tend to before I could leave. I circled back around through the alley and hopped the fence to another yard near our own.

Goliath, old and tired, struggled to wag his tail in greeting as he limped up to me and licked my hand. I knelt in the Adlers' yard and ruffled his fur, saying goodbye to the massive dog while I tossed pebbles at a bedroom window. Soon, Paul came out and joined me.

"Pauly, I need to ask a favor."

"Holy Cow, what happened to you?" he said. I hadn't thought about the bruises on my face. They were nothing in light of everything else.

"Nothing, I'm fine," I told him. "I'm leaving. I'm going to join up."

"Really? I'm jealous. Good for you. I wanted to, but my folks won't let me." Paul was a little younger than me and looked it. He'd need written permission to have a chance of joining up.

"So, listen," I said, "while I'm gone, I wanted to ask you to look after Maggie. Our mother isn't well, and our father...well, you know."

He nodded. "Of course, of course, I'll keep an eye on her."

"She'll need a friend," I said.

"She's got lots of friends." He sounded a little jealous.

"Well, she knows a lot of people, and they're nice to her, but you're a real friend, Paul. Even when you didn't have to be. I won't ever forget that."

He agreed, as I'd known he would. I felt a little better knowing that there would be somebody around who cared about Maggie. Over the next few days and weeks things would be hard for her. I didn't tell Paul about that, I couldn't, but I knew he'd help her if he could. It was the best I could manage.

"Alright," he said, "but only until I'm old enough to join up and do *my* part. Don't you win the war until I get there."

"It's a deal," I said.

I shook his hand and hugged Goliath one last time, knowing I'd never see the old dog again even if I did make it back there someday.

I walked the rest of the way alone and slept under a tree by the train station. The passenger train down to Seattle didn't leave until the next morning. I was worried that police might show up and stop me before the train arrived, but they didn't. When the train left, I was on it.

I signed up in Seattle. I'd assumed when I'd left that I'd be joining the army, just as my father had before I was born. I wished I could feel a bit less like I was walking in his footsteps, like I was becoming him. I had his name after all. I had his medal of Saint Francis. Hell, I even had his hat.

BE A U.S. MARINE!

The poster was simple, but it was all the encouragement I needed to take a different path. Marines went to sea, travelled, saw the world. If the plan was to get far away from home, then that seemed like a good way to do it. More importantly, my father hadn't done it first. I signed up on the spot, eager to leave.

It took a couple of days before I shipped out from Seattle, but again, no police showed up looking for the boy who'd killed his father. I signed a bunch of forms, went through a physical, and after I satisfied all the necessary requirements, did a lot of sitting around.

Other young men waited with me. Most of them came with parents or girlfriends or wives who tearfully saw them off. I sat alone and watched them, just hoping to be left alone.

One young man was dressed very conservatively. His father and mother came with him, as well as a young woman who immediately caught my eye. She was dressed just as modestly, they all were, and behaved demurely, but there was no hiding the fact that she was a beauty. She had golden blonde hair, fair skin, and just about the bluest eyes I'd ever seen.

The four of them joined hands and bowed their heads in prayer, the older man leading them quite loudly and publicly in asking for the safe return of his son, "if it please you, Lord." While they were praying, heads bowed and eyes closed, I saw the young lady open her eyes and look around. An enchanting look of mischief on her face. She seemed thrilled to be getting away with something.

Our eyes met.

I wasn't used to girls looking at me, especially not girls as pretty as she was. She noticed me looking at her and didn't blush. Instead, she smiled at me and winked. Winked. At me. Then she pursed her full pouty lips and silently mouthed "Shh", as if I were in on something terribly scandalous with her.

As the prayer was ending, she closed her eyes and bowed her head again with the rest of her circle, blending in as if she had never deviated from their pious display. The prayer ended and the man shook the young man's hand sternly and bid him goodbye. The woman embraced him in a motherly way and did likewise, dabbing at her eyes. The young woman threw her arms around the recruit and hugged him fiercely, kissing him on the cheek, until the older man cleared his throat and glared at her sternly, evidently embarrassed by such a public display.

She was gorgeous. Some guys had all the luck. It made sense, he was a good-looking young man. Fair-haired and well-dressed. I wondered if I could have gotten a girl like that if I'd been born with a face or family like his.

After they said their goodbyes and left, the young man began looking for a place to sit. There weren't very many left, and I made a point of looking away so as not to encourage him to join me. It was too late. He'd noticed me looking and smiled cautiously, walking right up to me.

"I beg your pardon," he said in a clear voice, "is this seat taken?"

I shook my head but didn't speak. He took it as a welcome and sat down beside me. He extended a strong looking hand toward me in greeting. I winced as he squeezed my right hand, but he didn't seem to notice.

"Pleased to meet you, name's Peter. Peter Madsen. But you can call me Pete." He smiled at me expectantly.

"Hello," was all I said, hoping he'd leave me alone. He didn't.

He looked to be sure that his entourage had left, double checking as if not wanting them to see what came next, before reaching into his bag and digging out a pack of cigarettes. He offered one to me. Not knowing what else to do, I took it and let him light it for me.

"I thought they'd never leave," he smiled. A girl like that and he was glad that she was gone? I took the bait.

"Your family?"

"Yeah, my father's a minister. Don't get me wrong, he's a good man, but I'm looking forward to being able to breathe a little. No drill sergeant is going to come close." He laughed at his own joke, but not in an obnoxious way. He seemed like a decent enough sort.

"Was that your girlfriend?" I asked, trying not to show my envy.

"What?" he laughed. "Heck no! That's my sister. Evelyn. Thank goodness. I pity the man she ends up with. If Father doesn't scare them all away, that is."

I'd seen scarier fathers but kept my opinion to myself.

The recruits were beginning to board. A man was calling names in the background.

"Where are you from?" Pete asked, still trying to get me to talk about myself.

"Montana," I said. Technically true. I had been born there.

"We're from Ballard, just a little north of here. You know it?"

I shook my head.

"Full of Swedes and Norwegians. We fit right in," he laughed. I didn't. Maybe if I kept quiet, he'd leave me alone. I should never have asked about his sister.

The voice called another name in the distance. Pete peered over my arm at the papers I held on my lap where my name was written in bold letters: Shepard, Francis.

"Isn't that you?" he asked. I hadn't heard my name called.

"What?"

"They called Frank Shepard, isn't that you?" he pointed at my name. My father's name.

Nobody called me Frank. My mother and sister had always called me Francis, to distinguish me from my father. Francis always sounded softer, smaller, kinder. A boy's name. To me, Frank was the name of a mean son of a bitch. A man to be feared and avoided. The kind of man who hurt people. A man I hated.

"Shepard, Frank!" the voice called again. Pete raised an eyebrow at me, expectantly.

I stood up.

"That's me."

PART 3

TERRITORIAL PISSINGS

CHAPTER THIRTEEN

1995

Rita hadn't died alone. According to the police report that Mack had managed to get to me, she had been with her boyfriend and some of his friends when they were attacked. There was blood from several people, and the trailer had been ripped apart, but there hadn't been any bodies present. That gave me a trickle of hope, until I read on.

A clear blood trail into the tidal marsh had led the police to the remains. Rita had been savaged, parts of her body were missing entirely, and bites had been taken out of what remained. Birds were picking at her entrails when they'd found her. They hadn't recovered any other identifiable bodies, though judging by the amount of blood in the trailer they expected to find several. They had found pieces. A man's finger, a foot, and...

I stumbled hurriedly past Mack and vomited behind a nearby cedar.

They'd found the gnawed leg of a small child, a baby, not far from Rita's mutilated remains.

"Jesus, Red," Mack said, catching up to me. "It's horrible, I know, but pull yourself together. We've got to track this son of a bitch down, like old times."

We'd been through a lot together. War, to start with, and years of cases. He'd wanted to be a cop himself when the war ended, but his injury hadn't allowed that. Instead, he'd talked me into going into business with him. Watson Investigations. I hadn't wanted my name on it. It was mostly divorce and fraud cases at first, but my nose has a way of leading me to trouble. Mack had known about my 'thing' from what he'd seen in the war, but years of working together on strange cases had given him an idea that there were other things out there, things that police weren't equipped to understand, much less deal with. For a few years, Mack and I had dealt with those things on our own, quietly. Sometimes, we'd even gotten paid for it.

My old partner was only seeing some new monster come to town, some boogeyman that he could talk me into hunting with him. That explained his attitude. He didn't really think for a second that it could have been me. He just saw a chance to play hero and recapture some of his lost youth. His faith in me was touching, but it made me feel even worse. I'd have to make him understand. I'd need his help.

"Mack, no," I said.

He cut me off.

"I know, I'm too old for this, but I'm not useless damnit," he said. "I think that maybe it's time to bring Owen in on this. He was too young before, but he's been a cop for a long time now. I think if we laid it out for him it would connect a lot of dots and he'd step up—"

"Mack!"

He stopped.

"You're not hearing me," I said. "I think I did this. I think I finally lost it, Mack. I killed that woman and, Jesus Christ, Mack, I killed that little boy!"

He looked at me with a patronizing expression and shook his head. "No. No you didn't."

"Yes, I did, Mack, I'm telling you!"

"Red," he said, "you were at your shack when I showed up. You were locked up like you always are. It's impossible. Frank, you're losing it. We need to talk about the drugs. I know you don't want to hear it, but they're becoming a real problem. You're confused."

He couldn't understand. The drugs were the only reason this hadn't happened years ago, and now they weren't enough.

"I broke loose, Mack," I said, "and the door was open when I woke up. I was loose."

That made him stop and take a reflexive step away from me. He furrowed his brow and thought for a moment while Blue whined beside me and sniffed curiously at what had been my breakfast.

"Okay," Mack said, "you're saying you remember killing her?"

"Yes," I said. He raised an eyebrow. "Well, kind of. It isn't clear like that. It's more like I dreamt it, but that can be what it's like when I lose it. Especially if I'm, well..." I trailed off.

"If you're loaded?" he said.

I nodded. He was kind enough not to rub it in.

"Think about it, Mack," I said. "She pissed me off. I wanted to hurt her. Hell, I barely kept from ripping her head off when you sent me. Then I 'dream' that I go and do just that and wake up to find that I've broken free. You're telling me that you think it's more likely that somebody else like me, something we haven't seen for years, showed up and chose her at random on the same night that I broke free and wanted to go after her myself? Mack, I know you don't want to believe that I did this, and I appreciate that, but don't be an idiot. It was always just a matter of time."

"No, you think about it, Frank," he sounded angry. "You think it makes more sense to think that you broke loose in your sleep, ran the seven or eight miles to that crappy trailer park, and then found your way back home and into bed? When you were too loaded to even remember doing it? Sounds to me like you're the idiot."

"You don't understand," I said, and it was true, he didn't. He couldn't. He hadn't lived with this thing the way that I had. He didn't know how strongly instinct could drive me, how the wolf could take over. He didn't know how many times I'd done something and had to piece together what I had done after the fact. The wolf returning to its den after hunting would be simple instinct. "I need to be alone."

We didn't speak as we returned to the Blazer, and I started on the way home. He didn't believe me. There was no way I could talk him into helping me with what I had to do next.

"I do understand," he said as we arrived at my trailer. "I understand more than you think. You're not the only one who's done things you regret."

"What? You think this is the same? This isn't me not keeping it in my pants, Mack!"

He looked at me like I'd slapped him. I'd never judged him for the failure of his marriage, never said anything. Who was I to judge?

"I'm just saying that I know who you are, Frank," he said through gritted teeth.

"No, Mack, you don't. Maybe you never did," I said.

"Bullshit," he said quietly. "You're my friend."

"No, Mack," I said, "I'm not. Get out of here."

"Fine," he said. "There's no talking to you when you're like this. Call me when you calm down, and we'll figure out what to do next."

I already knew what to do next.

He got in his shitty car and backed out of my driveway without saying anything more, but I could tell that I'd hurt him. Good. It would be easier for him that way.

Blue grunted at my side and gave me a queer look.

"Don't you start," I said. "It's for his own good."

I went inside, loaded the pipe from the contents of the stolen gym bag, and started to plan how I'd kill myself. It's no simple thing to kill a Garou. Not impossible, but far from easy. There are a few foolproof options but ripping my own head off or cutting my own heart out without anybody to assist me didn't seem likely. I'd had a half thought out romantic notion of kneeling like a samurai and accepting my death with honor while Mack stoically swung the axe. That wouldn't be happening.

I lit the pipe and took a small hit, enough to calm my nerves and settle my guts without putting me under.

People who want to put one of us down always think immediately of a silver bullet, but that's an invention of Hollywood. Silver doesn't do me any special harm. The silver medal of Saint Francis that I still wore was proof of that. Iron, that was the trick. Cold iron. Plain old steel. Silver would have been more exotic, but plain iron is harder to recover from than anything else I've encountered, except perhaps fire or salt. I don't know why exactly, but being pumped full of lead has never been as painful or difficult to heal as being cut with a simple steel blade.

I was vaguely aware of Evelyn's ghost sitting on her chair, staring at me as she always did. She was less solid than she had been during the full moon. Fading, like the wolf-spirit within me, in accordance with the cycle of the moon. I ignored her. The dope helped.

Steel jacketed bullets, that's what I'd need. They weren't especially common outside of the military, but they weren't impossible to come by either. I'd long made it a point to keep some near at hand. A steel jacketed .45 round to my temple should do the trick. Then again, it might not. I'd recovered before from things that I'd been sure would end me. A botched suicide attempt would only release the wolf to go on another rampage. I didn't want to come back to my senses days later to find that I'd killed another woman. Or eaten another baby. Jesus Christ. If there was anything in my stomach, I'd have been sick again.

No, to be certain of success I'd have to wait until the wolf was at his weakest. I'd have to wait until the new moon. Just as the wolf is strongest at the moment of the full moon, next to impossible to hold at bay, during the dark of the new moon it is practically dormant. I'd taken injuries before during the new moon and been worried that I might not survive long enough to heal. Those had been close calls. Waiting for the right time would be the key, but if I put a steel bullet into my head at the moment of the new moon there'd be no way to fail.

The way I was feeling, I'd have pulled the trigger that very night if I could be certain that it would work, but to do the thing right I'd have to wait about ten days. Fine. It was probably for the best. I had affairs to put in order. I had to be sure that the dogs would be looked after. I couldn't just abandon them. And there was Maggie. I'd been dreading the day that I'd have to live without her, and that day seemed to have been drawing near. I was relieved that I wouldn't have to face losing her. Thankfully, she wouldn't have to deal with the same pain when I was gone. She wouldn't even know the difference. If she had been in her right mind, I could never have done it, I could never have hurt her like that, but for once, her lost memories seemed a mercy. Still, I'd have to say goodbye. There was no question.

Only ten days. It seemed like a nice round number. A countdown. For the first time in years I felt that I had something to look forward to. I had ten days to live.

CHAPTER FOURTEEN

I left the shit and vomit in my trailer. The overpowering smell was a good excuse not to go inside and see Evelyn's ghost sitting on her favorite chair, at least not until the moon had waned and my wife's shade had faded more fully. I spent the next few nights with my pack, curled up with Blue and the rest of the dogs beneath the trailer.

The wolf still touched my dreams, but he colored them rather than dominating them as he would during the full moon, an influence that faded and sharpened with the lunar cycle. I dreamt of distant memories, the death of my father, my times at war. I dreamt of the lives I'd destroyed over nearly a hundred years. Most especially, I dreamt of Evelyn, of our first time together, of our wedding day, and of the way her blood had tasted on the night I'd killed her. I dreamt that part over and over, but now when I'd looked down at my bloody feast, I'd see Rita's eyes staring back up at me. I deserved to die.

Why?

The wolf didn't understand my guilt. It puzzled him, disgusted him, just as he puzzled and disgusted me. I ignored him, there was no point. For years I had tried to reason with my inner wolf, to change him, but it had never worked. He was older than reason, a force of nature that existed beyond it.

Weak.

I felt his judgement of my human character and felt him turn his attention to ignore me as I had turned my back on him. My dreams took me to childhood memories. I dreamt of hiding beneath the bed again as my father beat my mother. I dreamt of holding Maggie and comforting her as we silently prayed for it to stop.

"Francis..."

I looked at my baby sister's face and saw that things were different than I'd expected them to be. My arms wrapped around her were not my arms at all, but the thick grey legs of a wolf. My sister's grey eyes, so like mine and our father's, were gone. Instead in Maggie's face were two brilliant sapphire orbs, with a fleck of shining emerald in one iris. Andy's eyes?

"You're a good man, Francis." The words had been my sister's, but the voice was Andy's. What was going on? Why should that girl be in my dreams? She was nothing to me.

Knowing the dream for what it was, I forced my dream-eyes shut and willed the scene to change. It did. I was alone now, in the woods that had been my refuge as a child. Near where Maggie lived now with her nurses and medication. A safe place.

I walked in those woods, touching the trees and skipping stones as I had once done, hiding from my worries for a time. A tune crept into the air, faint and distant at first. I couldn't recognize it but knew it to be familiar. Now and again, a piece of foliage or a feature of the landscape would be different, more vivid, more grandiose. A maple tree that I'd once climbed stretched to touch the clouds. A creek that I had been able to jump across was a mighty river. It was pieces of my childhood but transformed, as though they belonged in the moonlit forest of my wolf dreams.

"Someone to watch over me..." the lyrics to the growing tune came clearly and startling from above me where a raven sat on a branch out of my reach, studying me as it sang Maggie's old song, a glimmering emerald fleck shining from one eye.

A fierce and powerful howl erupted from behind me, shaking leaves from the tree and launching the raven into a panicked flight which quickly carried her out of sight. The power of the howl was undeniable, a visceral force that drove me to the ground where I landed on hands which were already showing signs of fur and claws. I spun instinctively, snarling to face the intruding presence.

Atop an impossibly large fallen tree, not twenty strides away, stood a mighty dark wolf, hackles raised, and golden eyes locked on me in a snarl. His gaze and smell evoked a powerful instinct within me, to either fight him off and show myself dominant, or to lower my head now and acknowledge his dominance. My inner wolf didn't know which to do, he seemed torn in two directions and awaited my decision.

This other wolf didn't feel like a dream. Sometimes, in my Garou dreams, I'd encounter spirits in that primordial forest. They were usually wise enough to keep their distance from me, but such encounters could happen. The dreamscape had shifted more fully to match the moonlit wilderness of my wolf dreams, the surroundings dominated by towering pines and no longer mirroring my childhood memories. I'd never encountered another wolf spirit before, but I was certain that this was some sort of spirit and not some Jungian dream-creature of my own imagining. The smell of the beast alone cemented my certainty.

Fight, flee, or submit. The feelings were not words but urges from my wolf-self which were bone-jarring in their intensity. The newcomer wolf seemed perched in anticipation of my choice, ready to give chase or pounce.

No. I forced myself away from the instincts of my wolf-self and willed myself to stand. The grey paws which I had been standing on shifted, shimmered, came into focus, and I had fingers and thumbs once more. My change wasn't entirely complete yet. My hands were not entirely my own, hairy and dark things with sharp claws, but at least they had a more human shape. Along with the change in form came a change in thought, focus sharpened but remained tinged with primeval instincts. I pushed myself to my feet, standing as a man, and looking the dark wolf in the eye.

It growled, a low and thunderous sound that shook the needles on the ground and made my hairs stand on end.

"Who are you?" I said to the massive wolf.

It only snarled in response, snout low as it slowly crept forward.

"Answer me!" I demanded. This was my dreamscape. I should be safe here.

Then why didn't I feel safe?

The dark wolf drew back and leapt at me, my resolve crumbled, and I darted to the side, narrowly avoiding his snapping jaws as he landed where I had been standing.

I did the only thing I could under the circumstances. I ran. Desperately.

I jumped over stumps and scrambled under logs, weaving and darting behind enormous trees, desperate to put anything between myself and the beast that I heard crashing through the forest at my heels. In the way of dreams, I could feel his scalding breath on my back while simultaneously sensing that he was a turn or two behind me. I was keeping ahead of him, for now, but I was bound to miss a step, or to come to the end of my stamina, and he'd be on me. I knew with a certainty that the very thought of my impending failure was about to make that outcome a reality. I could feel the dream turning against me.

"Francis!" The raven with the emerald fleck in its eye called

my name from a branch above and ahead of me. A branch that was just out of reach.

"Francis, jump!" the bird called again.

There was nowhere else to turn, no place to hide, so I trusted the raven and leapt, arms outstretched. I knew it would never work, that I'd fall on my face and the beast would tear me apart. I was wrong. My fingers closed around the branch at the raven's feet.

I started to pull myself up, to hoist myself out of reach of the predator below me, but I wasn't quick enough. Fangs pierced the flesh of my right calf, driven deep by impossibly strong jaws, and the weight of the dark wolf pulled me toward the ground. I dug my nails into the bark of the branch and clung with strength derived from primal terror. I hung there with the wolf pulling at my leg, hearing the creaking of the wood and knowing that the branch would break, certain that my leg would tear free before the wolf released me.

As I watched, my hands seemed to diminish, becoming soft, frail, pink things that could never hope to contend with the force of the predator that had me in its jaws. My wolf had retreated, slinking back to the dark recesses of my mind in the face of what it perceived to be a superior predator. Above me, an emerald-flecked eye gleamed at me, and the raven launched itself forward, diving past my head to peck savagely at the wolf's face which still enveloped my leg.

The bird slashed and bit at the big wolf's snout, drawing blood. The wolf's only response was to bite down on me with even greater strength, a splintering crunch and a flare of blood red light in my vision accompanied the cracking of my bone as the fangs sunk into my marrow. I screamed, but somehow I kept my desperate grip on the branch, my fingers seeming to have almost grown into the wood, and the branch in turn having changed shape around my hands as if the tree itself were holding me.

I felt as if my leg were about to come loose from my body. Ordinarily, pain like this would summon my wolf whether I wanted his help or not, but he had surrendered to this dominant wolf.

"*Kraa!*" yelled the raven, before plunging her shining black beak deep into the yellow eye of the wolf.

Finally relenting, the wolf released my leg with a pained cry and dropped to the ground. He snarled and writhed beneath me, too preoccupied with the bloody jelly oozing from the wound on his face to give me a further thought.

The raven wasn't finished yet, however. She swooped at the wolf again and again, harrying him from his blind side as she croaked and called at him. He snapped at her, but she was too smart for the wounded creature. She disoriented him with cacophonous cries and kept out of reach of his maw as she took every opportunity to approach from his blinded side. She drew blood from his ear and again from his snout with her talons and beak before he ran off into the twilight forest, retreating.

As if the wolf's retreat freed me to wake, I sat up gasping and clutching at my leg, free from the dream and surrounded by my dogs. Blue huddled beside me and licked at my arm. Patton and Smedley both stood with their hackles raised, their eyes searching the night for whatever I was reacting to. I was drenched in sweat and pain throbbed in my right calf where the dream-wolf had maimed me, but my hands couldn't feel any blood or any other injury.

I pulled the pantleg up from my burning calf and lit my zippo to see by. My skin was unbroken, and the bone was intact, but the spot where the wolf had savaged my flesh in the dream, midway between my ankle and knee, was quickly turning an ugly shade of deep purple and blue.

"What the hell was that?" I gasped to myself. My breathing was frantic, and my heart was pounding like I'd just sprinted a mile uphill. It seemed like a good idea to fill the pipe and take another hit of dope before my wolf got out of control.

I extracted myself from Blue and the rest of the pack and started to limp toward the gym bag that I had moved to the Blazer. My leg hurt like hell, but it was fading quickly. I was halfway to the white Chevy when I realized that my wolf wasn't threatening to take over at all. I looked for the spot where I was accustomed to feeling him in my mind and found him pressed against the very back of that darkened cave. I imagined his eyes peering out cautiously from the shadows as he refused to budge from where he was hiding.

"Ha!" I laughed out loud in the predawn mist. At least I wasn't alone in having been terrified, and by what, a dream?

I decided to forgo the heroin for the time being and settled for rolling myself a cigarette. I sat there and calmed my nerves, slowly smoking one cigarette after another, centering myself on the familiar ritual of rolling them. Blue came back to my side, eyebrow raised as if concerned about me. She sat and leaned her comforting weight against me, and I ruffled her fur as we waited for the sun to rise.

In the distance I could just barely hear a croaking raven welcoming the dawn.

CHAPTER FIFTEEN

If I felt any guilt about the decision to end my life, it was centered on my dogs. They were the only ones I'd never disappointed, never hurt, the only ones I expected might miss me when I was gone. So, I took a few days to spoil them. We played together, hunting rabbits together in the brambly hills and wrestling on the ground. Most of the pack were enthusiastic to add me to their pile at night, though they didn't seem to enjoy the smell of the heroin I'd smoke before sleeping. Smedley, the old foxhound, gave me long disapproving looks. At first Blue was a bit possessive, especially when elegant Norma Jean came near, but by the second night even Nettle and Patton happily joined the pile.

After three days of enjoying my dogs and avoiding my responsibilities, it seemed time to put my house in order, so to speak. I decided not to bother cleaning the filth from the trailer. There was no point. I wasn't going to leave much behind. I'd come up with a plan. I'd use the canister of propane that Mack had provided on his last visit and burn the whole rusted mess to the ground on the night of the new moon. I'd light the match and then eat a bullet, trusting the flames to ensure that I didn't recover.

Evelyn's chair gave me pause at first. Should I burn the object that her shade was anchored to? Doing so would either free or destroy the ghost. I wasn't entirely sure which. I thought of preserving the chair so that she could endure, but I realized quickly how cruel that would be. I'd been selfish to keep her with me for as long as I had. I should have burned the chair years ago and allowed her to move on to whatever came next. Even if it was nonexistence, it had to be better than leaving her stranded and abandoned. That was decided. I'd die the way I should have all those years ago, with my wife.

I set my mind to the task of taking care of the living. Blue, Nettle, and Lenny followed me on an evening hike through the woods behind our trailer. Removed by a small creek and a thickly wooded hill was the house of my nearest neighbors, a pair of women who my dogs had introduced themselves to several years earlier. Lenny, my big slow-witted, sweet-hearted giant, hadn't shown up to dinner with the rest of the pack for several days. Worried, Blue and I had tracked his scent to a spot where he had clearly gotten into a fight with a pack of coyotes. Judging by the bodies of the coyotes, Lenny had been victorious, but the blood trail we followed from there had us worried that he wouldn't survive. His trail led to the elegant blue house where a veterinarian named Leslie lived with her girlfriend whose name I can never recall.

I'd stayed away from any neighbors in the years since my pack and I had started living in my little patch of wilderness, but the smell of my dog coming from the house necessitated an introduction. I'd been amazed that the short, plump veterinarian had been brave enough to approach a bloody dog three times her size. Most people are terrified of Lenny when they first see him, but Leslie had done just that. She had taken

Lenny to her clinic and very probably saved his life. After introducing her to the rest of the pack we formed a sort of mutual admiration, with my dogs occasionally sneaking to her house for food and attention when they needed it. Leslie had even introduced me to a badly abused and scarred young black Labrador, a rescue, who seemed too prickly to be adopted by anybody else. I named her Nettle, and she had quickly fallen in with the rest of my pack of broken and unwanted strays.

When we reached the edge of Leslie's yard, Lenny and Nettle both ran excitedly to the house, barking to announce their arrival. Blue stayed beside me beneath the trees, out of sight. I watched as Leslie answered the door and happily greeted the two familiar dogs who jumped and licked at her excitedly. She walked with them to a large barn behind her house where she fed them and pet them comfortably.

I thought about speaking to her, about making up some story about being sick or moving away, but I'd seen all I needed to. She was here, she would care for the dogs if they came to her, and they would come to her once I was gone. I didn't need to worry. Besides, I respected Leslie too much to feed her some lazy lie. It was better this way.

Blue and I walked back to the trailer, knowing that Lenny and Nettle would find their way back when they were ready, and we were met by Smedley when we were halfway there. The old foxhound had caught a rabbit and offered the remaining hindquarter to me, laying the piece of bloody meat before me in welcome. I rubbed the old dog, the oldest in my pack, and the undisputed dominant dog before Blue had joined our family, stroking his ears and ruffling the scruff of his neck. After taking the meat, I took a bite of it in accordance with my status in the pack hierarchy before offering the rest to Blue, who ate it greedily. I was relieved and a bit impressed that old Smedley could still hunt for himself at his advanced age. Blue and Smedley played together rowdily as I arrived back at the trailer.

It had grown dark, and in the dim light I could easily see the flashing light throbbing faintly in the window. That damned answering machine that Mack had foisted on me. I never should have plugged the phone back in. The call would be from Mack, no question, there was nobody else that had my number. Hell, even I didn't know what it was.

I started a fire in the metal drum beneath the rain-shelter and rolled a smoke while I prodded at the flames. I gave serious thought to ignoring the message. It would be best for Mack not to hear from me again at any rate. If I gave him the cold shoulder along with the rude send off when I'd last seen him, it would make it easier for him when I went missing. The light was accompanied by a low but irritating electronic beep that grated at my ears every two minutes, and I'd have to go inside to silence it. Besides, my stomach was aching for food, and I could sense my wolf slowly relaxing and being drawn out by the hunger. All my food was inside.

Fine, damnit.

The trailer reeked. The first thing I did was throw the windows fully open and leave the door wide. Tybalt slinked in behind me and quickly dove after a small mouse that scurried from my soiled bedding. It got away. The faint impression of Evelyn's face matched the disgust I felt for myself, but the image of my dead wife quickly faded from view. I grabbed an armful of canned stew and cans of tuna fish, then pushed the large round button on the flashing machine as Mack had showed me when he'd first brought it.

"You've reached Frank Shepard's home for wayward mutts," Mack's voice played from the greeting he'd recorded for me when it became obvious that I wouldn't make one of my own, "leave a message."

Beep.

"Frank, it's Mack," a tired and slightly slurred version of the same voice began. "I've been doing a lot of drinking... thinking, I've been doing a lot of thinking, and I want to just get something off my chest. You saved my life, and not just once. I owe you. I always will. That's why I can't just leave you alone when I see you throwing your life away like you have been. Just because you ain't gonna die doesn't mean you don't have a life to save. You need to stop being such an ornery old man and let somebody save it goddamn it! You've always been a miserable son of a bitch, but you at least used to get out and see the world, not just lock yourself up with your dope and your dogs and..."

Beep.

Mercifully, the message had been cut short. Jesus, he must be drunk. I had just reached the fire drum with my load of canned treasure when the message came to an end, my Garou ears having no difficulty in hearing the muffled voices from outside.

"You've reached Frank Shepard's home for wayward mutts," the greeting message played again, "leave a message."

Beep.

"Shit," I said, hanging my head and wondering how much of this I was going to have to listen to.

"Damn thing cut me off," Mack's voice said, "where was I? You used to be somebody damnit. You used to do things that mattered, we both did. We helped people. Now what do we do? You sit off in the woods and get high, growing your beard and howling at the moon or some shit. And I post bonds for junkies and delinquents who look like valedictorians and accountants next to you. I swear, if you hadn't walked out on the business, if you weren't such a self-loathing, pig-headed, son of a..."

Beep.

"Shit Mack," I grunted to myself, "tell me how you really feel."

"You've reached Frank Shepard's home for wayward mutts," the recorded greeting played for a third time, "leave a message."

I knew there was a way to stop the messages from playing, but I'd never figured it out, I'd never needed to.

"Goddamn machine!" Mack said with a heavy sigh. "Anyway, I'm just saying, life doesn't have to be like this, Red. You don't have to punish yourself forever. I want you to come back and work with me, like the old days. But this time, I want your name on the door next to mine; 'Shepard and Watson Investigations.' Not bad, right? We can still do something worth doing. Something good. It ain't too late. Hell, you may have all the time in the world, but I don't. So, pull your head out of your ass old man..."

Beep.

"Not gonna happen, Mack," I said as I opened a can of stew with my knife, propping the open can on the bit of wire grate above the flames to allow it to heat up.

"You've reached Frank Shepard's home for wayward mutts," the machine played for a fourth time, "leave a message."

I turned and walked toward the trailer. This was getting ridiculous, I didn't need to know how to work this machine to shut it up, I'd smash the damn thing.

"Last time, I promise," Mack began, "Just come down and see me when you cool down, Frank. Use my place upstairs, take a shower, shave, maybe put on the old suit, see if you don't feel different about—"

A loud recorded crash abruptly stopped what Mack had been about to say.

"What in the hell?" Mack's recorded voice shouted as a

deep familiar growl rolled out of the machine. I froze in the doorway. What was I hearing?

"No!" Mack shouted distantly as a thud told me that he had dropped the phone. Violent cracking sounds followed, with a distorted roar and the sounds of gunfire.

"Eat that, you ugly son of a—" Mack's voice was cut off by a sharp crashing sound chased by the sounds of snarling and tearing.

"No! No! Stop!" The words were screamed, and yielded to wordless shrieks of panic and pain that slowly gave way in turn to low moans and wet gurgling sounds.

Beep.

"Mack!" I yelled at the silent machine as I waited for it to play another message that never came.

I ran to the phone and frantically punched in the number that my friend had written in black ink onto the phone itself when he had bought it for me, the only number I'd ever needed and hadn't bothered to memorize.

The phone rang, rang again, rang a third time.

"This is Mack Watson," my old friend's familiar voice answered, and I released a breath in relief that I hadn't known I'd been holding. "I'm not able to come to the phone right now. Please leave a message with your phone number and I'll get back to you as soon as possible. Have a nice day."

Beep.

"Mack?" I yelled into the phone, my short-lived relief giving way to panic. "Mack! Mack, you son of a bitch! Don't you do this! Mack! God damn you, Mack! No! Mack!"

Nobody answered. I dropped the phone and ran to my Blazer. I didn't call her, but Blue knew that something was wrong and arrived at the white Chevy just as I did. She jumped in as I opened the driver's door. I slid in after her and we sped down the overgrown driveway and headed to Mack's office.

CHAPTER SIXTEEN

It was a small miracle that I wasn't arrested on my drive to Mack's office. I turned what could sometimes be a one-hour drive into a frantic thirty-minute race against time and didn't stop for any traffic lights or signs along the way. Blue was tossed against the side door on one sharp turn, but after that she braced herself for the rough ride. I didn't roll a cigarette or think about stopping to access the bag of dope in the back of the SUV, even though I could feel the hackles rising on my inner wolf in response to my panic about Mack.

What the hell had that noise been? My brain reached for feeble excuses, hoping what I had heard might have been a television in Mack's office, or even a stray dog, but I knew I was reaching. I knew exactly what I had heard. A large and fearsome predator attacking my oldest and only friend.

What I didn't know was whether or not that predator had been me.

I dismissed the thought at first. After all, I had no reason to hurt Mack. Why would I do that? It hadn't been the full moon, and I was much farther away. Sure, I'd been angry at him, but that wouldn't be enough would it? Maybe it would. After all, that had been why I was planning to end my life, the realization that I could no longer rely on myself to control the wolf, that I couldn't trust myself not to kill. How then? The distance to Mack's office from my trailer was substantial, about thirty miles cutting across country, more by road. I knew that I could cover that distance by foot in a couple of hours if I were drawing on the wolf. I thought about where I had slept the night before. I'd hunted with my dogs well into the night, chasing rabbits. Where had I stopped? As usual, I had taken a fair amount of the stolen heroin that evening and couldn't be entirely certain where I had lain down to sleep at the end of the night, only that I had awoken among my dogs beneath the trailer.

No matter how unlikely it seemed, I had to admit to myself that it was possible. Possible that, now that I had lost control to the wolf, that it had latched on to my anger and frustration at Mack and followed the familiar route to his office to act out those feelings in the only way it knew how, by tooth and claw. Possible then, too, that we had returned to the den to collapse with our pack and rest after the hunt.

Mack didn't buy it. He had too much faith in me, but I knew it was possible. Mack's misplaced faith in me might have gotten him badly hurt, if not killed. I was crossing my fingers that I would find my old friend alive when I arrived.

The flashing blue lights were as clear as the moon in the sky outside of Mack's building, signaling to the night that something horrible had happened there. I was too late; the authorities were there ahead of me. I didn't know what I would do, but I kept approaching, slowly now. I had to find out what had happened to Mack.

Blue barked beside me out of her half open window while we were still a block away from the office. I'd finally stopped at a traffic light as I considered my next move.

"Hi there, Blue," a soft voice said from the passenger window as pale hands reached in to ruffle the dog's fur.

I nearly jumped out of my skin, turning and snarling loudly at the unexpected voice. Andy's blue-with-emerald eyes looked in from the window as Blue licked happily at her slender fingers. The girl took a sudden step back from the vehicle as she saw the violence looming in my face. Blue whimpered.

"You?" I snapped. "What the hell are you doing here?"

"Nice to see you too, *Francis*."

That stunned me. Nobody but Maggie called me that. Not even Mack had ever known me by that name. I didn't appreciate the disarming effect this had on me, not at all.

I must have looked utterly dumbstruck and disarmed because the teenage girl stepped confidently back to the window. She looked tired, like she hadn't gotten much rest since I'd seen her, or she was itching for a fix. Maybe both. Her mesmerizing eyes looked both sad and frightened, but still not frightened of me. Her cheeks were wet from fresh tears and the blue streak of her hair partially concealed the bruises on her face which had faded to a sickly yellow. She was dressed in a black hooded sweater proclaiming the single word in white print, *Never mind*. I didn't know what it meant, but it made me think of Poe, thus misquoth the raven.

The traffic signal changed to the go position. There were cars approaching from behind and I'd have to move soon.

"Get out of here, kid," I hissed. "Something bad happened."

"I know."

The cars were getting near.

"You know? What do you know?"

"I know that if you don't open the car door and let me in soon, you'll be holding up traffic. I know that the longer I stand here talking to your window the more it will look like you're looking to 'party'. And I know that those cops down there..."

"In!" I said as I reached over and unlocked the door.

Andy Morgan slid into the front seat, easily fitting her narrow frame beside Blue. The cattle dog gave the girl an enthusiastic face licking as I put the Blazer back in gear and continued toward the crime scene. As I drove slowly past, careful to follow the speed limit, one police car as well as an ambulance were pulling out of the alley behind the building, where I usually parked. As they turned onto the street ahead of us, I noticed that their emergency lights were off. They were in no hurry, a fact which did little to comfort me.

I drove past Mack's building and turned up a side street, driving for two blocks before pulling into a different alley and parking the vehicle.

"Alright kid," I said. "Spill it. What do you know? And don't get cute. I'm in no mood."

"I can see that," she said. She had that same odd expression of looking just past me that she had worn when we first met. "You're scared."

"I'm angry and impatient is what I am! Now, what happened to Mack? Do you know?"

"I'm sorry," she said, turning her eyes downward. "He's dead."

I'd known it. There was no other way that what I had heard on the phone could have ended, but that didn't make it easy to hear.

"No..."

"I'm so sorry," she said. "He was sweet. I liked him."

"No," I said, "no, no..."

"I don't know much," she went on. "There were police here three hours ago when I showed up."

"No," I started to pound my fist on the steering wheel, softly at first, but harder as I went on. "No. No! NO!"

Crack. The wheel snapped under my fist. Andy pressed

herself against the passenger door and held Blue close to herself. She reached out one slender hand and placed it on my shoulder.

"Francis..."

I turned on her, reflexively preparing to put my fist through her head. What was she thinking, touching me in a state like that? She didn't even know me. Not afraid of me? Her mistake. I'd show her how wrong she was not to be—

Those eyes again. They caught my attention, not so much pacifying my wolf as distracting him. It was as if the engine had been revving, but she'd grabbed the gearshift and put everything in neutral for a moment. Those eyes. No wonder I'd dreamed about those eyes. The raven in my dream had those eyes. Thus, quoth the raven? Francis? I was lost. The rage washed away and left bare the uprising of fear and grief that it had been concealing.

I turned away from her and wiped at my eyes with the back of my sleeve. She kept her hand on my shoulder and neither of us spoke for a minute until I'd collected myself. Blue nuzzled at my hand, and I let her slip her snout beneath it and rubbed her head.

There was so much I wanted to ask, so much I needed to know, but Mack was still foremost in my mind.

"What happened?" I said. "Tell me everything."

"Like I said," she answered, taking her hand from my shoulder, "I don't know very much about it. The police were already here."

"Then what did you hear? You know something."

"Yes," she hesitated, "but I didn't hear anything. I don't talk to cops."

"Then what?"

"I—I dreamed it," she said, "I know that sounds crazy."

"Not really," I said, thinking about my most recent dreams. Let he who is without crazy dreams cast the first stone.

"I knew you'd get it," she said, not looking at me, "but it's not something I talk about very much."

She knew I'd get it? What was that supposed to mean? I'd learned from long experience that more questions can sometimes get in the way of the answers.

"Understandable," I said, waiting for her to go on.

"Sometimes I dream true things, that's all," she said. "I always have. You know what déjà vu is?"

I nodded.

"It's like that but all the time. I don't always remember my dreams until they come true. And sometimes I just dream strange things that I know aren't real, but that doesn't mean that they aren't true, you know what I mean?"

"True but not real?" I said. "Like what, a metaphor?"

"Yes!" she seemed excited that I was taking her seriously. "Like metaphors or symbols. Sometimes I dream about people and things, but they aren't themselves in my dream, but they still are. Y'know? When I was little, I'd dream about cartoon characters or animals. Sometimes in my dreams I'm not even a person, I just fly around and watch it all..."

"Like a raven?"

It was her turn to look stunned and disarmed. She gaped at me.

"You—you remember?" she said disbelievingly.

I only nodded.

"Oh my god! That's never happened before! You have no idea how exciting this is. I've shared dreams with people before, but they never remember it. Nobody ever believes me."

"That's why you called me..."

"Francis? Yes," she nodded but looked away, embarrassed, like I'd caught her going through my diary or my underwear drawer. "I'm sorry. I don't do it on purpose. Sometimes I just hear and see things. I can't help it."

That scared me. How many of my dreams, how many of my memories, had she already seen without my awareness? How much did this child already know about me? Was it even possible to keep a secret from somebody like this, somebody who could just wander into my dreams and wade through my memories? That thought scared me, terrified me. That kind of vulnerability, that kind of intimacy, was not something I wanted. It felt like a threat.

That thought was familiar to the wolf.

Threat? Attack. Kill.

I pushed the wolf down without much difficulty, the very human grief I was feeling for my friend along with Andy's presence were enough to smother him and force him back into silence for the time being.

I wanted to know more about this, about Andy and her dreams, but later. My dead friend was all that I could think about at that moment. I had to bring her back to the issue at hand.

"Andy," I said, "tell me what you dreamed about Mack. What happened to him?"

"Okay," she began. "Last night I dreamed about him. I dreamed that he was here, where I met him, but he was also in a bar. It was a bar, but it was here, you know?"

I nodded. He had certainly sounded like he'd been drinking. Not real, but true.

"Right," Andy continued, "well, circling all around him in the air were memories, like old black and white pictures. He was looking at them, and taking more drinks, and he had one hand reaching out for somebody who had his back to him. He kept trying, but he couldn't reach the person's shoulder."

"Who was it?" I asked.

"Let me tell it," she said. "I'm getting there. I didn't know at first because this guy was dressed in a suit and wore one of those old-fashioned hats, like an Indiana Jones hat, you know? A detective hat, like in the movies."

"I don't watch movies."

"Wait, what?" she stopped. "You don't watch movies? Who doesn't watch movies?"

I was sorry I'd said anything.

"Andy, the dream?"

"Right," she said with a nod, "so Mack was trying to reach this guy but couldn't. I sort of floated around to look at his face, and I didn't know who it was at first because his eyes were, well, they were moons. Just two full moons. But then I looked closer and realized it was *you*. It was hard to tell at first because you were shaved and wearing a tie and that hat, but it was you."

I swallowed, feeling the guilt rising in me to join the grief.

"But then you were gone," she said, "and there was this monster where you had been. Like, well have you seen an *American Werewolf in London*? Or *The Howling*?"

I looked at her and said nothing.

"Oh, right, sorry. It was a monster, like a wolf-man or something." She grew quieter but went on. "It... well it—it killed him. It was bad. I—I'm not sure what it meant."

True, but not real? It sounded pretty damn real to me. It sounded like Andy had watched me kill my friend, even if she had to dress up what she saw with the Hollywood monster movie bullshit that made sense to her.

"Anything else?" I asked her.

"Well," she said quietly, "yeah. I yelled for it to stop, and the monster thing, it looked up and saw me. It looked me right in the eyes, and it had those same moon-eyes from before."

That settled it as far as I was concerned. The monster had the same eyes she had dreamed on my face? Not real, but true. Andy's dream was telling her that I was the monster, but she wouldn't let herself believe it. She kept talking.

"So, when I woke up, I had to know if he was okay. I called, but nobody answered. So as soon as I could, I took the bus and walked—it took me half the day to get here—and the police were here. I knew he was dead. I just knew it."

"You haven't heard anything officially, though? You haven't seen the body?"

"Well, no," she said, "but I *know*. When I know something, I know it. I can't explain."

"Stay here," I told her, opening my car door.

"Wait, where are you going?"

"I have to be sure."

"I am sure!" she yelled.

"I have to see."

"No! Those police aren't going to let you walk in there. They're going to think you had something to do with it. Trust me."

"Maybe I did," I said.

"What?"

"Just keep Blue company." I left the engine running as I closed the door, cutting off whatever the teenager had been about to say in response. Two blocks away I could see the lights on in Mack's window. A single police car was parked outside on the road.

I slipped into the darkness, the way only a predator can.

CHAPTER SEVENTEEN

Most people have no idea what they are capable of once they overcome fear. I didn't require the wolf's strength to scale the two-story building beside Mack's offices. It was a simple matter to shimmy up the rusted drainpipe and old bricks to make it to the roof. The crumbling wall and creaking metal would have scared most people off. The idea of falling and injuring themselves would be enough to stop them. I knew I didn't have to worry about that. I hadn't had to worry about simple injuries for a long time. Not just because I was confident that I'd recover with unnatural speed from any minor wounds like those, but because I genuinely didn't care anymore if I was hurt. I deserved it, and worse, I welcomed it.

I made it to the roof without difficulty and silently crept along to the edge of the building nearest Mack's. Flattening myself to the roof, I held my breath and listened closely. My senses were sharp enough that it was a simple matter of listening past the sounds of traffic and the city around me, of tuning out the distractions until I heard what I was searching for.

"...for your loss Ms Archer," a man's voice came from the ground floor of Mack's building. "I need you to try and remember everything you can about Mr. Watson's most recent clients. Is there anybody you can think of who might have wanted to kill him?"

Kill him. That settled it. Mack was dead, but I still needed to see the crime scene, to smell it. I had to know if I had done this.

"Ha!" I could hear the heartbreak in Marilyn's voice as she scoffed at the question. She'd been crying. Hard. "His clients? Have you had a look at the list I gave the officer? Mack worked with hopeless cases; his clients were lost causes. Mack didn't know how to give up on people, even when he should've known better."

"What does that mean? It sounds like you're thinking of something specific?"

"No," Marilyn backpedaled. She didn't like me, and I couldn't blame her. I knew that she'd wanted Mack to cut me loose years ago, and frankly she was right. Bitter or not, Marilyn was loyal. She knew that Mack trusted me, and that was enough. She'd never mention my name. "It's just that a lot of his clients were mixed up with some dangerous people. There are a lot to pick from."

The interview was being conducted downstairs, away from the upstairs crime scene. Another police car was approaching, sirens blaring and lights flashing as it pulled in behind Mack's Suburban. This was my chance.

Pulling on the wolf's strength within me, I crouched, and launched myself across the gap between the buildings. I landed softly on the edge of the other roof, relying on the nearby siren and engine to drown out what little sound I might have made. The siren quieted and a car door slammed shut as I crawled along the rooftop to Mack's upstairs window facing the alley.

"What's this number here?" the officer said downstairs. "He dialed it several times around the time he was killed."

I lowered myself from the rooftop to hang in front of the window before finding the ledge with my toes and crouching on it. The window slid up easily. Mack opened it when he smoked and wouldn't have seen much point in keeping it latched.

"Oh," Marilyn said from downstairs, "that's just an old friend of his."

Good old Marilyn. They didn't make them like her anymore.

"Does this friend have a name?"

The smells of tobacco, blood, fear, and gunpowder washed over me with the warm air from Mack's apartment. His body had been removed and pictures had been taken, but investigative equipment and paraphernalia remained among the blood stains and smashed furniture.

"Yeah," Marilyn said, "that's Frank's number."

She'd held out as long as she could. I'd never expected her to lie to the police for me. I wouldn't have wanted her to. A door opened downstairs and urgent footsteps quickly came to a stop.

"Is it true?" a new male voice demanded, out of breath.

I didn't have much time. Things were still going on downstairs and somebody could decide to come back up to the crime scene at any moment. I needed to find something that would give me some answers. The smells of the room were too jumbled. There was something, somebody familiar, beneath the odors of blood and gunpowder which overpowered the room.

"Owen?" Marilyn said in her motherly tone. "Oh son, it's true. I'm so sorry..."

"Don't you call me that!" the man yelled. "Shacking up with my father does *not* make you my mother!"

I heard Marilyn's intake of breath, sharp and sudden as though she'd been slapped by his words.

The door to the stairs had been broken open from the outside, part of it still hanging on the frame above the shattered fragments on the carpeted floor. The empty shells to the right of Mack's desk told me that he had fired toward the door from his seat. The chair itself was on the ground. Perhaps he had stood quickly and knocked it over before firing at the intruder. The bloody mess in the corner told me that Mack had only made it a few steps from the desk before he was taken, and the amount of blood filled me with guilty relief that I hadn't seen the body.

Or had I?

"Easy, Watson," the officer said in a firm but soothing voice. "It isn't her fault."

"Yeah?" Owen Watson said. "Well then, whose fault is it? You have somebody in custody for killing my dad?"

I was going about this all wrong. If it had been me who had killed Mack, looking at things from his perspective wouldn't jar my memory. I had to approach this the way the killer did and see if anything came back to me. I approached the door, careful not to make any sounds that would alert the group downstairs.

"No, not yet. Listen," the officer said with the tone of a man speaking to somebody he knew well. "I know that this must be incredibly difficult, but I'm going to have to ask you to leave the scene. Given your relationship, you know there's no way you can be involved here."

I imagined having just broken through the shattered door and surveying the scene before me. The desk across the room would be the only thing between me and my prey. I'd advance before he had a chance to shoot. One step, perhaps two. I looked down at the dark carpet and noticed the discoloration that could be trace amounts of blood. I lowered myself to the ground to examine it more closely.

"No, no way," Mack's son growled the words. "Not until I know you've got something to go on at least. I can help."

"You know as well as I do that the lawyers would have a field day if you have your hands in this case, Mr. Watson."

"Detective Sergeant Watson," he corrected sharply.

"Not in this county you're not," the officer said.

"I can't work the case," Owen said, ignoring the man's point, "but I'm still family of the victim. That means I could have information that could help. Let me answer what I can. I wouldn't trust anything that woman says."

I tried to ignore the exchange between Mack's son and Marilyn, and I knew that if Mack had been here to hear Owen talking that way about Marilyn, he'd have cuffed the kid upside his head in an instant. But he wasn't here. I pushed the thought down and focused on the scene.

Blood.

The smell was unmistakable. If I could trust the wolf with anything it would be to smell blood. There wasn't much of it, and mingling with the thick coppery smell of Mack's blood that flooded the room, it was difficult to discern much about it. I sniffed again, touched my finger to it, and dabbed the finger on my tongue, inhaling slow and deep.

"Fine," the officer said. "Stay to answer questions. But no harassing Miss Archer, and no getting in my way, or you're out of here. Deal?"

"Deal," Owen said. "Where did it happen?"

"What did I just say?" the officer said. "I'm asking the questions."

The blood was not Mack's. It was distinct. Almost familiar. I knew this smell, though I wasn't sure how. The disturbing familiarity of Mack's scent was overpowering everything. If it were my own blood I was smelling, what else would I expect? That would mean that I had been shot, if it had been me, and I didn't wake up with any fresh injuries.

Would I have had any injuries? When the wolf was at the surface, fully in control, it took a lot to injure a Garou. Bleeding from wounds not inflicted by iron would stop almost instantly. I supposed that would account for the very small amount of blood, and my healing could be damnably quick with the wolf in control. This could really have been me, but I couldn't remember anything.

"Alright, Ms. Archer," the officer continued. "You were about to tell me about Frank?"

"Frank?" Owen said. "Frank Shepard had something to do with this? Why am I not surprised?"

Shit. It might be time to leave.

"No, no," Marilyn said quickly, "the officer was just asking about the calls Mack had made. Frank isn't connected."

"Like hell!" Owen said. "If Dad was talking to that junkie loser, they're mixed up in something shady."

Okay, so Mack's son wasn't a fan of me.

I crept closer to the kill spot, from which dark blood stains spread like vines across the walls in all directions, some even painting the ceiling. This kill had been messy, angry. Personal? It sure felt that way. I had to keep myself from thinking of the gory scene as being the remnants of my friend, otherwise I wouldn't have been able to function. Luckily, living with a bloodthirsty monster in my skull has given me ample experience compartmentalizing my thoughts. Still, it would have been nice to have taken a hit of that dope before coming in here. The blood smell was going to my head. From the corner of my eye, coalescing above the place where my friend had died, shadows and mist came together to form the semblance of Mack Watson. My friend's spirit had lingered! If I'd been his killer, he'd certainly let me know. I hurried eagerly to examine the corner where the specter was beginning to manifest.

The floorboards of the corner must have been weakened by the struggle when Mack was killed, because as I stepped forward, the old floor creaked and made a very noticeable crackle sound. I froze, instantly.

"What was that?" Owen said, "Is somebody else upstairs?"

"No," the officer said.

Two sets of footsteps came thundering up the stairs. The ghost hadn't manifested yet. Whether I had what I'd come for or not, that was my cue. I lunged at the window and scrambled through it as I heard the first footsteps crash through the broken door.

"Halt!" Owen yelled from behind me, oddly professional in his word choice at that frantic moment.

I didn't look back, there was no point in letting him identify me. I launched myself forward toward the other roof without any preparation, catching myself on the edge of the neighboring building just as I heard three distinct explosive pops from Owen's handgun.

I fell.

I didn't know why at first. There was no pain, not yet, but I landed hard on my back on the pavement of the alley below and stared up at the dark sky and wondered what the hell had just happened. First the warm, wet feeling spread across my chest, and I saw the exit wound near my right armpit before the feeling of being shot finally caught up with me. My right arm had given out as a hole had been punched through my shoulder blade, along with my right lung and the muscles of my back and chest. I don't mind saying, it hurt. A lot.

I fought to draw breath as a man leaned out of the window of Mack's office and stared down at me. There was no mistaking the resemblance. Owen looked remarkably like his father. A younger, fitter, angrier, more heavily armed, and less charitable version of my dead friend looked at me with all of the hate that I would expect from somebody who was convinced that I had killed his father. The bitch of it was, I couldn't argue.

"He's hit," Owen yelled to the officer behind him. "Come here and cover him, I'm going down there."

Owen's head was replaced by a middle-aged white man who didn't bother to level his gun at me as he called the situation into his police radio, I'm sure I looked more than subdued. Probably, he expected me to be dead before help could arrive. I knew that none of us would be that lucky tonight, and that if I let them corner me, I might well kill all of them when the wolf took over.

The pain was excellent fuel, just what I needed to bypass the guilt and grief I had been drowning the wolf in. I had to be careful not to release him entirely, but I needed to open the door a crack and let him lend a hand. I coughed up a cup-worth of blood as I felt the deepest tissues mending themselves first. Vital organs were always the first to repair themselves, which was why anything that doesn't kill a Garou outright likely won't kill them at all. A chance to recover is all I need.

I rolled to my left side, relying on that arm to bear my weight as I pulled myself to my knees.

"Hey, hold it right there!" the officer in the window yelled in disbelief as he watched me rise.

I could hear Owen's footsteps on the stairs within as he flew down them. I got my feet under me as he burst through the back door to the alley. Both he and the officer above levelled their sidearms at me.

For years I've made a point of not letting people see what I can do when I can help it, especially not the authorities. It was somewhat liberating in that moment to realize that those rules didn't matter for once. I was going to die soon anyway. Let them see. Let them wonder. As long as they didn't catch me, I'd be out of their reach before long anyway.

Yes. The wolf was eager to run and lick our wounds or to pay back those who had given them to us.

Flight, not fight.

I pushed that thought at the wolf like a muzzle and didn't loosen my grip on his mental chains until I felt his agreement.

"On your knees you son of a bitch!" Owen yelled as he approached me slowly, revolver levelled at me. "Please, please just give me a reason."

I bent my knees, slowly lowering myself toward the ground. A look of satisfaction came over Owen's face. He had me. He could relax. I saw his trigger finger loosen almost imperceptibly as he reached with one hand for the cuffs on his belt. That was the moment that I sprung, leaping not away but instead directly at him. He had thought himself safely out of my reach, and normally he would have been right, but he only knew how to anticipate the threats presented by normal humans. He hadn't realized yet that he was hunting a monster.

The distance and speed with which my leap propelled me left both officers completely stunned. My left knee collided with Owen's shoulder, knocking him to the ground and spinning him around, maybe even cracking his collar bone before I landed on my feet behind him. Now that Owen was between us, the other officer didn't dare fire a shot. I didn't bother to run down the alley. Instead, I ran up onto the Volvo parked outside of a neighboring building, using the car as a platform from which to launch myself into the hedgerow between buildings.

"God damnit!" I heard Owen yell as he recovered his footing, but by then there was a car and several bushes between us, and I was rounding the front corner of a house.

Out of sight of the two police, I quickly cut across the street and between more houses, putting several blocks between us before deciding that it was time to catch my breath and recover.

Touching a hand to my wound, I was startled by the thick hair sprouting from my knuckles and the hard curve of my nails. I shouldn't have been surprised, with that sort of injury and with the sort of speed I'd called on from the wolf, it was no wonder that I had begun to change. I needed to stay out of sight until I could make my way back to the Blazer, which sat parked on the far side of Mack's office. Using a nearby van as a starting point, I scurried up to the rooftop of a nearby house and pressed myself against the shingles, letting the wolf repair some of the damage in my shoulder while the moon bathed me in her waning light.

It didn't take long for sirens to overwhelm the sounds of the neighborhood. I was reluctantly impressed with their response time but frustrated that they were scouring the streets for me before I had made it to my vehicle.

Soon I could hear people talking within houses, speculating about what was going on. They had heard gunshots and sirens twice in one night. They were scared. I heard a mother whispering comforting nonsense to a child in the house I rested atop. I'd really fouled things up here. It was past time to go.

Examining my wound, I decided that I was fit enough to travel. The bloody hole through the front of my shirt made me thankful that I had left my jacket in the Blazer. At least I'd have something to cover the mess with. I rolled my right arm and winced at the pain. It was tender and far from fully functional, but it would have to do for now. The wolf lingered near the surface, sharpening my senses and filling my limbs with strength, but not threatening to take over. I said a silent thank you to the universe that this hadn't happened a week ago. I'd never have kept him in check.

Carefully and quietly, I jumped from rooftop to rooftop. Waiting each time to be sure that nobody was looking in my direction or had been startled within the house I'd landed on. At the end of the block, I lowered myself between two vehicles and began to make my way discreetly toward Andy and Blue. It required patience and cunning, but avoiding notice wasn't impossible. I scrambled into a dumpster to avoid a roving car, but he passed me by soon enough.

I crawled from beneath a parked station wagon once the

street ahead was empty and rounded the corner to where I had parked the Blazer, prepared to slip into the driver's seat and slip away into the night, but somebody had beat me to it. They were gone. The Chevy, my dog, the girl, and the gym bag full of the heroin that I was very much wanting to smoke right about then.

Gone.

CHAPTER EIGHTEEN

I was wounded, grieving, and hunted, but that wasn't a first for me. The healing and grief required time, time that I could only provide if I managed to evade my hunters. Pain and loss would have to wait. I pushed them down deep and tossed them to the wolf like a bone that he could chew on but never quite crack, much less digest. Feelings like that baffled the wolf, kept him occupied.

Flashing police lights reflected in the distance from several directions. I huddled between two old cars and took my bearings. The interstate highway was nearby to the east, and the ocean was over a mile to the west. The police would be focusing on making certain that I didn't gain access to the highway by car, or that I didn't slip away north or south on the city streets on foot or by car. They'd be shutting down, or at least monitoring, the on-ramps to the highway while they searched the streets. I could hide well enough, but only if they didn't bring police dogs to sniff me out. I had to leave, and I had to do it by foot. They'd be looking for a man on foot to go north or south. I decided to make a priority of defying their expectations.

I wasn't about to swim my way to freedom, so I crept

towards the highway. Interstate 5 was a massive road, bigger than anything we'd had when I first learned to drive. Four northbound lanes were separated by a wide bank from the four southbound lanes, and on the eastern side of the highway was suburbs and then relative wilderness. The only way to cross the highway on foot was by overpass, which would be conspicuous and all too visible. It was later in the evening, and so traffic was light, but that still meant a steady stream of vehicles with no more than twenty seconds or so in between them. There was no way to do this unseen, so I had to settle for speed.

I bided my time behind a thick hedgerow near the overpass, waiting for my chance. I wasn't concerned with making it across the road, that part would be easy, what concerned me was minimizing my exposure. The more people that saw me, the more likely it would be that the police would be notified. Busses and trucks carried radios, and Mack had been trying to talk me into carrying a clunky cellular phone for a couple of years now. I swallowed a fresh wave of grief as I realized that I'd never have that conversation again.

Later, damnit.

A bus passed and only cars were approaching from the north. I dashed. I don't know what the drivers of those cars would think that they saw. A blur, hopefully. At worst, they'd think they saw a man illegally crossing the highway and convince themselves that he couldn't have done it as quickly as they first thought. If they got a clear look at me, I might become another local bigfoot story. Something that happened to a friend of a friend. I hopped the barrier to the grassy embankment that separated the north and southbound traffic, and I realized that I wouldn't have the luxury of waiting to cross the next series of lanes.

The bank on which I found myself was steep and utterly devoid of cover, a fact which I couldn't have seen from where I'd been hiding. Likewise, I hadn't been able to see the northbound traffic until I'd gotten here. I was sliding down the bank and was exposed in oncoming headlights for everybody to see. No point in waiting. I propelled myself off the guardrail and landed in the middle of the highway, coming to a crouch on my feet and left arm. The lights and horns disoriented me terribly, leaving me unable to see what was coming or how far away it was. I hesitated, and the wolf reacted, pushing my body in a frantic scramble across the rest of the asphalt.

Horns and screeching tires spurred me on, but as I was nearing the opposite rail, I felt the impact of steel colliding with my hind half. The impact launched me into the air and sent me spinning, both legs shattered beneath the force of that blow. For an impossibly long time, I sailed through the air before landing and rolling on the other side of the road. I tumbled through grass and brambles before colliding with a vine-covered tree trunk.

The sounds of horns and shrieking brakes continued above and behind me as traffic reacted to the impact, but I had been thrown mercifully free of the road. I had made it across, but my situation hadn't improved. I'd been seen, and with my shattered legs, I wasn't going anywhere. The pain was breathtaking, eclipsing everything.

Cars are far more dangerous to me than guns. It's the damn steel. Sure, there are exceptions, the occasional fiberglass car or steel jacketed bullet, but by and large I'd much rather be shot. I've never understood it, but something about steel cuts through whatever resilience the wolf grants me against harm. When that car hit my legs at a mile a minute, I was every bit as vulnerable as a regular man.

Fortunately, there was no steel under my skin preventing my recovery. A steel bullet or arrowhead would have had to be removed, but my legs would only need time. Time that I didn't have. If I stayed near the road, they'd find me soon.

That panicked thought mingled with the pain that was already beyond my control, and the wolf answered their call. It was my turn to watch what happened next from the back of my mind as the beast made our choices for us. Using my arms, the wolf turned our body over and began to crawl away from the road, dragging our ruined legs behind us. The pain was unbearable, but it only strengthened the wolf, stoking his anger and panic. I watched as the hands that dragged us downhill grew sinewy and dark with hair, the nails stretching into claws that served better to pull myself with.

As I moved along the ground, pulling myself beneath a fence and through some family's messy backyard, I felt the bones of my legs drawing together. As is so often the case, the healing hurt much more than the injury had. Involuntarily, I roared with the pain, shaking the windows nearby. A car alarm began to scream in response not ten feet away and a light turned on in a nearby house.

No!

The wolf wouldn't hesitate to protect us, and since he couldn't run away with my broken legs, he wouldn't flinch from hurting anybody who came too close. I continued crawling away from the shrieking car alarm, but the pace was torturously slow. I could feel the crackling bones of my legs as they knit themselves together piece by piece. Within my skull, I threw myself against the bars of my psychic cage, desperate to regain control before the wolf took another life. I didn't make a dent, the pain was too strong, the situation too dire, and I had been too shocked by Mack's messages to numb myself with chemicals before going out among the sheep. I was a helpless spectator of my body's actions.

I was crawling across the residential road, just outside of the illuminating glow of the streetlight, trying to reach the bushes in the yard across the street. The only thought coming from the wolf was to escape, to put as much distance between us and our pursuers as we could before finding a hole where we could collapse in exhaustion and lick our wounds. Looking toward the dense bushes that the wolf was dragging us toward, I saw a barefoot homeless man standing still as a tree and staring directly at us.

He had darker skin and hair, Mexican or Indian in his features. His hair fell freely to his shoulders and a sparse beard grew in patches about his face. A length of rope held his dirty jeans in place, and his denim jacket was unbuttoned to reveal a shirtless patch of lean bare belly and chest beneath. It was a cold March night and any normal person would have been painfully cold in that attire, but I wasn't looking at a normal person, his eyes made that clear.

They were wolf's eyes. A golden yellow, the way that my own eyes would look at that moment, the way they always appeared when I succumbed to the change. Where my eyes matched the changes on the rest of my body, the hair, the claws, the fangs, this man before me was showing no other outward signs of change. I met those eyes, and my wolf realized instantly that we had seen them before. They were the eyes of the dark wolf that had hunted me in my dreams. Seeing the recognition on my face, the wolf-eyed, shoeless man stepped out from the bushes and approached me.

Run! Run! Hide!

My inner wolf lost all control in his desperate fear of this other wolf, all that mattered was to get away. I clawed frantically at the pavement of the road, dragging my ruined lower half behind me. The other man caught me with no difficulty, kneeling casually and grabbing hold of me by the ankle, sending a fresh bolt of pain searing up my spine.

With no control of my actions, I snarled and turned on the man, snapping my teeth and swiping at him with the bloody claws of my left hand that I had just splintered against the road. He simply leaned back and held on to the twisted foot, keeping easily out of my reach. In desperation, I tried to sit up to reach my own leg, willing even to bite my own limb off to escape this creature.

"Stop," the voice rumbled in a whisper. The man locked eyes with me as he spoke, and I fell back onto the pavement. My submissive wolf had bared our belly and throat there on the road. The sudden warmth and sour smell of urine made it impossible to deny that I had pissed myself.

I'd have been embarrassed, but the agony and panic didn't leave room for such a human emotion.

The dark man reached forward and grabbed me by the throat, and my wolf offered no resistance. With his other hand, the man drew a cold bowie knife the length of my forearm from within his jacket, and quickly pricked my skin with the steel tip as he pressed the blade to my throat. The message was instinctively clear to us, my man and wolf selves. The jaws of the alpha were at our throat and he could end our life at any time he chose. It would have saved me the trouble if he had killed me, but my wolf had no desire to die. We froze.

Though he was smaller than me, the man had no difficulty in lifting my broken body with one hand. He carried me to the cover of the bushes, bare feet utterly silent as I struggled to breathe. My feet barely grazed the ground as he ran, holding the blade in one hand and holding me by the back of the neck with the other. I doubt that I could have managed such disorienting speed on my best day, even unencumbered, but he managed it while barefoot and carrying me. He never broke a sweat.

I was utterly helpless to act; the wolf was still in control and he had decided to submit. My human mind struggled to catch up with everything that had happened in the last hour. Blue and Andy were both gone. The best case scenario would be that

Andy had been scared off by the police and had taken off in my Chevy, but I couldn't be certain of that. The existence of this new man-wolf who had me by the throat forced me to consider things in a new light. Had he been following me? For how long? Had he attacked Andy and Blue once I had gone? For that matter, had he been the one who had killed Mack?

The possibility that I hadn't been the cause of my friend's death invigorated me. I didn't care how much more powerful than me this newcomer was. I didn't care how broken my body was. I silently swore to myself that I'd eat his heart for what he'd done. Whatever it took, before I died, I'd avenge my friend. I just had to make sure that I lived long enough to do it.

The man-wolf dragged me eastward, carrying me miles through the sparse residential area, leaping through deserted industrial lots, even pulling me across the brackish Snohomish River before dropping me unceremoniously in tall grass on a slippery, muddy bank where the river diverged into a series of sloughs before joining the sea.

Sitting on his haunches, he locked his eyes on me and pressed the wet tip of his knife to his tongue, tasting the drop of my blood that he had drawn when he captured me. I heard him inhale slowly as he considered my scent. His lined face was impassive as he watched me, yellow eyes never wavering.

I gasped greedily for breath in the mud, my head swimming and my vision sharpening as oxygen returned in a rush. I looked back at him. His eyes gave the impression of age and quiet confidence. Locking eyes is a challenge for dominance, and my inner wolf immediately wanted to look away, but I didn't agree. I looked at the small dark-skinned vagabond before me and considered how easy it had been for him to carry me, and I thought of how easy it would be for him to have murdered my friend. I was helpless before this old wolf. Mack would never have stood a chance. I took the rage that came with that thought, the anger at the creature who had ended Mack's life—whether it was me or the stranger—and fed it to my inner wolf. The anger strengthened me, gave my wolf the fuel he needed to meet those ancient eyes. My lip twitched in the beginning of a snarl, and I had the satisfaction of watching the stranger's eyebrow raise slightly in surprise.

It lasted barely a moment, and then he was on me again, straddling my body and pressing his blade to the skin above my heart. With his free hand he grabbed me by the side of my head, forcing me to face him as he leaned in toward me. I felt the heat of his breath on my eyes as his weight pressed the steel tip through my skin. I winced.

"Be still," he said. His voice was soft, but it cracked from disuse. It had strength but creaked like branches of an old willow.

I glared at him as my inner wolf struggled to look away, the old wolf only grinned in mild amusement.

"I have questions," he said.

"Go to hell," I said. He had questions? Not nearly as many as I did.

"You will answer," he said as he pressed the knife more firmly into my flesh, clearly implying that the consequences of refusing him would be painful or even fatal.

"Do it!" I spit the words at him, and he recoiled as if struck. He hadn't expected that.

"You wish for death?" he said, looking more closely into my eyes, as if to confirm the question for himself.

"I wish for you to fuck yourself."

He considered me for a moment, weighing the defiance in my face against the way my legs still twisted unnaturally in all the wrong directions. Finally, he seemed to reach a decision. He rose to his feet and stood at a polite distance, sheathing his knife within the folds of his jacket.

"I am Hiram," he said. "Will you speak with me?"

I've heard it said that you can catch more flies with honey than vinegar, and it's just as true of wolves. The stranger, Hiram, had withdrawn from our struggle, even though he would have beaten me easily if I'd forced him to. I've always been a stubborn son of a bitch, as Mack had been fond of reminding me, and I would have made this man kill me before I'd backed down. He'd been wise enough to recognize that fact and had decided that he had nothing to prove. That befuddled me and defused my immediate anger. I was still suspicious and in pain, but without the immediate conflict to drive me on, my rage was deflated, and my strength and suicidal defiance went with it.

We sat there in silence for several minutes. Hiram kept his distance and presented no threat, waiting patiently for me to steady my nerves and regain full control of myself. While we waited, my legs continued to straighten and mend. They were not fully healed, that would take more than a day without giving way to the wolf, but they were improved. My left leg even felt as though it could bear my weight for a short time.

After watching my wolf features fade and my legs mend, Hiram extended his hand to me in an unspoken request for me to accompany him, and after a moment of hesitation, I took it. I couldn't walk. Not even close. The other man put his arm around my waist and bore the majority of my weight. He allowed me the dignity of appearing to hobble on my left leg.

Wordlessly, he led us through the mud and tall grass. I couldn't help but marvel at the strength in his hand and arm as he supported my weight. He could just as easily have been breaking my spine. I reminded myself that I may very well have to kill this man and resolved not to let myself become intimidated in the meantime. He'd get his answers, but only if I got mine, and then I'd know which of us needed to die first.

Hiram had a truck nearby, parked at the end of an unpaved

road which had been hidden by the grass and reeds around it. It was an old Ford pickup, older than my Blazer but also far better maintained. Where my Chevy looked old and worn, Hiram's simple grey truck seemed merely well-used. Beside the truck was a small pile of charred wood where he had recently had a modest fire. A tarp in the back of his truck covered whatever else he possessed.

He set me beside the coals and quickly but quietly added small sticks and dry reeds to the charred pile. Soon, a small fire crackled and warmed my feet. Reaching into the back of his truck, Hiram returned with a piece of smoked meat. He tore it neatly in half and offered me a piece. I took it.

It is much harder to kill a man you have shared food and a fire with. I wondered if Hiram felt the same way, and if that was why he was offering me his hospitality. He ate his meat wordlessly and added a piece of wood to the fire. I bit into the food I'd been given. Venison, barely smoked. The flesh was still pink and moist. I devoured it and decided not to put myself into this man's debt by asking for more.

"Did you kill Mack?" I asked. A little rude, perhaps, but I couldn't exchange niceties with the man who had killed my friend. To hell with manners.

He raised an eyebrow in evident surprise.

"No."

"Why should I believe you?"

"Why should I lie?" he asked.

"Because I'd kill you if you did!"

His brow shifted again in a clear display of incredulity, and he chose to ignore the threat.

"What is your name?" he asked instead.

I hesitated. Why should I tell him anything? I'd heard that names could be powerful things, but then I'd heard that from a crazy old woman who also believed in fairies and genies.

Besides, this Hiram had already given me his name, and if I were being honest, I had to admit that he already had all the power over me that he needed if he meant me harm.

"Shepard," I said.

He nodded in acknowledgement and unhurriedly finished his meat.

"Who was it that made you?" he asked.

"What?"

"The Turnskin who made you," he said, "who was it? And when?"

Turnskin? That was a new one for me.

"I never knew her name."

PART 4

OVER THERE

CHAPTER NINETEEN

FRANCE AND THE WAR.
THE PAST.

Against my better judgement, Peter Madsen became my friend. I didn't do anything to deserve his friendship. I just failed to try hard enough to avoid it. The outgoing son of a preacher decided that we would be friends, and I was never consulted.

We attended basic training together in California. We were too busy learning how to stand in line and wipe our asses to socialize, which suited me fine. Every time Madsen approached me to try and strike up another personal conversation, our Sergeants readily provided me with excuses to ignore him. The excuses ran out in October when we were shipped to Quantico for further training. A train ride from California to Virginia is the perfect battlefield for a conversational ambush.

"So," Madsen said as he claimed the seat beside me, "you never told me what church you went to?"

"That's right," I said. Undeterred, he laughed at what he took as a joke and slapped me good naturedly on the shoulder.

"You're pretty funny for a quiet guy, Frank."

"Sorry," I said. He practically fell out of his seat.

"Quiet but funny, you're a regular Charlie Chaplin."

"If you say so," I said.

It was a long ride. Pete Madsen was a pleasant enough sort of fellow, but he never stopped trying to be everybody's best friend. He was like a cat. The less you wanted his attention the more of it you got, and I seemed to want the least of it.

He talked at length about his family. He went on about his father, the Reverend Madsen, who was some flavor of Methodist, and how he had heard 'the calling' and brought his family west from Kansas to preach in the corner of civilization, as he saw it. He talked about his mother mostly by referencing her cooking. He'd go on and on about missing his mother's blackberry pie or biscuits and gravy. Madsen talked about food at the worst times. It was when he talked about his sister, Evelyn, that I paid the most attention. That stunning girl who had smiled at me in Seattle was hard to forget. Peter talked about her mostly as a little pest who had always gotten him into trouble and who could always get her way.

"Catholic?" He seemed appalled when I told him that I had been born into Roman Catholicism.

"That's right," I said.

"But...why?"

"What do you mean, why?"

"Well, because they're idolaters, Frank!" he insisted.

I shrugged, having no interest in defending my mother's church. He seemed hurt, like I had done him wrong and now owed him some sort of apology. He transfixed me with a look that seemed to say, now what do you have to say for yourself?

"I don't know," I said. "It's not like I picked it."

"What do you mean?"

"Well, come on Madsen," I said. "What do you think your

father would have said if you told him you didn't like your church and wanted to go to a different one. Or no church at all?"

He stared at me, mouth agape, as he considered the impossible scenario.

"I would never..."

"Yeah, I know," I said, "but what would he say if you did?"

"I don't know," he said, "but I'm sure he'd say it with a belt, and he'd keep saying it until I came to my senses."

"My old man wasn't as nice as yours," I said.

He seemed to understand and didn't press the subject further. Though, he did look at me sideways whenever my saint's medal fell out of my shirt, and he always made a point to try and include me when he prayed. I think that encounter only solidified his decision to become my constant companion. Now he saw me as a heathen in need of salvation.

I resigned myself to his companionship. After all, I supposed that I couldn't go through the entire war without talking to anybody, and there were worse people to be paired up with.

One guy, Barnes, never shut up about how he was going to come home with a chest full of medals and get any girl he wanted. To hear Barnes tell it, you'd think that the war had only gone on so long because he hadn't been in it yet.

Another fellow, Cervantes, had to be deloused when he'd first arrived, but not before he'd infested the entire training barracks with scabies and lice. Even after the beating we'd all given him. Cervantes couldn't seem to keep himself clean. The only use he seemed to have for a toothbrush was polishing his boots. The sergeant joked once that he'd fit right in with the Brits.

Having Madsen, the preacher's son, at my side, served to keep everybody else away. I'd rather be stuck in a trench beside a friendly guy who couldn't shut up than beside a guy who would get me killed with his need to prove himself, or a guy whose breath would force me to live in my gas mask.

At Quantico we learned the 'new style' of warfare that the Brits and the French had been using in the war. There was a lot of training with gas masks, and more digging than shooting. We did jumping jacks until our blisters had blisters, and I shoved my bayonet into enough sandbags to have bled the German army dry. It was damn tedious stuff, and most of us were eager to get to the real war just to get a break in the monotony.

There was a lot of bellyaching in Quantico. The guys talked a lot about how they'd never worked so hard in their lives. One or two bragged that life in the Marine Corps was nothing compared to what they were used to back home on the farm. I just enjoyed the steady supply of food and clean sheets. I'd never had it so good. No drill sergeant ever beat me half as hard as my father had. I didn't complain, mostly because I preferred to keep my mouth shut, but the guys seemed to think that this made me some sort of tough guy. After a couple of months of training and regular meals, I had put on ten or twenty pounds of muscle, and I think I may have even grown an inch.

In October, they put us on another train to New York, where we were supposed to take a ship to the war. The night before we shipped out, some of the guys decided to celebrate our last night in the states, and we went into the city looking for a way to blow off steam. Madsen pestered me into going along, and I figured I'd probably never get another chance to see New York.

Early in the night, the boys talked Madsen into trying his first sip of booze. It was just a beer, pale weak stuff that my father would have mistaken for water, but to Peter Madsen it may as well have been gin. He drank half of the beer and immediately ran outside and vomited in the street. Not from the taste, or anything else, but out of sheer guilt.

"I think I'm going to die!"

"You're going to be fine," I said.

"No, I'm not," he said, "one drink of liquor can destroy your liver, Frank."

I rolled my eyes, but he was too busy retching to notice.

"It's not liquor. It's just beer," I told him.

He heaved again in response.

"Madsen," I said, "Do you think those other guys inside are all going to die? They're on their second or third round by now."

"I deserve it, Frank," he said. "I promised my mother I wouldn't drink. It's a sin!"

"A sin?"

He nodded vigorously which set him off on another round of heaving.

"Didn't Jesus drink wine?" I said.

He looked up at me like I was crazy. I could see the wheels turning as he considered what I had said.

"Well, yes, but..."

"There you have it," I said.

He had nowhere to go, and he knew it. He could either accuse Jesus Christ of sinning, or he could back down. Given the choice between blasphemy and debauchery, Peter Madsen chose to get good and soused.

Three hours and two gallons of weak beer later, we had to carry Madsen back to the barracks. He couldn't walk, but he sang the whole way. After that night, Peter Madsen preached a lot less, and I liked him a lot more.

The next morning, on October 31st, we boarded our ship for France. Madsen's first hangover allied with seasickness to ensure it was a day he'd never forget.

CHAPTER TWENTY

Most of us had never seen a ship, let alone sailed on one the size of the Von Steuben. She was about eight or nine-hundred feet long and had a crew of more than twelve hundred. Of the thousand Marines on board, most of us had come from towns smaller than that ship. Earlier in the war, she had been named the Kaiser Wilhelm II, before being captured from the Germans and rechristened the Von Steuben.

It took me about a week to stop puking and get my 'sea legs', as the sailors said. Madsen seemed to get all his puking out of his system on that first day and was his usual chipper self again. Pete was smart enough to leave me alone for that first week, but after the first week I was playing cards and smoking cigarettes like everybody else.

Madsen had really loosened up after that night in New York. There were fifty or so nurses on the ship with us, and most of us found them a welcome distraction. Before New York, Pete would have guilted us for every whistle or glance we sent their way, but now he joined in with the rest of the admirers.

A week into the voyage, right around the time I was becoming accustomed to being at sea, I caught him kissing a brunette nurse in a dark corner. Later, he tried to tell me that he'd been whispering to her, but his hand under her skirt hadn't been whispering. He'd given himself permission to sin, and he didn't seem to believe in doing anything half-way. I decided that it was none of my business.

But Madsen doubled his nightly prayers. He seemed to expect divine retribution for his backsliding ways. Having never lived without supervision and punishment, he was certain that punishment would find him, even in the middle of the Atlantic.

God's justice seemed to find him two days later when we collided with another ship in our convoy. It was around sunset. All of the lights had been extinguished, and the sudden sound of tons of steel colliding and twisting had us on our feet in an instant. The recent fate of the Titanic being fresh in our consciousness, many of us assumed the worst.

"I knew it!" Madsen said. "I knew that God was watching!"

"What are you talking about?"

"You led me astray!" he pointed his finger at me in accusation.

"You're nuts!"

"Oh Lord," he closed his eyes and turned his face heavenward, "I pray for your forgiveness. I have sinned against you. I have dishonored my father and my mother. I have been led astray by false witnesses..."

I threw my hands up and walked away to see what was happening and if we needed to abandon ship. We didn't. Another ship in our convoy, the Agamemnon, had collided with the Von Steuben. The two ships had turned into each other and the anchor of the Agamemnon had torn apart a portion of our ship's bow. The collision had been so sudden and forceful that one soldier had been thrown from the Agamemnon and ended up on the Von Steuben with us. It was the damnedest thing.

Barnes and I found a sailor who had explained what had happened to us. He assured us that we were not in any danger.

"Nah," he said. "Trusty old Vonnie can take a lot worse than that, don't you worry."

He'd been right. We were underway soon, limping along a little slower with some hasty repairs but still expecting to reach France within a couple of days.

"It's going to be alright, Pete," I said. "It was just an accident."

Madsen was still kneeling beside his bunk when I returned hours later. I wondered if he'd moved from that spot. He opened his eyes and rose to sit on the bunk.

"My prayers have been answered then," he said.

I didn't say anything. If believing that he had a personal line to the almighty kept his spirits up, why should I care?

The next morning didn't do much to ease the tension. There were rumors flying through the ship that somebody had sighted periscopes in the distance. This close to Europe, the danger from German U-boats was on everybody's mind, and it seemed possible that we had survived yesterday's mishap only to be sunk today. Madsen immediately resumed his prayers. I figured it couldn't hurt to follow suit and may have muttered a prayer or two over my Saint Francis medal myself.

By midday, we were joined by a half dozen American destroyers that had been sent from France to escort us the rest of the way. We breathed a collective sigh of relief, and Madsen gave me a look that seemed to say, 'you see?'

From there, we thought we were home free, but we soon learned our first lesson about letting our guard down. The next day, one day away from our destination, we were attacked. Even with our new destroyer escort, U-boats had gotten close enough to take a shot at us.

There is a special kind of terror that comes with watching

your own death coming at you and knowing that you can do nothing to prevent it. Nothing inspires fear quite so much as utter helplessness. Standing there, we watched the torpedo speed through the phosphorescent water on its way to taking us out of the war before we'd even seen a German. Men cursed, prayed, and held their breath as we braced for impact.

The impact never came. The torpedo missed us, narrowly passing in front of our damaged bow. The destroyers opened fire, they hit nothing, but the U-boats were warned off from any further attempts.

It was explained to us later, by giddy sailors, that it had been the damage from the earlier collision that had saved our lives. The engines of the Von Steuben had been working at full steam, but the hole in our bow left us slower than the U-boats had anticipated. Had we been undamaged, the torpedo would have sunk us.

"You see," Madsen said, "His hand protects us."

"What are you talking about?" Barnes asked him as we disembarked in the port of Brest.

"Mysterious ways, my friend," Madsen said. "The Lord works in mysterious ways."

CHAPTER TWENTY-ONE

We spent Christmas in Bordeaux, far from the front. After arriving, we had taken a train south from Brest and spent the next two months training with the French. The French soldiers had been in the war for years at that point, and it showed.

They looked thin and old somehow, tired. The circles under their eyes gave them a haunted look, as if they had seen things that they didn't know how to tell us about.

We, in turn, must have seemed to them like something from a story. We were taller, cleaner, more fit, eager to get to the fight and get the war over with. Ragged soldiers in patched uniforms marveled at our weapons and gear. They seemed like an army of vagabonds.

When we weren't training, we were familiarizing ourselves with the French ladies. The temperance movement that was sweeping the United States back home hadn't taken root here, and wine and other spirits were freely for sale, if sometimes in short supply. Most anything we wanted could be had cheaply, or even traded for with American cigarettes and other simple items that meant little to us.

"*She'll do it for wine, she'll do it for rum, and sometimes for chocolate or chewing gum!*"

The song we picked up from the British soldiers about the ladies of Armentieres certainly rang true even down here in the south. Those of us who wanted female company didn't have to look far when we had liberty.

"*The cooties rambled through her hair; she whispered sweetly 'C'est la guerre'.*"

I wrote a letter to Maggie every week, mostly to ask after her and to make sure that she was getting the money I sent, but I felt that certain details of life in France were better left omitted. Her letters found me in Bordeaux as the year drew to an end, but they were far from timely.

Dear Francis,

Happy birthday! I received your last letter and want to assure you that we are well. You shouldn't worry. We have received the money that you sent and have put it to good use, but I worry that you aren't keeping anything for yourself. The police still haven't found Father's killer, and we worry that they may be giving up on the case. Mother is as well as can be expected, but she needs more and more of her medicine. The Adlers have been wonderful, even helping me find a job. Paul sends his best. I think of you often and hope you are well. Keep yourself safe and come home soon, I'll never forgive you if you don't!

Your Sister,

Magdalena Shepard
October 4, 1917

She enclosed little sprigs of mint with her letters, very dry and almost scentless by the time they reached me, but I imagined the fresh smell from memory. It touched me that she had thought to write to me on my birthday, but I was worried to hear that she had started working. I had hoped that the money I was sending would be enough to let her finish school. I worried about what she might not be telling me.

"You might forget the gas and shell," Barnes sang a verse of the familiar song as he staggered drunkenly into the barracks, *"But you'll nev'r forget the Mademoiselle!"*

Madsen managed to convey his disapproval with a silent shift in his body language. It was no secret that Barnes spent his every spare franc on wine and women.

"Ooh, what's this?" Barnes snatched Maggie's letter from my hands before I knew he'd even noticed me. "Does Shepard have a girl back home? Does she know about the Mademoiselle?"

"Give it back, Barnes," I said low and clear.

"'Dear Francis,'" he read. "Francis? Oh really?"

"I'm warning you, Barnes."

"What's the matter, *Francis?*" Barnes laughed, "Don't be embarrassed. It says here it was your birthday? Well happy birthday, Francis!"

I snatched at the letter but the drunk Marine managed to anticipate this and kept the paper out of reach, stepping back from me.

"Barnes," I said, "I'm not laughing."

"'We have received the money that you sent,'" he read on. "You're sending this girl money? Hey fellas, listen to this. The Mademoiselles aren't good enough for old *Francis* here, he prefers American whores—"

And just like that, Barnes was on his back. I had stepped in without thinking and landed a cross to his nose with my scarred right hand. He was on the ground before I processed what had happened. I'd heard the word whore, and almost instantly I was feeling the skin of my knuckles tear against the bones of his face. Barnes stared up at me in amazement, his broken nose pouring blood onto his face.

I stepped forward and knelt on his chest, taking his collar in my left hand and pulling back my right to hit him again. Before I could, somebody had a hold of me from behind me, their arms wrapping around mine and pulling me off Barnes, who continued to gape in stunned disbelief.

It was Madsen. He held me back as I gathered my senses, and Barnes touched his fingertips to his nose and winced.

"It's broken!" Barnes said through a mouthful of blood.

Madsen released me when I stopped struggling and put himself between us, holding me back with one hand on my chest and extending the other to help Barnes off the ground.

"You son of a bitch!" Barnes said as he held his face in both hands, blood dripping between his fingers.

"Easy Barnes," Madsen said. "It's over."

"Like hell it is! I'm reporting this!"

"Of course," Madsen said, "that's the right thing to do. We'll all go and report it together."

"What?" Barnes and I said in unison.

"Sure," Madsen said. "Let's go and explain the whole thing. How Madsen came back drunk after a night of whoring and stole Shepard's personal property and insulted his sister."

"Hold on now," Barnes said.

"You wouldn't want to tell just part of the story would you, Barnes?" Madsen said. "That wouldn't be truthful. You wouldn't expect me to bear false witness."

"I didn't know it was his sister," blood was dripping through his hands to the floor.

"Of course you didn't," Madsen said, "and that's why I'm sure that *Frank* here," he emphasized my name to the drunken idiot, "would be happy to accept your apology and call it even."

"Like hell I will," I said.

"Because he knows that the alternative," Madsen said, pretending he hadn't heard me, "would be to report this whole incident and spend Christmas digging latrines or standing watch, if we're lucky."

Barnes and I glared at each other but said nothing.

"Now apologize, Barnes," Madsen said, "and go get yourself fixed up. Who knows, maybe some French nurse would love to ask you all about what happened."

"Fine," Barnes spat the word. "Sorry."

"Good," Madsen looked at me expectantly.

After a moment I nodded at Barnes in acknowledgement, and Madsen seemed to take that as being good enough.

"Alright then," Madsen said, "now go get cleaned up, Barnes, you're leaking all over our floor."

The bleeding Marine stormed out of the barracks and left us alone with the mess. Madsen didn't say anything to me. He just reached to the ground and returned Maggie's letter to my hand.

"Thanks," I said.

"You can thank me by cleaning the floor."

CHAPTER TWENTY-TWO

It was the end of winter when we finally boarded a train to the front. Finally, after months of training back home, and four more months of training with the French near Bordeaux, we were going to have somebody to fight other than each other.

We disembarked in a place called Dugny, near Verdun. Everybody had heard about Verdun. Earlier in the war it had become the stuff of nightmares, where countless men had died and where the earth itself had been blasted to hell. The action had shifted a bit since those days, and we Americans were meant to get a little experience away from where the fighting was heaviest so that we would be seasoned when the time came for the real fighting.

It was dark when we were brought into the trenches, in order to avoid being seen by the Germans. The enemy was less than a mile away in some cases and would be quick to call in an artillery strike if they knew that reinforcements were being brought in. Still, the Germans knew that something was going on. They fired star shells into the night sky. The magnesium exploded above no man's land again and again and slowly drifted downward on parachutes, casting an eerie light into the trenches where we were concealed.

We'd been training for the trenches for months, but actually seeing them was another matter. They were bigger than I'd expected, deeper. These trenches had been in use for years now and were dug ten or twelve feet deep into the hillside. In order to fight we would have to climb up ladders to reach the firing line.

I was amazed at the sheer size of the network, complex winding things that we could easily have gotten lost in if it weren't for the French guides showing us the way. Little alcoves were dug everywhere. Men slept in some, and in others, little cookfires would be lit, where soldiers heated grey bacon in unwashed mess tins.

Most jarring of all were those haunted eyes of the French soldiers. They looked at us as if they didn't believe we were finally there. They seemed resigned to the monotony of life in the trenches, doubting any sign of change. When the sun rose, and I had my first real glimpse at the battlefield, I began to appreciate that look in their eyes. Our lines gave way to a forest of barbed wire beyond which lay no man's land, that desolate stretch of blasted earth and unrecovered corpses that rested between the German trenches and our own. It was a dark and hellish scene, unlike any I'd ever imagined or read about. Nothing seemed to grow. Dead wood covered the ground thickly enough to walk on. The twisted remnants of trees sometimes remained standing amidst the rolling mounds of broken earth and watery shell holes where men's bodies had been left to stew. The men I was joining had fought in that field. The bodies abandoned on the field had been their friends and comrades, and there was no guarantee that they—that we— wouldn't meet the same end.

Dante himself couldn't have dreamed up such a place.

It was there, near Verdun, that we first heard about the creatures of no man's land. Most of us took what we heard for tall tales that the French would tell to try and frighten us, but Peter Madsen took the stories to heart.

"Promise me you won't leave my body out there for those things to eat," Madsen whispered to me one night on watch.

I nodded.

"I mean it, Frank," he said. "Promise me! If you promise not to leave me, I'll promise not to leave you."

"Of course. I won't leave you, Pete," I said to shut him up. Not that I believed in ghouls that came out at night to feed on the dead and dying, but rats were real enough and I didn't like the idea of being food for the greasy, fat vermin that were everywhere in the trenches. I didn't like the idea of dying at all, and I wished he'd quit talking about it.

"Promise me!"

"Fine, fine," I said, "I promise."

"Good," he said with relief, "and I promise I won't leave you either."

I figured it went without saying that we wouldn't leave each other. Something about being in that hell hole made the men beside me something closer than brothers. Even a jerk like Barnes, with his newly crooked nose, was somebody I'd fight or die for now that it came down to it. I couldn't imagine leaving any of the men out there. But I imagined that the others who had been fighting this war must have felt the same, and there was no lack of bodies left behind, nonetheless. I'll admit, it did make me feel a little better having his promise.

Madsen seemed like two different people. Sometimes, when we had leave, he chased women and wine more than any other man I knew. At other times, especially when he was frightened, he'd seem the most devout and puritanical of us all, refusing wine or smokes and glaring with disapproval at any man who even spoke about a woman with desire. He bounced readily between piety and debauchery, and it was Madsen the pious who feared the things he believed lived between the trenches.

"There's nothing out there, Pete," I once told him to try and ease his agitation. "Well, nothing but the Germans."

That was bad enough. Why worry about bogeymen and monsters when there were thousands of real men only half a mile away waiting to kill you and leave you for the rats?

"I know they're there," he said. "I saw them."

"Saw what?" I scoffed.

"Demons," he said.

I looked at him, not answering. I knew better than to find myself in a disagreement with Peter Madsen on matters of religion. I was no atheist, but I didn't really know what I believed anymore. Certainly not with any great conviction. Peter had absolute certainty. He was utterly convinced, not only in the existence of God, but in God's plan for him as well as the existence of the Devil and all his demons. Peter's fire and brimstone preacher father had raised a god-fearing man, at the very least.

"You don't believe," he said.

"I believe you, Pete." That wasn't what he'd meant.

"Pray for faith, Frank," he said. "It's the only thing that will save you."

I looked at him then, really looked at him, and noticed, for the first time, the subtle, crazed gleam in his eyes when he spoke. Had it always been there, or had the fear finally made him snap? I didn't know. But I saw it then and decided that my friend might be a little bit nuts.

"You pray," I said. "I don't think He takes my calls."

He chose to ignore my joke.

"Do you remember," he said, "when we arrived at the front? When I prayed with those wounded men?"

"Sure," I said. Madsen prayed with everybody he could, but when he saw somebody close to death, he always tried to say a prayer with the wounded. It had been no different when we had arrived near Verdun. The injured men in the hospital trench had drawn Peter Madsen like a carrion fly. I had kept my distance. Most of us did. Why remind ourselves of what could happen to us on the front? I'd rather face it when it happened and avoid it while I could.

"Well, one of them, the poor bastard with his legs gone, he'd been left in no man's land for two days before his friends found him and brought him back."

"That's terrible," I said, not wanting to think about it.

"Yes, but what's more terrible is what he saw when he was out there alone, in the dark."

"I can only imagine."

"No," Madsen said, "you can't. That's what I'm trying to tell you. Can you guess what happened to his legs?"

"Shrapnel?" I guessed.

"No," he said. "He'd been knocked out in a blast, saved by his helmet, but when he woke up, he was whole. He said that he lay there and tried not to move or make a sound, because he didn't want to give away his position. He thought he'd be safe as long as the enemy didn't know he was alive. He had some broken bones, some bruises, but he thought he'd just have to be patient and he'd be alright."

"Smart," I said. "Wait for your chance."

"He waited for dark to fall, so that he wouldn't be spotted when he crawled back to safety. He let himself sleep through the day, surrounded by his dead comrades, saving his strength. But when he woke up that night, he wasn't alone."

"Germans?" I said.

"That's what he thought," Madsen said. "It was the movement that woke him up. Somebody was moving the body next to him, looting the body he thought. He couldn't see who it was without turning his head, so he stayed still. Then he felt somebody tugging at his boots, looting him!"

"What did he do?" I asked, finding myself sucked into Madsen's tall tale.

"He was startled, he kicked and looked at who it was," Madsen paused dramatically. "It wasn't a man at all. It was some sort of demon, something ape-like and pale with tiny black eyes and twisted, dripping teeth and long bent claws. It had been chewing at his foot. Tasting him!"

"Pull the other one," I said.

"I'm serious, Frank!" Madsen insisted. "I'm telling you, I saw the man's eyes. He wasn't lying. He was in agony. Why would he lie? Nobody suffering like he was would stop to play a childish prank on somebody."

"Maybe not," I said, "but he might have lost his mind from the pain. Did you think of that?"

"Yes, that occurred to me, but I haven't told you everything yet," he said.

"Go on then."

"So, there he was. He saw this monstrous... thing... nibbling at his boot, and he realized that it wasn't alone! The rustling around him at the other bodies had been more of them. These ghoulish things had been *eating* the bodies around him. New and old, from the freshly killed to the putrid bodies that had been in that shell hole for a year or more. He said that one of them was perched beside him, on the body of his friend, Guillaume—I think he said his name was. He repeated it over and over again when he told me this part. The ghoul was crouched on Guillaume's chest and was hunched over, eating his face! He said that Guillaume's jaw was missing, along with his nose and one of his eyes, and that his one remaining eye just stared cloudily at him as the thing's jaws cracked into his skull, and the ghoul began licking at the bloody flesh inside!"

Barnes and Cervantes were sitting up now, eyes wide. It had been their turn to sleep while Madsen and I kept watch. I had no idea how long they'd been listening.

"What did he do?" Barnes asked. His voice sounded a little different ever since I'd broken his nose.

"He yelled and kicked at the thing by his feet. Kicked it in its face, again and again. He was in a panic," Madsen said.

"Wait," Cervantes said, "that's not true. You said he didn't have any legs, so he couldn't be kicking."

Cervantes, always a little dim, seemed especially proud of himself for catching Madsen and exposing his ghost story as a hoax.

"He hadn't lost them, yet," Madsen said. "That came next."

"Shut up, Cervantes," Barnes snapped. "Let him tell it. What happened next, Madsen?"

Cervantes looked crestfallen but remained silent.

"The ghouls were startled. They drew back and cowered, scampering out of the shell hole and out of sight." Ghouls. That was the second time Madsen had used that word to describe his demons of no man's land, and it stuck with me. "The soldier caught his breath, and he started to think that he'd imagined it. Maybe poor Guillaume had been mutilated by an explosion or rats? He didn't know, but anything made more sense than the idea of flesh-eating monsters."

"He was right about that," I said under my breath.

Barnes glared at me and I rolled my eyes. Madsen went on spinning his tale.

"After he gathered his wits, he started to crawl out of the shell-hole. It was night, he'd been waiting for exactly this opportunity. He just needed to get to the rim of the hole, and then he could get his bearings and get back to his line. Back to his friends and the safety of the trench. Whether it was Germans or monsters he was worried about, the plan was the same.

"He said the hole was hard to climb up. That the sides were slick and muddy, and that the bottom was full of a dark, watery soup made of mud and old flesh, teeming with flies. He said that he slipped and slid back several times, and that soon he was hearing noises in the darkness. A scuttling sound. A scurrying, but he couldn't see anything. Finally, he made it to the lip of the hole, and he was relieved to see that his lines were closer than he'd dared to hope. So long as he avoided any German snipers, he'd be safe in minutes.

"But that's when they came back. He was looking toward the safety of his trench, *this trench*, when something closed around his ankle and pulled him back into the pit!"

"Shut up, Madsen!" Cervantes said, poorly pretending that he wasn't scared witless.

"You shut up, Cervantes!" Barnes shoved the man. "Let him tell it."

Madsen raised a disapproving eyebrow at Barnes in rebuke and didn't continue the story until Barnes looked appropriately abashed for laying hands on Cervantes. The pause in the story only seemed to heighten the fear for poor Cervantes though, the anticipation to know what happened to the French soldier was giving him time to imagine all sorts of horrors.

"He told me that he screamed as he was pulled back," Madsen said. "That his comrades were so close. He screamed for help, but in no man's land, ten yards may as well be ten miles if the Germans see you. He screamed louder still, louder than he thought he could, when he felt the fangs sink into his flesh. He says that it was like the teeth of the things were dipped in mustard gas. They burned as they tore into him. He tried to struggle, to kick and beat at them. And at first, he did, but he said that the burning spread out from the bite, and he lost all his strength.

"He lay there on his face, nearly drowning in the mud, and he couldn't move. But he says he could still feel what was happening. That's the horrible thing. He felt first one and then another of the horrible things start chewing at his feet. He felt them bite pieces off, heard them snapping bones and swallowing the pieces, and then move further up his legs. He couldn't even scream anymore."

"That's horrible," Cervantes whispered. Barnes glared but said nothing.

"He said that by the time they had gotten to his knees, that he could hear even more of the creatures approaching to feed with the others. One of them was biting into his shoulders when he heard the voices of his French comrades calling to him. He said that the creatures scattered, scurrying away as they heard the men approaching. That they were almost completely gone by the time he saw a friendly soldier look down into the shell hole."

"So, nobody else saw any of these ghouls of yours then, Madsen?" I said. Barnes gave me a dirty look.

"Actually, Frank," he said with a patronizing smile, "I talked to the men who brought him back. They said they had heard his screams and came looking for him while it was still dark, and they believe him."

Barnes looked at me as if that settled the matter definitively. I ignored him.

"So, a man was badly wounded on the field. He lost his legs and had some horrible fever dreams before he finally woke and screamed for help," Cervantes said. "Unless there's some evidence. I mean, you said the ghouls were gone before the soldiers got there? Why should we treat this as anything but the nightmares of a dying man?"

I hated to admit it, but I agreed with Cervantes. A story like this would need some evidence if I was going to take it seriously. And there wasn't any.

"I said that they were *almost* gone when the soldiers arrived," Madsen said. "The first man at the pit did see something."

"What did he see?" I said.

"He said he saw a shape scurrying out of the shell hole and into the darkness. He said it looked like a pair of naked legs, pale grey, and oddly shaped. Stringy. Twisted. And that he could have sworn that there were long, black claws on the ends of its toes."

"Wow," Barnes muttered in hushed awe.

Cervantes looked pitiful, clenching the fabric of his pantlegs in tight fists and looking at his feet.

"That's not evidence," I said.

Barnes looked at me like I'd just slapped a nun. Cervantes looked up hopefully. Madsen smiled and laughed softly.

"Alright," Madsen said. "Some people won't believe until they put their fingers in the wounds. I doubted it too. But like Thomas, I saw the wounds. I saw the missing legs and the way the flesh was torn, like it had been bitten and ripped."

I didn't say anything, but privately, I reminded myself that Madsen was no expert on battlefield injuries.

"But what truly convinced me," Madsen said, "was the wound on the man's shoulder. It was clearly a single, powerful bite. The marks where the teeth had cut away the flesh were clear, like biting into an apple."

"Can you show us?" I said. This was getting uncomfortable. I could tell that Madsen believed what he was telling me, he wasn't a dishonest man. But it wasn't his integrity that I doubted. It was his judgement. A man ready to believe in a talking snake, and pillars of fire and salt, might be ready to believe just about anything under the right circumstances.

"No," he said. "They were moving out when I met them. The wounded man was being sent to a hospital, but the medics didn't seem to think he was likely to make it."

Nobody had anything else to say. The way that Barnes and Cervantes looked at Madsen made me think of converts who had just found their prophet. The two men closed their eyes and pretended to sleep until it was their turn to relieve us, but I knew that they would be kept awake as they imagined the things out there waiting for us.

Beside me at the firing line, Madsen said a quiet prayer to himself as he often did. I looked out over the barbed wire and broken trees and wondered which shell hole might have been the one from the story and wondering what might be lurking within them.

I tried not to think about it and forced myself to keep a sharp eye out for enemy movements. I wouldn't have admitted it at the time, but I wasn't just watching for Germans.

CHAPTER TWENTY-THREE

When I imagined war, I thought of heroic last stands or glorious cavalry charges. The sorts of things that I'd read about as a child. I'd never read a novel about artillery, about what it was like to hunker down in the mud and brace yourself for hours as the world shook and thundered all around you. Waiting for the next shell to find you and wondering if you'd even know it before you were blown to kingdom come.

It wasn't so bad when we were the ones firing. We'd sit on our lines, cooking bacon over candles and smoking our cigarettes as the big French guns behind us pounded the German lines. For more than a day, we would hear the short bursts as the guns fired behind us, followed by the thunderous explosions from the German side of no man's land. You couldn't hear the man next to you, but it was bearable. We knew that every shell could mean one less German cannon or machine gun. One less thing for us to worry about.

The German retaliation came a day later. We braced ourselves against the sides of the trench and took cover in dugouts. The French soldiers laughed at us when the shelling began and some of us hit the deck. They knew how futile such measures were.

I remember panic setting in as the shockwaves of shells exploding behind our lines rattled my bones. My vision blurred as the thunder shook my eyes and knocked the breath from my lungs. Every muscle in my body completely locked and refused to move as I pressed myself against the wall and covered my ears with my hands.

Nearby, I could see Peter Madsen moving his mouth in prayer, his eyes closed. I couldn't hear a word of it. My ears were useless.

I soon realized that the Germans weren't aiming for the trenches, but for the artillery and ammunition kept hidden in the wooded hills. That was small comfort, given how near we were to those hills and how inaccurate the massive explosives were. They were covering the hillside in smoke, knocking down every tree in their search for valuable targets.

I don't know how to explain the feeling of sitting there and waiting to die while the world was torn up around us. It was far more terrifying than any combat I've ever been in. Probably because there was no illusion that we had any ability to fight back or defend ourselves. It was just hour after hour of hammering terror, and the sort of fear that you feel as a burning ache in your bones, as every muscle in your body pulls you in all directions only to hold you frozen in place. The feeling of wanting to scream, to cry out, but not even being able to force your jaw open to let it out.

When the shelling finally stopped, it was the silence that was deafening. The air seemed to throb in my ears like a low siren, and the world still seemed to vibrate as my body continued to shake violently in little spasms that I hadn't even been aware of when the bombardment had gone on.

It was over. My vision blurred as my eyes welled from the

relief of it. Soon, I began to make out the sound of men's voices nearby.

They were shouting. I couldn't make it out over the ringing. A single word, being shouted more closely now, but still incomprehensible. Was it my ears or my brain that refused to work?

I saw Madsen's face widen in recognition as he heard the shouts. He turned to me and I saw his mouth move. He shouted the word at me, and I could almost hear it. I just stared at him.

He leaned forward and shook me by the collar as he repeated it.

"Gas!"

All around me, men were scrambling to retrieve their gas masks and put them on. Madsen had his on when he returned and shook me again.

"Frank, move! Gas!"

I couldn't do it. I don't know why. I wanted to, but my body wouldn't listen. As I tried to stand and scramble to my mask, my arms and legs only shook more violently, and my jaw rattled. I could see a thick, yellowish haze dripping thin tendrils along the edge of the trench not far off.

Madsen saw it too. Soon, we heard screams that became choking howls from that direction, as men who had failed to secure their masks encountered the mustard gas. A faint smell of garlic crept into my awareness.

Madsen looked toward the encroaching gas and again to me and seemed to reach a decision. Before I knew what was happening, he had pressed his mask to my face and was securing it around my head. His bared face looked down on me with puffed cheeks as he held his breath.

"What, no..." I tried to say, but it came out as nothing more than a chattering mumble.

Madsen staggered to the wall where we kept our gear and

retrieved my mask for himself, securing it hastily to his own face with one hand as he came back to me. The yellow haze was close enough to touch when he reached me, put my arm around his shoulders, and began to drag me from where I'd frozen. My trembling legs tried to help him, as he all but carried me out of there.

My mask on his face was poorly secured, and he kept reaching to it with one hand, adjusting it. Between carrying me, adjusting the mask, and trying to keep one step ahead of the gas, Madsen lost his footing and we both sprawled to the wet mud of the trench floor. We had gone as far as we could.

I landed on my right side as Madsen tried to steady me as we fell. He let go of the mask and it fell from his face as he failed to catch himself, his face landing roughly in a shallow greasy puddle.

I thought maybe we were safe, that we had moved far enough from the dangerous area. Thanks to Madsen's selflessness, I was safe even if we weren't far enough away, his mask was fitted tight to my face. I felt barely able to breathe through the thing, adding to my panic.

"Ah!" Madsen cried out from beside me.

I managed to roll over to see that he was clutching at his face with one hand as he groped for the mask he'd dropped; his eyes were clenched shut against the gas.

I began to feel an itch on my side where I had fallen to the ground, where I was wet from the puddle. An itch that quickly began to burn. What had been in that puddle? Was it water at all? My brain couldn't make sense of it.

"Ah, God!" Madsen screamed, clutching at his face with both hands now and bent over with a fit of coughing.

Somehow, that brought me back to myself. The screams of my friend reached me in a way my own pain couldn't. I picked up the fallen mask and pulled my friend down beside me, struggling to press it to his face. First, he pushed me away, instinctively protecting himself, but then he realized what I was doing and greedily snatched at the mask, pressing it to his face.

The pain in my side was incredible. I wanted to splash water on it, but realized then that was the worst thing I could do. I remembered what they had taught us about mustard gas. That it reacted to moisture, which was why it was so dangerous for a soldier's eyes and lungs. When Madsen and I had fallen into the puddle, we had given the gas something to react to. Moisture on our skin for it to burn. It ate away at my skin, searing with incredible pain on my right hip and part of my ribs. I could feel it reacting to the moisture of my armpits as well. I imagined my skin bubbling and sizzling. Poor Madsen, though, had fallen face first into the puddle. I didn't know how badly he was hurt before I'd gotten the mask onto his face.

He sounded like a man in hell, screaming and choking out God's name and finding no relief. He didn't stop screaming. Not until the medics arrived with the morphine.

CHAPTER TWENTY-FOUR

Nobody comes back from war, not really. You can win, you can survive, but that person who left home never really returns. If war can't kill you, it will change you. I started to understand that over the weeks I spent with Peter Madsen in a French hospital.

We were lucky, really, to be sent to a French facility, as American doctors didn't have any experience dealing with mustard gas. I spent day after day laying on my left side as they treated and changed the bandages on my right. The blisters oozed and skin sloughed off, but I was told that I was quite fortunate. I didn't need to be told. A visit to Madsen's bedside showed me exactly how much worse it could have been.

The side of his face was a horror. The flesh had bubbled and melted off part of his jaw and chin, his right cheek was sleek and red, and the right side of his mouth was twisted in a perpetual, suffering grimace. He'd been wise to keep his eyes tightly shut until help arrived. He'd saved his vision, but he hadn't been able to completely hold his breath in the shock of the searing pain, and some of the gas had gotten into his lungs. As a result, he breathed with an agonized wheeze and avoided speaking over a whisper after doing so would start him on a torturous coughing fit that might not stop until he was given more morphine.

He mostly lay quietly and read his bible or wrote letters to his family. When I visited him, he listened more than he spoke, though I'd never been the talkative one in our relationship.

"I'm sorry, Pete," I said when I sat by his bed for the first time.

He didn't respond, didn't look at me, just kept his eyes on the ceiling and drew his soft, shallow breaths.

"You saved my life," I told him. "I owe you."

He winced as he turned his head, the bandages covered his wounds, but the movement clearly hurt him. I saw his eyes begin to water from the pain, but he didn't acknowledge it.

"No," he breathed the word, barely even a whisper. "You owe God."

I wasn't going to argue with him, not now that he was probably relying on his faith more than ever. I couldn't imagine what he must be thinking. The scars he'd gotten when he saved my life would be with him forever. My own burns were excruciating. Only the morphine that reminded me so much of the feel of my mother's old medicine even began to get me through it.

"Well," I said, "thank you just the same."

He touched my hand to save himself the words. It reminded me of a priest giving a blessing.

"You'll be going home soon," I said. I didn't know what else to say to raise his spirits.

He didn't answer. I left him to his silent prayers.

I spent my time in the hospital reading and sleeping. I learned a fair amount of French by listening to the nurses and the wounded soldiers. I visited Madsen, but he mostly remained silent.

"You'd do the same," he said to me once after I thanked him

yet again. I wasn't sure that I would have. Not at all. I hadn't even had the courage to save myself. How could I pretend that I'd have gone back to help somebody else? I could see in his eyes that he believed it, though. He didn't doubt that I'd have done the same thing for him. His confidence left me ashamed, and yet I resolved to live up to it. I'd be sent back to the lines soon, but Peter Madsen would never fight again. I felt that I owed it to him to do better if I got the chance to redeem myself.

For three weeks I drank only coffee, warm milk, and wine as we were told that the water wasn't safe to drink. I'd never liked milk, so I alternated between being pleasantly drunk or being jittery and restless. I preferred the former.

Madsen and I both received letters from home while we were in the hospital. Maggie said that she was beside herself with worry and demanded to know that I was alright. I assured her that I was just fine and would be rejoining my unit by the time she received word from me. Madsen's letters were entirely different. His sister Evelyn was kind at least, though she teased him a little. "I'll bet you're relieved to be coming home," she said, and "you're still the lucky one, I've been here with father while you've been seeing France." I suspected that she was joking with him.

"You don't know my sister," Peter said when I told him as much. "She thinks the world revolves around her. Nobody else's suffering will ever come near to hers in her mind. She's a spoiled child."

"If you say so," I said, but I didn't think he was being fair.

His mother wrote mostly to remind her son that whatever had happened would be for the best and to reassure him that "everything is part of the Lord's perfect plan." I silently thought that any plan which relied on a good man bearing unendurable agony and living with disfiguring scars was far from perfect, but I kept that opinion to myself.

Peter's father, the Reverend Madsen, was the oddest of them all. "Son, I was disappointed to hear that you had been wounded. You should be thankful that you have been given this second chance to mend your ways and learn how to better serve the Lord."

"Well," I said to Pete after reading his letter to him, "at least he's sad that you're hurt."

Madsen chuckled lightly. That was a mistake. The small laugh quickly turned into a series of wheezing coughs. I watched his body rise in pain with the spasms and my friend's face turned purple as he struggled to gasp for air. Finally, he clutched the sheets to his mouth and his rasping coughs took on a wet quality. When he pulled the sheet away, I saw that they were stained with crimson chunks. I didn't want to think too hard about what that might be.

Sometime later, after the nurses had calmed him with more morphine and forced him to sip some wine, he spoke again in a slow whisper.

"Frank," he hissed, "my father isn't sad, he's disappointed. In me."

"What?" I said. "That's ridiculous, how could he be disappointed that you were wounded? You're a goddamn hero!"

He raised an eyebrow at me in disapproval of my cursing.

"Sorry," I said.

"You don't understand my father," he whispered. "When I left, he told me that the Lord would protect me and keep me from harm if I had faith. For him, the fact that I was wounded can only mean that I didn't have enough faith. It's a personal failure."

"That's nuts. You don't believe that crap, do you?"

He didn't answer, only watched the curtains dancing in the late Spring breeze. I could see that he did believe it, or at least he couldn't be sure that he didn't. He just didn't want to tell me something that he knew I would ridicule; he didn't have the strength for it.

"You're not a failure, Pete," I told him. "You're the bravest man I know."

He patted my hand with his but said nothing.

I didn't talk to Pete Madsen again in France. I was shipped out the next day to rejoin my unit. The train ride back to the front was a lonely and anxious experience. Apparently, sometime since I'd left home, I'd grown used to having friends. Pete had tried my patience with his constant preaching and nonstop chatter, but now that he wasn't with me, I had to admit that I missed him.

It was nearing the end of May when I rejoined my unit near the Marne. While I'd been out of the action, the war had taken a turn. Russia had withdrawn from the war entirely following their own revolution, and this had freed up the German army on their Eastern front. With more forces at their disposal, they had pushed hard toward Paris and had gotten as far as the river Marne, only fifty miles or so from the French capital.

The French had asked for British assistance, but our English allies were busy to the north. That left the tired and battered French with little option but to rely on the help of their untried American friends. There was no more time to get our feet wet with softer assignments. It was time for the USA to join the war in earnest.

CHAPTER TWENTY-FIVE

"...do you want to live forever?"

A sergeant I didn't know was standing tall in the waving grass and beckoning to the marines behind him to stand up and charge. All along the tree line there was similar movement as grizzled old non-coms cussed at the fresh-faced young men to get to their feet and charge.

You'd think that it would take more than a couple of shouted words and a near suicidal gesture to make a bunch of young men stand up and run toward the guns that were firing at us, but I'll be damned if I didn't find myself on my feet alongside Barnes and Cervantes as we charged into the open wheat field.

All around us, Marines dropped in their tracks as German bullets found them. Some lay still and lifeless while others stumbled and thrashed, clutching at fresh wounds and calling for help, yelling for a medic, crying for their mothers. I knew beyond a shadow of a doubt that I was about to die. It was more than a possibility. It was a certainty. There was a strange freedom that came with that certainty. A fearlessness. Sitting in a trench as I waited for shells to find me—not knowing if I'd be alive in the morning—inspired a sort of soul-rending fear that I've never experienced anywhere else. But running toward certain death alongside the men I'd trained with didn't leave any room for that sort of fear. It wasn't bravery. Bravery is making a choice to overcome fear. There simply wasn't any fear to overcome. My body just acted, placing one foot in front of the other as my vision narrowed and the sounds of battle blurred together into a keening howl made up of gunshots, screams of pain, barked orders, and my own pounding heart.

It was like that for weeks, trading shots with the Germans across wheat fields and coming bayonet to bayonet among the trees of Belleau Wood. This was nothing at all like the warfare we had been preparing for, the trenches and the artillery and the gas. No, this was real battle. Often, we clashed in small groups, coming upon each other in the woods and finding ourselves more grateful for our bayonets and shotguns than our rifles. I wish I could write about how terrible those days were. I want to be able to say that I hated every moment of it, but I'd be lying. Dealing and expecting death alongside the men I was fighting for made me feel... alive, fully alive, in a way I'd never experienced. I found in those days that I could enjoy killing, and that I had a talent for it. Later, when I had the time to reflect on what I'd done with the appropriate horror and humanity, I'd fail to invoke that same confidence, but in the moment, in the heat of battle, I felt certain. I felt sure. I imagined the feeling to be something like what Madsen and other believers must feel from their faith. The sense of being free of doubt and hesitation for the first time in my life because I absolutely knew what was expected of me, and I did it.

Every day I'd wake up convinced that I would join the better men than me who had spilled their life's blood in the French soil. I didn't keep count of the dead, not of the friends I lost or of the Germans I killed. I was just determined to do my part, to take as many dirty Germans with me as I could before I inevitably fell. In my heart, it wasn't a matter of *if* I was going to die, only of when and how. It was the certainty of my own death that freed me as much as anything else. For once, I wasn't an outsider. I wasn't the harelip with no friends. I wasn't a freak. I was one among many, and I was going to die as a part of something. That thought made it all worth it. Looking back, I think that was the reason that I wasn't scared of dying. I'd been afraid every day of my life before then. Afraid of being alone, of being worthless. There in the wheat fields and little woods of northern France, I wasn't alone. I had value. I had a family. I think it was that the idea of dying with purpose, with brothers, felt immeasurably more welcoming than living without those things as I had before. Hell, I think I even wanted to die. I never wanted to go back to who I'd been before, the solitary freak. I'd die with my brothers; I'd die with respect.

I knew beyond a shadow of a doubt that the day would come when my name would end up on the ever-growing casualty lists. And I was right.

CHAPTER TWENTY-SIX

Being shot doesn't hurt. Not at first, anyway. I didn't even realize that the shot fired at me in the dark had struck its mark. It had seemed like the Germans who had snuck up on our position where we tried to rest in the shadow of the little farmhouse couldn't hit the broad side of the barn door that I was leaning against. They'd snuck past our lookout. I don't know if he had fallen asleep or if they had just managed to avoid notice, but he was dead now. They were standing where Cervantes was supposed to have been keeping watch—the silhouette of one spike-helmed German dipping his bayonet into my fallen friend —when Barnes had yelled wordlessly and awoken the rest of us.

They'd been about to execute us in our sleep, but now they had a fight on their hands. Some of us never made it to our feet, but I did. I felt and heard the bullets of our ambushers tug at my hair and shoot stinging blasts of dirt and grit from the ground where they struck. It was chaos. With only the moonlight and the muzzle flashes to guide us, I couldn't be sure that I hit any as I emptied my magazine. There was no time to reload, so I did what we had been trained to do. I took hold of my rifle, pointed the bayonet toward the enemy, and charged. They couldn't have been more than twenty yards or so away, and I had my eye on the one who had killed Cervantes. While my friends and enemies exchanged fire around me, I roared through clenched teeth as I bore down on the man I meant to kill.

Much as we liked to speak of them as drooling barbarians, the Germans had been well trained. My target dropped to one knee and lined up his shot with practiced discipline. There should have been no way that he could miss me. There was a flash and a crack as his rifle fired. I think I may have laughed out loud as I realized that he had missed such a clear shot. He'd blown his one chance to stop me. I was on him, the steel of my bayonet sliding easily into his chest as I put my weight behind it and let myself fall on him. He gave a sputtering, gurgling groan as he dropped his weapon and pawed clumsily at my rifle barrel pressed against him. Blood bubbled from his mouth as I wrapped my fingers around his throat and squeezed.

"Yes," I hissed at him for no reason I could fathom.

His eyes bulged and the blood he was drowning on spattered my own face as I leaned over him, close enough to kiss. My grip on his throat loosened. Loosened? Yes, somehow the strength in my hands was fading. That was odd. So was the light-headed dizziness that I was becoming slowly aware of. That didn't matter now, I told myself. Only the kill mattered now. Think about that later.

"Bitte..." he spat at me, panic fading from his eyes as he finally stopped struggling and lay dead.

My hands fumbled at him now, feebly patting at his neck. The weakness spread through me, and I found I couldn't hold myself up any longer. Without meaning to, I collapsed on the dying German and rolled off beside him.

Two things happened then at once. I became aware of the bloody hole that had somehow appeared in my guts, and I saw the other Germans rushing toward me with their bayonets raised. There was nothing I could do. I thought to roll away, to reach for my weapon, to kick at them, but my body didn't respond to any of these commands. Instead, I lifted my right hand a little, maybe inches from the blood-soaked grass, and managed a single confused word.

"Wait..." I said. That was the best I could come up with.

They didn't.

A German plunged his own bayonet into my belly, below where his dead comrade had shot me. I marveled at the cold, pinching feeling in my guts and how it shot out in tendrils of searing agony as he twisted the blade before withdrawing it. I may have screamed. I don't know. I hope not.

He stood there for a moment, satisfied that he had finished me off. I had to agree with him. I'd seen my share of mortal wounds lately and there was no denying that I had a matching pair. He looked then to his fallen friend beside me, taking a knee and shaking the dead man by his shoulder.

"Gustav!" he said. "Gustav! Aufwachen! Gustav!"

The man was distraught, his voice cracking as he called his friend's name. Gustav was beyond help. As was Cervantes just beyond him. I'd done my duty.

It struck me as somehow absurd then, the way that we had fallen in line to stab each other. Gustav killed my friend Cervantes. I killed Gustav, then Gustav's friend had come along to kill me. Probably a friend of mine would kill this man in the days to come and the cycle would continue, like a morbid set of dominoes that just kept falling forward. The image was ridiculous. An Austrian domino fell onto a Serbian domino which fell onto a Russian domino which in turn fell onto dominoes draped in other flags and uniforms. French, German, Belgian, British, American. And here I was, another American domino falling onto a German, doing my part to keep the intricate game going.

I couldn't help it. I laughed. I looked at Cervantes, at Gustav, at what may well have been some of my own intestines shining in the light of the full moon, and all I could do was laugh.

The German who had stabbed me didn't like that much, but I couldn't help it. Even the rolling waves of pain that shot through my guts and up my spine and down through my limbs with each barking laugh couldn't stop me. It was just all so damned stupid.

He kicked me in the side, hard, the force of his boot driving the air from my lungs, cracking my ribs. Even that couldn't stop the laughter. It silenced it a bit as well as adding a groan of pain to the wheezing sound I made through the amused rictus of my clenched face. Tears streamed from my eyes, my mouth grimaced in pain, but the silent laughter still shook me.

Disgusted, the German regarded me as if I were a broken thing. I couldn't argue.

"Verrückter Amerikaner," he said, and spat on my face.

He raised his rifle in his hands once more and brought the heavy stock down on my face, finally stopping my laughter and consigning me to dreamless blackness.

I never should have opened my eyes again. Wounds like mine were a death sentence. But after a time, how long I couldn't say, I remember a slowly-growing awareness of sounds around me. Wet, tearing sounds that reminded me of animals eating, of dogs gnawing on meaty bones.

I heard voices, distant German voices shouting orders, too far away to make out the words. There was no gunfire, no sounds of battle, just the moist rending and cracking sounds nearby and the distant voices of enemy soldiers.

Those sounds were what woke me. The disgusting hungry

sounds of scavengers feasting on the dead. The damn Germans had just left us here to be chewed up by dogs. Those tearing sounds could be curs chewing on Cervantes. Soon they would be coming for me.

To hell with that.

If I was going to die, and there seemed to be very little question about that fact, I was not going to die on my back as a meal for some farmer's feral dog. Slowly, being careful to avoid notice or pain by moving too quickly, I reached out beside me in search of a weapon. I winced against the pain in my gut as my torn muscles shifted and my fingers fumbled over muddy rocks and sticks. Nothing. I'd have to look further and hope to find something before they were on me. Dogs or Germans, it made little difference at this point. I was going to die fighting.

My right eye wouldn't open at first. It was held shut by a thick layer of my own congealed blood from the head wound the German had left me with. After blinking several times, I managed to force both eyes open, only to find that my vision was a dark blur featuring a shining bone-white orb shining down on me from the night sky. I shook my head to bring the moon into focus, and instantly regretted that choice as waves of nausea and pain flooded me. The agony forced a groan from my aching face and immediately the scavenging sounds froze. I'd been noticed. Damn.

I could see a shape beyond my hand now, a long solid bar with a glistening tip on one end which was exactly what I'd been hoping for. A rifle with a bayonet just out of my reach. I'd have to roll over.

The thought was horrifying. Simply moving my arm had pulled at the flesh around my wounds and brought barely tolerable pain. Moving my entire body would be more than I could take. It occurred to me then to just give up. I was going to die anyway. Why torment myself further before peace came?

The rustling of a large creature coming right for me from where the feeding had stopped answered the question for me. Because pain was preferable to submission, there was no question for me. I'd spent enough of my life submitting and cowering. That was behind me. I'd be damned if I was going to die that way now.

Seeing no point in trying to keep quiet anymore I pushed myself toward the weapon with a torturous scream. I felt the ripping and subsequent pouring as my punctured guts pushed against themselves. My fingers closed on the stock of the rifle. I pulled it to my chest as I used the momentum of my roll to bring myself again onto my back, the scream still echoing from my parched mouth. It was then that I first saw the thing that was coming for me.

CHAPTER TWENTY-SEVEN

"Monster" is an overused term. My father was a monster. The men who deployed disfiguring gas on countless strangers were monsters. The world is full of monsters. But the things I saw coming for me that night in the French countryside were literal monsters of a sort I wouldn't have believed existed if I hadn't seen them myself. I hadn't believed it when Madsen told me his story about them. The flesh-eating creatures that came out to feed on the battlefields at night. It was a story too grotesque and bizarre to take seriously, except that the things crawling toward me were exactly that. Grotesque and bizarre, and they demanded to be taken very seriously indeed.

They looked vaguely ape-like, with overly large shoulders, long stringy arms and comparatively squat legs. They scurried on all fours, using the knuckles of their front limbs as feet while their long, filthy, digging claws were folded toward them. The creatures were roughly man-sized but hunched and coiled in a simian manner. Unlike any ape I'd ever heard of, they were pale and utterly hairless. Their skin was a wormy grey color that seemed to glisten subtly beneath the moon. Their faces were what struck me as truly monstrous, with tiny black, unblinking eyes the size of pennies set close together beneath their sloped, pallid foreheads. A pair of large, flat nostrils flared just below them, and beneath that was an unnaturally wide mouth with dozens of jagged, needle-like teeth jutting from a protruding lower jaw. The things advanced quickly and silently, encircling me from all sides. They snuffled at the night air as they tasted my scent and began to drool heavily.

I'd never stopped screaming from the pain, merely changing pitch as horror and disgust mingled with my agony to form a visceral battle cry. I braced for the half-dozen ghouls to fall on me.

The boldest of the creatures lunged forward and swiped at my boot with its spade-like talons. I jerked my boot out of its reach and thrust my bayonet at it, jabbing it in its meaty shoulder and feeling the tough flesh part under my blade. I almost managed to ignore the agony in my guts as the thing chittered and screeched in pain, a thick black ichor oozing from the wound I'd given it.

Good. I could hurt them. If they were going to eat me, I'd make them pay dearly for the meal.

In unison, the pack of ghouls began to emit an unnerving chittering sound that seemed like an eerie union between the sounds of a rattlesnake and some strange insect. They drew closer as one, a step at a time, coming in for the kill. As they drew near, a stench of rancid meat wafted over me, drawing tears.

"Do it!" I yelled. "Come on!"

Every hair on my body stood on end in sudden answer to a piercing howl that split the night. Something in my bones wanted to cower in response to that sound. It was an instinct so deep that I knew my ancestors had huddled in caves and branches in times before language in fear of that howl. The ghouls must have held a similar instinct. They cowered in unison and their ominous chittering was at once replaced by a low and fearful screeching. The wormy ape-things turned their heads away from me, sniffing and licking nervously at the night air.

The one that I had stabbed was the first to find its courage and come for me while the others were distracted. It drew back on its squat hind legs and launched itself at me through the air with a silent grace I wouldn't have expected from such a revolting figure. I raised the bayonet to meet it and pressed the stock of my weapon against the muddy ground beneath my armpit. A moment later it fell on me, its slavering fangs inches from my face and its dirt-caked claws ripping at my shoulders. The smell of its rotten breath was sickening, and burned my nose and eyes. I had no doubt whatsoever that a bite from that putrid maw would lead quickly to sickness and death if the creature itself didn't finish the job.

I felt the weight of the creature on my weapon, and I drew on all my strength, regardless of the pain in my guts, to keep the ghoul from reaching me with the jagged little teeth that snarled and snapped inches from my face. In a fury, its forelimbs clawed at the earth around me as well as at the edges of my shoulders and arms in its frantic attempt to pull itself toward me, even as it pulled my blade deeper into itself.

Around us, the other ghouls were snarling and thrashing as well, but not against me. Something else had joined us in the little clearing. A shape that I registered only as a peripheral blur as I struggled with the creature on top of me. Whatever it was, the new thing moved with frightening speed and collided with the ghouls in an explosion of growling fury. All I could see clearly were the dozens of malignant little daggers dripping ichor and snapping hungrily toward my face as my panicked strength slowly gave way to pain and exhaustion. It had me.

All at once, the weight of the slavering thing was gone as

its clammy body was knocked from me by another clawed arm, this one covered in coarse hair. It was only then that I managed to catch my first glimpse of what had attacked the ghouls.

At a glance, I might have said it was a woman, because she was clothed in a long and tattered dress which was soiled with dirt and blood. Though her body was covered in hair, the hair about her head was longer and finer, somewhat like a mane. These things could have suggested the shape of a woman, at least at a distance in the darkness, but only for a moment. Nothing else about the creature seemed womanly or even human. Her limbs were lean but powerfully muscled, with sharp predatory claws evident on her fingers and toes. The fur was thickest on her head and shoulders as well as her forearms and calves, and her face was predatory and hungry. Sharp fangs sat exposed in her open mouth. Not the putrid and needle-like things that the ghouls had, but the imposing flesh-tearing canine teeth of a predator. Her nose flared wildly as she gulped in the night air and her yellow wolf eyes regarded me with a sort of hungry wariness, as if she was of two minds as to whether she considered me friend or food.

She had dealt with the entire troop of ghouls in mere moments. Their torn bodies lay strewn about the little clearing, and bits of their innards dripped from her clawed hands. She hunched and considered me in the moonlight, her shoulders rising and falling rapidly with excited breathing.

I decided that I must be going mad. There was nothing else for it. I was wounded, bleeding, and struck in the head. It was that last blow that must have done it. I'd known men to say and do truly strange things after a solid blow to the head. It was either that, or I had already died and found that the other side was peopled with nothing but monsters. That didn't seem right, though. If I were dead, would my damn guts feel like they were on fire? No, I wasn't dead, but I was dying. There was no doubt about that.

I closed my eyes as tightly as I could and opened them again, trying to clear my vision and make sense of what I was seeing. The savage woman was closer now, perched above me with her head cocked to one side. Her lip twitched in the hint of a snarl as she snuffed at the air above me. Her yellow eyes gleamed golden in the night and the light of the moon illuminated her long mane like a halo from behind her head. She struck me as beautiful then, not in the way that a woman is beautiful, not the beauty of desire. No, it was the sort of beauty I'd seen when I'd watched a hawk take a rabbit as a boy, or the beauty of a fox on the hunt. It was the beauty of nature, wild and deadly and completely unrestrained. The terrible sort of beauty that was best appreciated from a distance, the beauty of a great storm or a raging fire. She was majestic. Those other things had been like diseased rats or weasels. Here was a wolf.

"Beautiful..." I managed to say as my strength gave out utterly. I doubt I'd have been able to find the strength to say more, let alone move. I was in my last moments.

She drew back on her haunches as if the word had startled her. Shouldn't I be whimpering or screaming? Perhaps pleading for my life or losing all reason in the face of something that shouldn't exist? Perhaps in better health I'd have done one of those things, but I knew these to be my last moments, and I was still determined not to waste my last breath on fear. She regarded first me, and then the dead ghoul with my bayonet jutting from its back.

I was fading fast. I couldn't see. The night had seemingly grown darker. I was vaguely aware of a dim light where the moon was and a coldness spreading across my body. The pain in my belly was gone now, replaced with a merciful numbness. I forced a ragged breath, realizing that my breaths were no longer coming without conscious effort. This wasn't so bad. A bit like falling asleep, really.

Then the feeling of her on top of me, her long hair dangling in my face. Her scent, a musky, wild smell, surrounded me. This was nice. Her face pressed against mine, sniffing at my mouth and cheek. I didn't have it in me to be afraid now. I didn't have it in me to be much of anything at all for much longer.

Pain. Sharp hot pain in my chest below where my left shoulder met my neck, near my heart. A biting pain. A bite. She held her fangs in my flesh as I tried and failed to cry out at the pain. I stiffened, but she wouldn't let go. I felt my blood pooling beneath her mouth and trickling down my sides, and still she would not let go. Finally, after working her teeth in my flesh for long, agonizing moments, she withdrew.

Her weight was gone from me. Her scent was gone. She had left me to my death. I began to drift, not sure anymore how much of my last moments had been reality or a fever dream. The last thing I heard was her keening howl in the distance, and I felt something in my blood rise in answer, something new.

And then I died.

PART 5

RUSTY CAGE

CHAPTER TWENTY-EIGHT

"I never knew her name," I told Hiram.

The dominant man-wolf crouched across the small fire from me, holding his hands out to warm them.

"It was a female then," he said.

I nodded.

He considered that information for a moment, nodding like a man who had just confirmed his suspicions. I hadn't told him any more than he'd asked, those five words were all he needed. The memories that came to me with his question were mine, and I wouldn't share them unless I deemed it necessary. A lifetime of privacy, especially a life as long as mine, was not an easy habit to break even if I'd been interested in doing so.

"How much did she teach you?" he asked.

"Teach me?"

"Yes, after she changed you. How much were you taught?"

"I never saw her again," I said.

"You were abandoned?" he asked with disgust in his soft voice.

I shrugged, never having thought of it that way.

"Did nobody help you through your change?"

I laughed bitterly. I thought of how I'd woken up beneath French soil. Apparently, I'd been found and buried by somebody who had decided they couldn't manage to recover my body. I'd been dead and had been treated accordingly. I remembered clawing my way to the surface days later, gasping for breath, mad with hunger and thirst.

"No," I said.

"You managed to survive on your own?"

I remembered that first German patrol who had been unlucky enough to encounter me as I wandered the French woods, lost and disoriented. I remembered the taste of their blood and the feel of their bones cracking beneath my hands after they had shot me on sight. I remembered the way the wolf had come to the fore then for the first time, taking out all my fear and anger on the unfortunate soldiers.

I only nodded again in answer to Hiram's question.

"An unguided change can be very difficult," Hiram said.

I thought of the look on Barnes' face when I'd stumbled back to our lines that night, the horror and panic in his eyes as he saw his dead friend covered in dirt and German blood. He'd screamed and fired at me, remembering stories of the monsters of no man's land and utterly certain that what he had seen was some sort of flesh-eating monster wearing his dead friend's face.

He was right.

Barnes had never been a good shot, and after his first shot missed, I ran off into the night with the speed of the wolf behind me. With my predator's ears I'd listened from the darkness as he told the other men what he had seen. I heard as they laughed at him and mocked him for his cowardice and superstition.

"How long?" Hiram asked.

I only looked at him and raised an eyebrow.

"How long since your change?" he clarified.

"Years now," I said.

Hiram raised his eyebrows in apparent surprise. The lean man's yellow eyes regarded me with what seemed like fresh respect.

"Truly?" he asked.

I nodded.

"Impressive," he said.

"Why?"

"Well," he began, "there's no reason you should know this, but most Turnskins, even with guidance, lose themselves to their bestial sides after only a few moons."

I nodded my understanding. I knew too well the temptation of finally stopping the struggle and letting the wolf have his way. It had been a close thing for me more than once, a sort of suicide that would require no real effort, only surrender. It was especially tempting in those first days, before Evelyn, and before I found my way back to my sister. It had been those two women, love for my sister and guilt over what I'd done to Evelyn, that had given me the spine to refuse that particular temptation. I simply couldn't abandon my sister again, and I couldn't stand the idea of fully becoming the monster who had killed my wife.

Only one part of Hiram's statement struck me as odd.

"What sort of guidance?" I asked him.

"A maker has a responsibility to those they turn," Hiram said as he poked at the coals of the fire with a gnarled stick. "A responsibility to teach them about what they are. The secrets of our kind. How to live as a true Turnskin and not merely some mindless monster."

His yellow eyes regarded me again then, as if evaluating my worth. I was struck again by the fact that his eyes stayed the yellow of the wolf while the rest of him showed no sign of change, remaining utterly calm.

"Even with mentorship," Hiram went on, "not many are

able to find the sort of balance it takes to go on as one of us. Many of us, the great majority in fact, give in to one extreme or the other and lose themselves in time."

I sat silently, massaging my mending legs, and waited eagerly for him to continue.

"To live as a Turnskin is to walk a razor's edge," he said. "To misstep is to risk falling and never regaining one's footing. On one side is the temptation of giving in to the wolf, of becoming too enamored with the power of your wolf self and the pleasures of the hunt. Giving too much to the wolf means giving up too much of the man. Once given, it is never reclaimed."

I nodded. I knew this already. I'd lived my life for decades now instinctively avoiding this very fate. It was exactly what I dreaded, exactly what I was prepared to finally kill myself to avoid.

"On the other side," Hiram went on, "is the risk of fighting the wolf completely. Of denying utterly the very thing that makes you a Turnskin and rejecting half of yourself out of fear or disgust. Such as those live, sometimes for a year or more, exhausting lives of constant vigilance. They torture and isolate themselves until their strength is gone and they finally have to unleash the part of themselves that they've been starving and imprisoning. In many ways, they end up worse than those who gave in to their wolves in the first place. Because in time, no matter how hard they may struggle against it, the wolf will break free."

"That doesn't make any sense," I objected. "How is holding back the wolf any worse than giving in to it?"

Hiram looked at me sadly, as though I had just confirmed for him exactly which side of the razor I'd been hanging from.

"Because the wolf isn't some separate thing to fight against, or some monster for you to guard against. It is half of your true self now. Sharing your life with the wolf is the only way to have a life. A real life, anyway."

I scoffed.

"So, what?" I asked. "You just have to be a monster half of the time and then you get to live happily ever after the other half? Eat a little girl in a red hood once a month and then go about your life behind a picket fence with a wife and kids?"

This man was insane. Whether he'd killed Mack or not, it was clear that he was dangerous now. Instead of being a mindless monster, he had some sort of grand philosophy that justified his monstrousness. He wasn't a maniac, just a psychopath with delusions of enlightenment.

"No," he said sadly. "You don't understand."

"Oh, I think I understand just fine…"

"*No.*" He growled the word softly, but it resonated with a low and rumbling power that silenced me and held me in my place. Somewhere in the back of my mind, my wolf was whining. I yelled at it silently to shut up.

"I smell dogs on you," Hiram said flatly. "You take care of them?"

I nodded, not trusting my voice to refrain from cracking.

"That's good," he said with a hint of admiration. "It may explain part of why you still have some reason. Let me ask you something. Do you chain your dogs, or do you lock them in a cage?"

"What?" I asked, perplexed.

"Do you chain them, or do you cage them?"

"I…neither," I said.

"Why not?"

"Because that's no kind of life for a dog." I thought of Blue and the rest of the pack. I thought of how they roamed the acres of woods around our trailer and sometimes vanished for hours or even days at a time before returning, exhausted and happy with a scrap of rabbit or field mouse dangling from their mouths alongside their lolling tongue.

Hiram nodded and smiled. I saw what he was getting at.

"No," I argued. "That's wrong! A dog doesn't go around killing people. A dog isn't a bloodthirsty monster!"

"No?" he asked. "No dog has ever been a killer? No dog has been a danger to those around them?"

"Don't be ridiculous." I was losing my patience now. He seemed to be deliberately obtuse. "Sure, *some* dogs have been that way, but they're the exception. Those dogs are different."

"What makes them different?" Hiram asked with the voice of a kindly grandfather trying to calm an unreasonable child.

"Those dogs have been mistreated or they're sick. A dog that's been kicked enough will bite." I saw what he was getting at, but I couldn't agree. "But the thing inside me isn't a dog, damnit! You've got to see the difference."

"Of course, I see the difference," he said. "But do you see the similarities?"

"Between a dog and the thing in me? No!" I lied.

Hiram sighed, the skin of his leathery brown face wrinkling in a slight frown.

"What would you do," he began, "if a dog came to you, or even a coyote or a wolf if you wish, who was angry, dangerous, an animal that you knew had been locked in a cage for so long that it was half mad with starvation. This creature was kicked and whipped, neglected, tortured. Would you call it evil? A monster?"

"No..." I said with quiet reluctance.

"Would you hate it?"

I shook my head.

"Would you help it?"

I said nothing.

"Would you help it?" he repeated.

"If I could," I finally agreed.

"And if you couldn't?" he asked. "What if it was too far gone? What if it had hurt people and you couldn't help it heal? If it didn't want to be healed? If, despite all your efforts, you were convinced it would do it again?"

"Then I'd kill it... as kindly as I could."

He nodded.

I looked up at him then, understanding dawning.

"Are you going to kill me?" I was surprised at the fear cracking in my voice when I asked this question. Coward. I thought I'd wanted death.

"That depends," Hiram said, not unkindly.

"On what?" I asked.

"Do you want to be healed?"

CHAPTER TWENTY-NINE

The sunrise found me in the passenger seat of Hiram's old Ford. I'd accepted his invitation to come with him as if I'd had a choice in the matter. I wasn't going to get far on my mending legs yet, and at any rate, he'd already shown me that he could make me do as he wished if it came down to it.

We'd driven through the rest of the night without saying much. I chewed on our earlier conversation, turning it over and over in my mind. I still thought that he was probably wrong. That if he believed that the monster inside me was worthy of sympathy, he must be warped. Though, I had to admit, part of me hoped he was right. Maybe, just maybe, he could help me.

Besides, if he was wrong, I'd prefer to keep an eye on him. I'd only known a few other Garou in my time, or Turnskins to use Hiram's word, and each and every one of them had needed to be put down. Mack and I had encountered a few over the years and had done what needed doing. Now, Mack was gone, killed by one of the monsters we had used to hunt. A monster like me. Now there was no Mack to help, and Hiram was simultaneously stronger and more rational than any man-wolf we'd ever encountered before. I truly didn't believe that he had killed my friend, and Hiram seemed convinced that I wasn't the killer either. But what were the odds of there being a third Garou on the loose? Odds, ha! If I were to play the odds, I'd have to bet that Hiram and I would come to blows sooner than later, and if he was willing to let me heal and regain some strength before I had to put him down, then I'd be an idiot not to seize that advantage. Judging from how easily he'd tossed me around the night before, I'd need any advantage I could get.

He'd driven us east, into the mountains. Past the little town of Oso and the logging town of Darrington and beyond until we were rumbling along on barely maintained, unpaved forest roads. I wondered where he was taking me, but refused to give him the satisfaction of asking. As the sun crawled out from behind the taller mountains to our east, I saw that we had climbed above the blanket of clouds and could see for miles. The forested hilltops rose in all directions from the rolling fog like verdant islands in a milky sea. Not for the first time, I found myself wishing that I could still see the deep green that I could smell all around me. Instead, my inhuman eyes revealed the trees and ferns to me in shades of deep yellow-grey.

As we rounded a corner, a small black bear looked up from a lingering snowbank to regard us tentatively before lumbering off into the trees with deliberate slowness.

Hiram laughed softly under his breath at the bear and his lazy lack of concern. That baffled me. This man, this monster beside me seemed to take genuine pleasure in the nature around us. His face spoke of a quiet satisfaction at the sights and smells all around. Once, when the sun had just crested the mountain tops, he had stopped the truck for several minutes and closed his eyes, sitting still and reveling in the warmth of the fresh sunlight bathing his haggard face.

When was the last time that I'd taken genuine pleasure in simple things like that? Too damn long. Delusional or not, Hiram seemed to have a deep and sincere sense of peace. I found myself resenting the fact that I envied that about him.

I wasn't able to be present and unconcerned as he seemed to be. My mind was elsewhere. Where were Andy and Blue right now? Were they safe? My mind went to Mack and his family, his son Owen, and the pain and anger that had been in his eyes. I'd lost my last friend, but he'd lost his only father. He'd be looking for me. I thought of Rita and her little boy. I hadn't even known his name. It felt grotesque that I didn't know his name. Especially if I'd killed him. But had I?

Mack was convinced that I hadn't killed them, but that had less to do with the facts than with Mack's inexhaustible faith in his friend. That thought, and the realization that his faith was gone forever, that all the things he had done so freely for me and for so many others were done now, hit me in the chest with a far sharper pain than my shattered legs had given me.

My arms and legs were just beginning to itch. It was a little thing for now, but I knew it would get worse soon. Unthinkingly, I reached into my jacket pocket for my bottle of Vicodin before remembering that it was gone. That realization sent a small jolt of panic up my spine and a drop of sweat rolling from my hair and into my face despite the freezing mountain air.

"Where are we going?" I finally asked as I began to calculate how I'd get to my pills or dope from up in the mountains.

"Someplace you can heal." He didn't look at me.

"I'll be fine," I said as I massaged my legs. "They're almost as good as new."

"I'm not worried about your legs."

"Then what?"

"You're sick," he said matter-of-factly. "You need time."

"What I need is my medicine..." I muttered.

"No," he said. "I smell the poison in you. You've drowned yourself in it."

"I need it to keep the wolf back..." I said as I scratched absently at my arm.

"You poison yourself so that you don't have to face yourself. You've bound your wolf-self in chains of poppies and whiskey, you reek of it. Up here, we will break those chains and see if you are worth saving."

That thought frightened me. Did he really mean to keep me out here in the woods until he could force my wolf to the surface? No locks? No pills? The crazy bastard was trying to take me from one side of his so-called razor's edge to the other. He'd let my wolf out and let it consume me.

"No," I said nervously. "No. No. No!"

"Calm yourself," he said.

"No!" I threw open the passenger side door and let myself fall to the dirt and snow of the wilderness road. As I scrambled into the snow and trees on aching legs, I could hear Hiram stopping the truck and opening his own door.

"Shepard," he said my name in an even tone from the roadside. I ignored him as I tried to stand, slipped on my shaking legs and found myself scrabbling on all fours in the snow. The fear, the panic, that I felt at the idea of losing myself to my wolf was exactly the thing that he needed to waken him in his cage. I felt my wolf-self stirring within me in response to the adrenaline coursing through my veins as well as the sounds and smells of the wild all around me.

"No," I said again to myself. "No..."

Hiram's bare brown foot appeared with unnerving slowness before my face. How had he gotten there so damn suddenly? He dropped to a crouch in front of me, resting his hands on his knees.

"Shepard, stop this."

"No!" I screamed it now. Screamed my defiance at him. At my wolf. At the mountainside. I felt the claws beneath my nails itching to burst through my flesh, the fangs within my gums burning to tear into the man in front of me.

I launched myself at Hiram, taking him by surprise and sending us rolling end over end down the snowy hillside before we came to rest roughly against the fallen trunk of an ancient spruce. Squirrels barked their alarm to the rest of the forest as I snarled at the smaller man and reached for his throat.

I could see the surprise in his eyes. He hadn't expected the speed and strength that I'd managed to take him with, and neither had I, but that moment of surprise had passed now. Hiram's lip twitched slightly in the hint of a snarl and the yellow of his eyes deepened noticeably as he grasped each of my wrists in his iron hands. A low rumble emanated from his chest as he rose to his feet and forced me implacably to my knees before him, twisting my arms until my chest and throat were exposed.

"Kill me!" I roared at him with the last of my defiance as our eyes met. I couldn't hold his gaze. My eyes fell to the ground between us as my bellow gave way to choked sobs. "Just kill me. Please."

"Why?" he asked.

"I killed him," I cried. "I killed Mack. I killed the woman and her baby. I'm a killer. It's all I am. So just—just kill me."

I was disgusted with myself. Only the thought that I wouldn't have to live long with the memory of begging him on my knees for my own death with teary eyes made the act bearable. This was what I'd become. Once upon a time I'd been determined to die on my feet. Now I just wanted it to be over. Didn't I?

I'm sorry Maggie, I thought to myself. *I'm not strong enough. You'll have to forgive me for breaking one last promise.*

"No," Hiram said in his low rumble, "you didn't kill the man last night. And you didn't kill the woman and her child. You might be a killer, but those kills were not yours."

CHAPTER THIRTY

Hiram had tasted my blood. He'd licked it from the tip of his knife shortly after my hasty departure from Mack's office. According to him, he knew the smell of the killer, and I didn't match up.

I let him gather me up and lead me back to the truck. He explained more to me as he drove the rest of the way to our destination. I was too broken down, suffering too much with the dope withdrawal, and too raw to do much more than sit quietly and listen. His words ran together for me as I stared out the window at the deepening snow and ever taller trees that we found ourselves venturing into.

The gist of what he told me was that it was this other killer, a third Garou after all, that had brought him to Mack's office the previous night. To hear him tell it, he collected strays much the way that I did. Only, instead of stray mutts, Hiram took wayward monsters under his wing. He taught the Garou who could be taught. As for the ones who wouldn't or couldn't be taught, he put them down, as much for their sake as everybody else's.

As to which category I might fall into, Hiram offered no opinion.

After driving on for the better part of an hour, the truck came to a stop at the end of an overgrown dirt trail that might have once passed for a road. Hiram continued his explanations to me as he opened his door and stepped out into the wintry woods, leaving me to follow his example if I wanted to hear him.

"I wasn't sure when I first smelled you," Hiram said. "I needed to see you to be certain."

He paused for a moment as if expecting me to divine some special significance from this statement. When it became clear that the pair of opinionated chipmunks in the branches above us had more to say on the subject than I did, he sighed and continued to explain.

"I knew the smell of the one I was tracking," he went on, "because I know her. The odd thing was the fact that you and she have a very similar scent, confusingly similar, in fact. When I tasted your blood, I knew why."

He seemed intent on pausing to give me an opportunity to ask him to explain, but I was equally intent on disappointing him. If he wanted to tell me more, he would. I wasn't looking for some mentor to bow to and beg for pearls of wisdom.

"A Turnskin often has a similar scent to those who share their line. If you were to make another, that one would share your blood and would have a close connection with you."

"Wait," I said, "I've never made another like me. Honestly, I don't even know how. And if I did, I'd never do it. I've bitten people before, but they never turned into..."

"It takes more than a simple bite," he said. "That is folklore. Superstition. The one who made you had to mingle her blood with yours. It is true that this is most commonly done by a bite, but she would have had to have bitten her tongue or something similar in order for the bite to share her blood with you. Such things have been known to happen accidentally, but it is rare. More often, we pass on the gift to those we choose. It is a deliberate thing."

"Gift?" I spat the word incredulously as Hiram took several packs from under the tarp in the back of his truck. He tossed me a leather satchel, something like an old saddle bag, and I caught it on reflex.

"For one who learns to appreciate it, yes. But that is beside the point. I'm not saying that you made another, but there is one who once made you, is there not?"

I thought back to France, to the beast woman who had torn apart the ghouls before I could become their supper. I'd never seen her again. In truth, I never supposed that I would. She'd struck me as a mad, unthinking thing. A feral reminder of what I could become if I let the wolf have his way.

"Her...?"

"Yes," Hiram said as he began to walk into the treeline carrying several packs of his own. He went slowly enough that I could follow him on my still unsteady legs. "I believe that a woman I taught is the one who made you."

"What—how? How is that even possible? What—what is her name?"

"She left me some years ago now," he said sadly. "I wish it had been otherwise, but I wished her well and respected her choice to go her own way, though I feared she might come to a bad end. I never knew her birth name. When I first met her, she had lost the ability to speak. I gave her a name so that I'd have something to call her. I called her Yarrow, after the little flowers I sometimes caught her playing with when she thought I wasn't looking."

Though his back was to me and his voice was melancholy, there was something in his tone that made me suspect he might be smiling, if only a little.

"Yarrow," I tried the name on my mouth, still shocked to have a name to put to the ancient memory of the beast of Belleau Wood. Hiram seemed to take it as a question.

"Yes, do you know it? In Spanish it is called *plumajillo*," he pronounced the word with the effortless accent of a native speaker. "Though, it has many names, as plants often do. Milfoil, thousand-leaf, nosebleed plant—that last is because it was once used to stop bleeding from wounds—I'm sorry, I didn't mean to ramble. It isn't often that I have somebody else to speak to. I'm afraid I'm out of practice."

He shot me an amiable smile over his shoulder. But something in the flash of his teeth wouldn't let me forget that he was a predator who could just as easily rip my head from my shoulders and drink the blood from my skull as he could lecture me about the names and properties of wildflowers. I forced a nervous smile in return.

"As I was saying," Hiram continued, "Yarrow stayed with me for several years. We lived mostly in the wild as she slowly regained some sense of herself. I have to say, she impressed me greatly. She was eager to learn all that she could, though she was always a bit defiant and rebellious. I thought she would overcome those tendencies in time. The fact that she has turned you, and perhaps others, and that she has begun taking lives so brazenly, well... let us just say that I feel a sense of responsibility for what she has become."

"So, you're what," I said, "here to clean up her mess?"

"In a manner of speaking, yes."

"Well, good. You can help me get her!"

"No."

"What do you mean no? You said you were tracking her. Aren't you?"

"Yes, and I will continue to do so. But you are not ready to help *me*."

"Like hell I'm not," I said angrily as I struggled to keep pace with him. "This ain't my first rodeo, you know."

It was an unfamiliar experience to have somebody talking to me from a position of age and greater strength. I didn't much care for that shoe being on this foot.

"Yes, I assumed as much," he said. "The way you carry yourself, you were a soldier? You've seen battle?"

"Yeah, I've been to war," I confirmed without volunteering any more information.

"This isn't war, Shepard. It is a hunt."

"Either way, I'm in this," I said.

"We will see."

I harrumphed but didn't press the subject for now. I'd be going after the thing that killed Mack one way or another. If old man Hiram didn't want me to go, I'd like to see him try and stop me.

We walked a while longer through the snow and brambles as I thought about the implications of what he'd been telling me. A day ago, I'd been the oldest person I knew, usually by a very wide margin. I generally passed for a gruff thirty-something, or perhaps a spry forty on a bad day, but that didn't change the fact that my hundredth birthday was only a couple of years around the bend. This guy was older than me. That was clear. He looked older, maybe fifty-something at a glance, but that didn't mean much when I didn't even know how old he'd been when he'd become something other than human. I knew I was outclassed here, but by how much?

"How old are you?" I spit the question out without preamble. I figured that there was no sense in beating around any more bushes than we already were.

"I don't keep count," he said with a grin in his voice.

"Okay then, I won't card you. But how about a ballpark guess?"

"Well, let's see. When I was a boy, all of this," he gestured with his off hand to indicate the hills and the land in all directions, "was called the Oregon Territory."

I didn't say anything, I didn't want to give him the satisfaction of knowing how much that stunned me. Washington was far from one of the oldest states in the Union, but I knew enough history to remember that the Washington Territory hadn't been broken off from the Oregon Territory until sometime before the civil war. At a rough estimate, Hiram might be twice my age. He looked damn good, considering.

I laughed without realizing it. Hiram turned his head and raised an eyebrow in curiosity.

"Clean living," I said with a sad smile, remembering a bad joke I'd made to Mack when I'd last seen him.

He furrowed his brow in confusion but didn't ask for further explanation. We walked on in silence for perhaps another mile before Hiram decided that we had arrived.

He stepped into a small snowless space between three great pines and dropped his bags softly into the cold moss. There was a crude lean-to shelter and a thick pile of pine boughs before the cold remains of an old fire.

"So, what is this place?" I asked him.

"Just a place," he said without looking up.

"Alright," I said, "what now?"

"Now," Hiram said as he knelt by the coals and began the work of building a fire, "we eat."

That struck me as an excellent idea. The walk had done my legs good, they seemed fully mended now, but that didn't mean I was comfortable. The itching that had begun in my limbs had spread to my chest and shoulders, but my cravings for another fix were overshadowed by the wolf in his cage and his demands for meat. If I couldn't drug him into complacency, I'd better at least not let the damn thing get too hungry.

"Good idea," I said. "How can I help?"

"Go kill something."

I waited a moment, wondering if he was joking, but Hiram went about building the fire without any indication of a sense of humor. Well, fine, I could certainly hunt when I needed to. I looked around the little camp to take stock of the resources at my disposal and finding none I picked up one of the packs we had carried in.

"You won't find any prey in my bags," Hiram chuckled to himself. Just my luck, the man had a sense of humor after all, and it was a bad one.

"Of course," I replied. "It's just that I seem to have left my rifle in my other pants, and was hoping I might find some line to make a snare or maybe a sling with."

He turned to look at me.

"I can see that you are clever," he said, "and that can be a good thing, sometimes. The clever half of you can serve you well at other times, but this is not one of them. I know that you ignore the voice of the wolf within you, so I will say this once so that you can understand with your clever mind something that your wolf already knows." He turned to me then and met my gaze with his yellow eyes. His face was utterly devoid of any trace of humor. "In this place, I am the alpha. If you touch what is mine again without my permission, I will hurt you."

I dropped the bag and my eyes before I could think about what I was doing. Again, my inner wolf responded to Hiram before I had a chance to choose my response. I resented it. Deeply.

I turned my back on Hiram. It went against my instincts but that was the point. It was the only act of defiance that I could manage in that moment.

"Leave your boots," he said casually as he turned back to his pile of tinder and kindling.

"What?"

"Your boots, take them off and leave them before you go."

"Why would I do that?"

Hiram cleared his throat in the briefest rumbling growl that set all of my hairs on end.

"You ask too many questions," he snarled as he rose to his bare feet and rushed at me, teeth bared. I took a step backward and slipped, falling on my ass at the edge of the camp before scrambling to my feet again. Hiram relaxed his snarling lip and concealed his teeth, speaking more calmly. "Today I'll forgive that, because you haven't yet been taught any better. Today only, I'll explain myself to you. But it would be wise for you to learn to listen and submit."

"I've never been very submissive," I met his eyes briefly but still couldn't hold his damn gaze. It was infuriating.

"Or wise, I'd wager. Now, take off your boots."

I considered whether or not this was the time to test myself against Hiram. We'd only just arrived, and I hadn't learned much of anything from him yet, if there was anything to learn. Consciously, I doubted that he had much to teach me, but on a deeper level I think I sensed that he knew something I wanted very much to learn. He knew something about how to move through the world while feeling that he had a place in it, and that was something I'd never known how to do. I decided that there was time enough to fight with him tomorrow, so I kicked off my boots.

"You separate yourself," Hiram said by way of explanation. "You keep yourself apart from the people around you, from the world around you. You even separate yourself from yourself. That is not serving you well."

"So, you want me to stop separating my feet from the ground?" I scoffed.

"Yes," he said. "How can you learn to trust your senses when you hide from them?"

I wanted to argue with him about that. I didn't hide from my damn senses. Though I had to admit, if only to myself, that the smells of the forest were clearer to me than they'd have been if I had the cigarette I was craving at that moment. I rolled my eyes a little, but as I was still facing downward Hiram didn't see it.

With my feet now cold and bare, I walked across the soft floor of fallen pine needles, feeling them prick and give beneath my skin. There was an odd sensation, a stirring from the wolf's cage in my mind, but not the angry rattling at the bars that I was accustomed to. It was as if the wolf lifted his head and perked up his ears at the sensation of the forest beneath my feet, and the result was a sharpening of my other senses as the smells and sounds of the mountainside came into greater focus for me. Hiram had been right, damn him, but I wasn't about to let him know it.

Fine, I'd play his stupid game. I'd go chase squirrels barefoot in the woods. Why not? I'd run with my dogs, hadn't I? We'd even run down rabbits together. Of course, this time, I was going to do it alone.

"The strength of a Turnskin," Hiram said from behind me in apparent response to my unspoken thought, "is that we are never alone."

CHAPTER THIRTY-ONE

There is an eerie calm to an alpine forest at the end of winter, especially first thing in the morning. Distant cries of birds greeting the sun provided makeshift lyrics to the rhythm of melting snow falling from branches in a soft staccato all around me. My own footsteps, my breath, even my heartbeat joined the muffled symphony of the hunt.

Shortly after leaving Hiram's camp, I picked up a handful of small stones which I thought might suffice for taking a small bird or maybe a squirrel if I was lucky. I knew that the crazy old man who had sent me on this ridiculous errand probably wouldn't approve of the rocks in my hand, but that was half of their appeal.

It wasn't long before I came across a chipmunk. The little fellow berated me mercilessly from the perceived safety of his tree, barking an alarm to the rest of the woods. I froze in place and considered the possibility of hitting him with one of my stones. I just might be able to do it. If nothing else, it would shut him up.

Then I imagined myself returning to the camp with my kill, the mighty hunter with a half mouthful of meat proudly held before him. A chipmunk, Frank? Really? Why not just bring back a handful of snowberries and perhaps a bug or two to show my prowess? A chipmunk was little more than an overly hairy, tree-dwelling mouse when it came down to it. I imagined the look on Hiram's face when I returned with the noisy little chipmunk and reconsidered. I could do better than that.

I walked on, creeping softly on the balls of my feet, the icy cold biting at my toes. The angry little sentinel kept barking at me as I went, blissfully unaware of how close he had come to being tomorrow morning's turd.

A mile or so later, I found a trickle of snowmelt flowing rapidly downhill and paused to have a drink. As I knelt and extended my cupped hand toward the water I saw that my arm was trembling slightly, more from withdrawal than the cold. Because of my body's unnatural resilience the physical cravings would pass quickly, even if my desire for the drugs wouldn't leave me so easily. A drink could only help. I lifted the water to my lips for one slow trembling sip at a time, but the dryness of my mouth quickly left me frustrated with that approach.

Impatient, I dropped to my hands and knees and drank directly from the little stream, slurping greedily at the icy water. I'd been missing my coffee and whiskey, but I had to admit that this wasn't half bad. Not bad at all. It was as if I could taste not only the trees that the water had flowed past, but I imagined tasting the very clouds that the snow had fallen from. Earth and sky, taking a detour in my mouth on their way to join the sea.

Having nowhere else in mind to go, and thinking I must not be the only thirsty creature in the woods, I decided to follow the little stream downhill. Soon it was joined by other little rivulets and doubled in size before I heard the rushing waters of a more respectable stream nearby. This was encouraging. I thought the odds would be good that I might find something edible stopping for a mid-morning drink before bedding down for the day.

I stumbled upon a little game trail heading toward the crashing sounds of the water. It wasn't a trail in the way that people would easily use the term, being only a well-worn path of flattened grasses and bent branches. All sorts of animals used little paths like these. They usually started out as a bit of pressed foliage where a deer or perhaps some rabbits passed on their way from food or water to safety. Before long, other creatures take advantage of the path, either because they find it convenient, or because, like me, they are predators who are drawn by the promise of meat.

I knelt beside a pile of dark pellets and tasted the air. Deer. Female. And fresh. The scent stirred my inner wolf to wakefulness, and I found myself salivating in tune with his excitement.

Yes. Hunt. This is good.

Crouching low, I ambled slowly along the path, careful to absorb the shock of my steps in my knees and hips. I kept my head level as I went forward, pausing every few steps to test the air again as I searched for the scent of prey.

My body knew that I was close before I saw or heard anything to confirm the instinct. As I neared what I suspected would be the final bend before arriving at the running water, every muscle and sinew was poised to give chase. I moved one limb at a time, taking several shallow breaths between each movement. First my left leg, then my right arm, then my right leg, and then my left arm, and so on.

The wolf jerked our body to a sudden stop once I saw them. Three deer. Two young ones, yearlings by the look of them. One had a pair of velvety spikes just barely protruding from the top of his head, the other a lovely young doe with graceful lines and a twitching nose. These two drank greedily with no suspicion of danger. It was the third, their mother I suppose, who was wary. She was a big old doe with dark eyes and tall twitching ears, her belly swollen with the fawns that would be born someday soon. She was older and wiser. She knew to keep alert when taking water, she knew that water masked the sounds and smells of predators as well as prey, and she knew that creatures with sharp teeth needed to drink also.

The old doe froze and flashed her black tail high in the air as I rounded the corner. She looked right at me as I stood statue-still but seemed unsure what she was seeing. Responding to his mother's tail flash and sudden tension, the young buck also snapped his head up and looked about, not knowing where to look. The younger doe drank on, unaware of the warning signs her family were displaying. The three of them were perhaps ten long strides away from me.

Yes. Prey. Good. Careful now.

The wolf worried that I would scare them off. He urged patience. I felt him feeding his strength to my limbs, preparing for the chase. If we sprang at them now, they might get away, though I thought that we would likely get to one before they escaped. The wolf didn't like our odds and wanted to wait until the matriarch had relaxed her guard and see if we could stalk a few steps closer before the chase began. I agreed.

So, we waited. The muscles in my newly mended legs twitched and burned with the effort of holding the mid-stride position where I had frozen when the deer came into view. It took the span of a few breaths for the young buck to turn away and go back to drinking, apparently satisfied that there was nothing to be concerned about. The wind was with me, keeping my scent well away from the prey. Mother deer took her time, not trusting the strange shape she thought she saw near the thicket, even going so far as to take a tentative step forward to see if her movement would trigger a chase from some mysterious hunter. She knew her business. My wolf tensed hungrily as she moved and almost pushed us forward reflexively, but we held our position. Finally, the old doe lowered her head and joined her offspring in the noisy shallows of the rocky creek.

I lowered the leg I'd been holding above the ground, feeling it tremble slightly in relief as I shifted my weight. I took three slow breaths and then followed the wolf's urging to stalk forward. Low and slow now, very carefully. One step, no reaction. A second step, the old doe twitched an ear but didn't look up. Three more breaths as she relaxed, and I took a third step, then a fourth.

Yes! Good!

The wolf in my head was exultant, we had our prey now. From here we could launch ourselves at the prey of our choice and have them before the others knew what was happening. The old doe was fat and slow, easier prey perhaps, and more meat too. She was pregnant though, and while the wolf didn't give a shit about such things, my man's mind still found the idea distasteful. The young buck then. He was close enough, and he was enough meat for several days. Young and tender. I salivated at the thought of his flesh and felt the wolf's appreciation of the idea.

We were in utter accord, my wolf and I. We wanted the same thing and were moving slowly toward that common goal. I could feel how pleased he was with this morning's hunt, how fondly he anticipated the kill and meal to come.

He was so very pleased.

This monster, the thing that had caused me so much suffering, which had led me to do so many awful things. Even if I wasn't the one who had killed Mack or Rita and her son, that didn't change what I was, and it didn't change what the wolf had made me do in the past.

Evelyn.

I remembered my wife. My beautiful, willful, stubborn, mischievous, golden-haired Evelyn. Dead now for almost seventy years. Now only a ghost, bound to an antique rocking chair in my shit-smelling drug den, unable to speak or touch. Always watching me with those sad eyes. Never able to hold the baby she'd so wanted, let alone the grandchildren or great-grandchildren that she should rightfully have by now.

I remembered her face, the pain and the fear in her eyes, the pleading way she had screamed my name the last time I had ever heard her voice, the way that I still heard it in my dreams. I remembered the taste of her blood on the night that the wolf had gotten loose and murdered her. The same wolf that was so happy with me right now.

"Fuck you!" I roared suddenly at the top of my lungs. The deer leapt immediately into action, springing across the creek, scrambling up the bank and into the thick woods on the other side. I held myself in place and watched them go, making sure that the wolf saw their escape.

No! No! Why? WHY?

He didn't understand what had just happened. He couldn't understand it. Wolves don't bear grudges. He couldn't fathom that something so long ago could still matter.

"Because," I said under my breath to myself, "I hate you."

He couldn't understand that either.

The two rabbits and partridge that I brought back to camp made a more than adequate meal. I'd cornered the rabbits in their warren and dug them out and snapped their necks swiftly while several others ran away. The partridge had been a bit of luck. I'd seen him standing by one of the little ice-melt rivulets and had found a perfect stone sitting in the melting snow.

Hiram didn't comment on what I brought back when I deposited the three animals beside the impressive fire he'd managed to build during my hunt. He didn't need to know that I'd refused my wolf, that I'd gotten this meat with my human ingenuity rather than a monster's instincts, but that fact mattered a great deal to me. I was quietly proud of it, considering it a personal victory.

Hiram picked up the rabbits and drew his knife. With practiced ease he sliced open the belly of the first rabbit and reached within, pulling out the ropey grey intestines and other bits of viscera, throwing them into the fire. I was briefly relieved to find that he wasn't going to just bite into the thing. At least he had some veneer of humanity. My relief was short lived, however, as he plucked out a few choice morsels and ate them raw. The liver, the kidneys, perhaps the heart. He bit into the still steaming pieces of meat and let the red juices drip down his chin as he turned to me and met my eyes with his unblinking yellow stare.

My wolf, angry still at having been denied a proper chase and kill, recognized Hiram's display for exactly what it was. A display of dominance. Of course it came to that. He was doing exactly what I did with my own dogs, showing his dominant position by eating the first and best portion of the kill before any others were allowed to eat.

Fine. If his idea of dominance was earned by eating steaming rabbit guts, he was welcome to it. Let him think what he wanted; I knew who had killed the things.

After cleaning and eating his choice portion of the first rabbit he repeated the process with the second rabbit, again picking out and savoring the bits that he deemed best. After that he tossed one rabbit and the partridge to my feet, evidently leaving them for me to prepare how I pleased. His own rabbit was quickly skinned and left to rest on a rock near the coals, roasting slowly and making me swallow to keep from drooling.

I plucked and cleaned the partridge and skinned my own rabbit, skewering both animals on a makeshift spit that I held over the flames for quite some time after Hiram decided that his own rabbit, still blue and bloody, had cooked long enough. He was licking the marrow from bones and wiping his mouth when my own meal was just beginning to cook.

My own meat was rare, and I liked it fine that way, fresh and steaming.

After eating, we buried the scraps near the fire so as to avoid attracting scavengers and Hiram had laid down on his pine bed within the crude lean-to, soaking up the heat from the dying fire and resting his eyes.

"Now what?" I asked.

"Now, gather some more wood for the fire," he said without opening his eyes, "and then rest. The time for sleeping is midday and midnight. The wolf in you knows this already."

The wolf in me can rot in hell, I thought silently.

I relieved myself a little way from camp as I sullenly gathered fallen branches and pinecones to add to the fire. When I returned to camp Hiram seemed to be sleeping. I stoked up the fire and looked at him, curled on his side and facing the fire. It could be easy to attack him now while he was sleeping, it might even be wise to take that opportunity if we were going to come to blows eventually anyway. Easy and wise it might be, but I wasn't convinced it was necessary, and I was damn sure that it would be cowardly. Besides, I wasn't entirely confident that he wouldn't hear me coming anyway.

Quietly ashamed, I pushed the thought aside and cleared a spot on the ground on the opposite side of the fire from the sleeping man. Curling up on my side near the crackling warmth. I remember thinking that rest might be a good idea but that there was no way I'd let myself fall asleep.

Moments later, I was dreaming.

It was less a dream, really, than a nightmare. At first, I found myself in a pleasant enough scene. Trees and a stream I'd once known well, shades of green that had been lost to me except in memories and dreams like this. The emerald green fleck in

Andy's blue eyes occurred to me then. I was still baffled at how such a thing was possible in my waking life. Perhaps Hiram would know? Thinking of Andy and Hiram led me to remember another dream in which Hiram had appeared as a ravenous wolf and Andy, in the form of a raven, had helped me escape him. Yes, Hiram had been in my dreams, he might have a thing or two to teach me after all.

Remembering the earlier dream, I looked up to scan the branches for any sign of a sleek raven spying on me and turned around to be sure that there wasn't a stalking wolf preparing to pounce. No, there was nothing like that here. That earlier dream had been in what I thought of as the wolf-wood, that primordial landscape of impossibly tall trees and ancient mythic beasts that I would dream of hunting sometimes when the moon was near her fullness. This dream was not one of those. No, this little stream and the familiar trees shading it were from my long-ago childhood. It was the place I'd spent my days when I wanted to be left alone. I'd come here to skip stones and read books, to forget about the world after one of my father's beatings, or when I couldn't bear to show my deformed face at school. It had been my place. Only mine. Not even Maggie had come here.

In the way of dreams, thoughts of Maggie and my father began to change the scene. I didn't move so much as the world moved around me to match my thoughts. I saw the long-ago city of Bellingham where I had grown up, when it had been a logging and fishing town, reachable mainly by ship or train. The brick buildings and street cars shifted around me as a familiar hill placed itself beneath and behind me, pushing me toward the place I didn't want to go.

There it was, the drab little house I'd grown up in. Just as I remembered it, with weeds growing brazenly in the yard and paint peeling from the walls. Near the back of the house I saw a figure, a man's figure, pressed near a window. I didn't want to look. I knew exactly who I was going to see. I closed my eyes, turned away, but again my fears shaped my dream as I found myself standing directly behind my father, eyes wide and staring despite my intentions.

His shoulders rose and fell with excited breathing as he peered into the bathroom window, his hair hanging in greasy clumps.

"You've got some nerve," my father slurred the familiar words without facing me.

Alright. I knew what came next. I'd relived this particular memory more than once and was prepared to do it again. As my father began to slowly turn and face me, I raised my fists in the fighter's stance that he himself had taught me, ready to beat his face in as I had done that awful day. Only, my right arm didn't rise. It was shattered and helpless, laying in a sling at my side as it had after he had broken it when I'd been twelve. No, this wasn't right. That was a different memory. I should have both arms! As I puzzled at my helpless right arm and the memories of pain now shooting through it, my old man turned fully to look at me with a face that barely deserved the name.

His nose was utterly shattered, flattened in a wet, red mass into the swollen mound of his face. His jaw jutted out to one side, several teeth missing from bloody gaps. He peered at me from one grey eye that was nearly swollen shut. The other was beyond all hope, bloody jelly dripped from a tangle of flesh and bone that had once been his left eye. It was impossible for somebody to be walking and talking with a face like that.

"I always knew you were a monster," my father drawled as a thin stream of near-black blood spilled from his lip.

I was a child again. Broken, helpless, and afraid. I turned and ran for the kitchen door, tripping and scrambling to my feet in a flash as Frank Shepard Sr. walked steadily after me.

"Don't you run, boy. You stand and take this like a man, *Franthith*!" Even with his ruined mouth my father still mocked my childhood lisp.

I dashed through the flimsy wood door and into the kitchen, running into the next room before my father could follow and find me. I found myself standing in the old living room where my mother had sat in her chair and read her books or napped the day away in an opium haze. It occurred to me suddenly that the room was impossibly large. The chairs and table towering over me, disorienting me. My father's footsteps thundered in the distance like some terrible giant who would sniff me out and grind my bones.

Above me, a woman sat rocking gently in her favorite chair. She was wrapped in blankets and her hair hung in her face as she regarded a bundle held in her lap.

"Mama," I said, hearing my little-boy's voice, now much younger than twelve. "Mama, help!"

"Shhhh," she pressed her finger to her lips as she hissed without looking up. "Be quiet you little beast. You'll wake the baby."

"Mama," I heard my voice break, and I started to cry and clutched at her leg. "Mama, please..."

She pushed me away with her slippered foot, still not meeting my eyes. In her arms, baby Maggie had begun to cry.

"Oh, there, there little one," my mother said with a tenderness I could barely believe as she stroked the baby's hair and kissed her brow. "Don't cry. Shh. Don't let that little monster make you sad. Here, you take your medicine, and everything will be better..."

My mother reached to the table beside her and retrieved... a pipe? It was the same dirty metal pipe that I kept in my trailer. The one that I'd recently used to smoke Rita's stolen heroin. This wasn't right. My mother had never been a smoker. Where was the dropper and her bottle of laudanum? Before I could react, she pressed the dirty pipe to the baby's mouth and struck a match. The sickly-sweet smell that came with the smoke filled me with longing, even as my baby sister was choking on the fumes.

The thunder of my father's footsteps returned, louder and nearer now than it had been before. The walls shook and windows rattled as he drew near. I turned and fled from my mother's parlor, around the corner, and through the door that I knew would lead me to safety. Slipping into the room that Maggie and I had shared, I slid beneath the bed and huddled against the back wall, pressing myself still and silent against the floor as I covered my eyes with a child's certainty that what I could not see would not see me.

I heard the door open on its screeching hinges, heard the deafening boom of my father's slow steps approach and then stop at the edge of my bed, but I refused to look.

"Come here, you little coward," my father said as I opened my eyes and saw his monstrously huge hand reaching toward me. I pressed myself against the darkness behind me, but there was nowhere to go. My father's arm grew and grew, impossibly long, until I could smell the tobacco and liquor on his unwashed hand. I opened my mouth to scream, but no sound escaped my tight child's throat.

My father laughed.

Behind me, from the darkness, came a low threatening growl. I knew without thinking about it that the growl wasn't for me. Terrible and fearsome as it was, I had nothing to fear from it. My father, on the other hand, was another matter.

A pair of golden lights appeared beside me in the shadows under the bed, yellow predator's eyes that met my father's one monstrous grey one. Hot breath erupted into a deafening howl behind me and the eyes rushed forward, shining ivory fangs tore into the giant hand of my father, and his blood filled the world under my bed.

"Shepard," something struck me in the ribs, "Shepard, wake up. You're scaring away all the prey."

Hiram stood over me, regarding me with a furrowed brow and nudged my ribs again without consideration. I met his eyes in challenge and he raised one eyebrow in warning.

The fire had died to white ash with only a handful of scattered coals giving scant warmth. The shadows of the trees were growing long in the afternoon daylight.

"Are you ready to learn?"

I wanted nothing more at that moment than to crawl into an opium coma and never come out again. Failing that, I'd settle for whiskey, beer, weed, anything at all to keep from being present. But that wasn't to be. Lifting my dirty hand before me I saw that the tremble I'd noticed earlier was now completely gone. I may want to self-medicate, but my body was awake and ready for whatever was next.

"Fuck it," I said. "Why not?"

CHAPTER THIRTY-TWO

"How long is this going to take?" I said.

"It takes as long as it takes," Hiram said without looking back at me.

We'd been hiking steadily since dawn, and he'd shown no sign of slowing. The midday sun offered us what meager warmth it could as it peeked at us from behind scattered grey clouds. We'd moved camp every day after we'd arrived nearly a week ago, and he seemed intent on taking us even further into the mountains today.

Each day we would wake before dawn, eat whatever we had left over from the night before, and walk steadily until we reached whatever destination suited Hiram's fickle needs. Then, he would start a fire and send me out for more meat. Rabbits and squirrels had sufficed but I was getting sick of rodents and the like. The thing that baffled me about our daily treks was that they were never in the same direction. I'd have understood if he had been leading us perpetually further east or north or in any direction, really. It would mean that he had some destination in mind. Instead, we spent half of each day roaming in some new direction.

Early on I had asked Hiram where we were going.

"We'll know when we get there," was all he had said.

It had rained on us about half the time, the water falling as sleet in the mornings and evenings when it was colder. If we hadn't had the advantage of our inhuman resilience and healing, we'd have died long ago of exposure. Especially the perpetually shoeless Hiram with his open jacket and bare chest. He'd looked at me disapprovingly when I had put my own boots back on after my first hunt, but he didn't object. He had proved whatever point he'd been trying to make and was willing to leave that decision in my hands after that.

At night, before we went to sleep beneath the light of the fading moon, he taught me about the wolf-dreams.

"It is a real place," he told me, "or at least it was once."

"What is?"

"The wood where I first found you. You and your raven friend."

"You mean in my dream?" I said.

"The Dream doesn't belong to you Shepard, it belongs to all of us."

"All of us... Turnskins?" I tried his word and found it awkward on my lips.

"No, not only Turnskins," he corrected me. "Everything that dreams, everything with a spirit, can touch some part of the Dream."

"Then why didn't I ever go there before I was changed? Why don't any humans I know go there?"

"You did, and they do, in their own way. But not the way that you do now. Most people experience only little pieces of the Dream, and that is for the best. Most people are not prepared to protect themselves from the things that live there."

"Right..." I said skeptically. Now he thought that dreams were real. I wanted to dismiss him out of hand as somebody who had lost his grip on reality, but I couldn't simply dismiss the fact that he had bitten me in the wolf dream when I'd met him, and the bruise on my leg when I'd awoken had been real enough. The things that Andy claimed to have learned about me from my dreams were real enough too.

"Because they don't touch the Dream fully, the things of the Dream can't touch them, as I touched you. As your raven friend touched me," he rubbed his eye in memory of how she had pecked at the eyes of his Dream-wolf self.

"What is so dangerous? I haven't been hurt in my dreams," he raised an eyebrow in challenge until I amended my statement, "at least not until recently."

"It is safer for us than for most. We hunt in the Dream, and most things that live there fear us."

"What *things*? You keep talking about things that live in my dreams, what kind of things?"

"Not *your dreams*, the Dream," he repeated. Leaving no room to doubt the capitalization of the word. "You've seen them, the least of them anyway. Haven't you wondered at the little wisps that flit about and keep just out of reach?"

"The little lights? Sure, but they aren't alive, they're just... just lights."

He shook his head. "They're more alive than you know. Those are wisps, single minded little sparks of the Dream-folk. Spirits."

"Spirits, like ghosts? I've seen ghosts."

"Of course you have, we all do, but no, that isn't what I mean. What you call ghosts, those are just shadows. Pale echoes of things that once were. Not true spirits."

"So, what is the difference?"

"One is alive; one isn't. One is like a spark that starts a fire. The other is like the last light of a fading ember. Shades don't linger long, not without somebody to tend to them."

I thought of my sweet, sad Evelyn in her old chair, always watching me from the shadows with those disapproving eyes. No, I wasn't going to share that with Hiram. She was mine. She was all I had left of my wife.

"So, these... sparks, they last, then?" I asked.

"Oh yes," he laughed. "They can last for ages. They attach themselves to things, trees or animals usually, and they share the life of that host for a time, adding those experiences to their own. Most fade after a time, but they can last as long as there are people who remember them, people who feed them with their feelings and memories."

"What does that mean?"

"Well," he paused and searched a moment for the right words, "have you heard stories of tribal cultures? The Indians in this area tell stories of Raven for example, or of Coyote, or other animal tricksters. Do you know what I mean?"

"You're saying that old Indian stories about coyotes are real and based on ghosts... um, spirits?"

"Not coyotes, Coyote," he said the word as a proper name. "And yes, in a sense. Spirits, both great and small, are shaped by the world and their experiences much as anybody else is. The difference is that they have eternity to be shaped while most people have only a brief flicker of a life. Most spirits are quite curious, and more than a little mischievous. They love their games. When they find themselves with enough power to touch the world around them, they can make quite a mess of things. Wars have been started by tribes over which spirit is best or more powerful. Whether you want to call them angels, or demons, or spirits, or fairies, or even gods, they're a bunch of trouble if you ask me. And regular people are better off avoiding them."

I didn't say anything. I was deep in the woods with a nutcase. He may as well be holding a cardboard sign and telling me that the end was nigh, and that he was the second coming of Jesus sent to save us all from the Martians.

"You've got a talent for denial, Shepard," he said to me with a smile. "You deny your instincts, you deny your own senses, you even deny what you are."

"I know exactly what I am," I said. *A monster,* I finished the thought silently.

"No, you don't. You think that you are this," he shoved my shoulder forcefully, "but you pretend that the meat and bone is all of it. Meanwhile, you don't let yourself wonder how it is that the moon can call to you, how you can hunt wonderous things in the Dream, how you see the shades of the dead, or how a powerful Spirit shares your body with you and can turn that meat and bone into something else. How do you think you do that if you deny your Spirit?"

"I don't know," I said softly, "but isn't that better than pretending that I do?"

"It would be, if it were true," he said. "But you know, and instead you pretend that you do not. You lie to yourself. Let me show you."

"I don't lie..." I said.

"Come, let me show you. In the Dream."

"I... how? I only have those dreams sometimes."

"Yes, because you wait until you stumble into the Dream, but you can choose to go there if you wish. Even your little Raven friend, a little girl, knows how to do this. She is a talented Dreamwalker, don't you think you can do the same?"

"How?"

"Lay down. Find the moon. Let her fill your senses..."

So, Hiram had taken me on my first guided tour of the wolf dream, the Dream, as he called it. Pulling myself into the Dream was a matter of realizing that I wasn't pulling at all but letting go. It was a bit like one of those trick pictures where if you look at it just right you can see a sailboat instead of a block of shapes and colors, but only if you relax your eyes just right. You can stare at it all day, straining your eyes until your head pounds, but when you finally give up and start to look away, there it is. Then, once you've seen it, you know how to see it more easily afterwards. The Dream was like that. I pushed, I pulled, and I couldn't make anything happen. Then, after I'd given up and lay on the ground, staring up at the moon in utter defeat, I released a breath and stopped trying. And I slipped right in.

"What took you so long?" Hiram asked me as an enormous dark wolf. I just about jumped out of my skin. My wolf-skin, which I was wearing without intending to. Instantly, I was standing on two feet again but couldn't keep myself from retaining certain wolfish features. No matter what I did I had a bit of fur, or a long snout, or tufted ears, anything but completely human. I'd never liked that about the wolf dream. Pleasant and exciting as my dreams here could sometimes be, the wolf was always closer to the surface than I'd like.

I shook my hand, trying to make the fur and claws go away fully.

"What are you doing?" Hiram cocked his great shaggy head at me and made the words without moving his mouth.

"Trying to be... myself!"

He laughed, a loud roo-roo sound that seemed equal parts howl and laugh.

"You are yourself," he said. "How could you be anything else?"

"Show me how to make the wolf go away," I said as I rubbed at the canine ears that had popped up as soon as my hands were the way I wanted them.

"But this is his place," Hiram said.

"What is that supposed to mean?"

"This is the Dream, Shepard," he said with reverence as he gazed upward at the towering prehistoric trees that were greener and more vividly real than any memory of the waking world could ever be. "This is the place of spirits. Your wolf self is a spirit. You'll never fully hide him here. He is the part of you that most truly belongs here."

I decided to try my best to ignore the fangs and claws that had sprouted against my wishes and looked around me. This moment had never lost its awe for me over the years, standing here in the shadow of ancient giants, with the distant sounds and smells of creatures that may never have existed teasing my senses and driving me to hunt. The little lights that Hiram called wisps were bobbing in and out from behind trunks and branches in myriad colors, perpetually out of reach but blinking their little lights as if winking at us playfully, teasingly.

I couldn't contain the wolfish grin that tugged at the corners of my mouth as I sniffed at the moist and verdant air. Hiram-wolf cocked his head at me, and his great wet tongue lolled ridiculously out to one side of his mouth with no regard for dignity.

"Well," he said, "what are you waiting for?"

With that, he launched himself from his powerful haunches and ran in the direction of the alluring scents. Without thinking, I ran after him, finding myself on all four padded feet and matching his speed. I held back from letting the wolf have his full shape in small ways. I was unwilling to release him entirely, even as I followed Hiram in a hunt that ended with us taking a large and powerfully muscled woolly beast with one great, solitary horn. We feasted on our shared kill and howled our triumph to the moon that was always full and bright in that twilight realm.

. . .

When I woke, I found myself strangely satiated after the Dream feast. I wasn't full, not really, and I still needed to eat. But there was less urgency to it, and I found myself more refreshed.

After that, Hiram took me every night into the Dream, showing me the ways of the place. I didn't know if I subscribed entirely to his superstitious drivel about spirits and fairies and such. The place seemed more like some sort of primeval Jungian dreamscape, a sort of shared instinctive experience. Surely there were ways to explain it without resorting to all this talk of gods and demons. But there was no disputing that Hiram knew things that I didn't, and if he needed the language of superstition to share those things, then I decided that a little mumbo jumbo was a small price to pay. I'd eat the meat he fed me, and I'd spit out the bones if need be.

I learned to better understand the ways that I could choose my form in the Dream. As before, it was a matter of discovering the knack of not spoiling what I wanted with too much effort, of letting myself slide into what I wanted rather than to push or pull. It was like learning to ride a wave rather than fight against the current. Once I learned the basics of sliding through the Dream, I found that I could accomplish the sorts of things that make lucid dreaming so appealing. When I leapt, I could ignore the pull of the ground for a moment, no more than a heartbeat really, but it was enough to turn those jumps into brief soaring glides. Sometimes, all I needed to do was think about a place or a thing and I'd find myself sliding to it.

More than once, I found myself thinking of Andy, and wondering how much of this she already knew. What was she that she was able to venture here to our primal hunting grounds? Thoughts of Andy led me to lose focus. I'd remember her peculiar smell, the smell that wasn't unlike the powerful smell of the plants there in the Dream, and likewise the emerald fleck in her eye that matched the moonlit pine boughs above me. Once or twice, when thinking of the strange girl and her bewitching eyes, I'd spy a black-winged shape flitting in the branches far above, but whenever I turned my head to see if it was her, there'd be nothing there. Hiram, always beside me, never seemed to notice. Had it been her? Spying on me still? I couldn't be sure.

In the waking world, following Hiram across another alpine valley, I found myself worrying about Andy, and about Blue and the rest of the pack. I knew that Smedley and the other dogs would be fine. I'd had to leave them for a time before, and they were good at hunting as well as relying on the generosity of my neighbors who I knew would never let them starve. But Andy and Blue were in another situation entirely. The girl had left with my Chevy and my dog in order to protect herself. I couldn't blame her for that. Hell, I'd have told her to do exactly that if I'd had the chance.

Was she safe? Blue would look after her, I knew. The dog had taken a liking to the waifish teenager even sooner than I had, but there are some dangers that even a dog as good and loyal as Blue couldn't guard against. Drug trafficking bikers and a rampaging bloodthirsty Garou came to mind, and Andy seemed, somehow, mixed up with both.

I wanted to talk to her, and I was fairly sure now that I'd be able to do just that in the Dream, if she were willing. I suspected that Hiram was keeping her at bay, perhaps not intentionally, but I couldn't fault the girl for not wanting to come too close to the great wolf who had tried to snap her out of the sky when they'd last met. Perhaps, if I could manage to get to the Dream without Hiram, maybe then I could at least learn whether or not she was alright.

"How much longer until you decide whether or not you need to put me down?" I said as we crossed another rocky stream.

"Ah," he said, turning and dropping his bag. "Are you so eager?"

"I'd just as soon know where I stand."

"No," he shook his head. "Your mind is elsewhere. You're eager to be where your mind is. What is your hurry?"

"What's my hurry? The killer is still out there, or have you forgotten?"

"I've forgotten nothing," he said sternly. "Yes, there is a killer, and it may well be my Yarrow, but the moon is fading now. A mad Turnskin will be quieter for the time being. There will not be more kills until the moon begins to fill again."

He was right about the moon. It had been shrinking the past few nights from a thick crescent to a sharp sliver, and as it had done so, I had felt my own wolf quieting in his cage. It had helped that he had been finding so much release in the Dream of late, hunting spirit prey rather than people, but with the waning of the moon, our journeys to the Dream became more and more tenuous. Last night it had taken me longer than ever to slide sideways into the ancient forest, and even Hiram had seemed smaller and less present once we were there.

"But what if she isn't just mad? The murders haven't been entirely random. Going after Mack was calculated."

"Yes, but even the mad are not mindless," he said. "Besides, if our lost Turnskin does kill while you are here with me, far away, then we will have proved that you cannot be the killer, won't we?"

"At the low price of somebody else's life?"

"What would you have me do?" he said. "Put you down

now, to be safe? Tear out your throat and build you a cairn here in the mountains where nobody will ever find you and return to wait for the real killer to reveal herself?"

"Well, no," I said, "preferably not..."

The moon was so far gone now that my wolf barely stirred at the implied threat to my life. It occurred to me then, that it was almost the new moon, when I had planned to kill myself. Here I was, far away from my gun. But if I knew that the new moon would be the easiest time to kill me, wouldn't Hiram know that as well?

No, that was paranoid. Why would he have taught me for this past week only to murder me on the night of the new moon? He might be a little bit nuts, but he wasn't some evil witch who wanted to fatten me up on sweets so he could eat me once I was good and fat. On the other hand, I wasn't the only one who would be more vulnerable during the new moon, was I?

"You're afraid," I said suddenly.

"What?"

"You're up here because you don't want to risk facing the killer when the moon is dark, when you won't be able to rely on your wolf."

He glared at me with eyes that were beginning to look more brown than yellow.

"You're a coward," I said softly, meeting his eyes more fully than I ever had, knowing that I was correct.

He drew his lip back in a snarl, but his wolf wasn't behind it, and he struck at me, hitting my chest with his open palm and sending me stumbling backward, falling on my ass in the shallow, icy water.

"Do not confuse cowardice with good sense," he hissed at me.

I rose to my feet and lunged at him, taking him with my shoulder against his gut and pulling him to the ground. He'd struck first, and I'd had enough of playing the submissive beta. If we were going to have it out, now was as good a time as any.

We rolled there, trading positions on the rocks, elbows and knees colliding with stones and snowpack as often as with each other. We both grunted and cursed, neither of us snarling or growling as we would have a day or two earlier, the wolves within us being nearly dormant observers. This was a fight between two men.

He was older, it was true, but not so old as to be weak. And with his age came a great deal of experience. I put up a respectable struggle, and he'd feel it later, but it wasn't long before he'd taken my back. From behind me, he wrapped an arm around my throat, constricting my breath as I pried at his wiry arm to no effect. With his other arm he drew his bowie knife, bringing the cold steel blade to my throat in warning.

I'd long known about the danger iron posed to me. Hiram had even mentioned it as he had rambled on about his spirits and demons. Iron was the bane of the spirit world, he had told me, that was why it was used against fairies in old folk tales. I don't know about fairies, but iron, and the steel made from it, will do just fine against one of our kind. Whatever resistance our wolves give us against other injuries seems to give way to weapons of iron, leaving us every bit as vulnerable as anybody else.

I paused, determined to make a respectable show of it, prying once more at his left arm, but I couldn't escape his grip. Finally, struggling for breath, I tapped his arm three times in submission. A moment later he released me and left me kneeling in the stream, coughing for breath.

"Watch your tongue," he grunted with a pained voice, still holding his knife as he stood back from me on the rocks beside the stream.

I dragged myself to the other bank of the glacial trickle and sat there, catching my breath for a moment longer, then nodded at him in acknowledgement. It wasn't an apology, but it was all he was going to get from me. He put his knife away.

"You don't think you can take her without your wolf?" I croaked. "Why? Wouldn't she be just as vulnerable?"

"Yes, she would be," he said, "if she were alone and unprepared."

"You think she's not alone?"

"I don't know, but she made you, didn't she? Maybe she wants a pack of her own. She never was one to submit easily."

"I can't imagine..." I said wryly.

Hiram chuckled reluctantly and put a hand to his ribs where my knee had connected earlier.

I rose to my feet and found myself favoring my left ankle and rubbing at my throat.

"Hiram, I'm not willing to wait while more people die," I said.

"But you will," he said. "Unless you want to challenge me again."

"You're saying you'll make me?"

"Yes."

I felt my mouth tighten in anger. My wolf breathed heavily in the back of my mind, barely taking notice.

"It doesn't bother you that more people could die?"

Seeing that I had chosen words over violence, Hiram took a seat on a small boulder and put his hands on his knees.

"Shepard," he said, "it is good that you would avoid needless death if you could. It speaks to your character. You're not the killer you think you are. But people die. Death isn't evil, it simply is, and you can't take it on yourself to bear responsibility for the actions of others."

"Isn't that what you're doing? Isn't that why you're here?" His hypocrisy pissed me off.

"No," he said calmly, "I take responsibility for myself only. I taught Yarrow. She is more dangerous because of those lessons, and so I will do what I can to stop these killings if she is behind them. But her actions are hers, not mine."

"And that's good enough for you?" He could hear the judgement in my voice and furrowed his brow at me as he spat his answer.

"Yes, more than that would be arrogance."

"That's horse shit!" I said.

"No, it's just the way things are."

"And that's the wisdom you brought me up here to learn? To teach me not to give a crap if bad things happen so long as it isn't my business? That's the grand philosophy you've cultivated over the years? The Tao of Not Giving a Fuck?"

"Careful, boy..."

"Maybe you're the one who needs a teacher. Let me tell you something about the 'way things are', while you sit on your mountaintop, above the problems of the little people with their short lives. Some of those little lives are full of nothing but pain and fucking misery. You can hear them if you ever bother to come down off your mountain and listen. I hear them all the time. I hear them crying to themselves when they think nobody can hear them. I hear them praying to nobody to come and help them, to make the pain go away, to make it all stop, or just to hear them. And you know what, nobody answers. Nobody is listening. Nobody but me. And your idea of enlightenment is what... they can go fuck themselves?"

I thought of Mack, how he had prodded me again and again over the years to help with cases that were too big for him. I remembered the way he was always trying to make things better, to make the world better, usually one person at a time. I'd mocked him for it, told him it was pointless, but he always came back and dragged me out for 'just one more time' and I'd go. I'd told him again and again that it wasn't our problem. Another missing kid, another battered wife, another brutal pimp, another child rapist. There was no end to them. Why bother? But he never stopped caring, no matter how many times I'd called him a fool, or how many times I told him...

"It doesn't matter," Hiram said.

Hearing my old mantra out of Hiram's mouth finally brought things into focus. Mack was gone. He'd never talk me into helping another person, never push me out the door for another lost cause. He'd spent a lifetime trying to make the world better. Trying to make me better. Had it all been for nothing? Had it not mattered?

"You're wrong," I said, smiling a little from the corner of my mouth. I turned around, took my bearings, and began to walk away.

"Shepard?" Hiram said.

"Shepard, stop," he said more loudly as I got farther away.

"Shepard, where do you think you're going?" he yelled from far behind me.

"I'm going hunting," I said softly, to nobody in particular.

CHAPTER THIRTY-THREE

Anger doesn't keep you warm, at least not after the moment has passed. I ruminated on this little pearl of wisdom as I struggled to build a fire in the darkness.

I'd walked for hours, even running a bit after leaving Hiram, determined to get as far as I could before the sun set. With my wolf nearly dormant as the moon waned, I found it more difficult than I had anticipated to maintain the pace I'd intended. Also, as the sunlight left me, I became aware of how damp and cold I'd become. Yet another thing that wouldn't have concerned me if the wolf had been with me more fully.

After I realized that I was shivering and stumbling in the darkness, I'd decided that I had gone as far as I could until the sun rose. I'd taken nothing with me when I'd stormed away from Hiram, and I was a little surprised that he had neither tried to stop me nor caught up with me. It seemed that he was going to let me go. Maybe he hoped that I'd find this mad wolf he was hunting and solve his problem for him, or perhaps he'd just decided that I was more trouble than I was worth. Whatever his reason, the results suited me just fine. I'd searched my pockets for resources and found only a couple of dollars and a bit of loose change, a few small smooth rocks that I'd pocketed for hunting, and my battered old zippo lighter.

As the lighter was low on fuel, I tried to collect as much tinder as I could in the darkness. Everything seemed damp. In time, I found some dry chips of wood that I could tear away from the underside of an old, rotted log. By starlight, I could almost make out the legion of termites or ants that I knew I had disturbed as I dug into their home, but there was nothing for it. Before long I had a respectable little pyramid of dry rubble and crispy moss that would have burned nicely if my lighter had cooperated, but it didn't. I could produce a small flame for a second or two before it sputtered out, but nothing like the sustained flame I'd need to get things started.

I sat with my back against the log, facing the spot where I'd failed to produce a fire. I held my knees to my chest and took shallow breaths as my teeth chattered. I wasn't in any danger. Not really. However distant my wolf might be, I wasn't going to die out here, but that didn't mean that I couldn't spend the night suffering. That was just what I needed, to go off and pit myself against the Garou who had made me with an empty stomach and a tired body and mind. That idea did strike me as more than a little dangerous. Right then, I'd have happily spent my last dollar for a book of matches or a bit of lighter fuel.

"Your last dollar?" I said to myself as I rapped my knuckles against my temple. "You idiot."

Fumbling in the pocket of my jacket, I drew out a wrinkled and torn dollar bill and realized that I didn't exactly have anything better to spend it on at the moment. I prepared a space in my tinder and folded the dollar a little to maximize the airflow and then lit it carefully within the folds of my jacket. It caught. Quickly, but as carefully as I could with shaking hands, I pressed the burning face of our first president into the little nook I'd prepared within the tinder and shielded it from the wind with my hands as I hoped that General Washington could get the job done.

Minutes later, my one-dollar fire was warming my fingers and toes as I fed it with the sticks I had gathered earlier. The little light from the dancing flames helped me gather more fuel from the surrounding area, and soon I was curled up beside the fire with my back to the log, soaking in the heat and preparing myself for what would come tomorrow.

By my reckoning, I should be able to hit the North Cascades Highway sometime tomorrow afternoon, and if I was lucky, I could hitch a ride. As I am seldom lucky, I also considered the possibility that I may need to steal a car, but I hoped not. From there... hell, I didn't know where to go from there. Andy had my Chevy and without Mack I had no idea how to reach her. Thoughts of Mack reminded me that I was likely still wanted in connection to my old friend's death. If I just showed up to poke through Mack's phone book or notes I'd probably find myself arrested or shot, and this time of the month that bullet would pack more of a punch. Still, Andy was the key, that much I was sure of, if for no other reason than because I had no other ideas. Besides, the girl was the only common link I could think of between the murders so far. Well, the only common link aside from myself, that was.

I lay against the log, ignoring the feeling of the bugs crawling up my pantleg and under my shirt, and looked at the needle-thin sliver of the moon in the cold, clear sky. At least the moon was nearly dark. Andy should be safe for the time being.

Without trying to, and that seemed to be the key after all, I found myself sliding into the wolf dream. It was dim and a bit out of focus compared to earlier visits, and when I looked at my hands, I could almost convince myself that I could see through them and make out the shapes of the gigantic trees beyond. I was barely there.

The smells and sounds of the primeval forest were invigorating, as always, though they seemed somehow more distant than I'd come to expect. But then, I'd never been here before when the moon was this dark. I suspected that tomorrow when the moon was completely dark, I wouldn't be able to find my way here at all. It was probably only the practiced ease I'd developed under Hiram's tutelage and the habit I'd gotten into of coming here every night that had let me slip here at all.

Hiram?

The thought of him poked at my sleepy wolf's consciousness and I sniffed at the air but found no trace of his now familiar scent. My nose seemed feeble and clumsy, a nearly human thing. Did Andy find it as hard to find her way here on moonless nights?

Andy?

A thought occurred to me then, something that I had little hope would work but that I may as well try. I focused on my thoughts of the girl, of her bewitching green-flecked eyes and her peculiar maple-blossom scent, and I wished myself to wherever she was.

The terrain shifted, trees and mountains moving around me until I found myself a little ways from where I had been. But I quickly lost my focus and was standing still on ephemeral legs again, the trees even more dim than they had been.

Remembering what I'd learned, I realized that I'd been trying too hard. I was pushing and pulling when I needed to be letting go, and I'd almost pushed myself all the way out of the Dream entirely. It occurred to me that if I pushed myself out now, I likely wouldn't find my way back in until the moon returned in a couple of days.

It wasn't in my nature to let go. I'd learned white-knuckle control over decades of self-denial, and it was no easy thing to loosen that grip now in the face of urgent need, but I knew it was exactly what was required In the Dream. I closed my eyes and took a deep, cleansing breath, letting the faint taste of the woods clear my mind. I released the breath and some of the tension in my neck and shoulders went with it, but I didn't open my eyes.

I continued my breathing with closed eyes and thought again of Andy. She of the emerald fleck and springtime smell. Willowy Andy with her dyed hair and the new baby growing in her belly. I released another breath and thought I could feel the world shifting around me, but I tried to ignore that sensation, tried to let it go so that I could keep my focus on where I wanted to go. Andy, with her bruised face and strangely fearless way of looking up at me from her tiny frame, utterly convinced that I was no threat to her. I released another breath as the world fluttered around me and the smells changed. I kept my eyes closed and thought of Andy. I thought of the taste she had left on the cigarette she had half smoked and the way she had shielded Rita's baby with her own body when things had turned violent. The Dream world shifted once more around me and then grew still. I opened my eyes.

I was... in a city? I'd never realized that there were cities in the wolf dream. I'd never come to one before. Maybe that was because my wolf had never wanted to. It was a familiar but altogether alien scene. The buildings seemed like dim reflections of what they should be, more like a faded painting than real mortar and wood. Little blurs of shadow moved slowly from place to place, vaguely in the shape of people who paid me no mind. Was this real? I knew this place. At least, I thought I did. A small town not too far from Mack's place, a little closer to the mountains. Snohomish? Why was I here?

"Francis?" The voice echoed distantly from above me as I stood gaping at my surroundings on the street corner.

Snapping my head up and raising my ghostly hands to ward

off danger, my eyes locked on the glossy black raven perched on the side of a house.

"A—Andy?"

"Francis?" she said again. "I can barely hear you."

"Andy? It is you? I can't believe that worked."

"What? What did you say?" She dove off the side of the house and flapped her shadowy wings twice, coming to rest on the impression of a bench beside me. She fixed her eyes on me, the emerald fleck glimmering, and she came more fully into focus. Or maybe I did.

"Andy? Can you hear me?"

"A little," she said as the raven cocked her head at me and then looked around. "The other one, is he...?"

"He's not with me," I said.

"Good. Are you alright? I thought maybe I wouldn't see you again."

"Yes, yes I'm fine. Andy, where are you? I'm coming back. I need to find you."

"I'm moving around a lot," she said. "Blue and I are sleeping in your car right now." What could only be a smile formed on the corner of the raven's mouth. "She's such a sweet dog."

I couldn't help myself. I smiled a little at the thought of my dog keeping this strange girl safe in the back of my Blazer somewhere.

"Thanks for keeping her safe," I said to Andy, knowing that she was too proud to appreciate the thought in reverse.

"She misses you, I think," she said. "Where are you?"

"In the mountains. I'm walking out. Can you pick me up?"

"Sure, I think, but I think they're looking for me."

"Who is looking for you? The police?" I asked.

"Sure, them too, but that's not what I meant. Lodi and the other Perdidos. They've been riding all over the place. I can't go home." At the mention of home she looked up at the house she had been perched on when I'd found her.

"Is that where this is?"

"Yes," she said, "this is where my dad lives. I was worried about him. But he's okay."

"Andy, I'm going to clear this up," I promised her, feeling guilty that I had stirred things up with the bikers, and that this child was paying the price. I thought of the bag of heroin in the back of my Blazer with a memory of longing, but not physical need. Hiram had done me a bit of a favor by forcing me to detox in the mountains. "But I need to get back first."

"Where do you want me to go?" she asked.

"Do you know the North Cascades Highway?" I said. "Highway Twenty?"

"Um, I think so. I can find it."

"Good, I don't know exactly where I'll come out in the morning. Somewhere out by Marblemount, I'm guessing, but I can't be sure. Just drive east. I'll be the dirty bearded hobo walking the other way. We're bound to run into each other."

"Okay," she said nervously. "I'll do my best."

"In the meantime," I said, "just keep your head down and stay safe. That's more important. Don't let them find you."

"I know that," she said impatiently and a little offended, giving me a raven glare. "I'm not stupid."

"I know you're not." I stifled a laugh that I knew would make her angry. "That's why I'm asking for your help."

"Okay then," she said. "North Highway, Marble Mountain. I'll do it."

"North Cascades Highway," I said, "and Marblemount."

"That's what I said!" she squawked ravenishly.

A new scent tickled at the edge of my senses and my lethargic wolf raised his hackles reluctantly. It was a predatory smell, familiar. A wolfish smell.

I looked around and Andy, picking up at the alarm in my posture, did the same.

"What is it? Is it that other one?" she asked.

"I'm not sure," I said, still sniffing at the air. "I think so. We'd better go."

"Okay, but..." she hesitated.

"But what?" I asked.

"Just... what are you going to do?" She sounded like a little girl then, rather than a raven, forgetting for a moment to act tough and letting her anxiety show in an unguarded moment.

"Don't worry," I told her with a wolfish grin. "You've got the big bad wolf on your side now."

"You're not so bad," she said with renewed confidence and then echoed the long-ago words of my sister that she had fished from my dreams. "You're a good man Francis."

I wanted to let her believe it. I wanted to let her take comfort in the lie she had told herself about me, so I said nothing. Instead, I gave her a wink as I pulled myself up and out of the wolf dream. I didn't wake. Not yet. It was still a long way until sunrise, and there was time yet to dream the dreams that were only mine. Time to remember that I wasn't a good man at all. Time to remember that I was a monster.

PART 6

IT HAD TO BE YOU

Casualty Record Office,
2 – 7 – 1918
Sir,
It is my painful duty to inform you that a report has been received from the War Office notifying the death of:
(No.) 10795(Rank) Lc. Cpl.
(Name) Francis Shepard
(Regiment) 6th Regiment, 4th Brigade, U.S. Marines
which occurred with B.E.F. France
on the 24th June 1918
The report is to the effect that he <u>was Killed in Action</u>
By His Majesty's command I am to forward the enclosed message of sympathy from Their Gracious Majesties the King and Queen, I am at the same time to express the regret of the Army Council at the soldier's death in his Country's service.
I am to add that any information that may be received as to the soldier's burial will be communicated to you in due course.

A separate leaflet dealing more fully with this subject is enclosed.

    I am,

    Sir

    Your obedient Servant,

    W. Jacobs. Colonel.

CHAPTER THIRTY-FOUR

AFTER THE WAR.
  1919 AND BEYOND.

Maggie received word of my death in late July, 1918, something I learned of much later. I was preoccupied with my own changed circumstances, having spent the month wandering the countryside and trying to make sense of what had happened to me. Those first few nights after my change, while the moon was still bright in the French sky, still feel more like a half-remembered, feverish nightmare than a real memory.

Northern France was a haunted place, more so than even Madsen could have suspected, and I had thought him so naïve. The smells and sounds of war wove a cacophony of blood and suffering that I had only barely glimpsed before I'd been bitten. Everywhere I looked were ghosts. Years of battle had left thousands of shades wandering the hills and fields, and in those first days, I didn't know how to shut them out of my senses. The spirits of the dead seemed to bleed together in a senseless tapestry of pain and fear. They seemed drawn to me. Each night they would crowd around me, silently begging or threatening me until I was utterly overwhelmed. It very nearly drove me mad.

I was a creature of instinct in those first days, a monster, and I wasn't alone. The ghouls that had tried to eat me, the ones that Madsen had been so fascinated with, were everywhere. They were stealthy, silent things that lurked underground in burrows that they dug to hide themselves during the day, but at night they emerged to feast on the dead and dying. The fetid and rotting smell of the things that had so sickened me when I'd first encountered them now burned my heightened senses and triggered a blind rage in me that I was as yet unfamiliar with.

I don't know how to explain the effect that the smell of the ghouls had on me. It was stronger than disgust or anger. They smelled wrong. Their presence *offended* me and drove me to a righteous fury. Each night, I would follow their blasphemous stench and launch myself at them, killing a few before the rest would scurry back into their holes and tunnels to wait for safer feeding. I didn't know what exactly they were or where they came from, only that I had to kill them. All of them. But no matter how many I culled, there always seemed to be more the next night. It was as if they were bred by war itself. As if human death on such an unprecedented scale had broken something in the world. As if the war had opened a wound in the side of the earth and these things had swarmed to it like flies.

The ghouls weren't the only things I hunted in those first days. The sight of a German soldier was enough to send me into a mindless rage in which my actions were a dream-like blur. After such berserk outbursts, I would puzzle over the blood and gore caking my hands and chin while marveling at the wounds in my own flesh that mended themselves before my eyes. I was aware of the smell and sounds of others like me as well, like the one who had changed me, but they kept their distance.

Sometimes I'd find signs of their own kills, bits of ghoul rapidly decomposing in the morning sunlight, or German or even allied corpses with cuts and bites that I knew now hadn't been inflicted by bayonets. Sometimes I'd glimpse these others, at the edge of a clearing or across a field. Our eyes would lock and something in me would cower. My newborn inner wolf forced me to flee in the face of a dominant predator. It wasn't fear, exactly, but a deferential instinct not to encroach on the territory of a superior. A sense of rank that my human self could understand easily enough.

In my calmer moments, as I lingered just out of sight near the humans that I knew I no longer belonged with, I could overhear them talking about the things in the woods. "Garou," the French said with a frightened reverence. "Werwolf," a German soldier whispered fearfully to another. It was years later that I heard the word "Teufelshunde." Folklore held that the German soldiers used the word to describe the U.S. Marines who fought them there in Belleau Wood. Devil-dogs. I don't know the truth of that story or whether I had anything to do with its origins. I don't really care one way or the other.

Slowly, as the moon waned, I came more and more to my human senses. I scavenged clothes and chickens from a farmhouse and tried not to think too hard about what I might have been filling my belly with for the past weeks. I started to feel almost like myself again and began to give serious thought to what I was supposed to do with myself.

Was I a deserter? I considered returning to my unit and remembered how I had tried to do just that when I'd first risen as whatever I was now. Barnes had been horrified; he'd shot at me. No doubt, by now, he had told everybody what he had seen. Probably they had mocked him and dismissed his claims. Barnes was an easy man to dismiss, but if I returned to them now there would be a lot of questions to answer, and I wasn't sure that I would know how. Besides, I was feeling better now, more like myself, but could I be certain that it would stay that way? Maybe the nightmare of the past few weeks was behind me and would fade as time went on. I hoped so, but I couldn't quite be sure.

I toyed with the idea that maybe I'd gone mad. Maybe the past few weeks could be explained by shell shock or by that blow to the head I'd taken. I'd seen men behave in all sorts of bizarre ways. Some had even lost the ability to speak and had acted little better than animals. That idea seemed to make sense, but then I sniffed at the little bits of blood under my fingernails and poked at the pristine bits of flesh where I'd been injured before and knew that madness couldn't explain everything. Unless I was still mad.

The ghosts still swarmed around me near the battlefields, a bit dimmer and less insistent with the fading moon, but still present. It was the ghosts as much as anything else that made up my mind for me. I needed to get away from the dead. If I was a deserter, then I may as well desert properly and get the' hell away from the war.

I made my way across France on foot at first, without much of a plan other than to put my back to the fighting and my face toward home. A day or two away from the front and things got much better. I didn't realize at the time that the moon was fully dark. I just assumed that it was the war that was the problem, that the further I got away from the fighting the more like myself I would feel. For a while, my theory seemed to prove correct.

But then the moon came back.

I'd gotten a good distance from the front, having walked and kept my head down through farmland and eventually stolen a ride on a passing train. I'd avoided major roads and cities in order to prevent being taken as a deserter while I formed some sort of a plan to get myself home. I'd been heading toward the

Atlantic coast, thinking only that I couldn't go to Brest or Calais if I wanted to avoid being shot as a deserter. The warm July weather made it a simple matter to sleep outside, and though the war itself was further away by the day, there was no escaping the effects of the war. Every house seemed peopled by children, women, and old men alone, and a sort of mournful somberness colored the people I saw.

Speaking of color, I'd begun to miss the reds and greens that I had taken for granted my whole life. During the frenzy of my first change, I was preoccupied with so much of my world being turned upside down that a shift in my vision seemed trivial. My other senses had captivated my attention. I was constantly startled at how sounds and smells seemed to assault me. One night, I woke with a start from my sleep beneath a hedgerow because I'd heard some large creature coming near. It sounded like a large dog or perhaps even a horse tramping through the underbrush toward me, but it had turned out to be only a little field mouse scurrying over dry grass. Another day, I found myself salivating at the smell of meat roasting nearby and expected to find the home where it was being cooked around the next bend, but following my nose I found that the family who had shared the meal had lived at least three miles off and had finished the food long before I saw them.

These changes helped me overlook the loss of color in my world. The loss had been more than compensated for, really. I could smell all the green things in ways that I had never been able to see them in my earlier life, and both flowers and bloody meat lent a richness and depth to my senses now that could never be represented by something as dull as a color. Sure, I couldn't see greens and reds like most people anymore, but when I thought back on my childhood I felt that I'd seen plenty of red. Too much really. I don't miss it.

Although my vision was in some ways diminished, in other

ways my eyes were sharper than ever. I required far less light than I had before the change and found myself walking comfortably long after dark if there were any stars or sliver of moon at all to give me light. Discovering this, I decided it would be wiser for me to travel by night and sleep during the day in order to avoid notice.

Night by night, as the sliver of moon grew thicker and brighter to light my way, I found my senses growing sharper while the alien urges and instincts grew stronger. I tried to deny this at first, telling myself that I was merely tired and hungry, or perhaps that I was falling ill. I was far from ill, though. I felt rejuvenated and energized with each moonrise. There was a well of vitality and primal strength burning in my breast now that eclipsed the boundless and often misspent energy of childhood. The only thing I had to compare to it was the tireless invincibility that came with the heat of battle. I was intoxicated with the sounds and smells of the night, so much so that I forgot to pay attention to the information my senses provided as I reveled in them.

The men approached me from upwind, more out of luck than any sort of skill, I think. I was laying on my back, half-dozing with a belly full of stolen chicken as I marveled at the dance of the birds against the backdrop of the drifting clouds. I was smiling stupidly to myself like a drunken vagrant, which is exactly what they took me for.

"Identifiez-vous!" a man's voice called from nearby.

Without thinking, I scrambled to my feet and crouched defensively, baring my teeth at them. I don't doubt that I made an odd sight, having lived in the dirt and bushes for the better part of a month, unshaven and unbathed.

Two men and a dog stood before me. One man was old and grey. Too old to serve in the war. Too old really to do much at all without help. The other wasn't a man at all, but a boy, perhaps fourteen years old, almost old enough to falsify his age and enlist if the war went on much longer. Both men carried guns, shotguns I think, though I wasn't thinking too clearly about that at the time, and their dog stood in front of them, stock still and dutifully pointing at me with its own hackles raised. The men were dressed modestly, their farmer's clothes patched and well worn.

"Ce n'est pas un renard," the boy said to who was probably his grandfather as the old man leveled his gun at me.

The dog began to growl at me. It was that growl, as much as the implied threat of the gun or the shock of being taken unaware, that awakened the wolf. He'd been content, asleep in the back of my head after glutting himself the night before, and had seemed happy to warm us in the morning sun. But now he was being challenged. Challenged by an old man, a boy, and a mutt. It was the first time I was fully aware of the wolf rising to the surface, of my eye-teeth bursting from my gums and growing into fangs, of the sharp claws that had been my fingernails lengthening as the hair on my body thickened slightly and stood on end.

I met the dog's eyes and returned his growl, with interest.

"Mon Dieu," the old man gasped as the dog whimpered and ran back the way they had come with his tail between his legs, pissing itself in terrified submission.

The eyes of the old man and the boy echoed the terror of their dog. They each stumbled backward as I advanced a step toward them. Not looking where he was going, the old man tripped and fell backwards, squeezing the trigger of his shotgun as he fell.

The blast took me in the shoulder and the side of my face, tearing my clothes and skin and spraying my blood in a fine mist. It staggered me, but only for a moment. I met the old man's wide eyes and roared with more force than I knew was in me.

All of that vitality and strength I'd been feeling was driven before me in a primeval cry of predatory rage, and I shot forward toward the old man, determined to kill him.

Moving with a surprising quickness of his own, the young boy put himself between me and his fallen elder. He struggled with his trembling hands to bring his own gun to bear on me, but the fear had him, and so did I. With a swipe of my clawed right hand, I tore the gun from his hands and probably broke his arm in the bargain. With an unthinking swipe of my left hand I tore into his ribs and sent him flying out of my way. He landed more than ten feet away with a muffled cry of pain and surprise.

I watched, more than participated, as my monstrous body grabbed the old man by the throat and lifted him from the ground, bringing him to my face. I could feel the muscles of my jaw tensing with angry anticipation as I drew back my other hand and prepared to take his head off, waiting only for the old man to meet my eyes before I finished him.

But he didn't meet my eyes. Instead his eyes struggled to find the boy I had dispatched so easily, searching frantically for him.

"Laurent..." the old man croaked feebly as he searched for his grandson. There was fear on his face, but it was all for the boy. He'd saved none of it for himself.

The wolf hesitated. The man refused to meet our eyes. Had he submitted? At the same time, my human self came to a sudden realization. This was a good man I was about to kill. He had come out with his grandson, a boy he clearly loved more than his own life, in search of the fox who they thought had killed their chickens. They had found the culprit, and it was no fox. I was about to kill this man and perhaps had already killed his grandson. This was wrong. This was vile, and I could not be a part of it.

"No!" I growled through lupine fangs, but the wolf didn't release our prey.

He wanted this man. He had hurt us. He had to pay. It was right.

He is prey!

"Oh...la douleur..." the faint moan came from where the boy had fallen.

In response, the old man began to struggle, ignoring me entirely except for wrinkled fingers that pried feebly at my monstrous grip as he fought to turn toward the boy.

No, I replied to the beast who had taken my body, *he is not.*

One finger at a time I forced the fingers of my own hand from the old farmer's throat. Incrementally, my grip loosened, and bit by bit I felt my body's control returning to me.

In a last act of defiance, the wolf opened our mouth and released a deafening roar in the man's face. As this happened, I drew on every memory of my father. All the hate I'd had for him for hurting people who never deserved it. Every promise I'd made myself as a child that I'd never be like him. I pushed every ounce of that childhood loathing and disgust into my arm, and I shoved the old man away from me, releasing him to stumble to the ground.

Instantly, even as he caught his breath, he scrambled on all fours to where the young boy had fallen.

"Laurent," he struggled to make the words form at first, and then added more in a pained rasp, "Je suis la."

The wolf in me wanted them still, wanted both of them. It raged against me within my own head, but I had control now, if only briefly. As the old man tended to the boy, I turned toward the trees and hills and moved as fast as I could, running in long leaping strides across the French countryside.

CHAPTER THIRTY-FIVE

I signed on with a transatlantic steamer in La Rochelle. With the dearth of able-bodied young men, on account of the war, they hired me without any questions and quickly put me to work stoking the engines. It was miserable, sweaty work, but I was glad of it. Spending nearly all my time below deck and with strenuous work to occupy and exhaust my body helped to keep my new instincts subdued. The wolf in me seemed frightened by the small dark spaces and the smells of grease and coal smoke. At times that fear threatened to spill over into anger. On those occasions, I worked myself even harder, volunteering to forgo my own sleep and taking the shifts of other workers who had offered to pay me with some of the opium they'd smuggled on board.

I'd never had interest in opium, but now I remembered the warm and dazed feeling that the morphine had given me in the infirmary after my run in with mustard gas, and I remembered the long trances that my mother would enter after taking her 'medicine'. After three days without sleep, I needed rest but couldn't trust myself to let my guard down. Not with the moon waxing ever brighter over our Atlantic flotilla. I decided that a little medicine might in fact be just the thing that I needed.

A black skinned fellow whose name I never bothered to learn, and whose French was colored with a heavy African accent, showed me how to use his pipe, and immediately I knew I had found the answer to my problem. The agitated wolf in the back of my mind seemed to withdraw sluggishly, and I let myself drift into dreamless sleep.

It worked, mostly. As the moon grew, I found my temper growing shorter during my work shifts. The occasional swigs of rum helped to take the edge off, but it was less effective as time went on. On the night of the full moon itself, I sensed that I was particularly dangerous, having almost taken the head off a man who had looked at me wrong earlier. My motley shipmates had grown weary of my brusque temper and threatening glances and refused to give me more opium. Already, I smoked more than any of them. So, I worked myself to exhaustion and smoked all of the drug that I'd managed to bargain for, steal, and hoard, but it wasn't enough.

My dreams were red. Hunting dreams. Fighting dreams. I didn't know or care what I fought, they were just shapes, voices, but I lashed out at them just the same, releasing the furious instincts that had built up behind my poppy-smothered sleep.

I don't know when exactly I realized that I wasn't dreaming, but there were four or five large and sweaty men struggling to hold me down. A different man had their full weight on each of my arms and legs. Another burly bastard straddled my chest and had his hands on my shoulders, tendons bulging from his neck as he fought to pin me. Each one of them outweighed me individually, but even so, together they fought hard to keep me down as I thrashed and snarled in the dark belly of the ship.

No! Stop! I tried to take the reins from my wolf-self. These men were our shipmates. We were in the middle of the ocean.

This was not helping. But the wolf didn't listen. The moon was full, and these stinking apes were trying to make us submit, we should show them!

Between the effects of the opium and my own horrified resistance to what was happening, my body remained largely unchanged as I bucked and thrashed.

"Donne moi..." the man atop me grunted as he lifted one hand to reach for an object being held to him from another man. It resembled a wrench or hammer of some sort, but I didn't care. I cared only about tearing the throat from the bastard above me.

"Mon Dieu, ses yeux!" another voice declared fearfully as the big man accepted the wrench and brought it to bear.

His filthy gorilla arm swung the tool with all the force he could muster and brought it down against my skull. The heavy metal crushed through skin and bone in a way that the bullets had not. A wave of cold, electric shock flooded my limbs, and I went temporarily limp as he readied for another swing if he needed it. My vision was blurred now, and my head swam as I struggled to form a single image from the three figures I perceived above me. I blinked at him dumbly, utterly shocked at the sudden vulnerability brought on by my first encounter with cold iron.

It took a handful of heartbeats for my wolf, driven by panic, to reassert himself. The men had relaxed somewhat atop me, thinking me subdued. They had hurt me, hurt us, in a way that nothing else had so far. My instincts took complete control in that moment. We had to get out or kill the creatures that threatened us. There was no other alternative.

I snarled and threw myself forward, still unable to clearly see what I was doing. One arm pulled free from the man who had been holding it, and my hand found the big man atop me. In a flash I had rolled on top of him, reversing our positions.

"Merde!" a voice cried as meaty fingers pried at me from all directions, but they may as well have been pulling at the ship itself. I was immovable. I felt the changes coming over me, the burning itch in my gums and the beds of my nails as fangs and claws prepared to do the work of a predator. The stretching and hardening of my sinews and bones to accommodate the monster that was going to emerge.

The wrench struck my head again, brought up in a mighty swing from the man I was preparing to murder. And again. I felt the cracking of my skull and the shattering of my jaw. I fell limply to the deck and felt the hammering blows continue on my arms and back for a time as darkness flooded my senses.

"Je pense qu'il est mort..." I heard before I lost all awareness.

For once, there were absolutely no dreams. I'd have thought that I was dead, but I had no thoughts at all.

Slowly, a throbbing awareness returned. I had no sense of how much time had passed, just a steady booming that deafened me and sent wave after wave of dull agony through my skull with each beat of what I came to realize was my own heart. My first thought was regret. Regret that I was still alive. Why couldn't I have simply stayed dead? There should have been no coming back from what had been done to me. And yet, there I was, drawing deep and greedy breaths while the wolf within me huddled in the dark recesses of my awakening mind, licking at his wounds.

I opened the eye that wasn't swollen shut, and the dim light redoubled the pain in my skull, drawing a groan from behind my dislocated jaw.

"Ah, so you are awake," a thickly accented male voice said from somewhere nearby.

I tried to turn to face him, but found my arms restrained above me, my weight supported as I hung from my bound wrists. Each attempt to move drew fresh pain from the bruised and cracked bones of my ribs and neck.

"Do not try to move, mon amie," he said. "You won't be going anywhere."

Over the throbbing and pounding in my ears, I heard him move from where he'd been sitting and come towards me. A scraping sound gave way to a brief, blinding flash of light, and a sulfurous cloud tickled my nose as he struck a match. As the light faded, I saw the grey bearded face of the ship's captain as he held the match to a dirty meerschaum pipe. He drew deeply several times before successfully lighting the bowl and blowing the thick smoke toward me.

I coughed, and winced at the pain of it.

"I didn't believe the men when they told me what had happened," he said. "I had thought that they must have killed you over a hand of cards, or perhaps they had caught you stealing, or even trying to touch a man's cock. These things happen."

He puffed again on his pipe as he regarded me. My spinning vision cleared slightly in my good eye, and I saw that he had taken the precaution of standing just out of reach. We were in the hold of the ship, large crates and containers surrounding us on all sides, and my arms were bound tightly in thick coils of rope that hung from above. They held me upright with my back to one of the large containers.

"You looked dead to me," he went on. "We were about to dump your body overboard, but then you moved. With your head bashed in and your face ruined, you moved. And so, I had to wonder about the ridiculous story that the men told me. They say you are a devil. That you have the strength of ten men and eyes that burn in the darkness."

He laughed without humor.

"But you know how it is," he said, "sailors and their stories.

The whole ship is talking about you, you know. No doubt the story has grown with the telling. Probably by now they will be saying that fire flew from your eyes, and that you fought off twenty of them before the Holy Mother herself appeared to give them the strength to bring you down."

Satisfied that I was unable to move, he stepped closer and examined the silver medal of Saint Francis that I had worn since leaving home, holding it delicately in his calloused fingers.

"You are a Catholic too, I see?"

I did not answer.

"The men say we should give you to the sea," he said, "and maybe we will. They are hard workers but superstitious. You've spooked them. Who knows, there could be problems if I don't do what they want. Frightened men are dangerous men. What do you think?"

I said nothing.

"I agree," he said as though I had given him some vaguely insightful and interesting response. "It is best to be patient and think these things through. But I will not risk a mutiny. I need answers. I do not believe in devils and ghost stories, you see, but I need an explanation for the men, mon amie."

He paused and regarded me patiently as I dangled there, looking at him from my one half-opened eye.

"Yes, it could have been drugs I suppose, but then how do you explain your survival? A miracle?"

Again, he laughed.

"Look at you," he said. "A day ago you barely had a face, but now..."

He released my medal and rapped his knuckles against my temple, sending fresh waves of agony through me. A low growl escaped my throat as the wolf within me raised his spectral head to regard our captor.

"You are far from well, but you are much improved. In a few

more days, you might be able to go back to work in the boiler room. That is, if half the men weren't convinced that you are the devil himself."

With the wolf's renewed attention to our plight, the pain in my wounds redoubled. I squeezed my eye tightly shut against the pain as I felt the burning where the worst pain was. It felt like something was crawling beneath my skin, like hundreds of maggots writhing in my wounds. Except that rather than consuming my flesh, this writhing signified the rapid mending of my broken body. It was the slow itching and ache of natural healing, but magnified a hundred-fold, rapid and excruciating.

I heard a sharp intake of breath as the captain marveled at the small movements of my face. A click and eruption of pain from my jaw rocked me as the bones continued to move back into place.

"Mon dieu..." he said to himself. "What in the hell are you?"

I looked up at him then, opening my one good eye, feeling the other swollen eye burning with the pain of repairing itself, and I met the captain's gaze.

He took a sudden step back, dropping his pipe and almost stumbling before catching himself against a cargo container.

"Your eyes, how..."

A low growl met the snarl growing on my mouth as my wolf stared into the old captain. A satisfying stink of fear rose from the man, and my snarl twitched into an involuntary, hungry smile.

"I can't believe it... they were right... the men were right... Mère de Dieu..."

He turned and ran away in a panic, no doubt fetching some of his stronger men to come back and deal with me, this time to be sure that I was thrown overboard for the good of the ship.

My own fear of the situation I was in fed the wolf, lending him renewed strength and speeding my recovery. The pain of my healing, in turn, spurring the wolf even more. I felt my muscles harden and my nails sharpen into claws yet again.

With the captain gone, I turned my attention to the ropes that held me in place. Pulling myself upward, my growing fangs bit into the thick hemp as well as my own skin without regard for the pain. I chewed and tore and ripped at my restraints with the desperation of an animal who would chew its own foot off to escape a trap. Soon I burst free and fell to the ground where strength returned to my arms.

As the captain had observed, I was far from well, but I was growing stronger with each breath. Crouching there in the hold of the growling ship, my wolf growled back at the iron beast that had swallowed us and gave me the only choice that our instincts would accept.

Hunt or hide?

I'd had enough of killing and wanted to avoid any more death if I could. Well, that wasn't entirely true. Half of me wanted to avoid killing. Another part of me reveled in the idea of putting down the greasy men who threatened us, of hunting every soul on this ship until it was ours and ours alone. Thankfully, the part of me that knew better managed to nudge the other half toward the better part of valor.

We climbed effortlessly onto the hulking containers and silently leapt from one to another, hiding behind a tarp in a shadowy corner where men could not easily reach.

Soon, a gang of blustering sailors returned with the captain and found the broken, bloody ropes where they had thought they had me trapped. I smelled the fear and panic coming off of them in waves that turned quickly to anger at the captain as they sought to hide their fear behind bravado.

The rest of the voyage was short and uneventful for me. For the crew it was defined by fruitless efforts to find the devil that hid amongst them. Day after day the ship swarmed with groups of frightened and superstitious sailors who swept the ship for any trace of the monster among them. They told themselves that I must have gone, disappearing into the sea or simply vanishing back to hell where I surely belonged, but they didn't really believe it. Nobody ventured anywhere alone, and everybody kept a watchful eye over their shoulders. Men slept behind locked doors and prayed fervently to their favorite saints as I lurked in the shadows, with the patience and growing hunger of a predator who knows instinctively that silence and stillness are every bit as valuable as fangs and claws.

Less than a week after my disappearance, I overheard the men declare with relief that land was in sight on the horizon. It was only then that I moved from hiding, bursting from the shadows and knocking over a pair of inebriated deckhands who screamed like children at the sight of me. Before their alarm could spread through the ship and bring more men to subdue me, I leapt over the rail and plunged into the cold sea far below, disappearing into the dark waves and swimming toward the distant lights of shore.

Men shouted and cursed in my direction, one even fired a pistol several times at a patch of flotsam not far from where I swam, but they didn't see me. I'd escaped the ship with nobody having died at my hand.

The lights of the ship shrank gradually into the distance, and the faint lights of shore grew as I paddled through the night toward land. I swam steadily, pausing to catch my breath now and then as I floated on my back, but I was quickly spurred on by hunger as much as by fearful thoughts of amorphous sea creatures that may or may not live in the black depths below me.

Nothing came up from the dark to trouble me, and when the sun rose it found me gulping exhausted breaths on a marshy New England beach.

CHAPTER THIRTY-SIX

I began to rethink the wisdom of going home. When I'd left France, I'd had it in mind to return to my family, to my sister Maggie back in Washington. But now I had begun to realize that I hadn't left my monstrous self behind me in no man's land. I had brought the wolf with me and he had emerged again with the moon. How could I bring that home to my sister? I couldn't. I refused to be a danger to her.

I was a man with nowhere to go. No, I wasn't even a man anymore, not really. I was a monster. There was no denying it. I began to wander the country with no particular destination in mind. When there wasn't much moon to draw out the wolf, I would sometimes take an odd job to make a little pocket money. Simple labor mostly, but I'd always leave after a few days when I felt the wolf beginning to stir in me. Other times, I stole what I needed. I wasn't proud of it, but having become a murderous monster, it seemed absurd to balk at stealing a bit of food or a jacket if I could do it without hurting anybody. Any cash that I managed to earn, or steal would usually go toward buying any dope I could get my hands on. This often meant going into cities, which I was only willing to do when the moon was at its darkest.

So I entered into the first of the wandering times in my life. Every full moon found me in a new patch of wilderness where the wolf could hunt and kill his fill of wildlife. Despite my best efforts to put myself beyond the range of people, now and then the wolf's instincts would lead to a farm where we would feast on livestock. A time or two, a shotgun-carrying farmer would even rush out into the night to save his stock from whatever sort of predatory beast he assumed I must be. In those times, with our belly full of hot fresh meat, I would manage to push the wolf into choosing flight over fight. I didn't kill any farmers, but it was a close thing more than once.

When my lunacy had passed, I would spend the darker half of the moon's cycle travelling as far as I could from where I'd had my last hunt. I walked, I hitched rides, I rode the rails. I'd pick up what work I could and got my hands on as much bootlegged liquor or Chinatown opium that I could until the moon grew again in some new place and the cycle repeated itself.

I saw much of the country during my wanderings. Starting in New England and Boston, I walked inland through New York and into the Adirondack Mountains for a time. From there, I followed the mountains and hills into Pennsylvania and West Virginia. I spent some time in Kentucky, and managed to hop a train in Missouri that took me to Colorado. Each month I was somewhere new, and each month, without meaning to, I found myself a little further west. A little closer to home. To Maggie.

As I travelled the country, I saw my share of ghosts, especially at graveyards and old battle sites. Gettysburg was particularly difficult for me, so I quickly learned to avoid such places when I could. I didn't see any others like me, but I wasn't sure I'd know them if I saw them. Once, during a full moon in upstate New York, my wolf caught the scent of something that I thought could be another Garou, but the smell had put a primal fear into my wolf and we had run from that place as fast and far as we could until the sun rose.

Ghouls, it turned out, weren't only a creature of the old world either. Their stench mingled with the smell of human death at a remote farmhouse I stumbled upon in the Alleghenies. The family inside had died some time ago, of the flu I'd guessed—it had been bad that year-and nobody had found them. Nobody human, anyway. The pallid black-eyed creatures I'd met in France were gnawing on the corpses when I followed my nose to the open window. The sight and smell of them brought a furious growl from my throat, even though the moon had only been a modest crescent in the sky that night. The creatures snapped their heads up and hissed at me as the wolf took the reins and launched us into the dead home with claws and fangs at the ready. I never thought about attacking them. I'd just as soon have avoided them if I'd thought about it at all, but that same sense of disgusting *wrongness* came over me at the sight and smell of them and the rest was left to instinct.

I killed one of the ghouls and the other two scattered into the night, chittering in the distance as they crawled into their hidden holes in the woods nearby. I burned that house down when I left, but not before helping myself to the family's pantry first. I needed the canned beans more than they did.

It wasn't all ghosts and monsters as I walked from place to place. I had my dealings with people too, though I avoided them when I could, especially at first when I didn't trust myself not to turn into a murdering fiend at the slightest provocation. Eventually, when my needs were great enough and the moon was dark enough, I tried my luck with human beings.

I found that I could talk to people. I could work beside them, for a time anyway. Hell, one autumn night in Kentucky a widow woman who had needed work done on her house had even taken me into her bed. I was sure that I came across as a bit strange to most people, perhaps shell-shocked from the war as so many boys my age who had come home by then turned out to be, but if I was careful and paid attention to the moon, I wasn't a threat to my sister Maggie, was I? I wasn't sure.

Winter found me in the Rocky Mountains and my wandering stopped. There was nowhere left to go once the snow came. I had months alone with myself, alone with my wolf. We hunted and scavenged and set simple little traps that I'd learned about from reading my childhood stories of mountain men. At first, I thought I'd freeze to death, or starve, but neither of those things happened. My wolf, I found, kept me warm enough, and I learned to tolerate the taste of mice when I couldn't get anything more substantial.

When spring came, and I was able to travel again, I was a changed man. I had lost weight and gained hair for one thing. My clothes were worn thin and hung loose on my wiry body. I'd always been a broad-shouldered man, and a strapping boy before that. I'd grown up hungry and lean, but I wasn't used to being truly skinny. The wolf disapproved of the state of our body. His instincts told me that to be this emaciated was the mark of a bad hunter or of sickness. Coming down from the hills that spring we were ravenous. Hunters in the area told stories for years to come about the year that wolves had killed their livestock by the dozen. Needless to say, I moved on quickly once there was some meat back on my frame.

My time in the wild had brought me a sort of peace with my condition. I could live away from people. I could survive. It also brought a healthy respect for the sort of predator I actually was. There was no way that Maggie would be comfortable with what I had become. I decided again to keep clear of her, for her own sake. By now she probably thought that I must be dead. It had been the better part of a year since my change, since my 'death' in France. What else could she think? It was for the best.

I liked my life in the mountains, thoughts and worries for the world were left behind me for a time, and I let myself follow the instincts that had grown in me. I let myself live the life of a wolf. I moved through the mountains, seeing less and less of the people in the towns and farms below. I hunted, I slept, and I dreamt. I dreamt, sometimes, of home and of Maggie. I'd dream of her crying, struggling, but more and more I dreamed of a great primeval forest with strange lights where I could hunt creatures I'd never imagined.

Another winter came and went, and then another. Francis Shepard was long dead, and I decided to let him rest in peace.

CHAPTER THIRTY-SEVEN

It was Maggie who brought me back to myself, or dreams of her at any rate. Wolf dreams.

I was denned up for the winter again, this time in the Bighorn Mountains of Wyoming, where the hunting was very good. I slept on the skins of deer and elk I'd taken, and I had been giving thought to bringing down a big bull moose who had been encroaching on what I thought of as my territory. When I slept, I dreamed the wolf dreams.

Having hunted to the wolf's content in my waking life, the wolf dreams weren't just a time to stalk and kill. Well, not only. Dreaming I'd find myself wandering, following my nose. I told myself I wasn't looking for anything in particular, but I think a part of me was still trying to go home to my sister.

The faint sound of crying reached my wolf ears one night. The wolf in me was shocked to hear such human sounds in that dream place, the place that was ours. The man in me already knew what I was hearing and ran toward the sound of my crying sister, but I never found her. There was only ever more primordial wilderness, more endless wild, and the harder I ran, the fainter her voice became, until I lost it.

The first time I awoke from such a dream, I dismissed it as just that, a dream. I tried to put thoughts of my sister out of my mind and went back to my hunting and sleeping, back to the hazy sort of peace that I had made for myself in the frozen mountains.

The second time that I woke from the sounds of my sister's cries, I couldn't let it go so easily. I sat in our den, a warm hole under a tree that we had frightened a bear away from and claimed for our own, and I argued with myself like a madman.

"It's just a dream, damnit. Just a dream."

"But you don't know that, you don't know that she is safe, what if she needs me?"

"Just a dream."

"We should check, we should go and see. Just to see…"

"Only a damn dream."

"We'll see. We will see that she is safe, and then we will leave. She never has to know we are there."

"Just a goddamn dream…"

The next night I dreamed of Maggie's crying again, and my mind was made up. In the morning, I set out on foot, walking north and west until I found a westbound train to hop.

Within a week I was home, or what had been home once. The northwestern-most corner of the northwestern-most state in the country. I hovered at the edges of Bellingham like a wild animal frightened to come too close to a fire, lingering just outside of the glow of civilization.

I slept in the old creek bed where I had once played and hidden from my father as a boy, and I barely noticed the Washington winter that insured my privacy from the people of the area. From there I could taste the familiar but new overwhelming smells of the place I'd grown up, the industrial brine of the cannery overpowering it all, even from miles away.

I waited the better part of a week for the moon to vanish

from the sky while I worked up the courage to finally go home again. I'd stolen a set of workers clothes as well as what I needed to shave and trim my hair. I still looked like an unwashed vagrant by anybody's standards, but at least I didn't look as much like a bearded wild man who had woken up in a cave on a bed of skins.

My childhood home looked smaller somehow, darker. It was a haunted place for me, ghosts or no ghosts. I was certain for a moment, as I looked at it from across the street, that I could see my father out of the corner of my eye standing at the back window where I had last seen him, but when I turned to look directly at the place where I had beaten him to death, there was nothing there. I didn't know if I had imagined it or whether or not I'd have an unwelcome reunion if I dared come back here on a night with more moonlight to see the ghosts by. I didn't care to find out.

As I crossed the dark street, my nose and ears assured me that the house was empty. What else had I expected? It had been years now, hadn't it? How many years exactly? I realized then that I didn't actually know. Hell, I didn't even know what year it was. While I'd been off playing wild man in the mountains, the world had kept moving on.

I entered the house from the back door. It had come free from one of its hinges and it screamed at me faintly as I pushed it open. Inside, I found only traces of the life I'd abandoned. The old table where we had eaten, covered in dust and rat shit. The ice box lay open and empty except for bits of trash that had been lived in by the little creatures. The next room, where my mother had sat in her chair on the day I left, the room where my father had broken my arm as a boy, showed signs of more recent use by vagrants. Empty bottles and cans lay around a familiar and stained old mattress on the floor, and it smelled faintly of stale human piss. That mattress had been in the other room once, on the bed that I'd once shared with my sister when we'd both been much younger. The bed we had hidden under.

That was the last place I looked. The last place I could stand to look. I stood in the doorway and regarded our old sanctuary from the monster we'd grown up with. When I opened the door, rats scurried from a pile of human waste and discarded food, darting into hiding. The bedframe that had been the castle wall for two young children was broken and shoved to one corner. The room itself was filled with garbage, bits of broken furniture that had been left behind when Maggie and my mother had left for wherever they had gone, and one corner had become the toilet for whatever drunken vagrants had taken up residence.

For a moment, a white rage filled me. This place had been sacred to me once. The place where I'd promised my sister that I'd keep her safe. That I'd never let anything happen to her. Where I'd held her and whispered comforting nonsense to a little girl who had nobody else. And now, it was the room where some drunken hobos dropped their pants and did their business. My jaw clenched along with my fists, and I put one hand through the wall, the flimsy old surface giving way easily in an explosion of moldy dust.

Nearly as soon as the rage had filled me, it left. To hell with this place. It had never been special. It wasn't the room that had mattered. It was the love I had for my sister that I was thinking of. It was the promises I'd made to always watch over her that were sacred. Promises that I hadn't kept. It wasn't the defecating drunkards I was angry with; it was myself. Whatever my reasons, I'd abandoned Maggie just as surely as our mother had abandoned both of us from the day we'd been born. To hell with this place. Let the hobos have it.

I walked out of the little house with the only thing of value that place had left for me. The memory of what I'd sworn to my sister. If I could do nothing else with my life now, I could at least keep that promise. I could look after my baby sister.

CHAPTER THIRTY-EIGHT

The Adlers lived where they always had. Far enough away from my old home that the stink of poverty could be ignored, but close enough that a poor little boy and girl could walk there and play with the nice boy and his dog who had befriended them forever ago.

They had done well for themselves. The house was well cared for and a new Model T was displayed proudly in front. The old dog, Goliath, was no longer there. A wave of sadness hit me at the realization that he must have died while I was away. I lingered nearby in the night long enough to determine that my old friend Paul was not in the house, but that his parents and siblings were, though they all slept soundly.

I wanted answers then and there. I wanted to wake them and demand to know whatever they could tell me about my sister and mother, but I had enough sense to know how badly that would go. I was hunting information, and in any hunt the prey could be lost if the hunter wasn't prepared to exercise a little patience in the stalk. I told myself to wait, to take the lay of the land, and only to move in when I could get what I was after. I left the Adlers to sleep through the night and wandered toward the waterfront, taking in the smells of the sleeping little city while I waited for the sun to rise.

The sunrise found me across from the Adlers' house again, watching and listening patiently as they rose from bed and prepared for their day. Paul had been the oldest of three children, and though he was gone, his two younger brothers were still with their parents. Stanley had been a bit of a pest when I'd last known him, not more than ten or so I thought, but now he was a tall and lanky teen. He was the image of his older brother, if a bit thinner and with more freckles. Ben had been the baby, barely toddling back then. But now he was an exuberant school-aged boy with unruly hair that his mother struggled to tame at the breakfast table as he protested with dramatic whines until Mrs. Adler pinched his ear and made him sit still.

Mr. Adler left to conduct his business, struggling in the frosty morning to start his Model T, but then puttering down the street to whatever he did with his days. He'd know what I wanted to know, but he'd remember me too. The same for Mrs. Adler. Paul's parents had never cared for me or for my sister, and I would stand out in their memory as that red-haired Catholic boy with the hare lip and the good for nothing father. The good for nothing father who had turned up dead right around the time I'd left for the war. No, Paul's parents wouldn't be the best choice. When hunting, it was often the young that were the best prey. They were less wary, slower, more easily cornered.

Sometime after Mr. Adler left for the morning, Mother Adler was bundling up her two sons and hurrying them out the door to school with a stern reminder and another pinch on little Ben's ear to make him listen. Soon, she had returned to the warmth of the house where she went about her domestic business and the two boys were walking down the street. They had no idea that they were being stalked.

In no time at all, Stan met up with a couple of older children and told his little brother to "get lost".

"But Mama said you're supposed to—"

"Don't be a little baby," one of the new children taunted Ben.

"Yeah baby-Benny," a third boy said. "Is you too scared to walk a whole two blocks by yourself? Poooor Baaaaby."

The two newcomers laughed at their own rapier wit. Stan elbowed one of them.

"C'mon guys, lay off him," he said to his friends before turning to Ben. "Come on Benji, you can see the school from here. You keep saying you don't want to be treated like a baby. Don't be a tag-along."

Ben pouted a little but gave in quickly enough to the pressure of the three older boys, and soon Stanley Adler and his two friends had left the younger boy to walk the rest of the way on his own.

"Hey, aren't you Paul Adler's little brother?" I surprised the boy a block later. He was startled at first, both by my sudden appearance and the rough way I must have looked to him. He took a step back, and I suppressed an instinct to give chase and pounce. This wasn't that kind of hunt. "You look just like him," I lied, hoping that the little boy would idolize his older sibling in that way that young children so often secretly seem to.

He hesitated, my familiarity with his brother warring with his fear of the strange man who had come out of nowhere.

"Um, yes," he started to speak but then rubbed at his ear as he seemed recall one of his mother's lessons in manners. "I mean yes, yes sir. Who are you?"

"I'm an old friend of Paul's from school," I said. "I just got back in town and was heading to your house to see him. Is he home?"

"No," he said, still with a little hesitation. "Paul doesn't live with us no more." He said that last with a bit of obvious childlike sadness. This was an unhappy topic for him.

"What happened?" I said sharply, too sharply. I was worried that something had happened to Paul, and I briefly forgot to use my soothing voice. Ben took another quick step backwards, and I raised my hands, palms forward in an attempt to placate him. "I'm sorry, kid, I don't mean to scare you. Is he alright? He didn't go to the war, did he?" Like so many boys our age, Paul had been eager to enlist.

"Yeah, Paul was in the army, but he's okay. He was real mad because the war was over when he got there, and they sent him right back," he laughed.

I breathed a sigh of relief.

"That's good," I said. "So he's around then?"

"No, he's not around," Ben said. "He don't live here no more."

I was struggling to maintain my patience. I'd never been good with kids.

"So," I said slowly, "where is he?"

Ben just shrugged and said nothing. He looked away from me. I could tell that he was nervous and a little scared of me. Damnit. It would be so much easier to just scare the information out of him, but I wasn't about to bully the little brother of one of my only friends. I took a knee and put a hand on Ben's shoulder. I meant the gesture to be reassuring, but he stiffened in awareness that I had him now, and he wouldn't be going anywhere if I didn't let him go.

"Ben," I said, "I just want to visit my friend. Don't worry. You can tell me what happened. Where is Paul?"

Ben looked at his feet and squirmed for a minute before talking.

"Mama made him move away," he said angrily.

"Why did she do that? Where did he go?"

"Mama didn't like Maggie. She said she was a...a bad word."

Maggie? What did my sister have to do with this? And what had Mrs. Adler called my sister?

"What bad word, Ben? I promise, I won't tell you said it."

"Mama said Paul couldn't marry Maggie because she was dirty. She said she was a...H-O-R-E." As he misspelled the word my hand tightened on his little shoulder, making him wince. Mrs. Adler had said that about my baby sister, had she? I thought about visiting Mrs. Adler at home after this after all if I needed more information.

"Wait... marry Maggie?" I said.

"Ow, that hurts!"

I released the boy and he stumbled backward, sniffling.

"Where are they?" I asked, standing over the boy, no longer thinking about Ben's fear or comfort. My head was spinning.

"Leave me alone. I'm gonna tell!" he yelled.

Other people were beginning to look from down the block and across the street at the strange red-haired man standing over the yelling little boy. Damnit. I didn't need this kind of attention.

I took Ben's hand and pulled him to his feet, holding his hand tightly and doing my best to look like a father or older brother walking a kid to school.

"Let me go!" he said, smelling scared. My little act wasn't working. People were starting to come toward us.

"First, just tell me where they went," I hissed, "and I'll let you go."

"Let me go!" he screamed.

"Hey mister, what are you doing to that kid?" an older boy in his teens yelled from across the street. Damn.

"The city, they went to the city. Let me go!" I released little Ben Adler's hand as he kicked at me, and he fell again to the frosty ground.

The city? There was only one to speak of around there. It was where Paul had often said he wanted to live when he was old enough to get out of that little town. They'd gone to Seattle. I ran.

CHAPTER THIRTY-NINE

Within a week, I'd found her. It wasn't hard. Walking the same streets as Maggie, it was inevitable that I'd catch her scent. My wolf-self had never smelled her, but that didn't matter. Even among thousands of strangers, there was no mistaking the one person in the world I'd known better than myself.

I followed my nose and found them living in an apartment over a Chinese laundry downtown. It was a tiny little place with barely any possessions to their name. I listened to them from the dark street below as I watched their silhouettes move against the windows.

Over the sounds of the city, even at night, I caught only snippets of conversation, but I was soon embarrassed to be eavesdropping as it grew clear that these were two young people who were very much in love. They talked about their days, about their plans, about what they needed from the market, and about their struggles. Peppered among the concerns and worries of the young married couple was a constant stream of sweet nothings and affectionate nonsense. I was mortified to be listening to it in the first place, but I learned a great deal about their situation before I retreated awkwardly in the face of their... enthusiastic affections.

I wasn't overly surprised or pained to hear that our mother had died. Shortly after receiving a letter from the government confirming that I had died, the money that I had been sending them had dried up. Maggie had struggled to find work while our mother had retreated into her medicine. Too far into her medicine. From what I could gather, Paul Adler had stepped up just as I had once asked him to and made sure that my sister was taken care of. He even went so far as to give up on college and allow his parents to disown him in order to marry her, something I had definitely not asked him to do. He'd given everything for Maggie, and she loved him for it. Hell, so did I. He did more than I ever could.

As so many people were, Paul and Maggie were struggling. Elsewhere, the twenties may have been "roaring", but not in Washington. The end of the war had brought a recession to the northwest, and work was hard to come by.

I followed Maggie for the next few days, always from a distance, getting a sense of her routine. She worked the counter at a downtown candy store, a massive operation with an enormous moving pig on its sign. When the laundry downstairs from their home had extra work, she would pitch in there as well. Paul, having forgone his college education, worked the waterfront when there was any work to be had. Every day he either worked hard, or he worked even harder in search of work. He was a smart man with a good head on his shoulders. If given half a chance, I knew he'd do well for himself. The problem was that there weren't many chances to be had in a recession for a young Jew who had dropped out of college.

Every time I followed Maggie, I came a little closer to forgetting all the reasons that I had decided to keep hidden. I wanted to run up to her and take her in my arms, to let her know that I was alive and would take care of her, to promise her that everything would be alright. But that would mean letting her be part of this new world that I found myself living in. The world of ghosts and monsters in which I may be the most dangerous monster of them all. I couldn't do that. Not to her. So, I decided to help in the ways that I could. They needed money, and I would find a way to get it for them. I just didn't know how.

In the meantime, being so near to Maggie and Paul was making me feel lonesome in ways that I hadn't felt since my change. I hadn't felt nearly so far away from people when I was alone on a mountaintop. This new nearness left me feeling more apart than ever. I'd decided that Maggie and her husband could never be part of my nightmare world, that they should never be exposed to the horrors that I was growing accustomed to. I needed to talk to somebody. Somebody who could understand that world. Somebody who could accept it.

I found my way to Ballard, just north of Seattle. Walking distance for me. I found myself hunting another familiar scent. Pete Madsen. The man who had believed in monsters and spirits even when I hadn't. The man who had seen some of the horrors of the war with me before he was injured and sent home. I needed a friend.

I found him quickly and in the first place I looked, his father's church. This didn't surprise me, after all, Pete had intended to be a preacher. It was like him to want to stay close to his calling. I didn't see him, but I could smell him and hear his voice within the building, and his wasn't the only voice.

I waited in the lot across the alley from the modest brick church. I wanted to be absolutely certain that Pete was alone before I approached him, and I had no idea how long I'd have to wait for that opportunity. I didn't have long to wait.

A tall and imposing older man in a somber, dark suit emerged from the back door. I recognized this stern-faced man at once as much from his resemblance to my friend Peter as from the one time I'd seen him before. Reverend Madsen.

"See to it that the pews are properly polished this time," he said in a deep but brusque voice without looking back.

"Yes, father," a soft and familiar male voice called from within the building.

"And be sure to be in your rooms before services begin tomorrow morning," Reverend Madsen said. "I won't have you lurking about and frightening the congregation."

"Yes, father," Pete Madsen said again from just out of sight.

The elder Madsen put his hat on and walked purposefully down the alley, toward home I assumed, and the back door to the church closed as if of its own accord. I waited until Reverend Madsen had rounded the corner before approaching the door and giving a quick, firm knock.

"Coming, father," the muffled voice of my friend came from within as I heard the lock shift and the door began to open. "Did you forget somethi—"

When I'd last seen Peter Madsen, his face had been heavily bandaged. I suppose I'd known that he would have scars from the day he saved me from the mustard gas, but I honestly hadn't given much thought to how bad they might be. The familiar and surprised eyes that looked at me from within the church regarded me from a face like something from a nightmare. One side of his face looked much as I remembered, a bit wearier and more lined perhaps, but it was the face of Peter Madsen just the same. On the other side, the side that had fallen into the filthy puddle of the trench where he had saved my life, the skin of Peter's face was a smooth and shiny mass of melted flesh that reached the corners of his eye and twisted the side of his mouth into a startling grimace that left his teeth perpetually bare. I understood immediately what Reverend Madsen had meant about frightening his congregation. This was a face that would cause women to gasp and children to run away.

And yet, Peter Madsen looked at me first with confusion, then surprise, and finally with a shocked expression of concern that made it clear that, of the two of us, I might be the one most changed.

The greeting I'd prepared dried up in my throat as we stood regarding one another for a long moment. Finally, Peter broke the silence.

"Hello Frank," he said with a smile that only reached one side of his melted face. "won't you come in?"

CHAPTER FORTY

"You mean you never leave this damn building?"

"Frank, watch your mouth, please," Peter said softly over his cup of steaming tea. The look he shot me left no doubt that he was very serious.

"Same old Pete," I muttered.

"Yes and no," he said. "I see you've still got that blasphemous mouth of yours."

"Sorry," I said with a grin. "But seriously Pete, you don't go out at all?"

Peter Madsen lived in the basement of his father's church where he could remain out of sight. He worked around the church when nobody else was there. He helped his father prepare his sermons and did what handiwork needed doing, but he never left. His modest apartment downstairs had a shelf of books, a small table, and a single bed. Everything was neat and orderly. A spartan cell with one small window let the night air in at the level of our heads.

"It's for the best," he said, "but what about you, Frank? I'd heard you were dead. Barnes wrote me. He even said that he saw your ghost."

"I'm no ghost," I said after sipping at the unsweetened tea he had offered me. "Barnes saw me, but the guy was so jumpy, he took a shot at me. You know how he is."

"How he was," Peter corrected solemnly.

"What? When?" *So, Barnes hadn't made it either?*

"Near the end, while the brass was negotiating the terms of the armistice."

"Damn," I growled. Pete raised an eyebrow in warning. "Sorry, it's just... such a waste."

"We can't know God's plan for us," Peter said, "but if it was his time then it was meant to be."

I couldn't agree, but I bit my tongue. I hadn't come here to argue philosophy. I shook my head and raised the chipped teacup before taking a sip. A poor toast for our fallen friend.

"What happened to you, Frank?"

"That's a bit of a story," I said. "I don't really know how to tell it."

"You're changed," Pete said. "I saw it in your eyes, Frank. There's... something in them now. Something that wasn't there before."

"We're both changed, Pete," I said.

"No, that's not what I mean, and you know it. What happened to you, Frank?"

I sighed.

"I don't know where to start..."

"Then let's start with why Barnes thought you were dead. What happened?"

I told him about the German ambush in Belleau Wood where Cervantes had died. About how I'd been shot and left for dead. I told him about how I'd woken up later to the sounds of scavengers.

"You were right, Pete," I said quietly.

"About what?"

"About... the things. The monsters that feed on the dead. They came for me."

Peter's good eye widened. The burned flesh on the other side of his face pulled grotesquely taut in the expression. He said nothing, eager for me to tell him more.

"I fought them," I said. "I fought them as hard as I could. But I was going to die. There was no other way for it to end, Pete. I was going to die. I knew it. But then, something else came..."

"What?" he breathed, a desperate heat in his voice.

"I don't know, not really," I said. "It killed them, the monsters, the ghouls, it was terrible... I didn't see it. I thought it was going to kill me too. It spared me... but I was still dying. I thought I did die, but then... then I woke up."

"Like Lazarus..." he whispered to himself.

"But after that night, I was different. Just... different. The whole world was different."

"An angel of the Lord..." Pete whispered to himself. "It had to be."

"What?" I was utterly baffled by his response.

"It was a miracle, Frank. It had to be!" he said. "Don't you see that? God spared you. You must see that!"

"Pete, it was no angel. The thing that I saw was a monster. It was terrible. A killer."

"Don't be a child, Frank" Pete said feverishly, "Haven't you read your bible at all? What do you think angels are? Fat little cherubs with feathered wings and harps?"

That was exactly what I pictured when I thought of angels, but I wasn't about to tell Pete that. He was building up steam now, becoming more excited, manic.

"Frank, my friend," he went on, "angels can be terrible, fearsome beings. It was an angel who killed the firstborn of Egypt! Angels are the will of God on earth."

"Pete, I really don't think that's what it was…"

"Oh, ye of little faith," Pete laughed and clapped me on the shoulders. "I *know* that is what happened, Frank, I *know* it. God must have a purpose for you my friend, and he has brought you to me to help you find it. Thank you, Lord!"

"Pete…"

I didn't know how to argue with him. I didn't even know if I should. He'd been through so much, had lost so much, and now he was reaching out and grasping at what had happened to me as if it were a miracle. He seemed so desperately hungry for it to be true. His need for it to be true left me uneasy, left me frightened. I hadn't even told him yet about what had come after. About the wolf within me. About the things that I had done. If he knew, would he think it was a demon that had come to me instead of an angel? If I told him, would he change his mind? Could he change his mind?

The sound of a key turning in a lock upstairs startled me away from my worries. I jumped to my feet and looked back at the stairs to the basement, the only way in or out that I knew of. The wolf inside me raised his hackles with the fear that comes of a wild thing finding itself in a corner. Peter didn't seem to notice my alarm at all. He was still lost in his newfound calling.

"Pete," I hissed. "There's somebody upstairs."

"What?" he didn't know what I was talking about.

"I hear somebody coming…"

"What? I don't hear anything."

The back door of the church opened and closed quietly, and soft feet moved across the floor upstairs. I backed away from the stairs, into the shadows to the side where I thought I might be most hidden. My hands clenched tightly as I looked about the room for a place to hide or another way out if I needed it. I considered the small, lone window. It would be a tight fit. I might tear some clothes and maybe some skin, but I thought I could make it through if it came to that.

The door to the top of the stairs opened and soft light formed a frame atop them. Within the light a figure appeared, and I found myself understanding why Peter Madsen could believe in angels.

CHAPTER FORTY-ONE

Evelyn Madsen was even more lovely than I remembered, and that was saying something. When I'd first seen her, Pete's little sister had taken my breath away. I'd reluctantly become friends with him at first just so that I could hear more about her, and though Pete and I had eventually formed a bond of our own, the memory of that first fleeting glimpse of his enchanting sister still sometimes kept me warm at night through the war until my change left little room for such thoughts.

The girl, no, she was a young woman now certainly, wore her honey-colored hair in carefully maintained curls that fell to her shoulders. Her icy blue eyes sparkled in the shadows from above an upturned nose and full mischievous mouth. She was dressed modestly in a blue dress that looked drab beside her eyes, and though the dress itself was as modest as one could expect from a preacher's daughter, the frame beneath it was not made for modesty. In one hand she carried a plate of steaming food draped in a cloth napkin, the smell of which would have driven me mad with desire if the smell of the woman hadn't already thoroughly captured my senses.

"Mama made pork chops for dinner, Quasimodo," she called out to the basement in a playfully musical voice.

Pete was brought suddenly back to himself, shaking his head briefly as if doused in cold water.

"Oh, thank you, Eve. I'd forgotten about dinner," he said.

She raised an eyebrow and one corner of her succulent mouth at her brother as she reached the bottom of the stairs, but before she could say whatever witty response she had been preparing, she caught sight of me standing still against the far wall. She gasped faintly and nearly dropped the plate she had been carrying, but quickly recovered her poise and saved the food. She pressed her free hand to her chest, as if clutching at pearls that she didn't wear, and forced a polite smile to hide her surprise and embarrassment.

"Oh, you have company?"

I didn't move. Her shock had sent the barest hint of fear into her scent and now the wolf within me was appraising her with nearly as much interest as the man. I wanted her. We wanted her, and the look on my face no doubt conveyed the desperate desire that was washing over me. Evelyn saw it and a pleased hint of a mischievous smile touched her eyes before she forced herself to look away in practiced decency. I forced myself to look away as well, to the food she carried. If I had to lick my lips, I was at least grateful to have a convenient excuse near at hand.

"Oh, yes," Peter turned to me with a warm smile, "this is my very good friend Frank Shepard. We served together in France. Frank, this is my nuisance of a sister, Eve."

Very good friend? My surprise at his effusive comradery matched his sister's annoyance at his introduction of her. She shot him a disapproving glance.

"I'm so very glad to meet you, Frank," she said. She set the plate on the little table and extended a lithe arm to offer her hand in greeting. "I'm *Evelyn*." She emphasized the name as she shot another quick glare at her brother.

I froze. The wolf in me didn't know what to do. It was as if the rabbit we were stalking had looked right at us and suddenly moved closer. They weren't supposed to do that. The man in me didn't do much better. I was suddenly struck with self-consciousness at the thought of my ragged appearance and cleft lip. I felt like a dirty child who knew better than to soil something beautiful by touching it with my grimy hands.

"Don't worry, Frank. I don't bite." She gave me a subtle wink, concealed from Peter, that seemed meant to cast a hint of doubt on what she had just said.

Slowly, I took her hand in mine and struggled to remember what little manners my mother had taught me as a shiver ran through me at the heat of her soft skin beneath my calloused fingers.

"Likewise," I muttered. She stifled a girlish giggle and raised her perfectly arched eyebrow at me as if to ask if I was echoing her pleasure at meeting me or her assurance that she didn't bite. She met my eyes then as I stepped forward, and there must have been something of the wolf in them then because the flush that spread across her face then was neither feigned nor girlish. She looked away quickly and I released her hand, hoping that I hadn't scared her, but she didn't smell frightened so much as excited.

"Frank will be staying with us for a while," Pete said.

I was? That was news to me.

"Oh, that's wonderful," Evelyn said, still avoiding my eyes.

"That's not necessary," I said, "I'll find another—"

"Nonsense," Evelyn interrupted as she busied herself with the presentation of the plate of food she had brought. "It's the least we can do for a friend of Pete's from the war. That name is familiar, Pete, Frank isn't the fellow from..." she made a gesture at the side of her face, indicating her brother's disfiguring injury.

"Yes, that Frank," Pete nodded, confirming that he had mentioned me to her before.

I wondered what she had heard. Did she know me as the foul mouthed and cowardly son of a bitch who had gotten her brother mutilated? I hoped not.

"Well that settles it then," Evelyn said. "We won't hear of you leaving. Mother and Father will want to meet you. I only brought the one plate of food, Frank. You just come with me back to the house, and I'll fix you something and you can meet our parents."

Pete grimaced at the mention of introducing me to his parents, and I panicked a little at the thought of having to be social and polite for a second longer than I had to.

"I—I don't know," I said.

Evelyn considered me with her eyes for a moment and then nodded.

"Yes, well, maybe not tonight," she agreed. "Pete, your clothes should fit him. You should lend him some clothes and let him clean up a little, then he can meet father at the service tomorrow morning. You do go to church, don't you, Frank?"

I nodded. It wasn't entirely a lie. I had *been* to church.

"Good," she smiled before I could refuse and spoil her plans for me. "That settles it. I'll just go back and get another plate of food. I'll be right back."

"No, that's alright," Pete interrupted as she began to turn to the stairs. "He can have mine. I'm not hungry. Besides, father would want to come back and meet him now, and Frank just got here. He's tired. Isn't that right ,Frank? We should let him rest first before putting him through *that*."

Evelyn laughed.

"I suppose you're right," she said. "Saint Peter here probably never said a word against him, Frank, but our father can be a bit, well, difficult to deal with."

Pete looked at her with stern disapproval, but she pretended not to notice. Evelyn pulled out the little chair in front of the table where she had placed the food and motioned for me to sit.

"No, I couldn't," I protested, not wanting to take Pete's dinner. The man was already much thinner than I'd remembered him.

Evelyn must have seen the hesitation on my face as I glanced at Peter.

"Of course, you can," she said as she took me by the arm and guided me to the table. The heat of her pressed against my elbow. The softness of her, caused me to stiffen, but still she pressed on and herded me to the table. "He never eats. I usually find most of his dinner in the trash the next morning."

"Yes, please, Frank, help yourself," Peter said.

I allowed myself to be pressed into the seat, enjoying the touch of Evelyn's hands a little more than I should.

"Peter, you should go fetch a cot while your friend eats," Evelyn suggested.

"Yes, yes of course," Pete rose and quickly went upstairs to retrieve the cot before I could even consider protesting. Evelyn fussed at the table and quickly set the place for me, leaning over me and even placing the napkin on my lap for me, letting her hair brush the side of my face lightly as her hands moved the cloth across my legs. The closeness of her was maddening. Did she know what she was doing to me? No, of course not. How could she? She was Pete's sister, and a preacher's daughter too. I was sure she was innocent, even if the coy smile she shot me as we heard Pete returning said otherwise. I was reading her wrong, certainly.

Evelyn watched me eat as Pete set up the cot. Pork chops, a little cold but still moist and delicious, roast potatoes with a touch of salt and dill, and a pile of peas with onions and butter. I hadn't eaten like this since, well, since I didn't know when. It was all I could do to remember to use a knife and fork as I devoured the meal, not coming up once for air.

"Now that's more like it," Evelyn said with a pleased voice. "It's good to see somebody enjoy their food for a change. Did you like it?"

"Yes, very much," and remembering my mother's brief lessons in courtesy I added, "thank you Miss Madsen."

"Stevens," Pete corrected as he finished making up the cot.

Evelyn stared icy daggers at him but didn't say anything.

"What?" I asked, confused.

"Not Madsen," he went on, "Stevens. Mrs. Timothy Stevens, she's married."

Evelyn smelled every bit as angry as she looked.

"Oh, I'm sorry," I said to Evelyn.

"There's nothing to be sorry for, Frank," Evelyn said. "There's no reason that you should have known about that."

"Well, thanks again," I said, confused as to why she should be so upset with Peter. "It was delicious."

"Yes, thank you, Eve," Pete said dismissively. "Now if you'll excuse us, it's late and Frank would like to wash up and rest."

"Of course," Evelyn said. "I'll see you tomorrow at the service, Frank."

She shot me a smile and began to ascend the stairs. I opened my mouth to try and say that maybe I wouldn't be able to make it, but she cut me off before I could.

"Don't disappoint me, Frank." I could hear the smile in her voice as she closed the door.

CHAPTER FORTY-TWO

I didn't hear a word of Reverend Madsen's sermon. I didn't mean to be rude, but between the anxiety that came with being in a confined space with so many people and the sheer heart-pounding excitement that I felt from the light pressure of Evelyn's knee against my leg where we sat on the front pew, scripture was the last thing on my mind.

Peter had loaned me a nice pair of slacks as well as a neatly pressed and heavily starched white shirt for the occasion, both of which were soaked in nervous sweat before the sermon was half over. I felt utterly out of place with the fresh shave and clean clothes, but Pete had insisted, and I was determined not to embarrass him. Though, Pete at least would be spared having to witness my awkwardness, as he remained in the basement for the duration of the service.

I could understand the situation. There was no denying that Pete's face was far from lovely, but it bothered me a great deal that he was expected to keep himself hidden. Maybe it was the fact that I'd grown up with a comparatively mild facial deformity myself, or the fact that I knew he had earned those scars in the act of saving my own life in the war. The idea that he would be shunned for his scars felt shameful.

"It's for the best," he told me when he saw my surprise that he wasn't going to be joining me.

"Have you ever considered, I don't know, one of those masks? You're not the only one who came back from the war with scars. I've seen a few men with them. It's nothing to be ashamed of."

He didn't say anything, only looked down as he finished tying the necktie that he was lending me for the occasion. Just then, Evelyn opened the door to the basement and answered for her silent brother.

"He had one, but father threw it out," she said by way of greeting as she descended the stairs.

"What? Why would he do—"

I wasn't prepared for the way Evelyn would look in her Sunday finest. She was dressed in a long and modestly cut navy dress that even the most puritanical father could never find fault with. And yet she somehow managed to wear it in a way that hinted at the curves of her hips and the swell of her breasts more provocatively than any half-naked flapper in a jazz club. How the hell did she do that? She looked at me with that mischievous smile of hers, pleased with herself that her arrival had managed to stop me in mid-sentence.

"My, my, Frank, you clean up alright," she said as she looked me up and down, taking in my fresh shave and borrowed clothes. "Let me do that, Peter, you've got it all crooked."

Peter relented and left his sister to finish adjusting the tie. After that, she led me around practically as if by a leash, never letting me out of her sight as she shepherded me up the stairs and into the pew at the front of the church. The rest of the congregation began to file in and take their seats.

"Oh, this is Frank Shepard, he's a war hero you know," she

said to a busybody of an old woman who greeted Evelyn with a judgmental sneer as an excuse to find out who she was sitting with. For the sake of future gossip, no doubt.

My own experiences with church had been highly traditional and somber affairs. There was a reverent beauty to the small Catholic church my mother had taken me to as a boy, but the experience was always steeped in propriety and ritual. So, I nearly lost my composure when Evelyn grabbed my hand and pulled me to my feet as the congregation of Reverend Madsen's little church rose and began to sing. The singing wasn't so bad. It was the heat of Evelyn's slender hand pressed against the damp roughness of my own that put me off balance. I could feel the beating of her heart through the contact, and I realized with a pang of something like hunger that I could match that rhythm to the smell of her and the low pulse that I could hear with my wolf's ears even over the din of the discordant singing.

Yes.

The wolf within me sat up and took notice, considering my desire for Evelyn with a savage approval. Even as I sought to deny what I was feeling and wanting from her, the animal part of me was shameless in its ceaseless barrage of sensual impulses. I wanted to take the hand she had given me and pull her away from here, anywhere else, someplace green perhaps, and take her into my arms. The thought was delicious and dangerously distracting. I bit at my lower lip, hard, drawing a thin stream of blood in my mouth. The coppery taste along with the pain helped me to focus, bringing me a little bit back to myself, but the burning in my blood that her touch ignited couldn't be extinguished so easily.

"Father, this is Frank Shepard," Evelyn was saying. "Peter told us about him, remember? They served together in France."

The service was over? When had that happened? Had I

been so besotted with my imaginings of Evelyn, of her skin beneath my hands, beneath my mouth, of her body pressed against mine—stop it! Apparently, I had been exactly that distracted, because here was the elder Madsen, standing before me just as Evelyn stood beside me, extending a hand to greet me as his congregation slowly filed out of the church.

"Frank," the older man said, his weathered face considering me soberly with eyes that looked very much like his son's. "Did you like the service?"

"Yes—yes sir," I stammered clumsily, "very much so."

"And are you also a friend of my daughter's husband, Timothy?" He raised a bushy grey eyebrow.

"No father, he's never met Tim," Evelyn said through a tight mouth, "and you know very well that he never will. Tim isn't coming back."

My ears perked up a little at this new information.

"Just the same," Reverend Madsen turned to his daughter. "Wherever he may be, he *is* your husband."

"For now," Evelyn muttered under her breath, looking at the ground.

"And what does *that* mean, young lady?"

How had I gotten stuck in the middle of this? I could be anywhere else in the world right now. I could be stalking prey in the mountains. I could be curled up with an opium pipe or a bottle of bourbon, but no, I was standing in a necktie and a sweat-stained shirt while Evelyn and her father were about to have this out. What could I do but hold my tongue and hope they left me out of it?

"I talked to some people, and I've decided that I'm going to get the divorce."

Despite the awkwardness of my situation, I had to fight back a wolfish grin from spreading on my face as I considered the possibility that Evelyn might be more available than Pete had led me to believe.

"No, you are not!" He took Evelyn roughly by the wrist, causing her to wince in pain, and pulled her away from me toward the corner of the room where he believed that they couldn't be overheard.

The wolf within me wanted to growl a warning at him but I kept control of myself as I kept still and glared at the man from across the room, clenching my fists. Why was this my business? Why did I feel so protective of this woman? So... possessive?

Mine.

No. No, she wasn't mine. Much as I might want her to be. I had to control myself.

"It's not up to you, Daddy!" Evelyn hissed at him as she tried ineffectually to pry her wrist from his grip.

"It is so long as you expect to live under my roof, young lady," he said as he loomed over her in a blatant attempt at intimidation. "You're *my* daughter, and you'll do as I say. You made a vow, a holy vow, and you are going to keep it!"

"Only because you made me! I never wanted to marry Tim, and you know it!"

He slapped her then, hard. The few remaining congregants turned away, leaving the Reverend to tend to his own house as he saw fit. They hurried to leave the church. I took a step forward without intending it and felt the flesh of my cleft lip curl in a hint of a snarl.

"You should have thought of that before you spread your legs for him, shouldn't you! Now what is left for you? Nobody else will want you, you dirty, willful, ungrateful—"

Crack!

She slapped him back, her small arm flying with surprising speed, her hand collided loudly with his cheek. He released his grip on her wrist, the tender flesh red from where he had been crushing it, and stepped back in shock, his eyes wide and jaw slack in utter disbelief.

She stood upright then, uncowed by his attempt to intimidate her, and met his surprised eyes with a fiery glare. I knew that look. I knew I'd worn it myself the day I'd had enough of my own father's abuse and had stood up for myself and Maggie for the first time. I'd had my arm broken for that look. But Evelyn didn't look frightened in the least. She took a step toward her father to match the step he had taken back, raised her own hand and pointed one slender finger at him like it was a dagger.

"Don't you *ever* lay your hands on me again!"

She turned then and strode angrily from the church. She didn't meet my eyes, but I saw the storm raging on her face as she blew down the aisle like a thunderhead. There was no thought of anybody else, not of me, or her father, or the gossipy old busybodies who would be talking about this for years to come. In that moment she was utterly free in a way that I've seldom seen a woman before or since.

Her father watched her go, dumbfounded. It took him several moments to realize that I was still in the room and he turned his angry eyes toward me, seeking somebody, anybody at all, to blame for what had just happened aside from himself.

I met his eyes, and I smiled.

And why not? After all, I had just fallen in love with his daughter.

CHAPTER FORTY-THREE

For a time, both Evelyn and Peter became a constant fixture in my life. I stayed in the basement of the Madsen church for a time, though I'm not sure if Reverend Madsen was entirely aware of that fact. He avoided Peter's downstairs sanctum when he came to the little church, as he tended to avoid Peter himself. Evelyn was around every day, a fact which annoyed Peter but delighted me. She'd bring us meals and would sit and read to us, well past the point where she had worn out her welcome with her brother.

"I apologize for my sister, Frank," he said one day after she had left. "I know she's a pest."

"That's alright," I said, not knowing what the hell he was talking about.

I dedicated myself to making money for Paul and my sister, but also so that I didn't have to live on Peter's charity. Although I wasn't in any particular hurry to get away from his sister. The first week or two was easy enough, but I knew that the moon would be returning before long, and with it I would become a less than ideal houseguest.

Peter suggested I try to find work at the waterfront. "There's always work at the shipyards these days."

I shook my head. My erstwhile brother-in-law Paul frequently looked for work at the waterfront. I'd followed him there more than once, and it wouldn't do at all to have him spot me one day unexpectedly. I wanted to see him and my sister eventually. My time keeping civil with the Madsens gave me hope that a reunion might not be an entirely unreasonable idea after all, but not yet. Not until I was certain I would be safe for Maggie.

Having eliminated the shipyards and coming to the realization that I had few, if any, marketable skills, I turned my mind toward what I did know how to do well. Violence. Before the wolf, I'd found my place in the war. Fighting had been the only thing I'd ever been good at. Hell, even before the war I'd made money for my bastard of a father by taking beatings in the local fights, and I hadn't even had the wolf then to help me recover.

Now there was an idea. Taking beatings for money and letting the wolf do some good for me for a change? Why not?

As the full moon drew near, I decided to go to the woods for a week or so, telling Peter and Evelyn that I would be back soon but that I had some business to tend to. Evelyn pouted deliciously and complained, but eventually gave in when I promised I'd be back. Though I could tell she didn't believe me. Peter just gave me a knowing look, as if he understood, as if we shared some holy secret, and smiled. What did he think? That I was going up to the mountain to talk to God like Moses? Saint Peter, as Evelyn teasingly called him, was beginning to worry me. He didn't need any reassurances or promises on my part. He knew I'd be back, worse, he believed.

"Frank," her voice came softly from the corner of the church as I closed the door behind me to begin my brief isolation. I'd thought she had gone home hours ago. It was getting dark now, and I hadn't thought to find anybody waiting outside. I should have smelled her, but Evelyn's smell was on everything around me these days.

I tensed, having never been fond of being taken off guard, and especially not since the war, and the wolf. I didn't turn to face Evelyn as she approached, forcing the snarl from my face before I let her see me.

"I thought you went home," I said, still not facing her.

"That's not my home," she said with a trace of tightness in her throat. "Not for a long time."

When she reached out and took my hand to turn me towards her, my snarl was gone, but I tensed all over again for all the other reasons.

"What do you want, Evelyn?"

She was holding both of my hands in hers now and looking up at me, trying to meet my eyes as I avoided hers. The heat of her hands and the smell of her making me quiver ever so slightly in excitement. This wasn't safe for her. That was why I had to leave in the first place.

"Don't go..." she said softly, looking up at me imploringly while I still refused to meet her eyes. What would she see there now if I did? I could feel the wolf closer than he had been in weeks. All the strength and urges that came with him were swimming on the surface of my thoughts, and I knew even then from my brief experience that meeting somebody's eyes when the wolf was so strong would shake them. Nobody liked to be reminded that they were prey.

"I'm coming back," I said. "I promised, remember?"

She kept trying to meet my eyes, but why? Did she think that I was avoiding her eyes because I was lying to her? Damn. It occurred to me then that this was exactly what she thought. Her soon-to-be ex-husband had left after all. Why shouldn't I?

"Why won't you look at me, Frank?"

I didn't answer.

"Frank? Look at me, please."

"No." The word fell from my lips, low and gravelly, with more than a hint of the wolf in my voice. She didn't flinch.

"Why not? Why won't you just look at me?" She was pleading now, frightened. I wished I could make her understand that what she should be frightened of was me staying, not my leaving.

"For your own good," I said.

"What?" She stiffened then. "For my own good? Oh, well thank you so much for taking care of little old me. I don't know what I'd do without all you big, strong men telling me what's best for me. I'm so grateful."

There she was, the woman I'd fallen for. Though I still tried to keep that fact from her. Her fear quickly gave way to anger, to righteous fury. God, she was beautiful when she was angry.

"Evelyn, you don't understand..."

"Of course not," she said sarcastically, "I haven't had a man explain it to me yet. How could I understand? I'm just a girl. What could I know?"

"Evelyn..."

"Don't you 'Evelyn' me!" she yelled loudly, worrying me that she might soon draw attention. "I thought you were different, Frank. I don't know why, but I thought you were different from Peter and my father and every other man who thinks they need to protect me and tell me what to do. But you aren't, are you? You're just like them!"

"No, Evelyn, keep your voice down, please..."

"Fuck you, Frank!" she yelled as she pounded her small fist into my chest, right above my heart.

Without thinking or meaning to, I caught her wrist and held her hand where it had landed as I raised my chin and met her eyes. She saw me then, really saw me. I could see it on her face as the realization came over her. She saw that I was different all right, but not the way she had thought. She stiffened as she saw that I was a predator. She saw the hungry way I looked at her. She saw that I was dangerous.

Now she would be frightened. She would pull away and run. She would want nothing to do with me, and she'd be right. She should have run. She should have told me to leave and never come back, should have screamed.

But she didn't.

Instead, she met my eyes without looking away and a little shiver ran through her. Yes, she was frightened, I could smell that, but more than that, she *liked* what she saw. She liked that I was frightening, liked that I was dangerous. She didn't pull away, didn't even look away. She just gasped a little and leaned into me, letting me feel the excited tightness of her trembling body. Letting me feel her own heart pounding as excitedly as mine as she pressed against me. Her glossy lower lip quivered slightly as she looked up at me, and I became aware of the hardness of her nipples pressed against my chest through the wool of her dress just as she became aware of my own firmness pressed against her. She didn't pull away, and I couldn't.

Before I knew what was happening, I had dipped my mouth to hers and kissed her. I was vaguely aware of my hands grasping at her, clutching her as her hands moved over me. But I was lost in that kiss, in the way that she took my breath into herself even as I took hers into me. The frightened and angry tears she'd been shedding only moments earlier still rolled down her cheeks, adding salt to the sweetness of that kiss.

She jumped up, wrapping her legs around my waist, and I caught her effortlessly, savoring the way she felt under my hands. How could something be so firm and so soft at the same time? We were against the door of the church, and Evelyn reached her hand out to open it. We stumbled inside.

If I'd been thinking at all, things would have gone differently. I wouldn't have been with her there on the floor of her father's church. I probably wouldn't have kissed her. Hell, I never would have met her eyes. But whether I blame it on the wolf or on the man, I wasn't thinking, and I did do all those things. And despite everything that came after, I never quite have been able to make myself regret it.

We lay there after, in the darkness, on the floor between the pews. Both of us drenched. Both of us scratched, bruised, and blissfully oblivious. Her hair tickled my nose as her head on my chest rose and fell with my breathing.

"I—I didn't hurt you, did I?"

She looked up and met my eyes, her hair draping over both sides of my face and forming a little cave where our noses almost touched. I felt but couldn't see her breasts resting deliciously on my chest as she smirked at me.

"Yes," she said, "and I want you to do it again."

I was still trying to make sense of her words when another voice joined the conversation.

"When are you planning to be married?" Peter said from the back of the church.

CHAPTER FORTY-FOUR

For once, my wolf was eager to get back to civilization, as was I. After all, that was where Evelyn was. The full moon in the mountains had been different than others. It had been more manageable, as though the wolf wasn't as desperately hungry to act out his instincts. Instead, it was a jubilant few days. We hunted, we ran, we bathed in the rivers, and we howled our excitement to the moon like a lovesick pup.

Peter had disapproved, of course. He'd looked almost hurt when he'd found me with his sister, but we'd managed to come to an understanding. Yes, I'd marry Evelyn, and happily, but I needed a chance to get things in order first. I wouldn't be staying in his basement with him any longer. Instead I'd go and make myself enough money to support my sister as well as his, then we'd be married as soon as possible. In the meantime, Peter agreed to help Evelyn get her divorce and would try to smooth the way with their father. Evelyn, after hurrying to cover herself, sat there as her brother and I negotiated the details of her future.

She was excited, running to her brother and attempting to kiss his cheek, but he pushed her off in disgust. He looked at her still-disheveled hair and clothes with a look that told us both he knew where she had just been and would prefer that she not touch him. He loved her, he always had, but that brotherly love warred with things he'd been taught to believe. Lessons that had been beaten into the man struggled with the boy's heart. To him, she was dirty now. Damaged.

Evelyn still smelled scared when I left but seemed reassured that I had a reason now to return. She wasn't wrong.

When I returned to the city, I immediately sought out the places that reminded me of my father. The speakeasies and illegal joints where they served smuggled Canadian whiskey. From there, it was just a matter of asking the right questions. It didn't take long to find a spot that held fights, a basement dive downtown run by an Italian from the east coast named Sal Curcio. Sal didn't need much convincing that I knew how to take a punch. My face was a convincing resume. He gave me a shot in the ring against a big Irishman named Lynch, a mean-eyed son of a bitch who smelled of whiskey and reminded me more than a little of my father.

"He'll go down in the third round," I told Mr. Curcio. He only looked at me like I was crazy and shook his head, no doubt thinking he was about to watch another poor bastard get the tar beaten out of him. He was only wrong about which of us in the ring was the poor bastard in question.

I let him hit me, taking his blows to my body and face without bothering to avoid them. In the first minute, he knocked me to the ground and raised his gloves victoriously. Within my mind, the wolf growled, wanting to lash out and take the big man down.

Patience, I told myself, *he's ours.*

I stood up, dusted off my gloves, and smiled at Lynch.

The big man was surprised, but more than willing to finish what he had started. A minute later, I was on the ground again.

Take him!

Wait.

I stood up and smiled again. This time he was a little disheartened. He seemed sure that he had put me down with that last volley, and I'll admit that he had handed out some good licks. But I'd had worse, even before the wolf.

Round two began, and I smiled. The big man was winded now. He'd let me have it in the first round, and he was beginning to feel it. His punches were slightly slower, slightly sloppier, but they still hit hard. I went down three more times in the second round. I could hear people muttering in the crowd that they should call the fight. This was no contest and some of them didn't want to watch some poor idiot get himself crippled. Nice of them, but unnecessary.

"Kid, what the hell is this? You said you could fight?" Sal Curcio hissed at me in my corner after the second round. "I don't expect you to win, but at least put on a damn show! Another round like that, and I'm calling it, people are going to start leaving."

"Third round, I told you. Don't worry about me, Mr. Curcio," I said.

"I ain't worried about you, you crazy son of a bitch. I'm worried that you're going to cost me money." He sweated nervously and took heavy drags of a cigar. Silly me. For just a second, I'd thought he cared.

"Alright, I'll show them something then," I smiled at him.

"And wipe that damn fool smile off your face," he shouted at me as I stepped in for round three. "Makes you look crazy."

The bell rang, and I felt bad for Lynch. But only a little.

He was fighting on fumes now and swung wildly. It was easy to catch his punches on my gloves or to step out of the way almost lazily. I finally started hitting him back. Just love taps at first. He'd come barreling in and swinging hard. I'd block and dodge a few, and then after he overextended himself, I'd let him feel one, just one, to the face. He'd stumble for a second, not sure what had just happened. Then he'd look at me, and I couldn't help it, I'd smile.

He was angry now, but that was fine. Angry and tired is an old family recipe for a beating, handed down from my father. After a half dozen exchanges of dodge-tap-smile, I decided it was time. It started the same. He swung, I moved, and my glove stung his jaw, but then instead of dancing away I stayed in close, going to his body for the first time. I let the wolf have his wish and unloaded the last two rounds of pain and anger on the big man's ribs. Left, right, over and over in quick successive snapping punches. No haymakers. No desperate swings. Just an explosion of quick angry strikes to his body. He stumbled back, but I stayed with him, not letting up. I growled back in my throat, but nobody could hear it over the shouting of the crowd. I felt a crack in the man's chest and knew I should stop, but the wolf didn't agree. We doubled down for a moment on the injured man, feeling his ribs give under the blows.

Enough.

I hadn't come here to kill or cripple this man, even if he did remind me of my late unlamented father. It was time to show Mr. Curcio that I was a man of my word. After working over the Irishman's body, it was a simple thing to pop up and put him down for good. Two quick jabs to his face and one hard cross did the job. He teetered for a second, the last to know that he had just been knocked out, and then hit the floor hard.

I didn't have to buy a single drink for the rest of the night.

"You cost me a lot of money tonight," Mr. Curcio said, sidling up to me with a fresh cigar in his hand.

"How's that? Nobody left." I finished my whiskey and looked around at the crowded joint.

"I had money on Lynch."

"Ah," I said, "sorry about that. I told you, he'd go down in the third round."

"Yes, yes you did." He smiled dangerously. "Next time, I'll believe you. But after the whooping you took in there tonight, it'll be a few weeks before I can make that money back."

"I'll be back tomorrow. You can make it back then."

"Tomorrow? Kid, you shouldn't even be walking..."

"I'll be back tomorrow night," I said.

"After seeing the punishment you took tonight, there's no way you're going to be able to go a single round tomorrow," he said.

"And that's just what everybody else is going to put their money on, isn't it?" I said slyly.

"Yeah, cuz they ain't crazy," he said skeptically.

"Well, maybe I am." I downed another drink.

"I'll tell you what, kid," Curcio said quietly, leaning in conspiratorially. "Not everybody is going to bet against you. Not after tonight. If you was to, say, hold on until the third round before *you* go down, I could make some money back and cut you in for a piece."

No. We do not submit.

Yes, I had to agree. I had taken enough beatings without properly fighting back. I had saved all those punches that I hadn't been allowed to use in the ring, and all that had ended the day that I had given them all to my father, with interest. I wouldn't be taking any dives.

"Mr. Curcio," I said softly, "respectfully, I *don't take dives.* You put your money wherever you want, but you'll make a lot more if you put it where I suggest."

He stared at the side of my face for a long hard minute as I studied the glass in my hand.

"Alright kid, alright," he said, laughing. "I'll take a chance on you. Why the hell not? But if you cost me, you'll be taking more than one beating, you get me?"

I nodded and stood, shaking his hand and meeting his eyes briefly. To his credit, he barely flinched.

"I'll see you tomorrow night, Mr. Curcio."

I spent the next day dozing under a tree like a hobo while the wolf made short work of my cuts and bruises. I wanted to go to Evelyn, but I'd told Peter that I wouldn't come back until I had found work, and I meant it. I'd also told Evelyn that I'd be back soon, and I'd meant that too.

The next night I showed up at Sal Curcio's joint unwashed and with an empty stomach. This time I was supposed to go up against a scrappy looking Jew named Levinsky.

"Well, I'll be damned," Mr. Curcio said as he clapped me on the shoulder while I laced my gloves. "You actually showed up, and you don't look half bad. What's your secret?"

"Fresh air," I said without looking up.

"Hah, that's a good one," he laughed. "So, kid, how do you like your chances tonight? Levinsky is a killer. He's won his last five fights. Three by knockout. You still think I should be putting my money on you?"

I looked across at the other fighter. He was an older man with a weathered look on a leathery face. The kind of face that has taken its share of punches and doesn't mind the idea of a few more.

"He looks tough," I admitted.

"You havin' second thoughts?"

"Fifth," I said.

"What?"

"He'll go down in the fifth."

Mr. Curcio looked at me like I'd just told him I could fly, but he was good as his word. He took a chance on me.

That night, Smiling Frank, as he started calling me, had his second straight win. After the fight, I walked out of Curcio's joint with a pocket full of money and a plan to come back the next weekend. The very next day I spent that cash on a gold ring.

CHAPTER FORTY-FIVE

"What do you mean, she went to see my sister?" I growled the words at Peter through clenched teeth.

He stared back at me from his burned face, unflinching, smug.

"Just what I said," Peter said. "After you were gone, she decided that her own family wasn't good enough for her anymore, so she went looking for yours."

"And how would she even know to do that?"

I took a threatening step forward, hands clenched at my side, the gold ring that had been burning a hole in my pocket on my way back to Evelyn, now all but forgotten.

"I told her, of course."

I grabbed him by the shoulders, pushing him against the wall and holding him there with more strength than a man should have. He remained smug and unshaken.

"Why?" I snarled the word.

"Because you left, and she was going to leave too." He spat the words at me from inches away. "She couldn't wait to tell our father that you were going to be married. To prove him wrong."

"Shit..." I sighed and released my grip on my soon-to-be brother-in-law.

"Of course, he disowned her on the spot," Peter went on, not showing any sign that I'd laid my hands on him. "Told her to get out of his house. She was only too happy to oblige, telling him that she had a new family now anyway, one that actually loved her."

"Oh boy..." I slumped onto Peter's bed, sitting with my head in my hands. Evelyn had gone to Maggie? Maggie, who still thought I was dead?

"What else should I have done, Frank? Told her nothing and left her to wander the streets until you decided to come back and find her? Of course I told her."

I glared at him and was met by his eternally smug expression. He'd had no right! But then again, what else did I expect? Oh Evelyn, why couldn't you have kept your delicious mouth shut for just a little longer.

"She's your problem now, Frank," he said with a hint of a smile. "I hope you have better luck than we did. Now, I think you should leave."

"What?"

"You heard me, Frank," Peter said, taking a step toward me. "You aren't welcome here anymore. Now leave, and don't come back."

I stood up, looked at him, puzzling briefly at the look of hurt and betrayal on his face that I hadn't been able to see before, and did as he asked. I was at the top of the stairs and walking out the back door of his father's church when I heard his parting words to me, spoken soft and low so that only I would hear them.

"But if you hurt her, I'll kill you."

My wolf bristled, but I thought of Maggie and decided that I could respect his warning, even though I knew the threat was an empty one.

I walked alone for several hours, making my way back toward the direction I'd come from. Downtown, where Maggie and Paul lived in their little apartment. Where yesterday I'd won the money for Evelyn's ring by beating a man senseless. My head swam as I tried to anticipate what would come next. Evelyn and Maggie, two very different pieces of my life, colliding. What sort of mess would that leave me to clean up? Would Maggie even believe Evelyn, or would she think she was some crazy woman? Either woman could be so easily hurt by the other without either of them meaning to, and it would be my own damn fault. I had no idea what I was going to do.

Soon my feet had taken me to the Chinese laundry that my sister lived above. I hadn't decided to come here, hadn't wanted to, but where else was there left for me to go? Everything that mattered to me was here, and that scared me more than it had any right to.

I stood there, I don't know how long, hours maybe, just listening to the sounds of the street and wrestling with what I was supposed to do next. The sun began to set while I marveled at how ridiculous I was for being so frightened. I had been to war damnit, had fought and killed actual monsters, had even become one. Hell, I'd fought bears with my bare hands in the dead of winter, but my little sister and the first woman I'd ever loved made me nearly piss myself with terror.

"Francis..."

How had I not heard her coming? How had I not seen her? I think maybe I was standing there so that she would find me, so that I wouldn't have to decide what to do next. I don't know. Whether some part of me intended it or not, there was my little sister now, all grown into a lovely young woman. Tears welled in her grey eyes as she stood in the doorway to the building, her hair that I knew to be the same red as mine was a sort of muted gold to my wolf eyes, but there was no mistaking my Maggie.

My mouth opened as if I were going to speak, but I had no words. Instead I just stood there like a slack-jawed moron as my grown-up baby sister walked straight up to me with all the courage and confidence that I had been unable to find.

She punched me in the mouth with a hard right cross. I was surprised but impressed. When had she learned to do that?

My hands went to my mouth where she had bloodied my lip, but then wrapped around my baby sister when she surprised me again by flying into them. Maggie buried her face in my shoulder and sobbed loudly, alternating between squeezing me tightly and pounding on my back and ribs with her closed fists.

"You let me think you were dead!" She screamed the words into my chest. "You let me think you were dead! You heartless bastard! You let me think you were dead!"

People on the street were stopping to look at us now, the fiery redheaded woman screaming and beating at the man with the matching hair who stood there and took it as he held her. I didn't care. To hell with all of them. None of them could understand.

Minutes passed like that, maybe more. She cried more loudly than I ever knew she could after all the times that I had held her as she cried quietly under the bed so that our father wouldn't hear. She positively wailed, soaking the front of my dirty shirt with her snot and hot tears, hitting me with slowly diminishing fury. Finally, I just held her there, stroking her hair and muttering nonsense to her like I used to do as she sniffed and wracked with silent sobs.

"I'm sorry, Mags. I'm sorry. I didn't mean to. I didn't know what to do."

Finally, after the sky had grown dark and the stars had come out, she pulled her swollen, tear-streaked face back from me, produced a handkerchief with which she wiped her eyes and blew her nose, and then turned to face me.

"Well," she said, "are you coming up or not?"

CHAPTER FORTY-SIX

"Francis?"

Evelyn raised a teasing eyebrow at me and smirked playfully when she heard what Maggie called me.

"It's Frank, now," I said.

"Not to me it isn't," Maggie grimaced. To her, Frank would always be our father's name, the name of a brutal and dangerous man, and that was exactly why I had adopted it.

My welcome into Maggie's small home had been warm and a little overwhelming. Evelyn had practically leapt into my arms and smothered me with kisses in relief that I had actually come back. I found the public display more than a little embarrassing but the weight of her in my arms was entirely too pleasant to refuse. Paul and Maggie both smiled and looked away politely, Maggie giggling a little, until Evelyn found her feet again. After that, Paul pumped my hand and clapped me on the shoulder with sincere enthusiasm.

Soon we were all sitting on uncomfortable furniture and drinking a bottle of shitty red wine that Paul had been saving for a special occasion—Evelyn had two glasses—and everybody bombarded me with questions I hadn't prepared for.

"What happened to you, Franc—um, Frank?" Paul asked, making an effort to correct his childhood name for me. Maggie glowered a little every time one of them called me by our father's name, but she didn't object.

"Well, where do I start?" I said, trying to buy time.

"We got a letter saying you had died," Maggie said. "Just a little while before Mama passed, about three years ago now."

I'd never lied to Maggie before, and I didn't want to start now. The trick was to find the right amount of truth. Maybe I'd tell her more later, but right then with Paul and Evelyn listening in, I couldn't just come out with everything. They'd think I was crazy.

"Well, there was an ambush," I said slowly, studying my glass as I thought of how to put it. "I was hurt badly. It was dark. They thought I was dead. I don't blame them."

"But, three years?" Paul asked.

"Yes, I know," I said, taking a slow drink of the cheap wine while I thought of how not to lie to my sister and the man who loved her. "It took me quite a while to make sense of things after, after what happened, and after I was well again, I realized that I'd be seen as a deserter. So, I couldn't just report back, or I'd be shot."

"They wouldn't," Maggie gasped, "would they?"

"I wasn't sure," I said. "After some of the stories I'd heard, it seemed possible. Likely, even."

Maggie put her hands to her mouth, her eyes wide. Evelyn leaned in against me.

"How did you get back?" Evelyn asked.

"Well, I walked quite a while, and eventually found passage on a ship across the Atlantic." All the while stealing chickens in the night, howling at the moon, and nearly murdering a boat load of superstitious sailors, I neglected to add.

"And I suppose that took you three years?" Maggie said with a glare.

"No. No it didn't." I didn't meet her eyes.

"Then why, Francis? Why didn't you write? Why didn't you come home?" The hurt in her voice broke my heart.

Paul put a comforting arm around my sister, his wife, a thing that I was still getting used to.

"Maggie..." I began, "I don't know how to explain, not really. Things happened in the war. Terrible things. Evelyn's brother can understand some of it, but nobody who wasn't there really ever could. The things I saw... hell Maggie, the things I did! I can't talk about it. I just—I wanted to keep it all far from you. Can you understand that? I wanted you to be safe and happy and loved, and I just, I suppose I felt I wouldn't be good for any of those things anymore."

Her arms were around me before I'd realized I'd been crying. Maggie had crossed the little room from where she had been sitting and knelt in front of me, wrapping me in a sisterly embrace. Beside us, Evelyn kept an arm on my shoulder but said nothing. I fought back the tears, embarrassed that any of them would see me like that, not wanting their pity, wishing they'd stop looking at me.

"Francis," Maggie said softly, waiting until I looked up at her smiling face, "you're really stupid."

I couldn't help it. I laughed. We all did.

After that, they didn't ask any more questions for a while. Not that night, anyway. I guess tears are good for something after all. Maggie fixed dinner in their small kitchenette and Evelyn lent a hand while I sat with Paul.

"So," I said to him sternly, "you married my baby sister."

He stiffened, smelling a little nervous and fearful. The wolf in me was pleased that he was a little afraid of me.

"Well, yes," he said. "I just, well you see, I've always loved her Franci—Frank! Frank. And after your mother died, there was nobody else. I thought she'd say no when I asked her. I was sure of it, really, and listen, I know it isn't what you had in mind when you asked me to look after her, but I won't apologize. I can't. I just, well…"

He was rambling. I was half-tempted to let him keep going, but that would have been cruel. Instead, I put a hand on his shoulder and felt him stiffen as he fought the urge to jump.

"Paul, it's all right," I said with a smile. "She's happy. Just keep her that way. You don't owe me any explanation. Thank you."

He exhaled and visibly relaxed, clearly relieved that I hadn't responded differently.

"Maggie Adler, huh?" I said, trying out her married name. "That'll take some getting used to."

"Actually, Francis, it's Lena now," Maggie said as she carried two bowls of soup to the table, followed by Evelyn who carried two more.

Lena, the name our mother had always called her. Nobody called her by her full name, Magdalena.

"Not to me it isn't," I said, cocking an eyebrow at her.

She couldn't argue.

The meal was simple, but hot, and more than I was used to.

"So, Frank," Paul said, "what are you going to do now? There isn't much work around, I'm sorry to say."

"I've noticed," I said, "but I think I might have found something."

"Oh?" Evelyn asked.

"Nothing official," I said, "but this guy, name of Curcio, runs a joint not far from here. He says he has work for me."

"Why do I know that name? What kind of shop does he run?" Paul asked.

"He runs a bar," I said.

Maggie looked up with concern, Evelyn was interested, and Paul looked disapproving.

"A bootlegger?" Paul asked.

"I suppose so."

Maggie scowled, and Evelyn tried to frown, but I could tell she was a little excited at the idea.

"That's dangerous stuff, Frank. Illegal," Paul said.

"I don't plan on running booze, Frank, don't worry. Besides, if there isn't any legal work to be found, what am I supposed to do?"

"Does it pay well?" Paul asked, interested.

Maggie placed a hand on Paul's arm.

"So far, well enough," I said, reaching into my pocket and withdrawing the little gold ring I'd bought.

"What is that?" Paul asked, oblivious.

Maggie raised her hands to her mouth and stared.

"I don't really know how this is supposed to be done," I said, turning to Evelyn.

Her mouth dropped open and a little bit of soup dripped onto her chin before she snatched up a napkin and cleaned it off.

"Frank, is that..." she said.

"I think I'm supposed to get on my knee, right?" I said, getting out of my chair and lowering myself to the floor. Across the table, Maggie let out a tiny girlish squeal. Paul still seemed confused.

Evelyn had pushed her lips together so tightly that they seemed to disappear entirely.

"Yes," she said. "Yes, yes."

"But I haven't even asked you yet," I said.

She didn't care. She was out of her chair now too, and had knocked me on to the floor, smothering me in kisses again.

Maggie kept squealing.

Paul cleared his throat.

CHAPTER FORTY-SEVEN

I was happy. At least, I think I was.

At first things went even better than I could have hoped. For the first week, we stayed with Maggie and Paul, until I had more money for a place of my own. Paul helped Evelyn get the divorce that her father had forbidden. When Maggie saw that there was no keeping Evelyn and I apart, she insisted that we be married as soon as possible, for propriety, something that Evelyn and I didn't give a damn about. Maggie and Paul both stood with us as we took our vows before a judge we had never met, and just like that, I was a married man.

"I like her, Francis, I really do," Maggie whispered to me on my wedding day, "she's so... wild."

"I know," I smiled.

And she was wild. Completely unrestrained. A fact that Evelyn made sure to remind me of on our wedding night in the little room I'd found for us not far from Curcio's joint. She was no virgin, that much had been clear from the start. Evelyn knew exactly what she wanted and had no problem in taking it. Demanding it. A fact that was as true in our daily lives as it was in our bed. She quickly took charge of the minor details of our life, decorating our little home as she saw fit, choosing our meals, and doing more drinking than most people thought a lady should. I didn't mind. I loved her wild willfulness. There was no controlling Evelyn, and I never wanted to, which is, I think, why she loved me. That, and the fact that I was almost able to match her appetites with my own wolfish needs.

Almost.

I went back to Mr. Curcio on the weekends and made us both a lot of money. I never lost a fight. Sal Curcio and Evelyn both complained that I disappeared for a week at a time, though.

"You're leaving money on the table, kid," Curcio said to me, but didn't try to stop me. After all, I still fought more often than anybody else and without complaint.

"Why do you have to go?" Evelyn would pout at me. "Stay, please..."

She did her best to persuade me to stay, and she could be very persuasive indeed. But for everybody's sake, I left for my time in the wilderness.

I'd begun to make a name for myself in the boxing ring, Smiling Frank was quickly becoming somewhat famous, a fact that Evelyn enjoyed but which I was beginning to worry about. The fights let me vent some of the aggressive instincts that I suppressed for most of the week, but I knew it couldn't last. A fighter who heals overnight might not draw too much attention at first in a local joint with dim lights and a bunch of drunken fools for an audience, but an undefeated fighter that people came from all around to see started to gather whispers.

"What's your secret, Frankie?" anonymous spectators asked me. I shrugged them off easily enough, but something had to be done.

Mr. Curcio's operation was doing very well indeed, and not just on boxing bets. He was raking in the money hand over fist on a nightly basis, Prohibition was good for the bar business.

Even police would come to Curcio's for a stiff drink and an envelope of cash to keep them looking the other way. And it was more than just Canadian whiskey that Sal dealt in. Soon I was getting a steady supply of dope from the Italian bootlegger, as well, for those days when I needed a little help keeping the wolf at bay.

Evelyn found my stash once, but rather than disapproving, she only demanded that she smoke it with me and agreed not to tell Maggie.

Eventually, I told Mr. Curcio that I couldn't keep fighting.

"Yeah, I figured as much, kid, boxing is small time anyway. Listen, I've got something better for a guy like you."

Curcio wasn't just a drunken boxing fan, he'd been paying attention. He knew damn well that there was something different about me, something that kept me getting up when other men would have stayed down for good. He didn't ask questions. So long as I was making him money, he didn't care about the details, something I've always enjoyed about criminals, but he saw uses for a talent like mine.

He brought me into his operation. It turned out that Curcio worked for a bigger fish in the Seattle bootlegging scene. A guy named Olmstead. This big fish, the Gentleman Bootlegger as he was called, used to be a cop himself, and so he knew all the right people and all the right ways to keep the booze flowing. But there was still some danger in smuggling liquor. Olmstead had a sterling reputation because he insisted that the people who work for him not hurt anybody. He even passed down a rule that they couldn't carry guns, something that Curcio didn't agree with.

What Curcio needed was somebody who wasn't scared to take a hit and who was able to return that hit with interest, but he was especially interested in a guy with the sort of reputation that would keep violence from breaking out in the first place. A reputation like Smiling Frank's.

So, I went to work for Mr. Curcio on the condition that he do me two favors. First, he had to allow me my time to go off on my own once a month, to take care of my personal business. He didn't like that, but he agreed. Second, he had to take on my brother-in-law, Paul, who had kept struggling to find steady work, but he had to promise me that Paul wouldn't be allowed to get caught up in anything dangerous. He agreed readily enough to that request as well. Mr. Curcio had a head for business but wasn't great at numbers. He let other guys manage his books but somehow always seemed unable to plug all the leaks in his finances. He was only too happy to have an honest man handle his money for him.

"Now that I got a Jew working my books for me, I'm feelin' practically legitimate," he laughed.

Maggie didn't like it, but after I promised her that I wouldn't let anything happen to Paul, she reluctantly allowed it. Paul was hesitant at first but took to his new position like a duck to water, eager to prove himself in the best paying job he'd ever had.

Within a year, all four of us had moved into two nice houses near each other on Capitol Hill. Nothing as fancy as the mansions on Millionaire's Row where guys like Olmstead and Curcio had homes, but close enough to feel that we had done damn well for ourselves.

Evelyn seemed only too happy to play the part of a gangster's wife, as she saw it. She would hang out at Curcio's on the weekends, Mr. Curcio said she "classed up the joint", and drink and smoke and listen to the music. The place did much better for itself over the years than it had when I first walked in looking to make money on a fight, and by my second anniversary with Evelyn it had become a popular nightspot. Evelyn thrived in the spotlight. She didn't sing or dance, but she loved being sought after. Something I didn't worry about much, because nobody in their right mind at Curcio's would dare mess with the wife of Smiling Frank. After all, I was paid to be intimidating, and I did my job well.

Maggie never set foot in the joint.

Evelyn's social needs weren't quite met by carousing at Curcio's on the weekends or drinking and smoking herself into a hedonistic stupor before going to bed with her antisocial husband at night. She wanted parties, but that was one of the few things I ever forbid her. I refused to let my home be filled with strangers. I needed a peaceful place to return to where I could quiet the wolf and not be a risk to anybody else. Evelyn was safe from me, after all. She had ways of putting the wolf to rest.

Maggie was only too pleased to host occasional dinner parties with Evelyn, but those failed to live up to Evelyn's dreams, something she complained about from time to time.

"Why do you get to go off and have fun?" Evelyn asked me once when I was leaving for the full moon. She sat in her favorite chair, an elegant wooden rocker I'd bought her.

"I'm not having any fun, sweetheart," I said to her. "This is pure business."

"Liar." She said to my face.

"What did you say?"

"I said, you're a liar. Old Sally isn't sending you anywhere. He told me he wishes you wouldn't take off like you do, just like me. He says he doesn't know where you go."

So, Evelyn had been talking about me with Sal Curcio. Damn. I'd kept the details of my condition a secret from Evelyn, though Maggie had come to know some of it over the years. Evelyn, as much as I loved her, wasn't somebody who I could trust to control her tongue, so it seemed safer for her not to know. Just as Mr. Curcio told all of us who worked for him not to tell our wives and girlfriends—those who had them—the details of our work. For their own safety. I had decided to keep my wolf a secret from Evelyn for the same reason.

She had to know something. She couldn't share a bed with me and not know that I was different, but it was a sort of 'different' that she enjoyed. Evelyn hadn't spoken to her family, not even Peter, since we had been married, but some part of her must still be the Reverend's daughter. Some part of her would surely judge me, condemn me, if she knew I was a monster. Better for her, and better for me, that she did not know.

I glared at her, caring even less for her tone of voice than I did for being called a liar. My lip twitched in the hint of a snarl.

"Just because it isn't business for Mr. Curcio, doesn't mean it isn't business," I said.

"What sort of business then?"

"My business," I said, "and none of yours."

"You've got another woman don't you," she said.

"Wh—what?" I was blindsided.

"You've got some floozy somewhere. I know it," she went on. "You go away for a few days, and you come back acting all relaxed and drained, just like after we screw."

She stared at me, waiting for a response, but I didn't have one. I just stared back, dumbfounded.

"It's okay," she said as she lit a cigarette for herself and took a long, sultry drag. "Lots of the fellas have a girl on the side, it's part of the life, really. I just wish you didn't have to lie to me about it. It wouldn't be so bad, if you didn't lie about it."

"I'm not lying, Evelyn."

"Sure."

"I'm not," I said. "There's nobody else."

"If you say so." She didn't believe me.

I didn't know what else to say. The moon was high and

bright, and the frustration of this conversation was raising my hackles. I had to leave. I turned to the door.

"So that's it then," she said. "You're just going to go?"

"I told you," I said, "I have to."

"Don't go, please." She sounded so sincere, so vulnerable for once. All her fierce wildness and angry sarcasm dropped for a moment as she simply pleaded with me.

"I have to, really," I said. "But there's no other woman, get that out of your head."

"Then tell me where you're going," she said.

"I can't!" I snapped at her. "Damn it, can't you just leave it be? Just trust me."

"Sure," she said, "like you trust me."

I left.

PART 7

OF WOLF AND MAN

CHAPTER FORTY-EIGHT

THE CASCADE MOUNTAINS,
1995

I walked out of the forest sometime before noon the day after dream-speaking with Andy. There was no traffic. The road was still closed and covered with melting snow this far east into the mountains and wasn't likely to open for another month. I'd guessed wrong when I told Andy I'd be coming out near Marblemount. That was nearly twenty miles west of where I was now, down where they bothered to keep the road cleared year-round.

There was nothing for it but to start walking, so I did. It couldn't be that far from where I was to where the road was open, in the town of Newhalem if I remembered correctly. Then I'd either find Andy waiting for me at the end of the road, or I'd keep walking until she found me. It was cold as hell, with the mountain wind whipping off of the melting snow and delivering the added chill with a piercing swiftness. I pulled my field jacket close around my throat and relied on the same things to keep me warm that had been doing the job for the past week or more; constant movement, and my slowly awakening wolf.

The new moon had passed, and with it my date with my own gun back in my trailer. I was a little disappointed that I had broken another promise to myself, but I still owed it to Mack to get to whoever the hell had really killed him if it hadn't been me, and I knew he'd never forgive me if I didn't make sure Andy was safe too. After all, he had taken the teenage girl on as his responsibility, and once Big Mack Watson took somebody on as his personal cause, he never gave up on them. I was proof of that. There'd be time enough to eat a bullet when this was through if I still wanted that, and I think I did.

Drawing a little on my semi-dormant wolf, I managed to traverse the closed stretch of road in about an hour. I smelled it before I saw it, the familiar exhaust of my beaten-up old Chevy Blazer, perpetually in need of more oil. I looked over my shoulder, half expecting Hiram to be following behind me.

I smiled. Nobody was there. Good. If the old bastard was following me, he would have a hell of a time keeping up now that I had my wheels. I caught a whiff of cigarette smoke on the early spring air and doubled my pace. Bumming a smoke off of Andy sounded like just the thing right then.

Rounding the last corner, I saw it, the old white Chevy parked near a pile of snow that the road crews had left at the end of the open road. The engine was running, and the headlights were on, pointed right toward me. Getting into the warm cab sounded almost as good as that cigarette.

I waved, but couldn't make out any reply from this angle. The damn high beams were on. Somebody needed to teach this kid a couple fine points about driving, but it damn sure wasn't about to be me.

As I drew near the roadblock, I began to sense that something was wrong. There was blood in the air, fresh blood. I could see now that there were more tire marks in the slush of the road than my Chevy accounted for, and as I hopped the little gate that separated the open road from the closed pass, I could see from the tracks on the side of the road, that some of those tires had belonged to motorcycles.

What the hell was going on?

"Andy?" There was no answer.

I took a tentative step toward the Blazer, sniffing at the cold, wet air. Blood alright, and other smells as well. The fresh smell of the still burning cigarette came from the running truck, traces of Andy's distinctive scent as well, but more than that. Man smells. Wolf smells. Garou?

A high-pitched whimper and yip from just beyond the road snapped my head around. Blue, my cattle dog, peeked at me from behind the tree line. Something was wrong with her. She was in pain.

Immediately, my hackles rose, and the wolf stirred within me. A member of our pack had been hurt. Attacked. There was nothing more provocative to the wolf, or to me. I was beside Blue in two steps, kneeling beside her and placing a comforting hand on the ruff of her neck. She was bleeding from the head, one side of her face a sticky mess where she had been struck by something hard. I didn't doubt that her skull was fractured and wasn't entirely sure that she still had her left eye. The smell of blood had been coming from her.

I knew immediately what must have happened.

Andy had been followed after all. Los Perdidos, those damn bikers, had caught up with her at the end of the highway. And unless my nose was lying to me, with them had been Hiram's mad wolf, another Garou. Andy never stood a chance.

But why leave my Blazer for me? For the same reason they had hurt my dog and left her here for me to find. They wanted me to follow them. They wanted to make me angry, and they wanted me to come after them. For Andy, for Blue, for Mack. Well, I was going to give the fuckers exactly what they wanted, and I was going to make them regret it. They wanted to go to war? They didn't know what real war was. I'd show them.

Carefully, gingerly, I wrapped my arms around Blue and lifted her, whispering comforting nonsense to her as I nuzzled her ear. She licked at my chin, weakly, as I carried her toward the Blazer. With every step her whimpering grew louder, they must have hurt her badly for my normally stoic dog to complain this much. I was sure she had made them work to take Andy. Blue wouldn't have let the girl go without a fight.

"It's okay, love, I've got you," I whispered to her. "We're almost there, I'm gonna get you help, shhh."

She began to squirm in protest as I reached the door of the Blazer and pulled it open. I should have listened to her, but I was too angry to think clearly. That, no doubt, was the plan.

"Hello, asshole," the biker said.

He was sitting in the passenger seat, across from me. He was maybe in his early thirties, unshaven and brown-skinned. He wore dirty leathers and had a small double-barreled shotgun, cut to well below the legal size, and pointed directly at me.

I never had a chance to say or do anything, but Blue was snarling at him before I knew what was happening. He fired.

The shot tore into us, the brunt of it missing Blue but tearing through her front legs just as it ripped into the flesh of my belly. Blue and I both screamed in pain, an instinctive yowl that matched one another as only old packmates can. I fell to the hard slush-covered ground, still holding Blue protectively as we dropped before releasing her on the ground.

I writhed with the pain. Steel shot. There was no mistaking it.

"Ha! Got you, bitch," the biker said as he exited the Blazer and circled around to where I lay clutching at my abdomen. I was clenching my teeth now, snarling at the pain. Blue screeched in pain beside me.

"You... hurt... my... dog..." I managed to gasp.

If it had been anything but steel shot, the wolf would have risen to the surface by now and taken this bastard's head off. But as it was, this close to the new moon, with a belly full of steel, I was nearly helpless.

"You stole from us, *ese*," the biker said as he reached me, before digging the toe of his heavy boot into my ribs with a powerful kick of his long leg. I felt something crack and grunted at the pain.

Blue continued her crying, driving daggers of rage into me with each heart-wrenching whimper. I curled into a fetal position in an instinctive effort to shield my vitals. He kicked my back and shoulders twice more.

"Did you think we wouldn't find you?" He kicked me again. "You and that little *puta*?" Another kick.

I was growing dizzy, losing a good deal of blood. The wound wasn't closing, and I could smell my own coppery heat steaming up from the nearly frozen road.

"You're lucky," he said as he kicked me again in the spine. "You get to die here, but Lodi has plans for that little bitch. Woo baby!" Another kick. "And then, after I grease you, Lodi is gonna give me the bite!"

The bite? So, this Lodi guy was the other Garou? Not Hiram's lost cub? I wasn't sure that added up, but it was good to know, nonetheless. Even in my shock and agony, I tucked that morsel of information away for later consideration.

Blue screamed and writhed again, not far from me. Was she dying? I stretched out to reach my dog, to lay a hand on her and let her know she wasn't alone. The biker kicked me again in my exposed ribs for my trouble, and I couldn't reach her.

"So, what do you have to say before I blow your fucking head off, bitch? Lodi will want me to tell him your last words, so make it something good." He grinned down at me and pointed the sawed-off at my head. At this range, with steel shot, I didn't stand a chance. I'd finally get what I'd been wanting. I could die. Maybe I should have just let him do it. And I might have, except for one thing.

I told him what it was, but he couldn't hear me. Not with my voice so low, not with the sounds of my dog screaming beside us, sending daggers of rage through my spine with the pulses of her agony. Her pain reached me in a way my own never could. Reached my wolf in a way mine never could.

"What did you say? Speak up, asshole," he kicked me once more.

"I said," I snarled, "You. Hurt. My. Dog."

It was a good trap, really. Get me distracted, catch me unaware, make me sloppy, and drop me with a gut full of steel. Somebody had put some thought into it, maybe this Lodi fucker I kept hearing about, and it should have worked. But the thing they hadn't accounted for, the thing that I had spent my long life coming to terms with, the thing that kept me living by myself in the woods like some junkie hermit, was that no matter what the circumstances, no matter how dark the moon was, no matter how full of drugs or how chained up with steel I might be, nobody was safe if I was angry enough. Rage was the essential fact of my life. And I loved that damn dog.

He didn't know how I got on top of him. Neither did I. It happened too fast. I only know that I reached up and yanked the gun out of his hand, sending it unfired to the ground, and the next thing I knew I was atop him, straddling him. I don't like to think about what I did to that man in the mountains that day. I try not to think about it. When I do remember that kill, I try to make myself feel better by reminding myself that before he died, he was already unidentifiable. When I finally tore out his throat with my teeth, I was doing him a favor.

CHAPTER FORTY-NINE

Blue wasn't dead, but neither one of us was in good shape. I needed help. For her, but also for me. At times like this in the past, I'd have turned to Mack. Now, that wasn't an option. Nevertheless, like any injured animal, I decided to go to where I'd gotten help in the past. Mack's place. Without stopping to think, I tossed the dead biker's half empty weapon into the Blazer and lifted Blue into the passenger seat over her shrieking protests of pain.

"It's okay, darlin'," I grunted through my own pain. "We're gonna get you some help."

The drive seemed to drag on for years, with Blue whimpering and bleeding on the passenger seat. I clenched my jaw and grimaced while I drove with one hand on my belly. It was a small miracle that I didn't kill somebody with my driving. I was honked at and given more than one friendly finger-based salutation, but I barely noticed.

By the time I arrived in Everett, it was later in the day and my wound had stopped bleeding, but it was far from healed. The little steel pellets still burned beneath my skin and in my guts, causing my wolf to whimper pathetically in the back of my mind in harmony with Blue's cries of pain beside me. She had fallen asleep, or lost consciousness perhaps, but that hadn't stopped the horrible noises that she was making, only muffled them a little.

Mack's big, blue Suburban was parked in its customary spot in the alley behind Watson's Bail Bonds. I tried to park beside it, but succeeded only in taking the paint off the driver's side of the pristine SUV that Mack had taken such good care of. The screeching grind of metal on metal announced my arrival to anybody who cared to know. I had just enough presence of mind to pull the keys from the ignition before I unthinkingly dropped them to the floor of my Blazer, which I now noticed was soaked in my own blood.

I hadn't meant to drop the keys, but my fingers were being disobedient little bastards and wouldn't do what I told them. For that matter, I hadn't meant to run into Mack's precious Suburban, but my eyes couldn't seem to keep open long enough for me to do a decent parking job. Hell, in the long list of things I didn't mean to do that day I may as well add get shot by a pissant biker drug dealer with aspirations of lycanthropy. Come to think of it, the gap between what I intend and what actually happens in my life has always been wide enough to sink a ship in. Today was just par for the course.

I was drifting. My thoughts swimming back and forth from one topic to another. I had gotten where I had meant to go, but why had I come here again? Mack. That was it. He'd help. He always helped. Ever since I'd first met him half a century ago he'd never let me down. I fumbled with one hand at the door lever and tumbled out onto the cool asphalt.

"What the hell is going on out there?" A woman's voice yelled from an opening doorway. "You'd better have insurance, you son of a bitch, or so help me you're going to wish—Frank? Frank!"

Marilyn was standing over me, her golden hair streaked with strands of silver, and her middle-aged face still showing the peculiar mix of compassion and intolerance for bullshit that had endeared her to me as long as I'd known her.

"Hello... gorgeous..." I smiled at her deliriously.

"Frank," she said urgently. "What the hell did you do?"

She was taking my wrist to feel my pulse while staring in horror at the bloody interior of my Blazer.

"Don't worry," I said, "it's mine."

Another face appeared behind her, a darker face, older than hers, but still somehow possessed of a youthful spark. A man's stern face with smile lines that looked as though they hadn't seen much use lately. The face of my friend, Big Mack Watson.

"Mack?"

Marilyn looked behind her to where Mack stood, her shoulder passing through him as if he were vapor.

"You're delirious, you crazy asshole," she said. "We've got to get you inside and patch you up."

"No," I mumbled. "Blue. Blue."

"What?" she asked impatiently as she tried to pull me to my feet.

"Don't help me," I said as I pushed her hand away, "until you've helped my dog."

Marilyn looked down at me like I was speaking Portuguese. The ghost of Mack Watson smiled sadly and shook his head at me, but his shoulders rolled softly with a silent laughter.

"I'm... sorry..." I said, and then everything was dark.

CHAPTER FIFTY

Passing out *should* bring peace. Isn't that the whole point? Not for me. For me, it brought the wolf dream, faint and unfocused in the dim light of a growing crescent moon, but there just the same.

My wolf was barely there, the steel in our belly held him at bay, and so the normally vivid smells and sounds of the Dream were greatly muffled, as though I were experiencing it from beneath several feet of water.

I was only faintly aware of the frantic flapping of black wings, of panicked blue eyes with an emerald fleck, and a frightened cawing sound that seemed almost to be calling out my name.

I tried to reach out, but my hands wouldn't move. I was so barely in the Dream that I couldn't affect it.

"Andy?" I tried to say. "Where are you?"

Any answer the black bird may have had for me was drowned out by my own sudden roar of pain as burning glass exploded in my intestines.

CHAPTER FIFTY-ONE

I was tied down, thrashing against restraints that held me to a firm surface while a figure stood above me, digging in my guts with medieval torture implements.

I bellowed at the pain, clenching my jaws until I heard faint cracking sounds from my teeth and a faint clink as a little piece of metal was dropped into a bowl beside me.

"Look who's awake," Marilyn said. "Now hold still or this might hurt."

She dug into me again with the narrow steel tool and I howled with pain. She quickly pulled the torturous thing out of my flesh and looked at me with a mixture of apology and disbelief.

"Blue..." I said.

"Shh," Marilyn hushed me as she looked down at my wound, preparing to go in again. I squirmed.

"Where's Blue..."

"Hold still!" she snapped at me. "You'll tear something. Blue isn't here. I had a friend take her. Don't worry, she's in the best hands. Now let me take care of this before you do any more damage to my carpet than you already have."

"Is she... alright?"

Marilyn looked at me with sympathetic eyes. The one thing she had never been able to hate about me, the thing we'd always had in common, was our love of dogs.

"She's in bad shape, Frank," she said somberly. "I can't lie to you about that. I can't promise you that she'll keep that leg, but she's in very good hands. I promise. Now, will you please lay the hell down so I can get this over with? I figured you'd want this taken care of here, instead of at a hospital, all things considered."

All things considered? She must be referring to my current popularity with the police. I nodded reluctantly and clenched my jaw, bracing for the pain. As soon as the gleaming steel tools passed my skin, the searing pain returned, and I couldn't help but thrash as I moaned in protest. Marilyn pulled back and reconsidered.

"It shouldn't be this bad, not with your 'thing'. Maybe I really should call an ambulance," she said.

"No," I barked the word and then softened my voice for her. "Please, no hospitals. I can't."

It hit me then that she mentioned my 'thing', using Mack's old term for my condition. This puzzled me. In my semi-delirious state it took me a while to understand why.

Marilyn had known me for a long time, not as long as Mack, but for more than half her own life, since she'd been a young veterinary student with a dangerous attraction to unshaven older men. We'd met during a case that Mack and I had taken, back when the pants were tighter, and the music was better. She and I had gotten involved. I'd been lonely, and honestly, Marilyn had reminded me a little bit of my long-dead wife, at least superficially, with her golden hair and sensuous frame. I'd been the older man, more so than she could have realized, and she'd had enough of an adventurous spark to be drawn to what she thought my life was.

I'd been the hard drinking and devil-may-care private investigator. I think she had seen me as some leading man out of a film noir—though not nearly handsome enough. She had wanted to play the Lauren Bacall to my Humphrey Bogart, and I'd been tempted to let her. It had been a short and stormy affair, with all the urgent passion you'd expect from a man who hadn't been laid in a decade, but I hadn't been able to let it become what she wanted it to be.

In the end, she was nothing like Evelyn. Not once I got past the superficial elements. Evelyn had been fierce, rebellious, fiery even. Marilyn was sweet, caring, and as loyal a person as I've ever met. She was going to be a veterinarian after all. A certain amount of tenderness was a job requirement, though she did her best to hide it well.

Marilyn had known that there were things I was hiding from her. How I knew things that nobody else could after I'd smell or hear something they couldn't, or why I disappeared for nearly a week out of each month. She wanted me to let her in, to share those secrets with her, but I couldn't. Not after what had happened with Evelyn. I'd learned my lesson. I'd never told her about being a Garou.

I'd broken it off with Marilyn and expected never to see her again. But the thing about partnerships is that you don't get to make all the decisions, and Mack had other ideas. He told himself that he was consulting with her on another case. I think that she was trying to use him as a way to hang around me, at least at first, but the two of them became friends, and then, over the years, something more. It had ruined Mack's marriage, but Mack and Marilyn had been partners in every sense of the word ever since. For the last twenty or so years. Until he died.

I'd been happy enough for them I suppose, it hadn't been

any of my damn business, and they had both given each other what they couldn't get elsewhere. Marilyn got the trust and openness that I couldn't give her. Mack got a reliable partner who would always be there when they said they would. Good for them. They'd made each other happy. Marilyn's prickly attitude toward me over the last two decades was a small enough price for that.

Only... exactly how much trust had Mack given Marilyn?

"What do you mean?" I gasped.

"I mean you need medical help and if you won't let me do it..."

"No, you said, my 'thing'," I said. "What did you mean?"

She raised a perfectly formed eyebrow at me in an expression that seemed to say 'are you really going to make me play this stupid game while you bleed all over my table', but didn't say anything.

"Marilyn," I groaned. "How much do you know?"

"Oh for Christ's sake, Frank," she said in an exasperated voice as she turned from me. "I know everything Mack knew, of course. He told me everything."

"He had... no right..."

"Oh, go fuck yourself, Frank Shepard," she turned on me. "What did you expect? That the man I loved would lie to me the way you did? Or that I would be too stupid to ask any questions after knowing you for thirty years and going from the younger woman to being able to pass as your older sister?"

In truth, Marilyn could probably pass as my mother, but even stupefied by pain and on the edge of consciousness I knew better than to correct her on this point.

"Mack was a good man," she went on, "a damn good man, and you should have known better than to think that just because you were too big of a coward to tell me the truth that he'd be the same. He was a braver man than you'll ever be."

"You're right," I said in a gravelly voice.

That stopped her cold. She'd been expecting anything at all from me but agreement. We hadn't agreed on much since the nineteen-seventies. The customary hardness that she kept in her eyes for me melted away, melted into tears. She held a clean rag to her face and sobbed loudly, her shoulders rising and falling in beat with her broken heart. The restraints around my shoulders and wrists mercifully spared me from having to decide what sort of comforting gesture was expected of me at a moment like this.

"Marilyn..." I said softly from where I lay behind her.

She turned back slowly, took in the look of concern on my face, and broke out in near hysterical giggles, holding the rag to her mouth to muffle her laughter even as the tears still fell down her full cheeks.

"What?" I asked, puzzled.

"Well, just look at you," she said with a stifled laugh. "You're half dead, wanted by the police, tied down, bleeding all over my damn kitchen, and *you* are worried about *me?*"

I smiled weakly, relieved to see that she wasn't completely broken. I should have known better. She'd always been stronger than I'd given her credit for. Mack had been able to see that, even when I couldn't.

"Alright then, you big baby," she gestured at the open wounds in my gut. "What do you expect me to do?"

"Did Mack ever tell you... about iron?"

She looked puzzled as she gave it some thought.

"Yeah, I suppose he did mention it," she nodded. "He said sometimes, some of the things the two of you went after needed something special to put them down when regular things wouldn't hurt them, like iron or fire."

I nodded softly.

"That's right," I said, "and I'm one of those 'things'."

Understanding dawned on her face as she looked down at her steel surgical tools and grimaced.

"Oh," she said. "Damn."

"You're tellin' me..."

"Shut it," she said sternly, but with a hint of a friendly smile in her watery eyes. "So, now what?"

"My body will do most of the work, if we can get the steel out of me," I labored to say. "Do you have anything else you can use?"

And so, Marilyn ransacked her kitchen, bathroom, and crafting supplies for anything she could find to dig the shotgun pellets from my flesh. In the end, after giving a frighteningly long amount of consideration to a pair of disposable wooden chopsticks, she found a pair of plastic tweezers in an old travel kit of Mack's.

It was hard going. I may or may not have called her a couple of names that Mack would have punched me for if he'd still been around, but she knew it was the pain talking. Eventually, after agonizing minutes of Marilyn digging around under my skin, she removed the last pellet.

The instant it was gone, the constant whimper of my wolf in the back of my skull quieted, and the pain in my guts crested and began to withdraw. Marilyn cleaned the wound and bandaged it for me, raising an eyebrow as she did so at how quickly the bleeding had already stopped.

"Thank you," I said to her as she untied me, and I sat carefully up from the table, wincing a bit at the remaining pain as I felt the muscles of my stomach flare in protest.

"It's what Mack would have wanted," she said without looking at me.

I nodded agreement.

"Speaking of what Mack would have wanted," I said with a coy smirk. "Got any beer?"

She scowled at me but couldn't hold the expression for long and broke into a grin herself. Mack's answer to every problem had been a cold beer. She walked to the refrigerator and returned with two bottles of my dead friend's favorite brew, and we sat there, talking like old friends should.

There were tears, there was more laughter, and there was the trust that I'd been denying her for far too long. I told her everything that had happened over the past couple of weeks, starting with Mack's call about Andy Morgan.

CHAPTER FIFTY-TWO

"So, what are you going to do now?" Marilyn asked.

I'd recovered some of my energy and the pain in my belly was considerably lessened, but iron wounds are slow to heal, and it would be days until I was at anything resembling full strength.

"I can't let them hurt the kid," I said as I staggered to pick up my field jacket from where Marilyn had dropped it. My shirt had been a lost cause and Marilyn had thrown it away before I could object. My abdomen was heavily bandaged, and my jeans were serviceable, though they'd been worn for a week even before being soaked in my own blood.

Marilyn looked at me with a furrowed brow as I put the dirty jacket on over her clean bandages, but she didn't try to stop me. After all the years we'd known each other, she knew to pick her battles.

"Is there anything I can do to help?" she said. "I know I'm not Mack, but I've got to be able to do something."

"Well, if you don't mind," I said, "I'd like to have a look through Mack's old gun safe. Maybe see if there's anything from the good old days I could borrow."

"Of course," she said, as she walked me to the closet in Mack's office where the tall metal safe was half concealed behind several of Mack's old coats. She produced a key and opened it for me.

Mack's old weapons were laid out before me. An old pump action twelve-gauge, a well-loved thirty-thirty, and the colt forty-five he'd carried on all of our old cases. I remember teasing him a hundred times that he must have something to compensate for if he wasn't willing to pack something more concealable, but he'd just glare at me half-jokingly as he awkwardly loaded the pistol with his one good hand. It had gotten the job done more than once. There was no arguing that.

Behind the pistol I found the knife that Mack had kept since the second world war. It was fitted to function as a bayonet, but was far shorter than the sort of bayonets I had been trained with back before my change. Short or not, it was steel, and I might need it if I were going up against another Garou.

I held up the pistol and the old knife to Marilyn. "Mind if I borrow these?"

"They're yours," she said.

"No," I argued, "I'll bring 'em back."

"Bring them back if you want," she said, "but they're yours. Hell, the whole place is yours."

"What are you talking about?"

"Well," she amended. "A third of it is yours. Mack left it to you. Didn't he tell you?"

"What? No," I stammered. "No, he didn't. Why the hell—I don't want it, he knew that."

She shrugged. "Sometimes, a good friend is somebody who gives you what you need, instead of what you want."

I stared at her, prepared to continue the old argument with her that I'd had with Mack every time I saw him over the last few years. "Come back to work with me, Red," or "You need something to do with yourself, Frank". He'd go on and on about it, even talking about how maybe we should bring his boy in on the 'family business'. "Owen is a good boy," he'd said, "a good man. Stubborn as all hell, but who knows where he got that from?" Mack would laugh his ass off at that, like he did to all of his own jokes, but I would always tell him no. I wasn't coming back, and I wasn't going to tell any more people my secret. Not Owen, not Marilyn, nobody.

But Marilyn knew anyway, didn't she? And I'd needed her help, needed to trust her when I had nobody else to turn to. The way I'd trusted Mack.

Pack.

The wolf's voice in my mind was torpid and soft. He was still reeling from our encounter with the steel in my gut, and there wasn't yet much moon to speak of, wouldn't be for days. But he responded nonetheless to my train of thought. His instincts agreed with the direction my thoughts were moving. Wolves didn't hunt alone if they didn't have to. They were strongest as part of a pack. The bikers knew that. Why didn't I?

"You said a third of it is mine?"

"Yes," she nodded. "A third for you, a third for me, and a third for Owen. Though, that boy won't talk to me long enough for me to tell him, and there's no way he'd ever agree to work with me. He still blames me for breaking up Mack's marriage with his mother. Hell, maybe he's right."

"It's his name on the door," I said. "Watson's Bail Bonds should have a Watson behind the desk, don't you think?"

"Well, about that," Marilyn said. "Mack left a little stipulation in his will about the business. It's written in there that each of the partners has to agree to have a name on the door."

"Mack knew I'd never agree to that," I said. I'd told my old friend that the days of Shepard and Watson Investigations were well behind us both, but he never stopped dreaming. Now he was going to try and rope me into it as a dying wish? That was low. "No, I won't do it."

"He knew you'd say that," she sighed, "so he wrote it into the will that if both names aren't included, that the business has to be sold off."

Marilyn Archer had worked for Shepard and Watson before it became Watson Bail Bonds. She'd spent her life running this business. She knew it inside and out. It was as much hers as it was Mack's, and she deserved to keep it. I snarled a little at the trap I was in. Mack had maneuvered me into taking Marilyn's life's work from her just after losing the man she loved if I was going to insist on staying away from the business. The bastard had trapped me. He knew me well enough to know that I wouldn't be able to do that to her.

"That son of a bitch!" I growled.

Marilyn raised an eyebrow at me.

"I'm sorry, Marilyn," I said, "But damn it. He could really be a manipulative bastard when he wanted to."

"Yes," she smiled, "he really could."

"I'll need to think about it," I said, "and now isn't the time."

"That's fair," she said. "What else can I do to help?"

I'd been thinking of how I wanted to handle this as I loaded Mack's old Colt. I had the beginnings of an idea.

"First, I need a pen and paper," I said.

She produced the requested items almost immediately.

"And second?" she asked, as I sat down to write.

"Second, I need you to call the police."

"What?" She stared at me, disbelieving.

"You said Owen won't take your calls?"

"That's right."

"Well, I bet he'll come running if you call and report that I showed up at the scene again."

"Oh," she said. "That's a great plan, Frank. That'll definitely work. He'll come right here and shoot you again, brilliant."

Marilyn always had been fluent in sarcasm.

"I won't be here," I said, "but you'll give him a message from me."

I finished scribbling my hasty letter to Detective Sergeant Owen Watson, only son of my dead partner, and folded it in half, handing it to Marilyn, who accepted it from me dubiously.

"And you're just going to what," she said, "go riding off to save the day by yourself?"

"Not if you make that call I won't," I said. "But I'm going to do what I have to do to help Andy. That kid is in over her head, and the more time I waste, the more likely they are to hurt her. I can't let that happen."

I stood up, a little unsteady still on my feet, and made sure that the pistol and knife were both secured in my belt.

"Frank," she said, "they've had her all day. What if she's already... well, hurt? What then?"

"Then," I growled, "I make them regret it."

CHAPTER FIFTY-THREE

I'd rather not die in a trailer park, but when you've got to go, you've got to go. I reflected on the likelihood of my impending death as I drove through the dark floodplains just south of my home, where my pack of dogs, minus the injured Blue, would be waiting for my return. I'd have liked to have had them with me now, but they were safer where they were. Blue's blood soaked the passenger seat beside me, the smell of it keeping the fire of my anger stoked high as I drove.

I expected to find Andy where I'd first met her, in the rundown cathedral of white trash where the late unlamented Rita had looked over her, her ugly baby, and the bag of heroin that was no longer in the back seat of my Blazer. Believe me, I'd checked. I could really have used something to take the edge off of the pain that lingered in my rapidly healing gut, but I supposed that a little clarity and wolfish instinct might end up being just the thing I needed anyway. At least the moon wasn't full.

My plan was simple enough. The bikers wanted me dead. The why didn't matter. Whether it was for stealing their dope, some connection with this Yarrow person or just the crime of being another predator in what they saw as their territory, I didn't care. I was ready enough to die a few days ago. The way I saw it, I had a chance to get what I wanted and to make it count for something at the same time. Two birds, one death.

The trick, as with so many things, was all in the timing. I had to make a scene, get the attention of the bikers on me and away from Andy. Maybe even give her a chance to run, so that when the cavalry showed up, she would be safe, and they would be exposed. With any luck at all, the drugs would be back with them at the trailer park now that they had recovered them. But if not, my fresh corpse and Andy's testimony of her abduction should be more than enough to lock up Los Perdidos for good. The human ones anyway. For the others, I had Mack's knife.

I was counting heavily on the note I had left for Mack's son, Detective Sergeant Owen Watson, to rally the troops. Maybe I was being optimistic, but if I was any judge of character at all, I expected Owen to move heaven and earth to take down his father's killer. Whether he believed that was me or this Lodi character didn't matter, as long as he showed up in force.

In the letter I had told Owen that the people who had killed his father would be at Edison Court tonight, along with the abducted Andy Morgan. The last girl his father had tried to help. I mentioned Los Perdidos and their stockpile of heroin. But just to be damn sure that he showed up, in case he still only cared about catching me, I told him that I would be there too, and I promised him a full written confession after the night was over.

Of course, if I died, I wouldn't have to worry about delivering on that last part, and I was willing to take those odds.

As I pulled up to Edison Court for the second time, I considered my options. There were more than a dozen motorcycles present. Lights were on in at least three different trailers, and a bonfire burned between them. Five or six burly figures moved around the fire, raising cans to their lips and thrashing their heads to loud 'music'. They looked positively pagan as they thrashed about in the firelight, a small band of barbarians preparing to sack Rome. I didn't see Andy but assumed that she wouldn't be joining the festivities at any rate. Likely, she'd be inside.

If Mack were there, he'd have told me to take the careful approach. Something subtle. Perhaps turning off the engine and going in on foot, using the cover of darkness to find an optimal position, maybe even find Andy first and get her out unseen. He was always good at those sorts of plans. But Mack wasn't there. He was dead, and the hole in my life left by his murder left me feeling anything but subtle.

So, I opted for a more straightforward approach.

I floored the gas pedal as I turned into the trailer park, sending gravel flying high in my wake as I crashed directly into a cluster of four Harleys, knocking them over in a sickening crash of sparks and twisted metal. I came to a stop atop their wreckage as I slammed into one of the illuminated trailers, tearing through its corner walls. Before they had a moment to react, I had kicked open my own twisted door with all the strength my wolf could give me, drawn Mack's handgun from my belt, and fired two shots into the air.

"Where's the girl?" I yelled.

Fuck subtle.

My grand entrance had the desired effect. Immediately the men forgot their revelry and all eyes were on me. Several ran forward, profanities spilling from their lips more freely than the beer from the dropped cans. They half hunched for cover in response to my gunshots, but remained in the open, regarding the mangled bikes with horror and disgust. As though I had just poured gasoline on a box of puppies and lit them ablaze. If there's one thing I know about bikers, it is that you never touch a man's bike.

"What the goddamn fuck?"

"You're gonna fucking die, fucker!"

"No, no, no!"

The voices had one trait in common. They rumbled their shock and anger in a low, bestial, familiar growl. I levelled the pistol at them in a clear warning, realization dawning as I looked into six sets of yellow, wolfish eyes.

"Oh," I said, "shit."

Instead of one Garou and a group of wannabe bikers hoping to earn 'the bite' that the dead biker in the mountains had mentioned, I had driven right into a full pack of werewolf bikers.

"'Oh shit' is right, motherfucker," one particularly mean-looking son of a bitch said as he stepped forward, smirking. He was tall, perhaps a hand taller than me, with wild dark hair covering his head and face. He wore jeans and a black leather biker vest, open at the chest and with nothing else beneath it. His arms and chest were lean, leathery, and heavily tattooed. His face told me more than all his patches or tattoos ever could. His was the face of a man who had killed, a man who had been to real war.

"You must be Lodi," I said, levelling the gun at his face. He stopped, about five paces from me. The rest of his pack arrayed behind him.

"You must be fucking stupid," he replied with a hungry smile.

"I must be," I said, "but that hasn't slowed me down yet."

"You're supposed to be dead in the mountains," he said casually as he slowly drew and lit a cigarette, deliberately showing everybody present that he wasn't a bit worried about the filthy blood-soaked man with the gun. "But, since you're here and Rudy ain't, I suppose it must have gone the other way."

"Guess so," I said, putting two and two together. Rudy? Hadn't that been the name of Rita's man?

"So, aside from a messy death," Lodi paused to take another drag of his cigarette, "what the fuck do you want?"

The five bikers behind him were getting excited. I could see their features subtly shifting as the fire lit them from behind. Ears grew to points, fingers were tipped with sharp claws, snarls displayed growing teeth. I was well and truly fucked.

My own wolf stirred in response. I wasn't sure yet if he would back down and cower as he had before the superior strength of Hiram, or rise to the challenge and want to put these pups in their place. He was still reeling from the iron in our system, and I wasn't sure how much help he'd be.

"I just want the girl," I said, trying not to let them see my hands shaking and wishing that I could get one of those cigarettes he had in his pocket.

"Andy?" he said. "Fuck, you can have her. We all did."

Lodi smiled at me, a filthy grin through yellow teeth. I thought of Andy, the scrawny teenage girl with all the bruises I'd met in this very spot. I thought of the baby growing in her belly. I thought of the way Rita had said that they had passed her around, and I understood a bit more of the peculiar, broken strength the girl had in those unusual eyes of hers.

I shot him in the neck.

Immediately I discarded my original plan in favor of a new one. Kill every one of these sons of whores. This wasn't a situation for the police. They'd just get hurt. If this was going to be handled, it had to be handled by somebody like me. In retrospect, I think I was rationalizing why I did what I did. Honestly, I shot the son of a bitch because I wanted to. Because he was the kind of person who could admit to raping a teenage girl with a smile on his ugly face. I needed to hurt him. Everything else was excuses.

His hands rose to his throat, dropping his cigarette as he looked at me in disbelief and fell to the ground. Before he was off his feet, I turned to the monsters behind him, putting two more rounds in one and then another before the slide of the gun locked back, empty. Lodi and the two others fell to the ground, writhing and growling, their own wolves rising to the surface as they worked to heal the injuries that I'd just dealt them. The moon was high and bright, but a narrow crescent for all of that. None of us would be at our strongest.

The three uninjured bikers rushed me, snarling and howling. My own wolf was rising to the occasion in response to Lodi's words as much as to the blood in the air, but I had one last human trick in mind before I'd cede the reins to my inner monster. As the first biker reached me, a hairy man with an ugly mustache who smelled of pork rinds and cheap beer, I pulled Mack's knife from my waist and let the other man's weight and momentum do the work for me. I slid the steel deep into his heart. Instantly, his eyes widened and dimmed, the wolfish yellow giving way to a dull human brown. I turned with his momentum, and he fell to the ground, very dead, the knife still in his chest.

The other two were on me, and I was out of tricks. They slammed into me, claws and fangs sinking into the flesh of my left arm and right leg as their weight carried me to the ground. They were atop me, scratching and snarling, fumbling their way through instincts which were still new to them. Each puncture and tear in my flesh spurred my own wolf on, awakening him fully from his earlier hesitation. These sloppy pups thought to pin *us*? A lesson in dominance was in order. I took the pain they gave me, welcomed it, used it to fuel the monster I'd kept in check since before these assholes had even been born.

Yes!

The growl of triumph in the back of my head was so loud that it seemed impossible that others couldn't hear it. My wolf was deafening in his exultation. For the first time in decades, for just a moment, I gave it what it had always wanted, utter freedom.

We tasted the hot coppery fear of the first biker as our fangs tore into his throat. We relished the panicked little gurgling squeal he gave in response, how like prey he sounded as he thrashed away from us, leaving stringy pits of flesh and artery in our jaws.

The second one was lower, biting and clawing at our hip and ribs. We grabbed him by the hair, ripping his face from our side, not caring that a mouthful of our own skin came with it. He bit at our fingers, and we let him. He was too new, too unsure to do what needed to be done before it was too late. He bit to cause pain, to make us submit, rather than to maim. But there was no submission in us, and pain was only fodder for the wolf. As he bit down on our fingers, drawing blood, we tightened our grip on his jaw, and pulled. With the delicious sound of snapping bone and ripping meat, his jaw came free of his face. We mounted him then, holding the missing piece of his own face before his disbelieving eyes as we roared our victory at him, inches from what was left of his face. We could have ended him then, but there was no pity in us. Instead, we pressed our clawed thumbs into his eyes, blinding him as he could only gurgle in protest. Only then did we leave him, to drown in his own blood.

Yes! Yes!

In under a minute, three of these new wolves lay dead or dying at our feet. We howled our victory at the silver sliver in the night sky.

We fell to the ground, confused, as a loud crack sounded,

and the smell of sulfur heralded the new hole in our shattered knee. We snarled. Lodi had risen to his knees, one hand held to the wound in his neck, the other holding a large stainless steel revolver. As we regarded him, preparing to pounce and tear his head from his shoulders. He pulled the trigger again and knocked us to our back, opening a fist sized hole in our left lung.

Behind him, the two wounded wolves that I had shot pulled themselves from the ground, snarling and coughing blood as their injuries mended. We became aware of other movements and sounds. Trailer doors opening, heavy boots stepping, lights turning on. Perhaps another ten men had come out into the night, some unarmed, but several carrying guns, knives, and even hammers. These were no Garou. These were the human wannabes I had expected. Aspiring members of Lodi's pack. Those not yet allowed to party with the new elite of Los Perdidos.

I gasped for air as the wolf receded from my consciousness, busying himself with the work of repairing my body. My knee was an agonizing ruin and my mouth filled with blood as I fought to breathe with my one working lung.

Lodi stood over me, giving that same infuriating smile, the bottom of his boot was the last thing I saw.

CHAPTER FIFTY-FOUR

I could hear again before I could see. Muffled voices, growls, and shuffling sounds assaulted my throbbing head as I felt myself being moved.

"Can't we just kill this motherfucker?" An unfamiliar voice asked from above me.

"No!" Lodi's increasingly familiar growl.

"C'mon, prez," a third voice pleaded. "He killed Alonzo and the other two, and he fucked up my ride. He's gotta pay."

"Oh," Lodi replied with a smile in his voice, "he's gonna pay, alright. I'm bringing him to Yarrow, and what she's gonna do to him...well, let's just say she's got enough hate for this bastard to get real creative. Don't worry."

"But she told Rudy that he could cap him," the first voice argued.

"Yeah? You wanna be the next Rudy?" Lodi growled. A rustle of sudden movement and a weak gasping and struggling sound made it clear that he was sick of having his orders questioned. I still couldn't see, but I could hear where they were tussling. The third biker was still dragging me along the ground. I could hear the murmuring of the human bikers gathered around but keeping what they considered to be a safe distance.

"N—no," the gasped answer finally came.

"Damn right, 'no'," Lodi sneered. "Rudy was a pussy. He lost his nerve after Yarrow tore up Rita for fucking up. All she did was give him a chance to prove her wrong about him, but she wasn't wrong, was she? All she gave Rudy was a chance to slow this fucker down and get his whining ass out of our way at the same time."

"That's cold," muttered the one who was dragging me, his arms flexing against my head as he pulled me from under my shoulders.

The pieces were clicking together slowly in my foggy mind. I had thought that the killer Garou was either Yarrow *or* Lodi, but it wasn't "or", it was "and". This Yarrow, Hiram's lost wolf, had made Lodi one of us, just as she had once made me, and he had gone on to spread the curse among his biker brothers, giving her a true pack of Garou. What I couldn't quite figure is why the hell the Garou who had turned me, all those years ago in the fields of France, would hate me. What was I to her? A mistake to be cleaned up? A disappointment? I couldn't piece it together, at least not with my skull cracked and my face bleeding.

Whatever the source of her hate for me, it seemed like a bad idea to let Lodi deliver me to her on a silver platter for her amusement. I tried to move but found that my hands were cuffed in front of me. My shattered knee was half mended, but half of a ruined knee is still useless. I was no longer choking on my own blood, that was good at least. Instead, my breath wheezed as my damaged lung struggled to function. I was a mess. There was no getting away. No fighting my way out of this. The best I could hope for was to buy time, or maybe to force them to kill me here and now.

I twisted in the biker's arms and lunged with my mouth,

sinking my pathetically dull human teeth into the flesh of his forearm. He screamed and released me, but I didn't return the favor. I locked my jaw and sank my teeth deeper into his flesh as he hollered and kicked at me.

A heavy pair of boots approached quickly and kicked me twice in the head, dislocating my jaw. I fell to the damp gravel, my bell rung.

"You've got balls, asshole," Lodi's voice clawed at my tenuous consciousness as I fought to open my eyes. "Maybe we should do something about that."

I blinked several times and a riot of blurry colors slowly coalesced, sending daggers of pain into my aching head. The smiling biker held Mack's bloody knife in front of me, twirling it, as he waited for me to register exactly what he was threatening me with.

Slowly, the scenario around me came into focus. They had been dragging me back to my Blazer. One of the human bikers had pulled it around for Lodi, backing it off of the mangled Harleys. She was banged up and uglier than ever, but I was a little proud to see that the old girl still ran. They were going to load me into my own truck and take me somewhere. Where? Why wasn't Yarrow here, leading the pack? And where the hell was Andy?

"Where's... Andy?" I murmured.

Lodi kicked me directly in the balls he had just been admiring. I guess envy can make a man do ugly things. Unsurprisingly, I didn't have much to say after that.

The two betas lifted me and threw me indelicately into the back of the Blazer, my face pressed against the worn old seat. It smelled of Blue, and a little bit of heroin and Andy. I had to keep it together, for her sake. I had to see if I could do anything at all for Andy, I owed her at least that much.

Then, everything happened all at once. The biker I had

bitten was leering down at me from the open doorway of my own truck, when suddenly his eyes lost focus and his tongue lolled from his mouth. A massive knife handle protruded from one temple, and the tip of the blade jutted out the other, droplets of blood only just beginning to trickle down his slack face.

Hiram pulled the knife from the dead biker's skull with a silent snarl on his lips. He didn't so much as look at me. There was no time. Instead, he leapt away from his fallen prey even as the mortal bikers opened fire with a hail of bullets. Several of them hit my Blazer, peppering the passenger side door by my feet and shattering my rear windshield.

So, Hiram had been following me after all. He wasn't the cavalry I'd been hoping for, but at that point, my aching balls and I were happy to take whatever help we could get.

"Who the fuck is that?" Lodi's last standing beta said, fear quivering in his voice.

"Who cares? Shut up and kill the motherfucker!" Lodi shoved the beta biker toward where Hiram had vanished into the shadows before drawing his egregious revolver once again and firing into the night at my erstwhile mentor.

A mortal biker screamed from the other side of the trailer park and guns fired in response.

"Where did he go?"

"How does it move so fast?"

"Oh fuck, oh fuck, oh fuck!" The voices of frightened bikers reached me, and I couldn't help but grin.

A weight settled into the front of the Blazer and the driver's door slammed shut. We were moving, kicking up gravel as Lodi, smelling strongly of fear himself, began to wheel us away from Edison Court trailer park.

"What's your hurry?" I chuckled through clenched teeth and an unhealed jaw.

He only growled in response.

A sudden thud rocked the Blazer, and I could just make out Hiram, crouched on the hood of the speeding truck, the razor sharp talons of one hand sunk into the metal of its hood. His eyes so brightly yellow that they nearly glowed. He locked his golden eyes on Lodi, but the big biker kept his wits about him.

Simultaneously, Lodi hit the brakes and fired his compensation cannon through the windshield at Hiram. The old wolf was sent sailing off into the tall grass of the floodplain, and Lodi began driving again before waiting to see what had become of his target.

That was wise of him. Struggling to sit up, I could just see Hiram pop back to his feet, perhaps thirty yards from the truck. Instantly, he began to give chase. I knew he'd taken at least one of those big bullets to the chest, just as I had, and within seconds he was running faster than an Olympian. Even if my knee had been untouched, I'd still have been lucky to manage a weak jog in my condition, despite the minutes I'd had to heal.

Impressive as Hiram's efforts were, he was still injured. Slowly, we pulled away from him and he turned to deal with the remaining bikers who were still firing at him in the night. Lodi pulled my Blazer onto the country road and began to take us north.

Looking back, I could see the faint flashing lights of police approaching the trailer park from the south. Had my plan with Owen worked after all? So much for timing. Lodi and I were headed the opposite direction and would be long gone by the time the police raided Edison Court.

"What are you looking at?"

I looked forward in time to see the butt of Lodi's revolver whipping towards me, and again, all was darkness.

PART 8

DARK WAS THE NIGHT

CHAPTER FIFTY-FIVE

SEATTLE,
1926,

Maggie and Paul named their baby after me. I was honored, but I thought it was probably a mistake. After all, I was named for our father, a world class bastard, and I wasn't exactly in a position to judge him.

Still, little Francis Adler seemed perfectly sweet. Maybe he could make something decent of that rotten name if given half a chance. Once, Paul had called his son Frank, but Maggie's cold and angry eyes and the night he spent on the couch assured us all that he would never make that mistake again.

Evelyn was jealous. Not in a mean-hearted sort of way, she loved Maggie and adored that baby with all her heart, finding any excuse at all to hold him. It was just that she wanted a child of her own so damn badly. After several years together, and being anything but chaste, we were childless. Evelyn blamed me, and I think she was probably right. I thought perhaps it was a part of my condition, but I never told her that. When she wasn't drinking or socializing, Evelyn was with Maggie and little Francis, living vicariously through the motherhood of my sister.

I didn't see the kid often, not for a lack of pleading on Maggie's part. It was just that I thought by staying away that I could keep him clean. Innocent, of the things I did and the thing I was. I'd been a monster since before he was born, but working for Salvatore Curcio, I found ways to put that monstrous nature to good use.

The business of bootlegging in Seattle had been a peaceful one when I'd first fallen in with it. Mr. Olmstead, the Gentleman Bootlegger who ran the region, had insisted on no violence. He'd kept the peace by paying off the police he'd used to work with, and there had been more than enough money to go around. He'd flaunted his wealth; Olmstead was well known and more than a little well liked.

It couldn't last. After a couple of years, the powers that be decided that they couldn't let a guy like Olmstead break their laws so brazenly and publicly, so in the first conviction ever to rely on evidence obtained by wiretapping, he was put away. Without a gentleman like Olmstead on the throne to keep the peace, the local bootleggers got competitive, and things got rough. That was where I came in.

Mr. Curcio had some connections back east, and he had it in mind to be the new king of booze in the Northwest. Those of us that worked for him found ourselves doing a different sort of work. It wasn't just keeping the peace anymore. Now we started to shut down his competition. Before long, we were going to war.

Sin is a slippery thing. Maggie tried to tell me that, but I didn't listen. I started working for Curcio because I needed to help my family, needed to provide for Evelyn and look after Maggie. If the price of that was breaking an unjust law and dealing in illegal alcohol, fine, it was no big deal. And if once in a while I had to give a guy a good beating because he was getting in the way of business, so what? I'd done worse. So long as my family, my pack, was provided for. And when the time finally came that Mr. Curcio asked me to kill for him, well, I'd killed plenty in France, hadn't I? I was already a monster, a criminal, a thug, wasn't I? It was a smaller step than I'd have guessed.

Killing was still easy for me. Easier than ever, in fact. I'd been good at it before I'd been bitten, and after, well... I play the part of the reluctant killer, but that is a facade. Wolves know the joy of the hunt, the pleasure of a good kill, and I damn well enjoyed myself too.

Mr. Curcio kept his old promise to me and kept my brother-in-law Paul away from the violence. He was strictly the money man. I was sure that I could insulate my family from the things that I was doing, that I could lock all the killing away inside me where I kept my wolf and that I could lead two lives. For a while it worked. At home I pretended not to be one of the most ruthless killers in that part of the country, and everybody else pretended to believe it.

The fact was, I was a very bad man. Since then, people have tried to tell me that I am a good person, that I'm decent, but I know better. I've never told any of them this part of my story, never told them that I killed not because of war or instinct or survival, but because I was paid to do it. Because I chose to do it. Because I loved it.

On some level I knew that I couldn't keep the blood on my hands away from my family, away from my wife, away from my sister and her baby. So, I spent less and less time at home, and more time drinking and working. It was better that way, better that I kept my distance.

Besides, Evelyn had grown distant. Or maybe it was that I had kept her at a distance when she'd wanted me to let her closer. Either way, there was a coldness between us, and I didn't know how to cross it. It seemed like nothing could.

Then my wife became pregnant.

I knew before she did. I smelled it on her the way I had on Maggie.

I'd come home, drunk and dirty, with some fresh violence behind me, and ready to collapse into bed. She was up as she often was, smoking, drinking whiskey, and listening to music by herself in her rocking chair. I'd gone to kiss her on the forehead as had become my habit before slipping wordlessly off to bed, but this time when my face neared her, I smelled it.

I looked at her, disbelieving. After all this time? A baby? Did she even know yet? I had to tell her. She would be so damn happy.

"What are you smiling at?" she asked with a raised eyebrow.

"You," I said, "you're... glowing."

She raised her glass to me as if in salute, dismissing my observation as an effect of the alcohol.

"No," I said with the same stupid grin, "this is different. Honey, I think you should go see a doctor."

"Don't be ridiculous," she said. "I feel fine. And why are you smiling so much if you think I'm sick? Some husband you are."

I couldn't help myself, I laughed.

"No, honey," I kept smiling. "We're going to have a baby."

She looked at me with both eyebrows raised now, an expression of strained patience on her pretty face.

"Just how much did you have to drink tonight, anyw—"

I cut her off, covering her mouth with a kiss. A real kiss, the kind we had used to share, before the coldness had grown between us. She was stiff at first, but soon softened in my arms, giving way to the love she still had for me. No matter how deep she tried to hide it behind her scowls and her sarcasm.

Her arms folded behind my neck and I lifted her from the

chair, holding her. kissing her. Tasting the whiskey and smoke on her breath. Tasting the other strange scents that were new and confusing.

"I love you," I whispered to her. She moaned wordlessly in my ear.

I carried her to bed, and we made love. The long slow sort that is more about savoring one another than feeding any sort of hunger. That was there too, of course it was, but it was a different need than just something my body wanted. It was my heart's need for her. For her to be close to me again. For us both to let the walls down and truly be with one another. I just cherished her.

So caught up in the moment was I that I didn't pay attention to what my senses were trying to tell me. I dismissed the strange smells, the hesitant way my wife responded to me. I wrote it all off as part of her pregnancy. I ignored it all and made love to my wife for the last time.

CHAPTER FIFTY-SIX

Evelyn had gone to the doctor, reluctantly, at my insistence, and learned what I already knew. She was stunned, happy, but still disbelieving. And something else, a little bit scared. I was familiar enough with that smell that I had no doubt about what she was feeling, but I figured it was a natural enough response. After all, I was scared too.

How was I going to raise a child? A man like me? A *thing* like me? And what if I'd passed something on to the baby, what if it was somehow... wolfish. I couldn't know. This was all new to me.

I decided that I had to change. I had to change everything. I couldn't be a father by day and a killer by night, could I? No. Like Paul, I needed to move to a more respectable part of the business. Or maybe just leave it all together. Mr. Curcio would understand.

Salvatore Curcio was having coffee with his son Tony when I went to his home. Tony was a handsome young man of about my own age, with dark features and a smile that was too quick and easy to be sincere. Mr. Curcio had slowly been showing Tony the ropes as his business expanded, grooming his son to play a larger role in the operation as it grew. Tony, for his part, was a smart enough fellow, but took too many risks. He was the sort of hot-head who wanted to rush into a situation when others would prefer to wait and think. I liked that about him, if not much else.

"Heya, Frank," Tony greeted me. "What brings you around?"

"I came to talk business," I said to the elder Curcio. "Is this a good time?"

"For Smiling Frank? I'd be scared to say no," Mr. Curcio laughed. "Sit down. Have some coffee."

I did. I laid it all out for them. I told him how grateful I was for the opportunities he'd given me, but that I was going to be a father now, and thought it was best to make some changes.

"Evie's knocked up?" Tony said with evident surprise in his eyes before he managed to cover it with his slippery smile.

I puzzled at that for a moment, but Mr. Curcio quickly took my attention.

"Frank, that's wonderful," the elder Curcio said. "Congratulations. Really."

"Thank you, sir," I said.

"I understand why you'd want to make a change, and I can't blame you," he went on, "but now is a bad time. You've got to know that. We're in the middle of something big here. I need my best hitter up at bat."

I understood what he was referring to. Over the past year, the Curcios had become the biggest bootlegging operation in town, but that hadn't been good enough for Mr. Curcio. He said it was no good just being the big fish if all the little fish kept trying to get big too. What he wanted was to be the only fish. He was damn close to accomplishing it too.

There was only one holdout he hadn't yet managed to absorb or put out of business, an Irishman from Chicago with out-of-town backers who had arrived on the scene soon after Olmstead had been put away. A guy named Kelly. Kelly was a different sort of gangster than the rest of the local competition. Harder, more willing to dig in and bleed for what he wanted. That was why we hadn't yet managed to scare him off.

"Yeah, Frank," Tony added. "You can't just walk out on us right before the big show, can you? Not after everything my old man has done for you?"

"I suppose I have a few months," I conceded. "I'm not quitting, I just need to know that there's a future in this for me, something different."

"Frank, my boy," Mr. Curcio said, "After Kelly closes shop, there won't be any more need for this kind of thing, and I won't forget the people who helped put me on top. You'll always be taken care of."

"I'm not looking for any handouts, Sal," I said. "I just want a chance to do better for my wife, she deserves it."

"Of course!" Sal Curcio exclaimed. "What kind of man would you be if you didn't want that? It's what we all want for our families."

"I'm glad you understand, sir," I said.

"I'll tell you what, Frank," Mr. Curcio said. "Tony and I were just working out the details of our big move. You come by the bar tomorrow night, and Tony will give you your marching orders. It's about time he got a chance to get some hands-on experience, see what it's like to run this operation, maybe keep him from getting too eager to take over once he sees what a pain in the ass it is to be boss, right?"

Mr. Curcio smiled at me, clapped his son on the shoulder, and laughed.

"Whatever you say, pop," Tony gave his ephemeral smile, and I nodded my reluctant agreement. Tony was young, but he wasn't dumb. He'd do alright.

"In the meantime," Mr. Curcio said, "go spend some time with that pretty wife of yours. Show her a good time. Buy something nice for the baby. Huh?"

He withdrew a thick fold of green bills from his pocket and put them into my hand without giving me an opportunity to refuse, patting the money into place with his other hand on the back of mine.

"Thanks, Sal," I said. "If you insist."

"I do," he said with a smile.

So, I did what he suggested. I came home, surprising Evelyn with the most expensive bassinet that Mr. Curcio's ill-gotten money could buy and taking her to dinner.

That night I held her in our bed but didn't try for anything more. I was nervous about hurting the baby, and there was a tentative sort of tension in Evelyn. That and the strange smells of her pregnancy tickled at my mind, but I pushed the thoughts down.

My wolf was growing agitated, the moon was growing nearly full and I blamed my wandering thoughts on that. Not having anything to hunt, and not wanting to calm the wolf with Evelyn for fear of hurting the baby growing in her belly, I slipped downstairs and smoked a heavy load of opium from Evelyn's stash, thinking to myself as I drifted off that I should probably get rid of this stuff, to keep Evelyn from hurting the baby.

CHAPTER FIFTY-SEVEN

I should have seen what was coming. All the breadcrumbs were laid out for me, but I wouldn't let myself see them. I was young, dumb, and too in love to consider the truth of what was happening under my predator nose.

I met with Tony and a few of the other leg breakers in the crew at Curcio's joint the next night. We shared a couple of drinks and went over Tony's plan. It was straightforward but smart.

Kelly's operation was taking in a shipment of Canadian rye whiskey on a small beach north of Seattle, just before dawn. We'd show up after them, leaving two guys to block the road out with the car, while Tony and I approached the beach on foot from the other direction. We'd wait until the Canadian boat had delivered their cargo and were underway before moving in. We had business north of the border, as well, and didn't want to jeopardize it. Then, I'd do my thing and take out Kelly's thugs, preferably without making too much noise, while Tony took care of Kelly himself.

The four of us piled into the car and drove north, Tony and I sitting in the back seat, smoking as we went.

"You think of any names yet, Frank?" Tony said.

"What?"

"You know, for the baby," he said.

"Ah, no, we haven't gotten that far yet."

"Ah, I see," he said, taking a drag. "If it was me, I'd have a list a mile long. Two lists, one for boys, one for girls. Of course, Tony is a hard name to beat."

He elbowed me jovially in the ribs and laughed. I didn't say anything. The kid tried too hard. He got on my nerves.

"What are you hoping for?" Tony asked after a few minutes.

"What?"

"You know," he insisted again, when, obviously, I did not know. "The baby. Do you want a boy or a girl?"

"Honestly," I said, "I don't care, I just hope it looks like its mother."

He forced a laugh.

"I have to agree with you there, Frankie," he said. "That's one damn fine-looking lady you've got."

"Thanks," I said, not enjoying the idea of him thinking about Evelyn's looks overly long.

"How did a guy like you ever end up with a girl like that anyway?" he asked.

"I don't know," I said. "I don't understand it myself. You'd have to ask her."

"I'll do that," he said, unsmiling.

Before the conversation could get any more uncomfortable, we arrived at the drop point. Our car let us out near a trail, and the two men drove on further down the road, ready to play their part of the plan.

Tony carried a nickel plated .38 revolver. I held a familiar pump action shotgun, similar to what they'd given us in France, as we made our way through the darkened trees toward the sound of crashing waves. Above us, the sky was just beginning to turn grey with the promise of dawn still behind the mountains to the east.

"There they are," Tony hissed.

I'd seen them long before he had but didn't need to say so. Three men stood on the rocky shore, illuminated by the headlights of their own truck. Two of them were hauling crates and placing them into the back of the truck, while the third, a well-dressed man in a presumptuous hat, conducted hushed business with a pair of men on a small, beached boat.

"I see them," I said.

"Kelly is paying off the Canadians," Tony whispered unnecessarily.

"Yeah," I said, not knowing how else to reply to such an obvious statement.

"You go left," he said to me. "Get closer to their truck. Once you make your move on those two boys, I'll pop out from over here and back you up. Then I'll take Kelly."

Of course, the boss's son would sit back where it was safe while I went in to do the real work. I couldn't really complain; it wasn't as if I had anything to worry about. This close to the full moon, I was looking forward to a little violence anyway. I nodded to Tony, and moved off into the shadows, trusting my ears and nose to guide me as much as my superior night vision. Unlike Tony, I could see every rock and pebble on that beach. Every face stood out as if lit for the stage. I even saw one of Kelly's workers look around carefully to be sure he wasn't being watched before slipping a bottle from one of the crates into his jacket pocket.

They had no idea we were there. This was going to be easy.

Several minutes passed, and the two Canadians shoved off, launching their boat into the dark waters of Puget Sound. According to the plan, that was my moment to act. Quickly, I slipped from behind the trees and driftwood at the edge of the beach and crept toward the two men as their backs were to me. The well-dressed Mr. Kelly was still standing in the headlights of the truck and wouldn't be able to see me creeping up in the darkness.

I was most of the way toward the truck, too far away from cover to go back now, when everything went to shit.

Three gunshots rang out from behind me, none of them striking Kelly or his men, though one did make a loud crack as it struck their vehicle. The two workers spun. One reached for a shotgun in the back of the truck, the other ducking and pulling a small handgun from his waist. Kelly took cover behind the door of the truck, drawing his own fancy pistol.

I was utterly exposed, the shotgun in my hand and my creeping posture left no question as to my intent.

"Drop him boys. We're out of here!"

Kelly slipped into the driver's seat of the truck and the two men opened fire. I dove to the barnacle covered rocks of the beach, trying my best to avoid the blasts, but there was no cover. Bullets and shrapnel tore at me, shredding my coat and peppering my arms and legs. They had me, and if I'd been an ordinary man, I'd have been dead, but I wasn't an ordinary man. Already, my wolf was chomping at the bit, eagerly repairing the damage in my body and preparing to return it with interest. Tony may have jumped the gun, but any second now he'd come out blasting, and I'd have my chance to do a little damage of my own.

But he didn't come out blasting. He didn't come out at all. A bullet tore into my pelvis. Pellets from the shotgun tore into my neck and face. They kept firing as I tried to crawl away. Hot metal and bits of shattered rock tore into me again and again until I fell limp.

It wasn't a ploy. I was down. My body was utterly unresponsive, all but dead. I couldn't hear my own breathing. Couldn't feel the beat of my own heart. I honestly didn't know whether or not I was dying. Strangely in that paralytic shock, I remained conscious. I couldn't focus my eyes, couldn't draw breath to smell what was around me, but I could hear everything that happened around me.

"Get in," a voice yelled, "before more show up!"

The truck rolled along the rocky beach and away from me, its engine slowly fading into the night, swallowed by the sound of the tide. I was left alone with my thoughts and the waves.

I remember thinking that perhaps this was what death was like. Being locked in your own still body as it slowly rotted around you, helpless to move or speak, a silent witness to your own decay. The thought grew in me and sparked a desperate panic, but my heart didn't quicken, nor did my breathing, and that scared me even more.

Then came the sound of stone grinding on stone. Of feet shuffling across the gravel of the beach toward me. Had they come back, or had Tony finally found the guts to come out and lend a hand now that it was too late? I wanted to rip the coward's guts out, but there was no chance of that. I couldn't even brush the sand from my own face.

The feet stopped beside me, and a man grabbed my shoulders, grunting as he leaned in to roll me over onto my back.

"Jesus Christ Frankie," Tony's blurred face said from above me. "I didn't think it was possible, but you actually look even uglier."

He spat in my face.

What in the hell was this? He wasn't just a coward. The rat had stabbed me in the back all but literally. Those shots hadn't been an accident at all, hadn't been nervousness. He'd hung me out to dry.

Tony actually intended for this to happen to me. He had as good as shot me himself. That decided it. I *was* going to gut the son of a bitch, if I ever regained the use of my body that was.

As I was mulling over the most satisfying ways to end Tony Curcio's pathetic life, he stood and walked to my feet. What was the weasel doing now? Grabbing my feet, he began to pull, slowly at first, but soon he'd managed some inertia and was dragging my limp body along the beach. The thunder of the waves grew slowly louder, and it occurred to me what he was doing.

The number one rule of our little family business had always been to never leave behind a body, not unless we were delivering a message. Tony was going to push me out into the waves.

No.

The wolf stirred within me, his attention pulled ever so slightly away from his work repairing my body by the fear I felt at the idea of being cast into the sound. Would I drown? Could I drown? Or would I just sink to the bottom, still locked in this useless body, powerless to move as the crabs ate my eyes?

No!

I felt something. Little more than a tingling in my limbs. A faint burning in my lungs as blood began to flow again. I coughed, my own blood splashing my lips.

Tony dropped my feet.

"Well, I'll be damned," he said in a tone of mocking awe. "Pops always said you were a damn hard man to kill. Said there was something special about you. I just always figured he'd been sampling too much of the product. But here you are, still too stupid to know you're dead. I've got to say, I'm actually a little impressed."

He stood over me again, my eyes fighting to focus on him. I

thought I could make out the white flash of his liar's smile as he looked down at me.

"If it helps any, Frankie," he said as he pulled out his ornate revolver, more a showpiece than a real weapon, "nobody is gonna miss your ugly face."

He pressed the barrel against my head, and the world stopped.

CHAPTER FIFTY-EIGHT

I hate seafood. I mean, I never cared for the stuff before, but after that day, I could never stomach it again. Something about waking up with a stomach full of salt-water, tiny pinchers nibbling at my flesh, tangled in kelp, well, it left a bad taste in my mouth.

Everything was dark. I was floating. I had been wrong before on the beach. *This* was what death felt like. Amorphous, dark, cold. I didn't know who or where I was for a good, long while. The first thing I became aware of with any certainty was the pain.

My skull erupted in stabbing agony. I didn't have the words to describe the pain. I still don't. I didn't know why I hurt. I didn't even know what pain was. It was simply the only ingredient in my growing awareness of the world. Slowly, my brain formed something capable of feeling the pain of my own injuries again, and the searing pain in my skull gave the wolf something to focus on.

That two-faced mother fucker had shot me in the head. And then what? He had dumped me in the water!

I opened my eyes and drew a breath, or at least I tried to.

Immediately my body spasmed violently as it tried to expel the cold seawater that had filled my lungs, but there was nothing to replace it. There was nothing to see. Just foggy shapes and a faint sense of pale silver light in the direction I could only assume was up.

The wolf took over. I had nothing to offer other than fear and flailing panic. The wolf had one thing I didn't, rage. Rage that drove us upward, clawing and kicking, until our head broke the surface of the water and we began coughing violently.

With aching lungs full of air, I regarded my surroundings. The silver light that had shown us the way up was the newly full moon. What else?

Full? The full moon had been days away still when we had gone on our little trip to the beach. How long had I been down there? How was I even still alive?

No.

The wolf was right. Thrashing in the sound in the middle of the night was hardly the time or place to try to puzzle these things out. What mattered in that moment was that I *was* alive, and that somebody needed to die.

CHAPTER FIFTY-NINE

The lights drew me. First, the moon, but then, the distant and familiar lights of the city. For over an hour, I thrashed and dog-paddled my way toward the lights of civilization, all the while feeling the wolf working to restore my flesh. Finally, I crawled out of Elliot Bay and dragged myself onto the rocks beneath the piers of the waterfront.

I wanted to rest, to gather my strength, but what I wanted mattered very little that night. The wolf was at the helm, the moon was full and bright, and what he wanted was blood. I was too deeply tired to argue and didn't half mind the idea of tearing Tony Curcio's heart out at any rate. The wolf was going to have his way.

I felt half asleep, as much dreaming as watching through my own eyes as the wolf took our body on the hunt through the dark Seattle streets. To the few late-night pedestrians who caught a glimpse of me I don't doubt I was a true horror. I'd spent days adrift beneath the water of the sound, and I could feel that my wounds were not yet fully healed. The hunt took priority. What did they see as I dashed, snarling, from one dark alley to another, sniffing at the air and growling my anticipation of the kill as I drew closer?

I picked up the traitor's scent at his father's joint, the place where we did most of our business. Even this late, there was a lively business inside, but my nose told me immediately that Tony wasn't there.

I moved on, uphill, following the trail of his cowardly stink. I stopped briefly to make sure I had it before moving on blindly, with no care for where the scent led me. Never before had I been so fully in the grip of the wolf since I'd first awoken with these new instincts on the fields of France. Before now, I'd been careful to take myself into the wilderness during the full moon, far from where my predator's urges could lead me to do something horrible. But this time, that choice had been taken from me.

My reflection stopped me. I'd followed his scent to a familiar door. My door, I realized without fully grasping the significance of it. Peering in the darkened window, I saw nothing but my own face, and I was a horror. My flesh was pale and pickled, with half healed holes in the skin of my face and chest where my shirt had fallen away. Worse, a putrid purple wound throbbed and oozed on my left temple where Tony had shot me on the beach. Where he had given me the pain in my head that still left me disoriented and unable to focus. But beyond all that, beyond the corpse-pale pallor of my wrinkled skin, and the bits of seaweed still hanging from my ruined clothes, I had become a beast.

My ears were long and pointed. Tufts of hair had sprouted around them down the sides of my face. My fingers were curled before me into gnarled talons, tipped with long and jagged claws. My hare-lip, the thing I'd been so self-conscious of for as long as I could remember, was barely noticeable as it was pulled back in a snarl from a row of prominent predator's teeth, particularly savage-seeming in the faint light. Most startling of all were my eyes. That is to say, the wolf's eyes, because they weren't mine at all, not really. They gleamed golden in the reflected moonlight, focused and intent on the hunt. There was nothing of mercy or decency in those eyes. Nothing human.

I was truly monstrous. To this day, that is the image I see when I think of the wolf taking over. When I drug and chain myself. When I choose the woods and the company of animals over the city. It is the memory and the hate of that monster that keeps me there.

A woman's faint screaming interrupted my reflection. Evelyn's screaming. Muffled, as if somebody were doing their best to keep her from being heard. Somebody? Tony's scent had led me here, and now my wife was in danger? My woman? My baby? My home? My family?

Mine.

Pushing the door open and splintering the lock with casual ease. I slipped into the house and leapt up the stairs in a single motion towards the source of the screaming. It hadn't stopped. They hadn't heard me yet.

All I could think of was that I would save her, save my wife from the man who had tried to murder me. I'd rip him apart, and she would be so glad of it. She'd be safe, and we would be together. We would leave. We'd go far away from the city. Just the two of us. The three of us. But first, there was blood to be paid.

I realized two things as I began to open the bedroom door. The first was the sounds. The screaming continued, still muffled, as if a hand were pressed against Evelyn's face, but the way she screamed...it wasn't pain. No, I knew that sound. Knew it well. That was for me. That was *mine.* The second thing was the smell. There was no mistaking it. Her smell, the smell of excitement, of her sex, mingling with a strange oily smell that had been teasing my senses before, a smell I'd thought had been because of changes due to the pregnancy.

The door swung open and my eyes pieced together what my other senses had already known. There they were, together, in my bed. *Mine.* Tony Curcio, bare ass thrusting forward, atop my wife. *Mine.* He wasn't forcing her. Not at all. She bit into his forearm to muffle her own screams of pleasure and closed her eyes as she arched her back, pressing her pale breasts against him as he squeezed one of them in his oily, dark hand. *Mine.*

For several heartbeats I just stood there, taking in the truth of what was in front of me. Again and again he thrust into her, the wet sounds and excited odors rising to taunt me with each of her ecstatic but muffled screams. He groaned in the throes of his own pleasure, both of them oblivious to what watched from the doorway.

I had thought that baby had been mine. *Mine.* Evelyn had been mine. *Mine.* This home, this life had been mine. *Mine.* In an instant, I knew I was wrong about all of that, and the pain of that realization rose in my chest. It rose and grew until the agony of it eclipsed even the throbbing of the bullet hole in my head.

"*Mine,*" I growled with the wolf's voice, nearly incoherent with rage.

Evelyn opened her eyes then and truly screamed.

Everything seemed to happen at once. I don't know the order of things even now. The room exploded into action. Tony was cursing, staring at me in shock and terror as he scrambled toward the side table where he had left his gun. Evelyn was screaming, nonsense sounds at first, and then both of our names, Tony's and mine.

I know that I was on him before he could get to the gun, tearing into him, delighting at the way his bones cracked and the way that his screams were suddenly louder and higher pitched than hers. Then, she was on me, naked and panicked, furiously beating at me to release her lover, pulling at my arms, striking at my head.

"No! Frank, no!"

I snarled and spun, striking her with the back of one hairy hand and slashing her with the claws of the other before I could think what I was doing. The force of my blow sent her flying over the bed and into the wall on the other side of the room where she landed against a mirror, coming to rest in a heap of broken glass and broken bones.

The wolf roared our anger and pain at her from across the room as some part of me reeled at what we had just done. what I had just done. She was hurt, badly. I had done that. I had hurt the woman I had loved.

Just like my damned father.

That moment of guilt and hesitation was all that Tony had been waiting for. I heard the click of the trigger before the crack of the powder propelled the first piece of lead into my flesh. He didn't stop there. He fired four more times, emptying all five rounds of his pretty little revolver in a panicked spray that missed more often than it hit.

Two of the bullets tore into me, one in my stomach and one in my shoulder, but I barely felt them. They didn't hurt at all. What did hurt, was the one that struck Evelyn in her naked breast. Her eyes grew even wider and more disbelieving than they had been before, and she lifted a hand to the wound as if to verify that it was even real. She looked at the blood on her fingertips as if she didn't know what it was.

I did. I'd seen wounds like that before. I could smell the rich metallic aroma of my wife's blood mingle with the sticky smells of their tryst and the piss stink of Tony's mortal fear. He continued to pull the trigger long after he'd emptied the gun.

Click. Click. Click. Click.

His eyes bulged as I turned to regard him, unimpeded by the two fresh holes he'd put in me. The moon was too full, and my anger was too hot for little things like bullets to bother me. Little inconsequential lead balls that hardly mattered in the least. If only he'd known to use steel.

I roared at him and the piss stink doubled in the room by the time I was on him. His screams didn't slow me in the slightest. Neither did the pathetic blows he pummeled me with as I ripped into his chest, cracking open his ribs with my fingertips as I roared all my pain and fury into his eyes from inches away. Did he smell the sea on my breath? Probably not, by the time I'd exposed his beating heart and pulsing lungs to the night air I doubt he was aware of anything as trivial as smell. His world was fear. Fear and pain. And I let him wallow in it for a moment as I savored it. I savored the smell of his blood and fear. The wolf savored the victory over our prey even as my wife lay dying only feet away, watching the whole scene play out.

Finally, before his eyes lost all focus, I reached in with clawed hands and tore the heart from Tony's chest. He'd done nothing less to me. I let him see it, held it in front of him and watched for the faint flicker of comprehension in his eyes before I thrust it with all my strength into his mouth. I felt his teeth shatter as I forced the hot muscle into his throat. I kept pushing until I felt his neck snap and the wood of the wall begin to crack behind him. Only then did I let go, allowing him to fall to the floor, dead.

Yes!

The wolf was exultant. Pure satisfaction and primal joy crashed through me at our triumph over our enemy. This was right. This was good.

...Evelyn.

The thought was my own, not the wolf's. I floated it to the

surface of our mind from far away, trying to pull myself by tooth and nail back into control of our actions.

We turned to regard my wife. She had hurt us too, hadn't she? Perhaps we had more prey to kill...

No!

The look of loss and fear in her eyes was utterly alien to the Evelyn I had known. Her hands moved to her belly where her pregnancy was not yet quite visible, and her bloody breasts shivered with rapid little sobs.

"My baby..." she whimpered.

The wolf didn't know what to make of this, and in that hesitation, I drove a wedge between the wolf and my waking mind. I forced all my regret, guilt, and love for Evelyn into a single white-hot point and used it to pry him away. Reluctantly, he retreated.

"Evelyn," I said, not knowing what else I could say as I crouched near her, still covered in my own blood as well as that of her dead lover. I placed a hand on the bleeding hole above her breast, trying futilely to stop the bleeding. My own wounds bled onto her as I crouched above her, but I gave them no thought.

In disgust she recoiled from my touch and winced at the pain of the effort. There was no love for me in her eyes. She looked at me and finally saw what I had hidden from her for years. What I had tried to protect her from. I was a monster. How could she ever have loved this?

"My Evelyn..." I muttered, and the old anger flared in her eyes.

"No," she coughed the word weakly along with a mouthful of blood, "not yours. Not...anybody's."

She wasn't making any sense. She was bleeding out and soon would be gone for good. There had to be something that I could do. Anything.

I knew what she was feeling now. I too had once been shot,

bleeding and dying. I remembered it well. Remembered the way the ghouls had come for me, and then the way that the wolf-woman, my maker, had stood above me after the fight. The way she had given me her long, slow bite.

Was that how it was done? I had no idea. I knew so little still about what I was. All I knew for certain was that I had to try something before my Evelyn was gone forever.

"It's going to be alright, honey," I said.

"Liar..." she coughed.

"Shhh, I'm so sorry. I have to do this," I said, as I drew closer to her wounded breast, where my blood had spilled to mingle with her own.

"No... get away..."

She didn't know what she was saying. There was no time to explain it to her. It was up to me to decide, to do what was best for her.

Drawing back my lips, I lunged forward and sank my fangs into the tender flesh near her wound, above her heart.

She screamed again and thrashed against me, pulling at my hair and striking weakly at my head. But her strength was fading fast. I latched on, feeling her pulse through my mouth as her blood surged onto my tongue with each beat of her dying heart. I didn't know what was supposed to come next, what arcane secrets I needed to know to make this work. Nothing seemed to be happening.

Fear swelled in me. Panic. I couldn't lose her. I couldn't! Stubbornly, I held on, holding my fangs in her flesh and crushing her to me with my arms, even as she continued to paw feebly at me in protest.

Finally, her protests stopped, along with the beating of her heart. She was gone.

I'd failed. Evelyn was dead, and it was my fault.

CHAPTER SIXTY

I lay there for a long time, crying on her breast, holding her limp body as it grew colder. Gradually, the sky grew pale in the window and the moon sank low in the sky.

I couldn't leave her like this. Not like this. Shot, clawed, broken, and bloody. Not my Evelyn. I couldn't stand the idea of anybody seeing her this way. It would destroy Maggie and little Francis. And if they ever knew it was me... No. That could never happen.

I knew what I had to do. I had to protect them from this as best I could. Looking one last time at the broken and bloody body of my beautiful wife, I came up with something like a plan.

"I'm sorry, Evelyn," I said through the tears that drew lines in her blood on my chin. "I'll be with you soon."

I meant it.

I couldn't take her body anywhere for a proper burial. There'd be too many questions. What happened to her? Where had I been? And what the hell had torn open the chest of Tony Curcio? Far too many questions. This mess was mine to clean up, and nothing cleanses better than fire.

A found and lit an old oil lamp that Evelyn had loved. We didn't need it, electric light was readily available, but she'd always thought there was a romance to firelight that electricity couldn't match. She'd always loved romantic gestures. Well, I'd give her one.

I stood atop the stairs that led to the entrance of our home and took a deep breath, bracing myself for what I was about to do. I didn't want to live without her, couldn't live without her, but a bullet to the head and the depths of the sea hadn't ended my life. Maybe it was time to see if fire could do any better.

With a snarl I hurled the lamp to the base of the stairs. Instantly it shattered, and the fire spread along the floor and walls where the oil splashed. Soon the stairs and the walls had caught ablaze on their own, and the fire began to engulf the house, spreading upward.

It didn't take long for the heat and smoke to burn my lungs. Within me, the wolf stirred in fear. It was the primal fear that all creatures of instinct have for a raging fire, but I held him back, pushing him down as he struggled to rise to the surface once more.

Stumbling, I returned to the room I'd shared with Evelyn. The room where I'd killed her. The fire would reach there soon, and I'd be caught in it, along with her poor body. They'd find us together, clean of blood and scars. Clean. I held her one last time, cradling her head and stroking her golden hair.

The smoke filled the room before the flames did, but I didn't succumb to unconsciousness. The heat grew, and soon the flames were licking at the walls and catching at the sheets of the bed. The fire roared more loudly than anything I could have imagined, a great and hungry beast even more primal and implacable than the wolf within me.

No! Run! No!

The wolf threw itself against the cage I'd constructed for it in my mind, battering at my will with all its might, but I held fast. I thought about the way I had looked in the reflection downstairs. How hideous and horrifying I'd appeared. How I looked with the wolf risen to the surface. That had been what I'd looked like the last time that Evelyn had seen me. The face of a monster. The monster who had killed her.

No, I'd stay here and burn. I deserved to burn. Maybe Evelyn's father and brother had been on to something after all with their notions of hellfire and damnation.

I locked myself in place as the fire licked at my clothing and blisters began to rise on my skin. I couldn't help the growing growl that fought its way past my lips, but I refused to leave Evelyn's side. She'd always been so afraid that I'd abandon her. I couldn't let her fear come to pass.

NO!

The pain was maddening. More than bullets or fists. More than broken bones or the teeth of wild things. The fire was more akin to steel in its searing bite. I could feel that the wolf was right to fear it. Maybe I'd found a way to kill it after all.

I laughed, even as my hands fought of their own accord to drag me away from the fire. The smoke was doing its work now. My head was reeling, my vision darkening and narrowing to a single point. A light through the window, sinking on the horizon. The light of the moon.

CHAPTER SIXTY-ONE

I've tried and failed to kill myself many times over the years, with varying levels of sincerity and creativity, but that was the first. I don't think that I failed entirely, not completely. It certainly feels as though part of me died that day along with Evelyn.

I came to my senses in the forest, high in the hills beyond the city. I was a burned and blackened thing, every inch of me blazing with pain. As best I could reckon, the wolf had found its way to the surface as I had lost consciousness. Once more he had thrust us toward the guiding light of the moon, throwing my smoking body from the window of the burning house.

After that, instinct and pain drove us to run, and I didn't have the will to fight it. By the time the wolf slept within me again, and by the time the pain had subsided enough to make it possible to think like a man again, the moon was nearly dark. I'd spent the better part of two weeks licking my wounds in the wilderness, oblivious to what was happening in the city.

My head was finally healed, and I could think straight. The memories of all that had happened leading up to the fire hit me like a hammer to the heart. I had to go back, had to see if it was true, though I already knew that it was.

The house where I'd lived with Evelyn, where we were going to raise what I'd foolishly believed to be *our* child, was a smoldering ruin. I lingered there for hours in the darkness, grieving and coming to accept what I had done.

I'd actually killed my wife. She'd been unfaithful, taking Tony Curcio into our bed, but that didn't make it right. Besides, hadn't I been the one who had been unfaithful to her? Faith in her was all she had ever asked of me, and all I had ever denied her. Had I driven her to this?

"Francis?"

My sister's voice in the darkness brought me back to myself. I'd been sloppy. I couldn't be here, couldn't trust myself to be around Maggie and her family. Better that she think I was dead again. I'd thought she would be safe from me, but I'd thought Evelyn would be safe from me as well. Nobody was safe. Not if I was in their life.

"Francis?" she said again, drawing closer. "I knew it was you when I saw you from the window. Who else could it be?"

Her arms were around me before I could escape them. I said nothing, just let her talk and hold me.

"Oh, Francis, it's so horrible," she said. "I'm so sorry."

Sorry? She was sorry? For me? I was the cause of this. I didn't deserve anybody's sympathy, anybody's pity. Still I said nothing.

"Poor Evelyn," she said, weeping.

I let her draw me towards her home, where Paul and the baby were still asleep upstairs. Maggie made peppermint tea and served us both wordlessly as I stared at the new piece of furniture she had added to her parlor.

Evelyn's rocking chair. It was lightly charred on one side but otherwise remarkably intact. Maggie could see my surprise.

"We found it after the fire," Maggie explained. "There wasn't much else. I know how much she loved that chair. Having it here almost feels—almost feels like a piece of her is still here with us."

"Tell me everything," I said.

Slowly, Maggie painted the picture for me of what had happened while I'd healed in the woods. Tony's gunshots had been heard, and the police had been called even before the fire had consumed the house. When the fire had finally gone out, all they found had been the charred and smoking bodies of Evelyn Shepard and Tony Curcio.

According to Paul, Mr. Curcio had assumed that his son had been the target of retaliation by the Kelly operation after Tony's raid had gone wrong. I'd been assumed, by Curcio at least, to have died in that fight. Tony had reported as much, of course.

There were rumors about what Tony was doing in Evelyn's home alone, at night, after she'd been so recently widowed. Mr. Curcio did his best to spin it as though Tony had been comforting the wife of a dear and loyal friend. But people knew what was happening. The affair was too obvious, too brazen. I regretted the way people would think of her, but Evelyn never had been one to care about appearances or the opinions of others.

Maggie didn't believe it for a second. Her sister-in-law would never have betrayed me. Not in Maggie's eyes. My little sister always saw the best in people, even when she had to imagine it. How else could she convince herself so deeply that her brother was a good man?

Maggie had painted a different picture for herself. She knew that I was different. I'd never been able to lie to her. I'd kept certain details to myself, but she knew. She hadn't believed that I was dead even when Tony swore that he had seen me die. She knew I'd come back. What she assumed was that I had come home in time to try and protect Evelyn from Tony, that he had always been sweet on her and thought that he had a chance now that I was out of the way. The way his body was mangled... Maggie assumed that I had shown up too late, that Evelyn had refused the gangster's advances and he had shot her, and that I had torn him apart for what he had done to my wife.

The version of that night's events that Maggie told me was built of little pieces of fact, but they were held together by my sister's bottomless optimism. By her desperate need to believe the best about the people she loved.

Sweet Maggie, she held a monster in her arms and told herself he was some sort of tragic hero. I couldn't lie to her, but I didn't have to correct her. She'd been through enough. Let her have her illusions of her noble big brother. I couldn't take that from her.

I pulled out of her arms and rose to look at Evelyn's rocking chair, sliding one hand along the curving armrest where my wife had leaned nearly every night of our lives together. She loved to sit in this chair, smoking, drinking, listening to her music. Things she would never do again.

I looked up and away from the chair, finding the thoughts too fresh and painful. Instead I looked in the mirror that Maggie had hung on the wall nearby, and I jumped.

There I stood, gaunt and haggard, with dark rings under my sad eyes, unshaved and unwashed from my time in the woods, but that was to be expected. What I hadn't expected was the figure standing beside me in the reflection, with her hand on the rocking chair beside mine. Her blue eyes met mine with a piercing sadness. Evelyn.

I spun around, expecting to see my wife there, but saw nothing.

"Francis? What is it?" Maggie asked.

"I thought... I thought I saw..."

I turned back to the mirror, and there she was again, smiling sadly, and shaking her head faintly in disapproval. She sat in the chair now, and it seemed to rock almost imperceptibly under my hand, as if of its own accord.

So, this was what was left of my Evelyn?

"I'm so sorry..." I whispered to the ghost of my wife.

"What did you say?" my sister asked.

"I have to leave, Maggie," I told her.

I couldn't stand the idea of staying another minute in that house, with the ghost of the only woman I'd ever loved. It was too raw, too painful. But I could never explain that to Maggie. She'd think I was crazy.

"Yes, maybe that's best," she said, "for a little while at least. Give Paul a couple of weeks to fix things here, and then we can come up with some sort of story about how you survived. You take some time to mourn poor Evelyn. Oh, Francis, I'm so sorry."

"No," I said, "I have to leave. For good."

"What are you talking about?"

"Maggie," I said, "I can't be here. I can't be in your life. I just... I can't."

I couldn't explain it to her. I wasn't willing to paint the picture of her heroic brother as a dangerous monster who might hurt his own sister or her baby one day.

"Francis, I know you're hurting, but we need you," she said. "I need you."

I kissed her on her head.

"No, Maggie," I said. "Maybe you used to, but you don't, now. You've got everything you need right here. You've got Paul and the baby."

"Babies," she said.

"What?" I'd smelled it on her but hadn't let my mind process what my instincts already knew.

"I'm expecting again." She smiled at me as if that simple statement would solve everything. She couldn't understand that another innocent was just one more reason that I couldn't stay.

"That's wonderful," I said, and meant it.

"So," she said, "you can't go. We all need you."

"No," I said again. "You don't need me to hold your hand under the bed anymore Mags. You're not that scared little girl anymore. Now you're the one who gets to hold little hands. The way that mama should have held ours."

"Francis, no," she said, a hint of fear creeping into her eyes and voice as she began to realize that I meant what I was saying. She took my hand in hers, unaware of how recently my fingers had been covered in blood. "I'll always need to hold your hand. You're being stupid."

"Maybe so," I said, "but why change now?"

I smiled at her sadly and pulled my hands away and began to take my leave

"No," she said firmly. "No. I won't let you. Not again. You're not going to disappear again. Do you hear me? You're not going to leave me again."

But I was leaving, even as she told me not to.

"Maggie, I have to..."

"No, you don't!" She yelled now. My proper little sister screaming at me as I started to leave, for once not giving a damn who heard or what they thought. Maybe Evelyn had rubbed off on her. "You're not the only one who lost her, Francis! I hurt too; we all do."

"Goodbye, Maggie," I said, refusing to meet the accusation in her eyes as I turned away from her. There was no way I could make her understand, no way I could make this alright for her. It would have been better if she'd never seen me standing there in the darkness. Now there was nothing to do but to make the pain as quick as possible, for her sake.

I walked away.

"You're being selfish!" she yelled. "All you care about is yourself!"

I turned a corner and quickly bolted behind a tree, slipping into the shadows before she could follow me. She rounded the corner moments later and saw no sign of me. Still, she knew I could hear her. She was crying and furious, yelling her curses at me into the night.

"Fine! I don't need you!" She yelled, sobbing. "Go away, and don't you ever come back!"

I moved slowly away through the night, her words growing more distant as lights turned on in the nearby houses and she ignored the people shouting at her to be quiet.

"You're just like him," her last words reached me. "You're just like Dad!"

I stumbled a little as those final words struck home. They stung, deeply, as she knew they would. I knew that she was angry and hurt, that if I went back right then she'd apologize and say that she never meant what she'd said. She'd say she was wrong, and she'd be telling the truth, though she wouldn't know why.

The truth is, she was wrong. I wasn't like our father. I was much, much worse.

PART 9

NEARLY LOST YOU

CHAPTER SIXTY-TWO

WASHINGTON STATE,
SPRING, 1995

It was the silence that woke me as we arrived at our destination. The sudden stop of the humming of the Blazer's engine.

I was aware of voices, a man's and a woman's, though their words were muffled by distance and walls. Familiar smells mingled with the sticky metallic scent of large amounts of spilled blood. I tested my body, trying to move, and found that I was still bound in iron cuffs. The wolf had worked tirelessly as I lay unconscious. The hole in my lung was closed, and I could breathe again, if painfully. The bleeding had stopped from my shattered knee as well, but it was nowhere near ready to support my weight. With the moon so small in the sky and the fuel of my own anger denied to him as I slept, there was only so much the wolf could do.

I heard heavy footfalls approaching, a man's steps, and decided to play possum, closing my eyes and doing my best to appear unconscious. I didn't have much chance of getting out of this, but whatever chance I did have would be in taking them by surprise and waiting for an opportunity, if one ever came.

The footsteps stopped and the truck door opened by my head. I stayed limp, eyes closed. Immediately, a hand gripped my hair and a cold pinch pierced my neck. I could hear the depression of a plunger and the quiet movement of liquid in a syringe. I thrashed. I couldn't help myself, needles have that effect on me since I'd learned to hate them sometime in the forties. I can't stand them!

"Ah, so you *are* awake," Lodi's voice said. "She said you probably were."

"What—what did you..."

A pleasant and familiar warmth flooded my veins, washing away my pain and fear in its wake and replacing them with a wash of euphoria.

"What's wrong?" Lodi asked with mock concern. "She said you liked our product, said you couldn't get enough."

I looked up at him from where I floated, struggling to focus. The biker looked down at me with a cruel smile, and though some part of me knew that I should be afraid of what that smile foreshadowed for me, in the pleasant heroin haze he'd sent me into, I just couldn't manage to feel concerned. Everything was fine. Better than fine. There was nothing to worry about.

"Who..."

"Don't play dumb, asshole. Yarrow has been looking forward to this little chat with you." He grabbed me by my throat with one hand and dragged me from the backseat of my Blazer, tossing me roughly to the muddy ground. "Welcome home."

The blood smell was stronger now—almost overwhelming—with my face in the mud. Welcome home? Where the hell was I? Did it even matter? I sniffed lazily at the mud and realized that my face had come to rest not in mud, but in bloody dirt.

That was odd. It didn't worry me so much in my addled state as much as it confused me.

Whose blood was I lying in? And what did he mean by 'welcome home'?

Blinking, I struggled to raise my head and look around me for more pieces to this puzzle. The first thing I recognized were the lights, candle lights in the windows. Windows I knew. My windows. My trailer? Strange. Why would we come here?

I looked around some more at the dark ground near me and slowly realized that what had at first just been uninteresting and blurry shapes on the ground, were something more significant. There were perhaps half a dozen of them, some small, some large. The one nearest me seemed... fuzzy. No, not fuzzy, furry.

I pushed through the haze, trying to focus. This was significant, somehow. They wanted me to see this. There were features on the nearest shape that my mind wanted to make sense of. I looked again and saw it. The eyes. The staring, blank eyes above a massive snout. The sweet face of my big dog Lenny, locked in a pitiful expression of agony. Even through the heroin haze I managed to feel something at this realization.

"Wh—what? No..."

Lenny had been the biggest, the stupidest, the sweetest of my pack. He'd been the most intimidating at first glance, but he'd been useless as a guard dog. Any harm he'd ever done to anybody had only ever been an accident, the unfortunate side effect of being a big dopey puppy in the body of a hulking beast.

He'd nearly knock me down sometimes when I came home, standing up on his hind legs and bathing my face in that enormous tongue of his. His breath had been... just awful, but not nearly as bad as the smell coming from him now. The smell of his spilled guts resting in the dirt beside him.

I looked around again, trying to make sense of this. The other shapes... they couldn't be—could they?

But they were.

My entire pack was strewn about the patch of dirt in front of my wretched trailer, their bodies broken and mangled in various cruel positions I didn't want to think too hard about. Winston seemed crushed, as if his head had been stomped in. Atop him lay Norma Jean, she'd always been protective of him, a hole blown in the top of her golden head. Smedley, Blue's partner, had blood staining his muzzle. I didn't doubt that he had given as good as he had gotten, at least until they had ripped his head from his body and tossed it to the other side of the yard.

They were all there. My pack. My dogs. The collection of unwanted and broken strays I'd brought together over the years. I'd wanted to give them a home, a place where they could be safe, a family. They were all dead.

...no.

The voice of the wolf was distant in the back of my mind, fighting to make itself heard through the smothering fog in my veins. He was barely there at all.

I knew I should have felt something. Grief, pain, anger...but there was only a cold emptiness, a chemical numbness masquerading as painlessness.

"Oh, yes," Lodi laughed. "You see, you fuck with what's mine, and I return the favor."

"Carl, stop playing with him and bring him in here," a woman's silky voice rose from my trailer. "I don't have all night."

That voice sent tendrils of electric cold skipping across my bones. There was something about it. Something so impossibly familiar. Yarrow? The one who had made me? Was I about to meet my... maker? One way or another, that outcome seemed all but guaranteed. I half wanted to look up, wanted to see the face of that voice, but I was too scared, too tired, too damn high to care.

Carl "Lodi" Vargas grabbed me again by the neck, not

caring that he nearly crushed my windpipe as he dragged me through the blood and viscera of my pack towards the waiting trailer. I struggled weakly, unable to twist free or even to look up at what I was being brought toward. As I was dragged into the trailer I could see the remnants of my own filth on the floor. I struggled to look around me and that is when I saw a pair of bare, delicate feet, caked in dirt and blood, sitting in my dead wife's chair.

Evelyn's chair. Was she here too, watching this happen? The ghost of my dead wife? Almost certainly. She'd watched every shameful thing I'd done in this trailer over the years. Every try at poisoning myself. Every failed, half-hearted suicide attempt. She had sat silently in that chair with the same sad and disapproving expression. I wouldn't be able to see her, not without a reflection. The moon wasn't full enough for that, but I had no doubt that she was watching this now.

What did she think? Would she be distressed, or maybe pleased to watch me get what was coming to me? I supposed it only seemed fair that she would now get to see how it ended for me. After all, I'd been there when it had ended for her. Probably she would have the same expression she always did, disappointment. Pity and disappointment.

"Put him there," the woman's voice gnawed at my memories. "Fasten him to that pipe."

Lodi obeyed her, without hesitation. So, this was his maker? His alpha? I supposed that made us related in some strange way. I chuckled weakly as the thought flitted across my mind. I thought of my father, and I chuckled.

"What's so funny, asshole?" Lodi snarled as he finished locking my cuffs to a length of chain.

"...nobody hates... like family..."

"Isn't that the truth," the woman said, as Lodi turned me

over onto my back, and I got my first clear look at who was sitting inside my trailer.

In the far corner, in what was meant to be the dining nook, sat Andy. She was gagged, her eyes wide and wet with fear and tears. That emerald fleck in her blue eyes shining as brightly and conspicuously as ever. It occurred to me then that the ghost of Evelyn wouldn't be the only one to watch what happened to me. I didn't want Andy here for this. It was bad enough that I couldn't save her, but it was so much worse that she'd be made to watch this.

The other woman, the wolf in woman's skin, made no sense at all. My first thought was that I was seeing the ghost tonight after all, regardless of the moon. My second thought was that I was even more high than I had realized, because what I was seeing simply wasn't possible.

Sitting in my dead wife's old rocking chair, regarding me with pale yellow eyes, was my dead wife, Evelyn.

Not Evelyn as I remembered her, not the curved and mischievous young woman in her twenties with immaculate makeup and carefully styled blonde curls.

No. This Evelyn was older, looking to be approaching forty, just as I did. She was leaner, the gentle curves I remembered replaced with sharp angles and wiry muscle. She was barefoot, dressed in jeans and a simple button up shirt, her long blonde hair resting behind her in a tight braid. She was still beautiful, but in an icy, jagged sort of way. She regarded me with those hungry, predatory eyes and just the faintest hint of a wicked smile at the corner of her mouth as she rested comfortably in her old chair.

"Hi, honey," she said cruelly. "I'm home."

"Ev—Evelyn?"

"Once upon a time," she said. "It's Yarrow now."

"But, but you're dead, I saw..."

Lodi kicked me in the ribs, silencing me. Evelyn—Yarrow—shot him a disapproving glare. Across the tiny trailer, Andy whimpered in fear.

"Carl," the wolf with my wife's face said to Lodi, "take our little Cassandra outside, won't you? We'll be leaving soon, and I'd like a little privacy to catch up with my husband."

Lodi grimaced, but obeyed her command, throwing Andy over his shoulder as she tried to scream through her gag. He slapped her once on her ass, hard, and laughed to himself as he carried her out of the trailer. As they left, Andy met my eyes. The terror in those eyes pulled at me, pleading with me through my drugged stupor to snap out of it, to do something.

But there was nothing I could do.

I watched from the floor, looking up at the window, unable to raise myself up high enough to see outside. Able only to see the reflection of the interior of the trailer in the candlelit glass. I saw Yarrow sitting in her old chair, smiling cruelly down at me. And beside her, the ghost of my dead wife, still young, still pretty, still sad, still dead. Eternally disappointed.

CHAPTER SIXTY-THREE

I was going mad. There was no other explanation that I could think of. I'd finally lost my damn mind.

Evelyn was alive? Sitting here. A Garou, like me. Responsible for changing Lodi and Los Perdidos from small-time drug runners and thugs into a pack of supernatural killers. Her pack.

But, at the same time, Evelyn was dead. She had to be. How else could her ghost still be standing beside the chair with the same sad eyes she'd had since she had died?

Both things couldn't be true at once. I had to be mad. I *had* to be.

"Oh, honey," Yarrow smirked, "you look confused."

"How?" I was reeling. I didn't know what else to say.

"How, what?" she smiled sweetly. "How am I here? How did I survive? How did I know how to find you? How am I going to pay you back for what you did to me? There are an awful lot of 'hows' we could be addressing right now, Frank. You'll have to be more specific."

"You—you're dead," I said, looking from the ghost of Evelyn in the reflection to the monster sitting and speaking with my dead wife's face.

"Oh, her?" wolf-Evelyn gestured to her sad-eyed doppelganger in the reflection. "Honey, that's not me. Never was. Don't you know that?"

"W—what?"

She sighed, exasperated.

"Frank, you're really not very bright, did you know that?"

She waited for me to respond, but I just stared at her, numb, dumbfounded, lost.

"How long have you been like this now?" she said. "Almost eighty years? In all that time, you haven't bothered to learn a damn thing, have you? Why am I not surprised?"

"How?" I said, "How—how can you be a ghost and be here? It doesn't make sense."

"Frank," she rolled her eyes, "this is really basic stuff. I've got to say, I'm disappointed. But fine, if it will help you understand what is really about to happen to you, I suppose I can spare a moment to enlighten you."

I looked again to the ghost reflection, with her unchanging, pitying gaze and back to the speaking Evelyn as she rocked slowly in her old chair.

"What do you think that ghosts are, Frank?" she asked, rhetorically. "The souls of dead people, some superstitious shit like that?"

"I—I just..." I stammered.

"Of course, you do, don't you? Well, they're not people, Frank. They're shadows. Echoes. Don't you know that by now? When a person dies, they're gone. Poof. Nothing left. But that doesn't mean that they can't leave their mark. You've been in the Dream, you should know better, Frank, really. It's emotions that make ghosts, not souls. Intense emotions usually, the stronger the better. They leave a mark on the Dream, form a footprint—if you like—a print that lingers in the shape of the thing that made it. Get it now, dummy?"

She leaned forward and tapped her fingers against my cheek in a patronizing, flirtatious gesture. I thought of the ghosts I had seen over the years, the way that they fixated on a given emotion or obsession, and the way that they tended to fade over the years. But Evelyn, my Evelyn, the ghost who had been with me for all these years, had never faded.

"Then why... why is she..."

"Why is she still here? That pathetic shadow you've been living with?" she finished for me. "Because you're a sap, Frank. A big softy. You keep her here. You've been hanging on to that ridiculous image of me for all these years, the same way you've been hanging on to this old piece of crap." She tapped her knuckles on the wood of the creaking old chair. "She's not my ghost, Frank, she's yours."

"She's not real?" I said.

"Oh, she's real enough, as ghosts go," Evelyn said. "She's just not the real me. I've got to say, it may be pathetic and sad, but it is at least a little bit sweet to see that you've been pining for me all these years. It'd be flattering if it wasn't so damn creepy."

"You didn't die?"

"Oh, I died alright," she sneered at me. "But it didn't take. I have you to 'thank' for that."

"But I saw you...watched you burn."

"Yes, about that..." she reached to the floor and tapped her sharp nails on something I hadn't noticed before. An aluminum container, full of liquid, judging by the sound. "We'll get to that, don't worry."

Outside I could hear Andy struggling, thrashing futilely as Lodi shoved her into the Blazer and slammed the door. I fought to think of any way I could help the girl. She didn't deserve any of this, even if I did.

"Let the girl go," I said. "She's not part of this."

"Who, Cassandra?" Evelyn arched an eyebrow. "No, Frank, I think I'll be holding onto her."

"But why? Why should she matter to you? Let her go, Evelyn, please. For whatever I might have meant to you, just let her go."

"Seventy years apart and you still think you can tell me what to do? Fuck you, Frank. I'm in charge here. I'll decide what happens to her, not you."

"But why would you want her?"

"For the same reason you do, Frank. Don't play dumb. Our little Andy is too useful to throw away."

"Useful? How?" I asked.

"You really aren't playing, are you?" she said. "You're actually this dumb. She's a Dreamer, Frank. She sees things. Do you have any idea how rare that is? No, clearly you don't. Then why the hell did you come after her if you didn't know? Are you fucking her, Frank? Or did you just fall for her little damsel in distress act? Well, it doesn't matter. You really had no idea what she was, huh? Oh, well, it's a bit late to worry about teaching an old dog any more new tricks, don't you think?"

She hoisted the metal gas can into her lap and drummed her fingernails along it.

"So, you're going to kill me? Is that the plan?"

"Yes, sweetheart, I'm going to kill you. Are you really surprised?" she smiled with mock sweetness, her yellow eyes gleaming in the candlelight.

"I suppose not," I said, feeling my own wolf recoil at the anger in her eyes, even through the haze of the drugs in my blood.

"'I suppose not,'" she sneered. "Well, you suppose right, Frank. Although, I'll admit, I've had some mixed feelings about this. I suppose, in some ways, I should thank you. No, really. Think about it, Frank. If it weren't for you, what would my life have been? Married off to somebody my father chose to take me off his hands? Dead now, probably, for years? Thanks to you, I'm strong enough that nobody gets to decide my life for me anymore. Not my father, not you, nobody. That's worth more than you can probably understand."

She stroked the side of my face gently, caressing me like she used to as she spoke softly.

"Maybe I should thank you for that," she went on. "For the joy of the hunt. For the feeling of my father's blood on my hands...oh, that was a glorious night, Frank, let me tell you. He was my first kill; did you know that? Just glorious. Glorious enough to make up for waking up in the dirt, screaming. Enough to make up for being burned beyond all recognition. For the agony I felt as I healed for months. For months, do you understand? Still, it was worth it. Worth losing my mind for years, clinging to little fragments of memory as I slowly pieced my mind back together. It was hell, Frank, but it was all worth it."

She drew her nails along the side of my face, pressing them lightly into the skin of my throat, snarling.

"It would all be worth it," she said, "and I'd still thank you for it. All the pain, all the fear, all worth it, except for one thing, Frank."

She locked eyes with me then and I felt her nails growing sharper, growing into my neck, drawing blood as she tightened her grip ever so slightly. The hate and loss I saw in her gleaming eyes scared my wolf into utter submission. He'd be no help at all.

"You cost me my baby, Frank," she snarled and thrust my head back against the floor, slamming into the hard surface with a dull thud.

"Oh," I groaned.

"'Oh?'" she screamed at me. "'Oh?' 'Oh?' Is that all you have to say, you bastard? All these years, and that's all you have to say?"

"I understand," I said, and I meant it. I did understand. She hated me even more than I realized, but not for the reasons I'd assumed. I'd taken from her the only thing she'd ever really wanted, her chance to be a mother. Her chance to love somebody so completely. Somebody who would love her back with their whole heart, no matter what she did. I understood. That was what this had all been about.

"You can't possibly," she spat the words at me, "and don't you dare pretend that you do!"

"Is that why you did it?" I asked.

"Did what?"

"Is that why you killed Mack?"

"Oh, him?" She laughed. "He was working against my interests. He was nothing. He couldn't have gotten to Cassandra if you hadn't helped him. I had Carl kill him when I realized that he was your friend. When I saw that it would hurt you. That's all."

So, Lodi had been the one that killed Mack?

"And the dogs?"

"The dogs and that filthy cat too. You cared about them. You didn't have much that I could take from you, Frank. There isn't much you love. That's smart of you, really. But you took everything from me. It only seemed fair that I return the favor."

A thought occurred to me then. My sister. Maggie. Living alone at Larrabee Assisted Living in Bellingham, only half aware of who she was anymore. The person that I loved most in the world, utterly vulnerable.

"Maggie..." I said under my breath.

"I thought about it, I'll admit," Evelyn said. "I went to see her, you know. Spent some time talking with her about the old days, she knew exactly who I was. It was nice, talking with somebody who knew who I was, even if she didn't really understand. But no, I won't hurt Maggie."

"Thank you," I said.

"Thank me?" she sneered. "I should do it you know. She'd probably thank me, Frank. Do you think she wants to live like that? Losing little pieces of herself until there's nothing left? No. I left her alone, because it will hurt you more this way. You get to let her down one last time. She won't know why you don't come to visit her anymore—why you left her. She'll just know that you aren't there the last time she needs you, when she depends on you to help her end it. You won't be there. I'm probably doing her a kindness though, because even if you were there, you wouldn't do what she wants, would you? Not you. Not Frank Shepard. You know best. It doesn't matter what she wants, does it? Not if you know better. You knew what was best for me, didn't you? Why should she be any different?"

Even through the heroin, tears were pooling in my eyes. She saw this, and like a hungry wolf getting its first taste of blood, she bit deeper.

"I watched you with her, you know," she said. "Bringing her candies, singing to her. Why didn't you ever sing for me, Frank? I never knew you had it in you. That's how I found this place. I followed you here, to this shithole. I watched how you drugged yourself. How you chained yourself up, just like this. I couldn't help myself, Frank." She winked at me and smirked. "I had to break you free, just to see what would happen, what trouble you'd get yourself into. But, unsurprisingly, you disappointed me. You were always so damn stuffy, Frank! I was so bored. I had to go and rip poor Rita's throat out myself, just to have something to do. You barely needed the chains at all, you know." With her hand, she indicated the fresh chains that held me to the trailer. "Did we do it right? I wanted to get things just right for you. Was the heroin right? I had Carl give you the good stuff.

I hope you appreciate it."

Evelyn always had a little wicked streak, a playful sort of meanness that I'd enjoyed sparring with, but she'd never been like this. Never cruel. She'd become everything I hated about myself. She was a murdering, torturing, monster, and she delighted in it. What had I done to her?

"I'm sorry, Evelyn," I said.

"Oh, are you, Frank?" she dripped with sarcasm. "Are you sorry you took my baby from me? Oh, I'm so glad you're sorry. That makes everything all better."

"Yes," I said, "I'm sorry for that. I am. But I'm sorry I made you...this."

"No!" she put her foot on my chest and snarled at me as she held up the gas can. "You don't get to do that! You don't get to claim me anymore, Frank. I'm not yours. You didn't make me! I'm what I want to be. Do you understand that? Tell me you understand that, tell me you hear that before I let you die!"

Her lip was trembling with fury. She was screaming, she was enraged, and she was right.

"You're right, Evelyn," I said. "I was wrong."

"Wrong about what, Frank? Say it! Let me hear you say it before you burn."

"I was wrong to... to choose for you," I said. "I was wrong to think... to think that I knew best what you needed, what was right for you. I was wrong to think... you were my responsibility. That you were... mine."

Her eyes widened as she looked at me, softened a little. As if, at last, I'd given her some small comfort that had long been denied her. I thought maybe she was about to thank me, to put down the gas can and change her mind. I thought maybe she might actually forgive me.

"Police, put it down!"

A man's voice yelled from outside the trailer and two

gunshots rang out in the night. Evelyn's eyes narrowed again, and she pulled her gaze away from me, spinning to the little window and peering between the blinds.

Outside the sound of a loud pained growl answered the gunshots, Lodi's growl, low and dangerous.

"Carl, take care of him," Evelyn shouted through the window. "We're done here."

She turned back to me quickly, the cruel smile again replacing the soft expression that had been there so briefly.

"What's happening?" I asked.

"Nothing for you to worry your little head over, Frank," she said, opening the gas can. "It'll be over soon. I'm sorry to rush this, Frank, you deserve to savor this moment, but, you know how it is... shit happens."

She upended the can, pouring cold liquid around me, careful not to douse me in it directly, soaking the floor and walls nearby, even stopping to saturate her old rocking chair.

"This time you won't be running away when things get hot," she said as she spread the last of the fuel. "You'll get to know what it feels like to really burn. And don't worry, Frank, I know what you're thinking. What if the fire doesn't kill you? Well, it probably won't. That's what this is for."

She produced my old model 1911 loaded with steel rounds, the ones I'd been planning to kill myself with, from the drawer where I'd left it.

"Once you're nearly done, medium-rare I'd say, I'll put you out of your misery, permanently. Don't worry, Frank, I've gotten good at it. Better than you at any rate. I won't fuck it up."

More gunshots rang out outside, followed by growling and a man's voice, yelling.

"Oh, shit! Oh, shit! What the shitting shit? Oh shit!"

I heard the voice receding, running into the woods toward the road, and I heard Lodi's angry growls follow suit.

Was that Owen Watson's voice? Mack's son? It sounded like it, but how could he have found me here? Was I about to get Mack's son killed too? I pulled at the cuffs, but my limbs were weak, thick, floating in the warm heroin glow.

"Tsk tsk, none of that, or I'll have to put a couple rounds in you early, and that would ruin the fun." She levelled the heavy pistol at my head with one hand and smiled as she reached out for a candle. Without taking her eyes off of me, Evelyn dropped the candle onto the rocking chair, setting it ablaze.

Her eyes didn't leave mine as the fire engulfed her old chair and quickly spread onto the floor and walls, the flickering lights of the hungry fire reflected blindingly from the simmering golden coals of her irises.

Her smile grew inhumanly wide as the flames spread to my legs and caught on my jeans. I began to writhe and squirm, clenching my teeth, not wanting to give her the satisfaction of crying out in pain. The heroin helped, but even with the chemical assistance, I knew I'd be screaming for mercy before long.

So, this was it. This was how it was finally going to end. Not the quick and relatively painless death I'd planned for myself to be sure, but I found myself strangely at peace with the way things were ending. I'd spent so many years punishing myself for what I had done to Evelyn, hating myself, that it seemed fitting that she be the one to do the deed. Maybe it was the guilt, or maybe it was the heroin. No matter, I submitted to her, accepted what she was doing to me as no more than I had coming.

If only I could do something for Andy or for Owen. My one regret was that they would pay for my mistakes along with me. I'd have helped them if I could, but I couldn't. I was trapped. I was burning. I was going to die.

A second shape came into the trailer behind Evelyn from

the door. So, it was over already. Lodi had finished off Owen and come back to gloat over my death. I couldn't make out his features clearly through the flames, but he seemed smaller somehow, slender, girlish even.

"Did you take care of it?" Evelyn said to the newcomer without looking behind her. She didn't want to miss a moment of my torment.

A short length of sawed-off steel raised and pointed at the back of Evelyn's head as Andy Morgan's voice answered her question. "I'm about to."

Yellow eyes twitched in alarm, but there was no time for any other reaction. Inches away from Evelyn's skull, Andy pulled the trigger of the sawed-off shotgun that I had left on the floor of my Blazer. The one that Rudy had used to fill my belly with steel shot. The gun roared and Evelyn's head split like an overripe melon. Her body slumped sideways, falling onto the burning rocking chair. For the second time, I watched my wife die.

CHAPTER SIXTY-FOUR

Grief is strange. I'd mourned Evelyn for the better part of a century, living most of my life with the guilt of her death. A person might be forgiven for thinking that this would have hardened me against witnessing her death a second time, but anybody who has ever loved another person would know better. It didn't matter that I'd lived seventy years without her. It didn't matter that I'd only had minutes to realize that she still lived. It didn't even matter that any love she'd once had for me had long since given way to a seething hatred. All that mattered was that I had lost her again to violence and fire.

If anything, the pain was magnified by the weight of the past. Her face was gone, utterly destroyed by the exit wound of the shotgun blast that had torn through her golden head, and the woman who had come to be known as Yarrow, the woman who had once been my wife, Evelyn, was dead at my feet. Her own ancient ghost looked down at the mangled body resting in her old rocking chair, once more caught in a burning home, the eternal look of sad disappointment seeming more appropriate than it ever had.

The pain ripped its way out of my chest, emerging from my throat as a deafening howl.

Andy, my wife's killer, stood just beyond the flames that were beginning to bite into my limbs. She saw the pain that I was in and mistakenly attributed it to the trivial agony of my burning flesh. Dropping the now empty shotgun to the floor of my trailer, she made a brave but futile attempt to reach me but was immediately driven back by the intense heat and choking fumes. Her left arm raised and covering her mouth and nose as she coughed and blinked uncontrollably.

"Francis!" she cried out to me hopelessly as she was forced to retreat toward the door. My eyes never left Evelyn's blackening body.

A man's figure appeared beside Andy in the doorway, but my watering eyes couldn't make out his features through the smoke and flame. Lodi, no doubt, returned in time to witness what had happened to his alpha. Andy had wasted her chance to escape in an attempt to save me, and now she would pay for it. The girl had proven to be the only hero on the scene, and I could do nothing to shield her from the fate of all real heroes. A painful death.

But it wasn't Lodi who joined us in the trailer. The male figure leapt through the flames and came to a crouch at my feet, separating me from Evelyn's body. Hiram's weathered face loomed over me, looking from me to the body of the woman he had only known as Yarrow. He frowned, a pale shadow of my own grief passing fleetingly over him like a cloud across the sun in a strong wind. Then, ever the stoic, the feeling passed from his features and he turned to me, assessing my situation for no more than a heartbeat before reaching out with both hands and snapping the chain that held me in place.

"No..." I coughed and shook my head. "Let me stay with her. No..."

He ignored me, hoisted me over his shoulder as if I weighed no more than a small child, and carried me from the burning trailer.

"Is he going to be alright?"

Andy hovered over Hiram's shoulder, peering at me with a queer combination of fear and disgust. I gathered I must have looked pretty bad. I smelled more than felt the burns, an unpleasant but vaguely baconish aroma steaming from the lower half of my body. The pain would be bad, eventually, but just then thanks to the numbing properties of the heroin still being burned from my veins, as well as the overwhelming pain of Evelyn's second and final death, I didn't much care.

Hiram turned his head and snarled at Andy. She in turn took three cautious steps away from the old wolf's personal space before summoning a stubborn scowl and standing her ground.

"Well," she said, doing her best to act fearless in the face of his golden eyes, "is he going to be alright or not?"

"In time," Hiram answered with reluctance, turning back to face me.

"Oh," was all she said. It was more a relieved exhalation than a word.

"She's dead. She's really dead..." They didn't respond to me, but the growing blaze of my little trailer was all the answer I needed.

"What about Lodi?" Andy asked nervously, looking around her to the thick trees and struggling to keep her eyes off of the mounds that had been my dogs.

"He ran before he could finish the policeman," Hiram said flatly as he considered my wounds.

"Owen. Is Owen—" Is Owen alive? I couldn't quite form the words. Had Mack's son made it through this night after all?

"Shhh," Hiram hushed me as one would a delirious child.

"Is he—is he alive?" I grabbed Hiram's wrist in an effort to compel him to answer me. I doubt there was any strength in my grip.

"I don't know," Hiram answered without concern. "It doesn't matter."

"Like hell it doesn't!" I snarled the response with more force than I should have been able to muster, the anger at his disregard for the life of Mack's son feeding my wolf just enough to rouse me for the moment.

Hiram glowered at me as he brushed my curling fingers aside from his throat. There had been no real strength in them, but the implied challenge to his dominance rankled him.

"Help him," I said as I was pushed gently back to the ground. "Please, you've got to help him."

"Why?" Hiram looked genuinely puzzled. "Do you wish him turned?"

"What? No," Andy and I objected in startled unison.

"Then I am not certain he can be helped," Hiram said with the barest hint of impatience. "He was badly wounded when I saw him last."

"Try. Help him," I said urgently, and then to smooth his pride I added as an afterthought, "please."

"There's no time," he shook his head infuriatingly calmly at me as if explaining obvious truths to an irrational child. "The fire will bring others; you and I must leave, now."

"What?" Andy interjected. "You can't just leave? What if Lodi comes back?"

Hiram ignored her.

"Hiram," I struggled to sit up, wincing as my body fought me for every inch. "I'm not going anywhere. Not if we don't help Owen."

"You have no choice," he glared at me, the force of his

dominance focused through his yellow eyes. "I'll simply carry you."

"I'll fight you..."

He gave me a look of purest incredulity. We both knew that the idea of me fighting him, or anybody, in my condition was absurd. He narrowed his eyes and raised one brow at me.

"I mean it, Hiram," I said. "I know I won't win, but I'll fight. Every step of the way, I'll fight. It'll be faster to just help him."

His lip twitched in the hint of a snarl before he released a heavy breath and the tension went out of his face.

"Fine," Hiram said in a dangerous voice.

He stood and walked with utter silence and startling speed into the brush, vanishing utterly in the space of a breath. Was he giving in to my demand, or had he decided that I was more trouble than I was worth and simply abandoned us? I honestly didn't know. Either way, I was in no condition to do anything about it.

In his absence, Andy stepped forward and took Hiram's space beside me, regarding my wounds with a sympathetic grimace.

"Francis," she said. "Thank you."

"Don't—"

"No, I mean it," she cut me off. "Francis, you came back for me. You didn't have to, but you did, and I need to thank you for that."

"No, don't—" I grunted before she cut me off again.

"I mean it," she said stubbornly. "I know you're not normal, but, Francis, you're either the craziest or the bravest person I've ever met. I don't know anybody else who would have done what you did."

"Andy, don't—"

"God damnit!" She cut me off again. "Would you just let me

thank you without any of this cowboy tough-guy bullshit? I'm thanking you. Just deal with it."

"No," I said, "Don't—don't call me Francis."

"Oh."

She flushed briefly with embarrassment but was saved from responding by Hiram's sudden reappearance. He emerged from the shadows as stealthily and suddenly as he had vanished, but now he held the motionless and bleeding body of a middle-aged black man in his arms.

"Oh my god, is he alive?" Andy said.

"Yes," Hiram responded without looking at her. He looked meaningfully at my white Blazer, even more scarred and dented than before. "Can you drive that?"

Andy looked from Hiram to the vehicle and instantly took his meaning.

"Um, yeah," she said nervously. "Sure, I guess. But it looks pretty bad...can't we take your car?"

"I didn't come in one."

She looked puzzled for a moment, looking down at Hiram's bare and weathered feet as she tried to come to terms with the fact that he had travelled by foot to what she almost certainly considered the middle of nowhere.

Not waiting for her comprehension, Hiram carried Owen Watson to the back seat where I had recently been restrained and placed him in the truck with uncharacteristic gentleness.

"Go," he said to Andy without looking at her. Instead, he walked directly to my side without pausing, forcing her again to retreat before him.

He knelt beside me and hoisted me unceremoniously onto his shoulders. It hurt like hell. The pain was growing in my limbs as the shock and dope began to give way.

"Wait—" I started to say.

"No," he answered, and began to walk away from the road.

As Andy shrank in my vision, I called out to her. "Get him to the hospital as fast as you can!"

As the foliage rose to obstruct my view, I saw Andy climbing once more into the driver's seat of my Blazer, looking around anxiously as if fearful that Lodi would return. From a distance, I could hear the engine struggle and start before the Chevy rolled over the gravel of my hidden driveway.

Minutes later, we were atop a hill, and Hiram wasn't even breathing heavy when I heard a distant boom that could only have been the flames finally reaching my long-neglected propane tanks.

"You should have told me how old you are."

Even after weeks together in the mountains, Hiram kept returning to this same complaint. He'd made some assumptions about my relationship to Evelyn—to Yarrow as he still called her. He'd tasted the connection between me and my dead wife when he'd first taken my blood, and he had known her since shortly after I'd turned her into one of us. He'd spent years with her, helping her heal, teaching her, and despite how everything had turned out for her, I couldn't help but love the old wolf for that. He'd been there for her, cared for her when nobody else had, and I owed him for it.

I hadn't lied to him; I simply hadn't realized the faulty assumptions he had been making since we had met. He had known from our blood that Evelyn and I had been close, that one of us had turned the other. He had simply assumed that I must have been recently made, like Lodi and the rest of Los Perdidos. It hadn't occurred to him that a Turnskin as untaught and isolated as me could have been one of us for more than a couple of years. I defied his experience.

"You should have asked me," I said, not for the first time.

He glowered at me. It irritated him to have a student who didn't show what he considered to be the proper amount of submission and deference, but now that he understood that I was not some inexperienced pup he had come to tolerate my independent streak. But that didn't mean that he liked it.

"It's unheard of," he said more to himself than to me, "without teaching—without a pack—you should have gone mad."

"Who says I didn't?" I said. He shot me the now-familiar scowl meant to remind me that he didn't find me amusing. Hiram didn't find anything amusing. If more than a month in the mountains with the old wolf had taught me anything, it was that Hiram had no sense of humor.

He'd done for me what he had once done for Evelyn. He watched over me as I healed and grieved, and then, slowly, he began to teach me about what we were, about the ways of the Garou, of Turnskins as his native kin had called us.

"This is no joke, Shepard," he scolded me. He may have accepted that I was no pup, but at twice my own age, Hiram was far from accepting me as an equal. "You don't realize how dangerous it can be, caging the wolf for so many years as you did."

"I guess so," I shrugged, "but the alternative seemed worse."

"That is because you saw the alternative as submitting to the wolf," he corrected me, "but that is not the way. The choice is not between the wolf and the man, but between balance and imbalance. You are not two minds, but one."

I didn't respond. Hiram knew that I didn't agree with his view of the wolf. Slowly, under his guidance, I had begun to make a sort of peace with my inner beast, letting it out of his cage to roam now and then, but still struggling to keep it on a short leash. I understood Hiram's perspective. There had been times when I had viewed the wolf and man within me as an 'us' rather than 'it and me', but those times frightened me.

"Those who have gone long without learning balance seldom find it," Hiram said.

"And you put them down..." I added the unspoken conclusion of his statement for him.

"Yes," he agreed somberly. "For the mad wolves, it is a mercy."

"Is that what you're going to do to Lodi?"

We hadn't seen the leader of Los Perdidos since that night at my trailer. The night that Evelyn had died, and Owen had nearly joined her.

"If he is lost, if Yarrow failed to teach him balance, then yes."

I didn't give a fuck about Lodi's 'balance'. I thought about what he had done to Andy, to Mack, to Owen, to me. If I saw that son of a bitch again, one of us was going to die, and not because of philosophical differences.

"If?" I asked. "Did he seem like a well-balanced sort of guy to you?"

"Perhaps not," he agreed, "but that remains to be seen."

"Not to me it doesn't."

"You are no judge of balance, Shepard. You haven't yet mastered your own."

"I don't know," I said, "I think I'm doing pretty good."

"Not good enough," he added.

"Good enough for you to give me a night off though, at least, right?"

He scowled.

"Come on, Hiram," I scowled back. "We had a deal. I have business to take care of. There are people I need to see."

"Very well," he relented. "One night. But if you do not return..."

"I know, I know," I interrupted, drawing a thumb across my throat and grimacing theatrically.

He didn't laugh, of course.

"This is an important test for you," he added, "to maintain balance among the humans without poisoning yourself. Remember what you've been taught, and you will do fine. The full moon is still a week away. Avoid provocation and then return, and we will continue your lessons."

"And how long will that take?" I asked.

"How long will what take?"

"My 'lessons'? How many more months am I supposed to sit up here chasing rabbits and contemplating my navel?"

"Balance isn't something you simply achieve. It is a lifelong pursuit, a practice. As for how long until you have mastered yourself enough to be trusted on your own, who can say? You've denied half of yourself for so long that it has grown sick, feral. It could take years."

"I'm still not convinced that 'balance' is for me." I said. I still wasn't sure that a pipe full of dope, a bottle of jack, and some sturdy chains weren't the more practical choice.

"That is your choice to make," he said. "But you know what choice I must make should you choose poorly."

"I know you'll give it your best shot," I shot him my once-famous Smiling Frank provocative grin.

"You doubt that I could put you down?"

"Don't take it personally," I said. "I doubt just about everything."

CHAPTER SIXTY-SIX

"Do you like my tattoo?"

Andy turned her sleeveless left arm to me, revealing the fresh and vibrant ink still healing there. It was huge and ornate, and very much in keeping with what I knew of the girl. A huge blue-eyed, black raven dominated her upper arm, its wings spread wide and its beak open in a triumphant cry. Beneath it lay dark shapes. Silhouettes of burned buildings. Blackened skeletal frames of houses still ablaze in a raging fire. The flames licked upward at the raven, a broken chain hanging free from one clawed foot. I could make out the shades of yellow in the vibrant flames, the darker bits that I assumed to be orange and red were lost to me. The overall effect was that of a black feathered phoenix, free and reborn from the ashes of some great catastrophe.

I liked it, but I wasn't about to tell her that.

"Are you even old enough for a tattoo?" I said.

"Don't look at me," Marilyn protested. "I didn't know about it until after the fact."

"I think it's very pretty," Maggie opined, as she scratched

absently at Blue's head with one hand, the dog's tongue lolling happily from her one-eyed face.

"How old do you think I am, anyway?" Andy scowled at me.

"I dunno," I said with a shrug. "You're all kids to me."

I regarded the three ladies at the table with me; Andy, barely more than child despite her swelling, pregnant belly and fresh tattoo, Marilyn, a handsome woman in her fifties who was still determined to appear ten years younger with every cosmetic trick available to her, and Maggie, eternally the smiling baby girl I'd held in my arms so many years ago despite her wispy white hair and wheelchair. The three faces of the goddess, each sipping at their lemonades and iced teas while we waited for the festivities to begin.

"For your information, I turned eighteen last month," Andy said with a cocky smirk. "June twentieth. The last day of spring. And you still owe me a present."

"Eighteen? But you look..."

"Lovely," Marilyn interrupted me diplomatically, having come to know Andy over the past few months, and more aware than I of how sensitive the girl could be about her youthful appearance. "But that's not the point, honey. Aren't tattoos dangerous for the baby?"

"Psh," Andy waved away Marilyn and her matronly concern. "Only if you go to somebody who doesn't know what they're doing. One good thing about spending time with bikers, you get to know all the best tattoo artists."

Marilyn pursed her lips and regarded Andy's tattoo with overt disapproval but was wise enough not to refight a battle already lost.

"When are you due?" I asked, changing the subject.

"Not until late September," she said with a smile, the emerald fleck of green in her brilliant blue eyes sparkling at me brighter than ever. The girl still puzzled me. I'd grown accustomed to her peculiar gifts and even to seeing her in the Dream from time to time, but I understood less than ever about what exactly she was.

"I just love babies," Maggie offered, half following the conversation. I laid my hand on hers atop Blue's head. The dog drew back to lick at both of our hands. Maggie gave a familiar girlish giggle at the tickling tongue and Blue laid back down, leaving my sister to grip my hand and smile at me. How much did she understand? How much did she remember? I couldn't know, but it did my heart good to see her smiling so warmly.

"I'll be right back," Andy said. "Smoke break."

Marilyn scowled harder than ever, but Andy pretended not to see. There was no stopping her, however old she was. The girl rose and walked away from the outdoor tables at the memory care facility, strolling toward the treeline and the cliffs that overlooked Bellingham Bay.

"That girl just won't listen to sense," Marilyn grumbled.

"Yeah," I said. "It's almost like she's a person, with her own opinions and everything. Next you'll tell me she wants to make her own decisions."

Marilyn glared at me for a long moment before breaking into a reluctant grin.

"Who are you and what have you done with Frank Shepard?" she chuckled.

I grinned back.

"Okay, Okay, maybe I deserve that," I said. "But maybe she has to make her own mistakes? I remember you when you were young—uh, younger," I amended in response to the sudden flash of anger in her eyes. "I'm just saying, nobody could tell you to do anything either."

"It didn't stop you from trying," she said.

"Yeah, and how well did that work for me?"

"Touché," she said. "I just wish I didn't have to watch her learn the lessons I did the hard way."

"Was there another way you could have learned them?"

"Damn," she stared at me. "You need a drink. I don't know if I like sober Frank. You get all creepy and insightful."

"I know," I grinned. "I hate it. Don't worry, it's a small wagon and there aren't any seatbelts. I'm sure I'll fall off sooner or later."

Marilyn swatted my arm playfully and Maggie smiled at us both.

"Honestly, though," Marilyn said as she looked toward Andy. "She's a damn smart girl. Good head on her shoulders, when she wants to use it, anyway. She's been a big help around the office."

"What have you got her doing?"

"Oh, just clerical stuff mostly," she said, "but she's quick. A couple of times now she used her 'thing' and helped us close a couple of cases that I thought were going to stay open forever."

Marilyn wiggled her fingers mysteriously as if casting a spell to indicate the nature of Andy's 'thing'.

"Oh yeah? Are you going to bring her on full time?"

"Not until she finishes her GED," Marilyn said with a stern furrow to her brow. "That was my condition to letting her work for us in the first place. I wanted her to go back to school, but with the baby on its way she said there was no way. She wanted to just get to work full time, save up for a place of her own. The GED was our compromise."

I nodded in approval, taking a sip of the ice water I'd been nursing in lieu of something more substantial.

"Speaking of business, Frank," Marilyn went on, "I've got the papers right here for you to sign."

"Do we have to do this now?"

"When else?" she said. "You aren't exactly easy to get a hold of. While you're out playing mountain man, life goes on for the rest of us. Come on, it'll only take a minute. I've marked the spots where you need to sign and initial."

She presented me with a stack of papers in black and white, all very official looking. I picked them up and looked them over.

"Don't waste time, Frank," she said. "It's exactly what I told you it was going to be."

"And you're sure that Owen's okay with this?" I asked.

"He doesn't like it, but he knows it has to be this way."

"How's he recovering?" I asked, trying to change the subject.

"He's grumpier than ever, and he'll need that cane for a good while longer, maybe forever, but he's feeling better now that he's working again. After the Sheriff's office fired him for going off the reservation, I was worried. I thought he might do something stupid. That boy has always been too damn proud."

"But he's better now? He doesn't mind being in business with the two of us?"

"Oh, he minds alright," she laughed. "Every morning he shows up in the office and glares at me, and if he ever sees you, he might put another bullet in you. Even though he knows that it wouldn't do much now."

"What does he know?"

"Who knows? He keeps his cards close to the vest, that one," she said. "He knows that he saw some things that don't make any sense unless he believes what he hears from me and what's in Mack's old case notes. He's been going through those old files like he can't put them down. I've answered a few questions for him, but some questions aren't mine to answer. He still wants that confession you promised him. As to what's going on in his head, he's not letting on. He's a lot like his father that way."

"Yeah," I said, missing my old friend. "I'll get him what he wants. I think I'll sit and write out that confession, but it may take some time. Mack wanted to tell Owen everything years ago. It's long past time, I guess."

"You're damn right it is. Just...do me a favor and let me deliver it for you when you've got it all written down. We just remodeled the office. I don't need you two wrecking it again."

I laughed.

"I'm not joking, Frank. Keep your distance, for now at least. Now, stop trying to change the subject," she said sternly, "and sign the damn papers."

I signed and initialed in the indicated spots, looking carefully as I went before stopping at one troubling passage.

"Jesus Christ, Frank," Marilyn sighed, "what is it now?"

"This name," I said, indicated the proposed new name of Shepard and Watson Investigations. "I don't like it."

"Frank, we've been over this," Marilyn rolled her eyes. "It's what Mack wanted. None of us get the business if your name isn't on the door."

"I know, I know," I said. "But that don't make it right. It's not like I agreed to come back to work, after all. I'm not coming back anytime soon."

"That doesn't matter. It's just a name. Owen and I are going to run the business. We all know it's symbolic. Just sign the damn thing, would you?"

"Fine, fine," I said, picking up the pen and scribbling a few quick changes, crossing some lines out and putting my initials next to the alterations before handing the papers back to her.

"What the hell did you do?" Marilyn reached into her stylish purse and took out the reading glasses that she loathed wearing and examined what I had done.

I had drawn a line through the name Shepard and Watson, and in the margins nearby I had written in my amendment to the document.

"Watson, Archer, and Shepard?" She read the new name aloud.

"There's no way my name should be before Mack and Owen's," I said, "or yours."

Her face was hidden behind the papers that she held between us. For a long moment Marilyn said nothing at all. Then she lowered the papers and punched me in the shoulder, hard.

"You jerk!" she said with a tear-streaked smile. "You made me ruin my makeup."

She leaned across to me and kissed my cheek. I wrapped an arm around her and held her there for a moment, basking vicariously in her happiness.

"Thank you, Frank," she said, as she fanned at her eyes with her hands. "Now, don't look at me!"

I rose from the table, smiling.

"I was just about to go and have a smoke anyway," I said by way of excuse, "I'll be right back."

Squeezing Maggie's hand, I released it and walked slowly toward Andy. Blue followed on three legs.

"Nice view," I said to the pregnant girl in a feeble attempt to strike up a conversation.

"Yep," she said, not taking her eyes from the darkening bay. In the distance, across the water, an occasional premature firework would explode in the sky, sending blossoms of flame or showers of sparks.

"Spare a smoke?" I asked.

She turned to me with a skeptical eyebrow raised as her distinctive springtime scent tickled at my nose. The subtle aroma of green things, of pine and maple blossoms, blended nicely with the salty sea air and the natural smells of the towering pines we stood beneath.

"Really?" she said. "Aren't you going to tell me about how bad it is for the baby?"

"Why?" I said. "Don't you already know?"

She shrugged.

"Yeah, but that hasn't stopped anybody else."

"Then you've probably heard it enough," I said. "Besides, I'm not exactly qualified to give lectures on healthy living."

She snorted a laugh and quickly covered her face in embarrassment. I found it oddly charming.

"So, are you going to let me bum a smoke or not?" I said as much to move her past the embarrassment as to satisfy the craving that had been growing in me since I'd first smelled her light up.

She handed me a dark and pungently sweet little cigarette that smelled of cloves. What the hell was this? Was I supposed to smoke it or eat it? I regarded the thing in my hand for a moment before reminding myself silently of the mutually exclusive natures of beggars and choosers. I drew my old, battered zippo from my jacket pocket and lit it, coughing heavily at the first burning drag.

She snorted again. I pretended not to notice.

"You do seem, I dunno, cleaner," she said as she looked me over. "I mean, still dirty but clean. Ya know?"

I considered my unwashed clothes and unshaven face and smiled. It had been months since I'd drugged myself to make it through a full moon or rough day. It had been one of the conditions of Hiram's lessons. I didn't know if I intended to stay sober once I was left to my own devices again. There were plenty of nights where I sat up from dreaming of Evelyn or other horrible memories and wished that I could retreat from the searing clarity of those thoughts. But for the time being, it was good to know that I could at least survive without the drugs.

I considered her unusual scent as I had before, noticing that the smell of her pregnancy was of course more prominent. Her mysterious green scent, as well as the smell of her peculiar cigarettes, were both strong, but the sickly-sweet smell of opium that had been there when I had first found her hiding in Rita's closet was not there.

"Yeah," I said, "you too."

"Yeah," she said. "I just figured, the baby and all."

"Good for you."

"Yeah."

We stood there for a while, not saying anything, watching the distant and increasingly frequent displays of celebratory artillery. They were beautiful from a distance, anyway. Any closer and the flashing lights and thundering explosions would have tested my nerves and my sobriety.

"Andy?"

"Yeah?" she said.

"What are you?"

She turned to me with a grimace.

"What does *that* mean?" she demanded.

"I don't mean nothin' by it," I said, raising a hand in a gesture of peace as Blue nuzzled Andy's leg in response to her agitation. "I've just been wondering about you. The way you say you can see things—know things, or the way you can show up in people's dreams."

She looked around us quickly, clearly agitated that I was talking about this out loud and worried about who might overhear. Maggie and Marilyn sat at the table outside the care center, well out of earshot. The distant pop and sizzle of fireworks would have made it difficult even for my ears to eavesdrop from that distance, so I went on.

"And there's other things," I said, "you smell different. Your eyes are... well, unique. And those bikers, they wanted you for something. They said as much. You're different. I'm just asking how. What are you?"

She looked around us once more with obvious irritation, frustrated with me that I had raised the topic.

"Honestly, dude," she said, "I don't fucking know."

"What?" I hadn't expected that.

"Did I stutter?"

"No," I said, "it's just—isn't that what you do? Know things, I mean?"

"Sometimes. Some things."

"But not this?"

"Nope," she said. "Don't know and don't want to know either."

"Really?"

"Yes, really," she whispered angrily. "Why is that so hard for you to believe?"

"I don't know," I said. "I just, I guess I'd want to know if it was me."

"Why?"

"I don't know," I said, musing. "I suppose I'd just want to know who I was."

"I know who I am. I don't need anybody else to tell me."

This girl never ceased to puzzle me. She looked at me as if to gauge whether or not her answer had satisfied me, but it must have been apparent that I was not any less curious.

"Listen," she said. "I don't know why I'm like this. I wasn't bitten by a radioactive crow or cursed by some creepy voodoo priest or any shit like that, okay? Maybe it has to do with my parents. I don't fucking know, man."

She took a long drag on her strange smelling cigarette and exhaled dramatically.

"Your parents?"

"Yeah, I don't know," she said. "My mom died when I was little. My dad, he adopted me, but I never met my birth dad. So, I don't know. I'm weird. So what? I've seen some really weird shit, man. Ghosts, and fairies, and dreams that come true. Heck, this one time I even met a really nosy guy who dreams that he's a wolf and who keeps getting shot and getting back up again. He saved my life by fighting off a bunch of psycho-killer-zombie-werewolf-bikers. So, as weird shit goes, I feel pretty normal. Yeah, I'm different, and I don't know why. But I'm okay with that."

"Fair enough," I said, trying my best to take 'I don't know' for an answer.

"Now, can we go back and have some pie before it's all gone?"

I nodded and followed behind her, Blue doing her best to limp beside me as she still worked to adjust to life as a one-eyed tripod.

"Oh, Francis," Maggie said, beaming. "I didn't know you were coming!"

I had been gone for maybe ten minutes, and already she'd forgotten that I'd been here. I fought down the lump that struggled to form in my throat as Marilyn and Andy both gave me pitying looks.

"Surprise," I said with a forced smile as I bent to give my baby sister a kiss on the forehead and sat beside her.

Nurse Jeanette was handing out slices of apple pie inside the cafeteria. Marilyn motioned to her to indicate that we would like some as well.

"I'm glad you came," Maggie said with her childlike smile.

"So am I, Maggie," I said.

"Have you said hello to Paul? He's around here somewhere, he was just here a minute ago." She looked around us, confused, trying to find her long dead husband.

"Yes, Maggie," I said, "I said hello to Paul."

I didn't even have to lie. Paul Adler's protective ghost stood near my sister in the reflection of the care center's huge windows. If I let myself, I could see him in the reflection, looking down dotingly at Maggie in her chair, taking her hand in his though she didn't know it. I didn't have the heart to tell her that he had been dead for nearly forty years. I'd tried before, it had never gone well. And what was the point?

Maybe Andy had the right idea. Maybe it was better not to know too much. Maybe the only way to get through life with our sanity intact and anything resembling happiness was to learn to accept things as they were and be grateful for what little we had.

"Oh, fireworks!" Maggie declared excitedly, beaming with genuine happiness.

The pyrotechnics had begun in earnest above the bay, filling the sky with burning blossoms. The crack of the explosions sent Blue leaning into my leg with a quiet whimper. She was more skittish now than she had been before her injuries, understandably. I put a hand on her head and made comforting noises to her, reassuring her that she was safe. Soon, she quieted, laying at my feet.

"Happy Independence Day, Lena," Nurse Jeanette was saying to my sister. "I've got some apple pie for you."

"Oh, lovely dear, thank you," Maggie said, not taking her eyes from the show in the sky.

"Are these family or friends you have with you today?" The nurse said in an attempt to engage Maggie in conversation and test her awareness of her circumstances.

Maggie looked at us for a moment, confusion in her eyes. She looked from Andy, to Marilyn, to me, smiling at each of us in turn. When her eyes fell on me, recognition dawned again.

"This is my big brother, Francis," she said.

Nurse Jeanette pursed her lips in sympathy for us, clearly deciding that my elderly little sister was having a bad day. After all, she was in her nineties, and I looked to be somewhere in the ballpark of forty. She was clearly making no sense.

"Why does she get to call you Francis?" Andy asked petulantly.

"Seniority," I said.

"So," nurse Jeanette turned to me and said with an air of patronizing good intentions, "you're all family, then?"

"More or less," I said, looking at each of the four ladies sitting with me, my inner wolf regarding each of them from my eyes with protective affection. "We're a pack."

The nurse rolled her eyes at my strange response but didn't say anything. There were other patients who needed her attention. She left us with a plastic smile and went about her business.

"Ooh, look at the red one!" Maggie declared, pointing to a particularly majestic starburst in the night sky. "It's beautiful."

Only I couldn't see the colors the way she could. To me, it was just light. The reds and greens of the world were lost to me, something that other people could experience, but never me. It was something that I was missing, but looking around me, I came to realize that each of us were missing something. Blue was missing a leg and an eye but was sleeping contentedly at my feet. Marilyn had lost the man she loved but was continuing the business they had built together. Andy didn't have any answers about where she came from but refused to let those questions define her. Maggie was missing pieces of herself, and she smiled more brightly than anybody else at the table.

So what if I didn't see what they saw, if I didn't have what they had? That didn't change the basic truth of what Maggie had said. It was beautiful. Within me, even the wolf agreed. I didn't need the things that they had in order to find beauty in what I had been given.

I resolved, just this once, to let myself follow their lead and try to enjoy the show.

RATE AND REVIEW

We hope you enjoyed *The Pack* by E.C. Saulness. If you did, we would ask that you please rate and review this title. Every review helps our authors.

Rate and Review: The Pack

MEET THE AUTHOR

E.C. Saulness grew up in the Pacific Northwest and currently lives in the shadow of Wyoming's Bighorn Mountains. He has a face for radio, a voice for photographs, and a twisted sense of humor that only comes from having been both a sailor and a social worker. When he isn't coming up with new ways to torment his children he spends his days thinking up new ways to torment his characters, and ultimately his readers.

OTHER TITLES FROM 5 PRINCE PUBLISHING

www.ingramcontent.com/pod-product-compliance
Lightning Source LLC
Chambersburg PA
CBHW030746030726
47497CB00001B/149